"A genuinely engaging book, even for those who, like me, are not altogether convinced Jungians. Galipeau, who takes the Star Wars *sequence seriously and very much to heart, sees the Lucas films as embodying a collective social myth that speaks to the drama of the archetypal—the infinite—within us. And this accounts, Galipeau says, for the enduring effect and personal value of all* Star Wars *movies. In Galipeau's view, . . . the* Star Wars *sequence, whose narrative he examines in amazing and often quite subtle detail, serves people in the way our other eternal stories do. "The sequence successfully shows us our deepest conflicts and our most careful resolutions. These Galipeau reveals with the conviction and humanity of a very fine analyst, sensitive to the scope of Jungian psychology and to Jung's special grandeur, his value for those who want—who need—to understand themselves."*

—PROFESSOR LENNY KOFF
University of California, Los Angeles

THE JOURNEY OF LUKE SKYWALKER™

AN ANALYSIS OF MODERN MYTH AND SYMBOL

STEVEN A. GALIPEAU

OPEN COURT Chicago and La Salle, Illinois

To order books from Open Court, call toll-free 1-800-815-2280.

Open Court Publishing Company is a division of Carus Publishing Company.

First printing 2001

Printed and bound in the United States of America

Library of Congress Cataloging-in-Publication Data

Galipeau, Steven A.
The journey of Luke Skywalker : an analysis of modern myth and symbol / Steven A. Galipeau
p. cm.
Includes bibliographical references and index.
ISBN 0-8126-9432-5 (pbk : alk. paper)
1. Star Wars films. 2. Skywalker, luke (Fictitious character) I. Title
PN1995.9.S695 2001
791.43'75—dc21 00-068439

Dedicated to my sons,
Brendan and Owen

Contents

Illustrations

Preface

Movies have added a new storytelling medium to modern culture, offering us an abundant variety of tales with visual and auditory qualities far exceeding those in the written word or the old oral narratives of the traditional raconteur. Often a movie script based on an earlier written work is adapted to the big screen, but in the case of movies like the *Star Wars* series, the story is created especially for this artistic medium. In either case the imagination of the moviemaker communicates with the viewer in what is, historically, a relatively new art form.

Since ancient times the stories of cultures—their mythologies—have carried much of the meaning and significance of the struggles of the people of those times and places. The study of myth and symbol has become a part of many modern disciplines, from archeology and anthropology to religious studies. Joseph Campbell, the prolific author of many books on mythology, had originally been a professor of literature. He became drawn to understand the earliest products of the human imagination as found in our mythic heritage.

Myths have also proven of interest to the pioneers of psychology. One myth in particular, the Oedipus myth, appealed to Freud. C.G. Jung, who discovered deeper layers of the unconscious than initially postulated by Freud, believed that *all* myths could help us comprehend these extensive levels of the unconscious that all humans share—what he referred to as the archetypal layer of the psyche. Since mythological themes often appear in our dreams and other spontaneous creations of the imagination, understanding the myths helps us to understand ourselves better.

My hope in this book is that my personal Jungian approach may give additional meaning to the story of the first three *Star Wars* movies, which contain an abundance of symbolism linked together in a remarkable way in what appears to be a simple story. The whole series of movies, projected to number six, is called *Star Wars*, and each movie also has its own title. The first *Star Wars* movie (Episode IV) is often referred to simply as *Star Wars*, whereas I generally refer to it by its proper title: *A New Hope*.

With the release of the *Star Wars* Special Editions (Episodes IV–VI) in the winter of 1997 and *The Phantom Menace* (Episode I) in 1999, there is even more interest in and fascination with these films than when the first movie of the original trilogy was released over twenty years ago. The comments and questions of creative, thoughtful people over these years have further stirred my own reflections on the symbolic content of these films. As one woman wrote to me after hearing a tape of my 1997 lecture on *Star Wars: A New Hope*, "When I first saw *Star Wars* I felt there was something of great importance going on here but had no vocabulary for what I sensed. . . . When I started studying Jung a few years ago, I realized that it was here that many valuable insights into the film's meaning could be found."[1]

I hope to provide a rich assortment of insights into the deeper meaning to be found in these films—being aware, even as I do so, that new understandings will always emerge, just as they do when working on a fascinating dream. The symbolic richness of the storytelling in these films leads me to believe that the release of the three movies making up the *Star Wars* "prequel," telling earlier parts of the story, will further amplify what the film viewer has already witnessed in the first three movies—just as our dreams bring up past experiences and their meaning to shed light on our present and future. Similarly it is my belief that a closer exploration of the meaning of the first three films will add to the depth of the experience of viewing the films that are now being released. I would expect that we will gain further appreciation of Luke Skywalker's accomplishment at the end of *Return of the Jedi*, especially from a psychological point of view.

The early reactions by some critics to *Star Wars: Episode I—The Phantom Menace*, which appeared in 1999, clearly demonstrate how lack of an informed sense of the symbolic nature of the films can easily lead to misunderstanding of George Lucas's style of storytelling.

Yet the generally enthusiastic reception of the film testifies to its powerful mystique in our culture's imagination.

In the Epilogue, I provide a preliminary discussion of *The Phantom Menace.* It's too early to analyze this movie in the same detail as I have analyzed Episodes IV, V, and VI. The original trilogy was first released over twenty years ago and then re-released in 1997, when it was, once again, enthusiastically received by a vast audience. There is much more story to come in the new trilogy, and this will provide greater context for *The Phantom Menace.*

You don't need any prior knowledge of Jungian psychology to follow this book. To help readers who are not familiar with the terminology, a glossary of basic Jungian terms is included at the back. The notes for each chapter, also found at the back, provide background information and point to additional resources for exploring the symbolic and mythological themes described here.

Acknowledgments

Many people over the years have expressed to me a desire for a "Jungian" understanding of the journey of Luke Skywalker—whether it has been in a lecture or retreat that I was offering, or in some form of personal communication with me. This story has fascinated others as much as it has captivated me. Without this shared interest from so many people I would never have pursued composing this book.

Of course a good story must come from a good storyteller and I want to acknowledge George Lucas's creative efforts to bring the vision of his extraordinary imagination to our collective awareness in such an evocative form. At the same time, I want to acknowledge C.G. Jung's immense contribution to our understanding of the archetypal levels of the human psyche which help shed light on so many aspects of the symbolic manifestations of our imaginative life. In many ways this book is a "marriage" or "coniunctio" of the creativity of these two unique individuals of different generations and backgrounds.

The book has more clarity than it did originally thanks to the editorial assistance of Margaret Ryan. I thank her for her many valuable and constructive observations, and for her excitement about the material. I thank Louise Mahdi for opening the door for publication at Open Court and David Ramsay Steele at Open Court for shepherding this book along the way and for his helpful suggestions.

But most of all, I want to thank my family, beginning with my wife Tia. One of our earliest dates was attending one of the original showings of *Return of the Jedi*. Her enthusiastic response to this tale (and subsequently the earlier films) helped me realize I had found a true soul mate. She read the entire first draft of the manuscript and made many helpful comments, and was supportive in a great many ways so that I could find the time to complete this project.

Equally and maybe more magically valuable has been the enthusiastic response over the years of my sons Brendan and Owen (now 15 and 12). To witness the wonder of their reactions to these films at a variety of ages, and the ongoing enchantment that these movies hold for them has been a delightful aspect of the special privilege of watching them grow up. Our whole family has savored few things with such joint enthusiasm as the journey of Luke Skywalker (and now of his predecessors). In appreciation for the opportunity to view these films so many times through their eyes, I dedicate this book to them.

The Force . . . is an energy field created by all living things. It surrounds us and penetrates us. It binds the galaxy together.

The Force will be with you . . . always.

OBI-WAN KENOBI to Luke Skywalker in
Star Wars: A New Hope

The decisive question for man is: is he related to something infinite or not?

C.G. JUNG,
Memories, Dreams, Reflections

INTRODUCTION

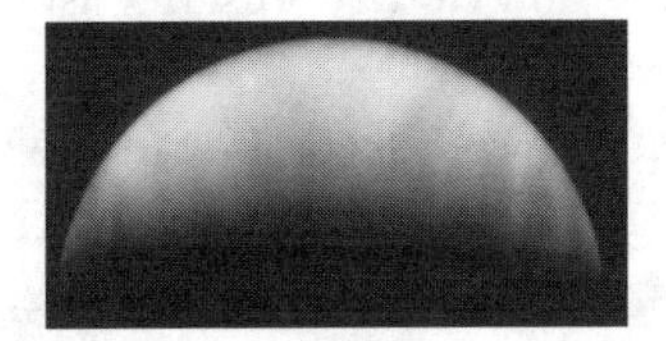

"Why Is the Force Still with Us?"

When I first saw *Star Wars: A New Hope* in 1977, I was deeply struck by the story and its many imaginative and mythological dimensions. In retrospect I have come to realize that this movie has defined for me what I most desire to experience when I go to the movies: to be immersed in a good story that genuinely moves me. Over the years I have enjoyed many other movies but have found none that has affected me as much as the three movies that comprise the original *Star Wars* trilogy. Each time I've gone back to one of them—and these times are now too numerous to count—I always find something new to absorb and ponder. This is a story that, for me and countless others, wants to keep telling itself, that invites us to come along again and again. The story of Luke Skywalker has become a modern fairy tale that has gripped the imagination of two generations—and it may be even more compelling to the second generation than the first.

As a Jungian analyst, my work with people includes reflecting on what their dreams mean—an age-old tradition found throughout the world. I've been impressed by how often the characters from these films have appeared in my own and other peoples' dreams. Indeed, the entire *Star Wars* saga can be approached as a *cultural dream*, one that has meaning for numerous people and symbolically depicts in important aspects the psychological and spiritual shifts taking place in our age. Like our dreams, the *Star Wars* story can be seen as a myth or fairy tale that represents aspects of our collective psychological life.

Seventeen years ago I was asked to lead a weekend camp retreat for the youth of a large church, to offer something that would capture their attention and help them explore the deeper spiritual values necessary for an authentic life. I suggested using *Star Wars* as the theme. The young people were not told what the retreat would be based on, only that they would be seeing a movie on Friday night. Even though the movie (*Star Wars: A New Hope*) had been out for a while and available on video, a group of over fifty adolescents sat riveted for two hours. They were completely captivated. During meetings over the course of the weekend, I explored with them themes from the movie that I thought would be relevant to issues in their lives. When the weekend was over I overheard one of the youth say to one of his leaders, "I can't believe that guy got all that out of that movie." I felt as if I'd given them a taste of what it might be like to spend time with Yoda. What one is looking for is there all along, you just have to learn how to recognize it, and understand how to use it and learn from it.

I believe that the story is at the core of the success of *Star Wars.* The storyteller, George Lucas, is a master of his medium and uses its multiple facets to involve his audience in his story, much like the storyteller of old who recounted ancient tales in the dark mystery of a winter's night. Lucas's style particularly reaches the child's psyche, or the young psyche in the adult—that part of the imagination that comes most alive in childhood when one is in bed at night and wonders about . . . the creatures lurking in the closet, under the bed, outside the window. Jung called this important imaginative place "the children's land," and said that it reaches not only back to our personal childhoods but to "a time when rational present-day consciousness has not yet separated from the historical psyche, the *collective unconscious.*"[1] The full wonder of George Lucas's storytelling is that he sets the story in a *futuristic* timeframe that exceeds and eludes that of our present-day rational consciousness—we don't have that kind of technology yet—and links it together with creatures of a more *primordial* nature.

Lucas created these movies in response to a gap he perceived in our culture. "It seemed to me," Lucas explains, "that there was no longer a lot of mythology in our society—the kind of stories we tell ourselves and our children, which is the way our heritage is passed down. Westerns used to provide that, but there weren't Westerns any more. I wanted to find a new form. So I looked around, and tried to figure out where myth comes from. It comes from the borders of society, from out there, from places of mystery—the wide Sargasso Sea. And I thought, Space. Because back then space was a source of great mystery. So I thought, O.K., let's see what we can do with all those elements. I put them all into a bag, along with a little bit of 'Flash Gordon' and a few other things, and out fell 'Star Wars.'"[2]

Linked to this realization about a need for a particular genre was Lucas's unique approach to filmmaking. Lawrence Kasdan, who collaborated on the screenplays for *The Empire Strikes Back* and *Return of the Jedi*, suggests, "'Star Wars' was a serious breakthrough, a shift in the culture, which was possible only because George was this weird character . . . He opened up people's minds."[3]

"I'm a visual filmmaker," Lucas explains, "I do films that are kinetic . . . I was always coming from pure cinema—I was using the grammar of film to create content. I think graphically, not linearly."[4] In response to criticism concerning his style of making movies, Lucas replies, "I feel 'Star Wars' did make a statement—in a more visual, less literary way . . . But of course if the movie doesn't fit what they think movies should be, it shouldn't be allowed to exist. I think that's narrow-minded. I've been trying to rethink the art of movies—it's not a play, not a book, not music or dance."[5]

Such an artistic approach is also quite important psychologically. Lucas's work begins with the images that spontaneously emerge from his imagination. He then organizes them by pushing forward with the creative use of his artistic medium, despite how others might react. He stays true to his own vision. Such devotion to his imagination—especially using a visual medium—allows a unique expression of the deeper mythological levels of the psyche, what Joseph Campbell called *creative mythology*. The implication is that good storytelling—that which emerges from a genuine connection to the imagination—serves an important psychological role, albeit for most of us, on an unconscious level.

Music and sound are also central components of the *Star Wars* storytelling experience, adding greatly to its emotional intensity. The sound vivifies the immediacy of the experience and the music stays with the viewer long after he or she has left the theatre. Most people would recognize the major musical themes of the *Star Wars* movies if they heard them.

In viewing sports, a spectator participates indirectly in an intense emotional struggle whose outcome is unknown, walking the edge between the "thrill of victory, and the agony of defeat." At times the action of *Star Wars* draws viewers into situations similar to athletic contests. (As a youth Lucas was drawn to the speed and action of auto racing.) For many people these various cultural avenues give access to a breadth and depth of emotional experience that might otherwise be missing from their lives. In the past this was an important aspect of the emotional appeal of religions. The unconscious need for intense passionate involvement can also draw some people into war. Each of these powerful collective phenomenon can give us a highly spirited experience that feels connected to something mysterious and beyond everyday life. Sometimes it's positive and creative; sometimes it's negative and destructive. When these more traditional avenues for finding alive "transcendent" experiences are lost, they have to be discovered in other places. As we shall see, this need for the transcendent is one of the subtle, but important, themes in the *Star Wars* myth. It is also a central concept in Jung's psychology.[6]

While the emotionally charged experience that Lucas offers the moviegoer in *Star Wars* was intended to restore a mythological genre, it actually follows the pattern of religious initiations that was meant to help initiates come to terms with the deeper dimensions of life. As Jung liked to point out, there is an inner drama that goes on within each of us that is as crucial, and often more crucial, than the activities of our external lives. Sometimes these inner experiences have "mythological" proportions, and, if properly understood, can help us deal creatively with the grimmer aspects of our daily lives. Myths and fairy tales have described such psychological dramas for countless past generations, yet they remain relevant for the modern psyche.[7] *Star Wars* can be seen as adding to humanity's mythology.

Those who worked on these films also became aware of the importance of the story as central to the films, not the technology or the special effects. Richard Marquand, who directed *Return of the Jedi*, noted, "If there is one thing that I have learned from working on *Return of the Jedi* it is simply that the story is what really counts. There have been a lot of directors and studios who have been misled by the success of *Star Wars* into thinking that special effects are everything. They're not. Special effects have their place—a very special place—in the *Star Wars* saga. But first and foremost comes the story . . . What we have here, in the *Star Wars* saga, is one of the greatest stories ever told."[8]

After the three original movies had been released, Sir Alec Guinness (Obi-Wan Kenobi) admitted that it was very difficult to explain why he did the movies. "I thought the dialogue was pretty terrible and the characters fairly meaningless—but there was a story value. I found I wanted to know what happened next, what was on the next page? In the end I thought: Why not?"[9]

Lucas's characters and dialogue have to be taken on their own terms to be appreciated. The characters, I believe, are to be most appreciated as a whole, not as separate individual personalities. They are best seen, as we shall see, like the various characters in a dream, not so much as real people. Interestingly, in a 1995 interview Lucas noted that he chose the cast as a group, based on how they worked together, not on the merits of each as an individual actor or actress.[10] Similarly, the dialogue serves many purposes, but it is not the conversation of fully fleshed out human beings, it is often used to tell the story and entertain as the drama moves along.

Star Wars is more alive today in our collective imagination than it was when the movies were first released. With George Lucas now bringing the three "prequels" to the screen, filling in the background of Darth Vader, Obi-Wan Kenobi, and the earlier history of the *Star Wars* galaxy, it will certainly continue to be so for quite some time. A 1997 magazine article by John Seabrook reports that for the previous two years *Star Wars* action figures were the best-selling toys for boys, and that a large percentage of these were actually bought by adults. Seabrook also reports that since 1991, *Star Wars* novels are, book for book, the single most valuable active franchise in publishing. Yet, until 1999, none of the movies has had an original release since 1983![11]

The title of Seabrook's article asks, "Why Is the Force Still with Us?" A great question! Hopefully the readers of this book will find many interesting psychological responses to this question in the pages ahead. Why does this seemingly "simple" story continue to have such an impact on people's imaginations?

By believing in the story he wanted to tell, even when his friends had thought he had "lost it," Lucas has ended up living a part of the tale he created. Numerous newspaper and magazine articles recount the wonder of Lucas's commercial success, as do a few books.[12] Lucas's first musings about his space adventure myth met very little acceptance. The skepticism created an environment in which Lucas was able to forego the usual director's salary in exchange for exclusive merchandising rights. The success of the first movie enabled him to make the second, thereby continuing to create on film the entirely new universe he had imagined. Out of his commitment to the story, to his own personal vision, the entire *Star Wars* franchise was born. For Lucas, the financial success meant the opportunity to tell more stories, develop other projects, and to develop the technology to tell the stories in even more imaginative ways. The *Star Wars* Special Edition releases offered Lucas the opportunity to bring to the movies the technology that he did not have available when he originally made them.

Seabrook summarizes Lucas's accomplishment this way: "It seemed to me an alchemic [sic] transformation was taking place: dreams were being spun into desire, and desire forged into product. In a world where the stories and images and lessons provided by electronic media seem to be replacing the stories and images and lessons people used to get from religion, literature, and painting, the lessons of Star Wars—[he lists those important to him]—is a very powerful force indeed."[13]

Seabrook also quotes Lucas from an interview he did with him in regard to Lucas's didactic intentions in *Star Wars.* "I wanted it to be a traditional moral study, to have some sort of palpable precepts in it that children could understand. There is always a lesson to be learned. Where do these lessons come from? Traditionally, we get them from church, the family, art, and in the modern world we get them from media—from movies." He adds, "Everyone teaches in every work of art. In almost everything you do, you teach, whether you are aware of it or not. Everybody teaches all the time. Some people aren't aware of what they are teaching. They should be wiser. Everyone teaches all the time."[14]

From what he learned through anthropology and his study of the work of Joseph Campbell, Lucas teaches us a great deal in his story and through his mastery of the medium he uses to tell it.[15]

So let's set off on our own journey of discovery. Using a psychological approach, we will now begin to explore what the *Star Wars* story and its rich, complex symbolism can teach us.

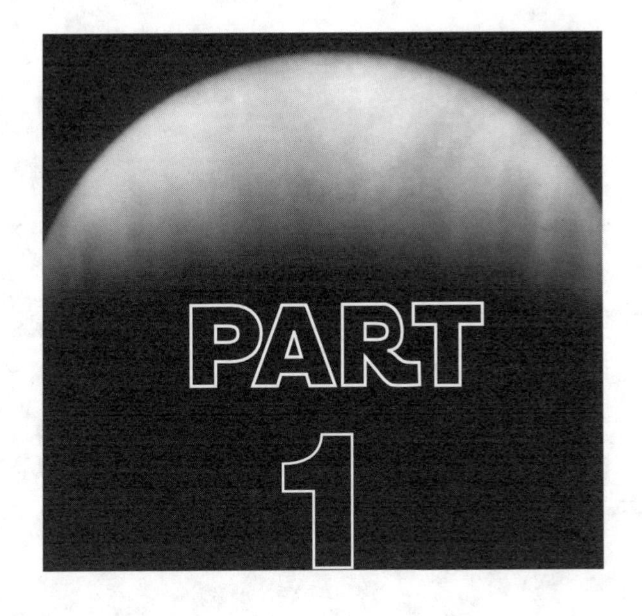

EPISODE IV

A NEW HOPE

CHAPTER 1

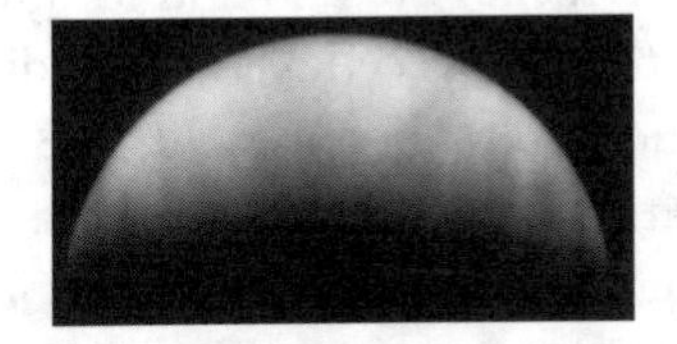

Setting the Stage: The Story Unfolds

A Galaxy Far, Far Away

In charting our course through the symbolism and psychology of the *Star Wars* movies, we will take our bearings from *location*. Each of the major visual locations has important symbolic significance to the story being told. But before we reach our first symbolic location, the dry wasteland of Tatooine, the opening sequence that begins each film serves to situate us in a broader context.[1]

After the studio and production company credits, we read on the screen:

A long time ago, in a galaxy
far, far away . . .

We read these words in silence—for a brief moment we are quietly left with our own thoughts. Like "Once upon a time . . . ," this is an introduction to *mythological time*, to *dream time* a timeless realm that exists only in the imagination. We are also told that we are in a far-off place, an obviously imaginative, mythological space, a "dream" land. Immediately Lucas is notifying us that he is telling us a story, thereby establishing his movie genre.

Next, accompanied by a stirring orchestral fanfare, we see the general title of STAR WARS. Title and sound jump immediately into our senses and then the title recedes into the distance, pulling us in as the music continues. As stars appear in the background the first word of this general title is augmented visually, and it becomes clear that we will be seeing "war" among the stars. The symbolism here, in this universe created by Lucas, changes from that of modern life. Darkness predominates: the void, the unknown, and the vast reaches of space, except for the glimmers of light. Modern life is dominated by the light of reason, the rational intellect, and our technological ability to cast light almost everywhere. A vast dark universe takes this security away from us, as does a darkened movie theatre. Depth psychology, with its focus on unconscious processes suggests that there is much more darkness and unknown primitive life within all of us than our modern consciousness is usually willing to admit.

The night-time sky, studded with stars, is where the imaginations of children and adults can meet. For it is "under the stars" that, from earliest times, the human imagination has thrived. It was envisioned, for example, that the birth of Christ was heralded by the birth of a new star in the sky. And all the names of our constellations come from the figures of myth and imagination that were thought of as residing in the night sky. These figures of imagination help us to orient ourselves in the night-time universe, the internal world of dreams. The 1996 movie *Dragonheart* utilized this symbolism at its conclusion. Up amongst the stars, Draco the last dragon, a creature of pure imagination, could reside and thus remain "in our hearts." In *Star Wars* Lucas has found a way to take this mythological association to the night-time sky to new imaginative heights.

The images and reality of war also stir us emotionally and imaginatively. In the *Iliad* Homer described the conflict between the Greeks and the Trojans in the Trojan War as not only a human drama, but a divine one as well. The gods were in conflict and had pulled human beings into their squabbles. Similarly the Hebrew Bible not only tells the story of the people of Israel, it also tells the story of divine conflicts. Which God or gods are to be served and receive the most honor? With which divinity or divinities will the people be in relationship? How will they relate to people who worship other divinities? Often battles and war result from these conflicts. Personal, cultural, and divine conflicts are all merged together at the same time in one drama. Repeatedly throughout human history, and even today, the impulse to fight or go to war was—is—in the name of some divinity or some sense of divine purpose. The god-like identity that took over Germany and Japan contributed to the horrors of World War II. The reality of war stirs up strong emotions on very many levels from the personal to the social, political, and religious. Jungian psychology sees such upheavals as being related to the activation of the *archetypal* layers of the unconscious.

The Story Begins

After the words STAR WARS on the screen we read the following as the exhilarating orchestral music continues:

Episode IV
A NEW HOPE

It is a period of civil war,
Rebel spaceships, striking
from a hidden base, have won
their first victory against
the evil Galactic Empire.

During the battle Rebel
spies managed to steal secret
plans to the Empire's
ultimate weapon, the Death
Star, an armoured space
station with enough power to
destroy an entire planet.

Pursued by the Empire's
sinister agents, Princess
Leia races home aboard her

starship, custodian of the
stolen plans that can save
her people, and restore
freedom to the galaxy. . . .

Before we see images of any sort, Lucas presents us with a *written* story, one that begins to disappear into deep space as it draws us further into this unknown universe. My sons, before they could read, would *always* ask me to read the text that began each of these movies. They wanted to know the story right from the start, and they wanted to know it *each* time it began to unfold before them. The written story sequence, which begins each of the movies, reflects the reality that movies have become a new mode of storytelling. They pick up, in a sense, where the written word leaves off.

The reach of Lucas's vision for these films appears right at the beginning of this first one, which is identified as "Episode IV." When I first read this in the theatre, I wondered if I was in the wrong theatre or had come late to the movie. When I realized I was in the right place at the right time, I felt thrilled that this story was a part of a much bigger one. I admired Lucas's creative courage in beginning the film this way from the start, even though he could not be sure that it would be successful.

The episode title "A New Hope" and the story text that follows offer a great deal to wonder about. We assume that there will be some possibility of hope amidst a conflict of "galactic" proportions that involves civil war, rebels, spaceships, an evil empire, spies, secret plans, a weapon of death with terrible destructive capabilities, sinister agents, and a princess rushing to save her people and restore freedom. This is some place we are heading into! The format Lucas uses to begin each movie creates considerable anticipation right from the beginning, immediately dropping us into the middle of the story.

As the written aspects of the story recede into the distance, the camera pans downward to give us a glimpse of a planet below. (We actually never learn the name of the planet during the first movie; we only experience it visually and metaphorically.) We see a spaceship fly overhead, pursued by a much larger one shooting at it, and overshadowing the screen as it passes overhead. We have an immediate involvement with the pursuit we have just read about.

Most of us can relate to the feeling of being pursued and the fear of being overtaken by something more powerful than we are. When we were children, our parents loomed large, prodding us to behave in certain ways. Bullies lurked in school or on the playground. As adults we may all too easily feel pursued by the demands of life, of work, of relationships, of parenting, and threatened by the darker elements in society. Inwardly, the psychological demands for growth and development can even feel like a pursuit. The archetype pushing the personality towards wholeness, which Jung called the *Self*, can seem to be, in essence, pursuing the ego for greater realization, using a variety of ways to gain its attention. The pursuit portrayed on the screen is clearly ominous; it seems likely that the smaller ship belongs to the rebels and the larger one to the evil galactic Empire.

The scene then shifts to inside the smaller ship. Despite the fact that troopers are rushing around, the antics of two robots or "droids" are the focal point. One is cylindrically shaped and emits beeps; the other has human shape and is verbal, *very* verbal—and provides the translation of the conversation of the beeping droid. The verbal droid is clearly a very anxious droid and expresses much of this side of the emotional component of what is happening. The other droid seems more adventuresome, more oblivious to danger.

These two droids play critical roles throughout the story and demonstrate Lucas's storytelling skill. They are opposites on a variety of levels—physical shape and color, disposition, and roles—highlighted by the comedic Laurel and Hardy/Abbott and Costello elements they bring. We soon see that these droids are more "human"—that is, involved in the unfolding drama in an alive and adventuresome way—than many of the human figures—who are actually more robotic. When we see Imperial stormtroopers blast into the rebel spaceship after it has been drawn up into the much larger ship, they are helmeted and faceless. In contrast, the faces of the rebel troopers are completely visible and their expressions help tell the story. The faceless cylindrical droid seems to have more personality than any other character to this point.

Now two more central characters make their appearance. First is the princess, whom we read about at the very beginning—certainly we assume it must be the princess. She's a young, mysterious lady in white, furtively hiding something in the cylindrical droid (which we later learn is an R2 unit). The droid suddenly becomes animated, and, as we learn through the commentary of the humanoid droid, now believes he has a mission. Eventually an ominous masked figure, dressed all in black, appears following the faceless troopers. Breathing in a labored and sinister way, it is immediately clear who the "evil" villain is.

At this point in the tale everything seems fairly black and white, symbolically speaking. However, the symbolism is also new. We're in the past—a long time ago—yet, given the nature of these spaceships, it is the future. There is the white-clad, virtuous, heroic princess and the black-clad evil villain. There are the two droids—gold and silver, human-shaped and cylindrical, verbal and electronic. The symbolic significance of all these characters will unfold throughout the narrative, and each will carry some element of its mystery. As the two droids depart on their adventures, we are embarking on a journey that explores through its imagery, many of the issues concerning what it means to be truly human.

The Adventures of the Droids Begin

When discovered by the stormtroopers the princess puts up a brief fight but is easily captured. Our story now has a "damsel in distress." However, this princess is no shrinking violet. She is brought before the darkly clothed figure who just tossed a rebel officer aside, and holds her ground. She does not become intimidated. Through their conversation we receive the first identification of major characters: Darth Vader and Princess Leia, the dark male villain and the light heroine. At this stage of the story they are archetypal embodiments of masculine and feminine principles, the two most important pair of opposites at work in every human being.[2] Here the two figures—and thus the two principles they represent—are in conflict, mirroring the most ubiquitous conflict on this planet: the darker aspects of the masculine principle dominating the feminine. This oppression exists in the external world, as reflected in society's mistreatment of women, and the struggle for equal rights, as well as internally, with those qualities of being associated with feminine nature. Indeed, the journey of Luke Skywalker can be viewed as a story about the wounding and redemption of the feminine principle, or *anima*, in a man living in a patriarchal and power-dominated environment.

At present the fate of the princess seems to rest with the droids, whose escape pod descends to the planet below. They are not fired upon, since Imperial sensors do not detect any life forms. But the dark figure, Darth Vader, realizes immediately that the princess must have hidden the plans in the escape pod and orders a detachment of stormtroopers to retrieve it. The pursuit is still on as we descend with the droids to our first major location, the desert planet of Tatooine.

CHAPTER 2

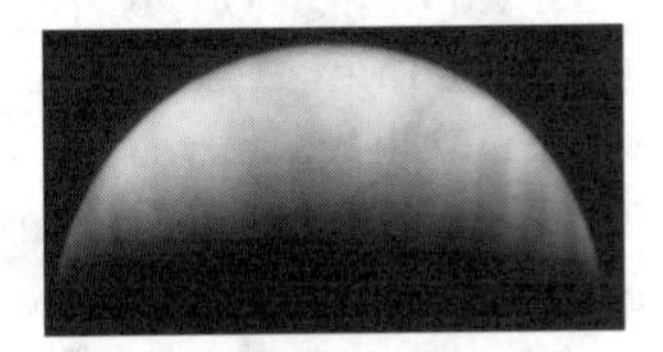

Tatooine: A Desolate Place

The Adventures of the Droids Continue

We experience the first "location" through the two droids. It's a desert wasteland that seems to stretch on forever in all directions. Artoo Detoo (R2D2, the cylindrical message carrier) is the adventurer and See Threepio (C3PO, the gold, human-shaped one) is his reluctant sidekick. Threepio is both narrator of and commentator on this adventure, as he often is throughout the saga. He comments on what we are seeing on screen: "What a desolate place this is!" Psychologically this is the realm where many of our efforts for transformation begin, where we come to find that life is dry, empty, and desolate. The dry desert is an image of being cut off from the principle source of life, which is often symbolized by water. For example, in the story of Moses, after the conflict in Egypt during which he kills an Egyptian overseer, he finds himself in the desert wilderness. His life begins to change when he comes upon a well, an important water source, and the women he meets at this desert oasis. (This was also true of his ancestor Jacob.)

How do we deal with encountering our own inner deserts? The two droids exemplify the poles of response: Artoo wishes to continue with his "mission," while Threepio wants to go the easier way.

The conflict between them leads to their separation. The theme of separation and eventual reunification reappears throughout the films, as it does throughout human life. The feelings that accompany such experiences usually have a great deal of influence on our most intimate relationships and how we feel about ourselves. In the case of the droids their differences lead them to part company, which evokes in Threepio the anxiety that he feels in being alone. Following each of these characters, we feel our own aloneness. One of the reasons these stories have such an impact on young people is that they are usually less defended against the anxieties that come with separation. This is but one reason that this relatively simple sequence is emotionally involving.

Threepio quickly discovers a transport, and we are left with our own suppositions about what happens to him at this point. Artoo journeys into a dry canyon where he comes upon some small, cloaked creatures who speak in high-pitched voices. These are the first of many imaginative creatures we encounter throughout the films. They represent the unknown, but can also conjure up more familiar memories of fairy tales and legends (see Figure 1). These little creatures work together to capture Artoo, eventually hoisting him into a giant sand trawler; *big* and *little* as symbols are juxtaposed and intertwined with these small creatures and their huge vehicle.

After Artoo is taken aboard the sand trawler, we soon discover that Threepio is already there. They are joyfully reunited, but like many fairytale heroes and heroines, they are concerned with where they are and what will happen to them. As is his custom, Threepio expresses a great deal of anxiety about their situation. Being held captive inside something giant conveys a "Jonah-in-the-whale" theme, which is repeated several times throughout this modern fairy tale. We also have the theme of the small but powerful person or dwarf, as in the Grimm's fairy tale of Rumpelstiltskin (a miller's daughter will owe her first child to a dwarf who helped her become queen unless she can guess his name). The fear of something terrible happening is often overly exaggerated by Threepio with exclamations like, "We're doomed!"

Figure 1

Fabulous beasts from another mythic era: the entry point for initiation and transformation. From Timothy Husband's *The Wild Man: Medieval Myth and Symbolism*. Swiss tapestry, T117–1937, © The Victoria and Albert Museum, London. Reprinted with permission.

Luke Skywalker

Amidst the droids' anxiety about their fate, the sand trawler pulls up at a small settlement. Later we learn it is a moisture farm: it's full-time work to find water on this desolate planet. Life is very precarious here. At this farm we meet the central figure of this part of the *Star Wars* epic: he, who from the Jedi point of view, is to be "the new hope." We meet him as a discouraged, frustrated young man, stuck on his uncle's farm, dreaming of going to the galaxy space academy with many of his friends. As he goes with his uncle to meet the Jawa sand trawler and the droids they bring, his aunt calls out his name: "Luke! Luke!" The music and sequence immediately set him apart. It also becomes clear that these Jawas are some sort of droid scavengers.

We continue to learn more about the droids, especially Threepio, a protocol droid who can be of use to Owen Lars, Luke's uncle, to program his moisture vaporators. Luke's uncle purchases Threepio and a red cylindrical droid from the Jawas. The two droids are, once again, in danger of being separated. When the red cylindrical droid breaks down, Threepio suggests to Luke that they take Artoo, a suggestion to which his uncle agrees. The mystery in the air is expressed by Threepio, when he remarks as Artoo joins them, "Why I should stick my neck out for you is quite beyond my capacity!" He's more *human* than he's supposed to be. As the story goes along we will encounter many "humans" who are *less* human than they're supposed to be.

The psychology of the film deepens significantly at this point and we learn more about Luke and the droids. First, we are given insight into the symbolism of the location. When Threepio asks Luke which planet they are on, Luke responds, "Well, if there is a bright center to the universe, you're on the planet it is farthest from." Symbolism of the center was for Jung an indication of the archetype of the Self, which he saw as the central organizing archetype of the personality. Thus we could say that psychologically at this point in his life, in this desolate environment, Luke had no center and was very far from knowing who he was and, in the language of the films, discovering his "destiny," his purpose in life.

For now, as he tells Threepio, he's "just Luke," after Threepio had been inclined to call him "Sir, Luke," a subtle introduction to the film's subtext, since Luke eventually journeys to becoming a Jedi knight. Luke learns of Threepio's name and that his functional area is human-cyborg relations and that Artoo is his counterpart. We would know little about this other droid without Threepio. Threepio also diminishes his own capacities when Luke discovers that the droids have been involved in the rebellion against the empire. Threepio dismisses his function as "not much more than an interpreter and not very good at telling stories. Well, not at making them interesting, anyway." In the final drama it will be Threepio's ability to make the story of the main protagonists interesting that will have an important contribution to the eventual outcome. There are many seeds for later character and symbolic development in this sequence.

As Luke is cleaning Artoo Detoo, an image bursts out of the droid of the princess delivering a part of her message, "Help me, Obi-Wan Kenobi. You're my only hope." This is one of the best depictions I know concerning a man's experience of what Jungian psychology calls the anima archetype: the feminine aspect of the transcendent Self, a key component of psychological wholeness. Usually this occurs in projected form; the qualities we are really experiencing in ourselves we attribute to another person. Usually a man's first experience of having a "crush" on a woman is not of that particular woman *per se,* but of the image of the feminine inside him that is now carried by an actual woman. It can be very intoxicating to receive the attention such a projection evokes in a man, for it creates the illusion that one is being "seen" or desired in a personal way. But the deeper reality is that the woman is not experienced for who she is.

Luke Skywalker is literally knocked off his feet as this image emerges. Such is the effect on a man of being "hit" by an anima image, which is usually first experienced through projection on an actual woman. If the woman is ever to be known as a real person, the man must separate the anima image from the woman onto whom he is projecting, and discover the meaning of the *inner image of woman* in his psyche. The same is true for women in regard to their internal images of men (the animus) and actual men. Much of the discord in relations between the sexes can be seen as stemming from the problem of *not* making this psychological differentiation and thus unconsciously expecting members of the opposite sex to conform to our inner image of them.[1]

This experience of the "image" of a woman, so well conveyed in the ethereal hologram, captivates Luke and diminishes his focused attention. In his consuming desire to hear more of this message, he absentmindedly removes Artoo's restraining bolt and then forgets to reattach it. This is how an anima experience works: it diminishes a man's conscious awareness of everyday realities so that aspects of his psychic life can, in essence, be seen, opening the door to the deeper dimensions of life.[2] Both inner and outer aspects of "anima" development unfold in this story: Luke's deeper connection to himself as well as to those with whom he establishes relationships during the course of his journey.

When we are touched by an image, a person, or an experience that opens up newer and deeper possibilities for us, those aspects of life that keep us imprisoned or hold us back can also be activated. When Luke removes the restraining bolt on Artoo to hear more of the message, the message disappears altogether and he becomes frustrated. Then the voice of his aunt beckons and he's called back to his daily reality. However, he leaves the job of tending Artoo to Threepio, quite forgetting himself and believing that the droid unit is too small to run away. Since the droid claims to belong to an Obi-Wan Kenobi, Luke wonders if he belongs to old Ben Kenobi, the strange hermit who lives beyond the Dune Sea.

A participant at one of my lectures asked about the symbolism of the restraining bolt and its importance. I'm grateful for his calling my attention to this symbol, as it is quite important at this juncture in the narrative. In the next scene, when Luke eats with his aunt and uncle, we see that his uncle has placed him under considerable psychological restraint. Luke longs to go to the space academy and his uncle states that he wants Luke to stay on for another season, until there are more droids. By removing the restraining bolt from the droid, Luke has unwittingly set the stage for removing the restraints on his own life. Similar experiences are common on our own planet and in our own time. Many people, for example, are moved to become further involved in life by helping others, and through such work discover their own needs for such help themselves. By seeing and responding to another person's plight, they are beginning a journey to find help for *their own*.

At the dinner table with his aunt and uncle, Luke is told to have the droid's memory erased and that this Obi-Wan Kenobi doesn't exist any more and probably died the same time as his father. The "wizard," Ben Kenobi, is just a "crazy old man," his uncle tells him. After Luke leaves, his aunt notes that he has "too much of his father in him." As the drama unfolds, it becomes clear that part of the restraint on Luke is intended to keep knowledge of his family's past from him, and also any knowledge of larger political and spiritual issues in the galaxy. Memories of such are to be "erased" and possible links, like the old hermit who lives out by the Dune Sea, are to be discredited. This happens far too often in families: the real truth is withheld, ostensibly to protect the child for his or her "own good," but it also severs the youngster's connection to a vital part of his or her history, thereby banishing aspects of the true personality.

In his frustration that he is obviously going "nowhere," Luke leaves the family meal to finish cleaning the droids. But first he stops to watch two setting suns—a brief pause in the narrative that comes with symphonic musical background—a moment that also holds interesting symbolic significance. In most mythologies the sun is associated with the father and the male principle (an important exception is Japanese myth). The two setting suns Luke watches can have numerous meanings; I would like to suggest two. First, Luke has had two "personal" fathers, his own father, whom he hasn't known, and his uncle. The sun is setting on this particular familial configuration. Second, Luke will soon be faced with the conflict between two archetypal male views concerning the dark and the light sides of life. The tendency to identify with one pole or the other is particularly strong when there hasn't been much personal experience of the father (as is true for Luke). This tendency is also strong when the father-figure (in Luke's case, his uncle) has not been particularly connected to the son's hopes and dreams and relates to him out of his own fantasies of what he thinks his son should be.

Luke soon learns that the new R2 unit has taken off and fears his uncle's response. He also criticizes himself, exclaiming, "How could I have been so stupid?" This self-recrimination is the opposite side of a positive anima experience. Enlivened and fascinated by the princess in the message, Luke became lax in his accustomed ways of functioning. This unexpected interruption of the norm is absolutely necessary psychologically when new life possibilities appear. Unfortunately, we tend to feel critical of the effect the new experience has on our old way of doing things. The battle against this internal self-criticism, compounded by the demands of outer authority figures (such as Luke's uncle) is very difficult, especially in a patriarchal environment. Often the new enlivening experience is in danger of being lost completely.

Due to the altered consciousness induced by the image of the princess, followed by the droid's suggestion to remove the restraining bolt to hear the whole message, Luke has unwittingly opened the door into a lifetime adventure! Artoo Detoo, the droid who "excels" at getting others into trouble, according to Threepio, has now drawn Luke into his journey, much as he did Threepio. Artoo's silver color, following connections made in alchemical symbolism, suggests a link to the feminine principle, one that continues to animate Luke's life in new ways. The droid, the message carrier, is very much related to the image it brings to this young man. For fear of the Sand People, Luke will have to wait to pursue the droid until the next morning.

Obi-Wan Kenobi

As the new day dawns, Luke sets off with Threepio on his landspeeder in pursuit of Artoo. They catch up to him, but when Artoo's scanners pick up something, Luke is eager to check it out, believing that it might be Sand People. He soon proves to be right, but has underestimated them, and they set the jump on him. One quickly knocks Luke down and bellows out a victorious howl over him that reverberates throughout the desert canyon.

The Sand People are obviously more aggressive than the skittish Jawas. They are fierce and more nearly human, yet they too are faceless (we saw only bright eyes inside the hoods of the Jawas). They use elephant-sized creatures called Banthas to travel. From a Jungian perspective, we have entered the world of the *shadow*, the dark face of the unconscious that now gets to speak. One of the reasons we try to be in control, to not do "stupid" things, is to avoid this aspect of our psychic life. For both children and adults (as it was for Luke at his uncle's moisture farm) the fearful reality of the shadow is particularly threatening at night, but it also can jump out at us in our daylight experience (as it did with Luke). Shadow symbolism, which appears throughout the movies, will soon appear in its more helpful and personal forms when Luke gets to the city of Mos Eisley.[3]

As the Sand People quickly scavenge Luke's landspeeder a loud animal-like cry resounds through the canyon. Startled, they take off, and then we see a robed figure carefully picking his way over the rocky terrain. The figure moves over the unconscious Luke, whose body has been dropped by the Sand People near the speeder. He checks Luke's pulse and puts his hand over Luke's forehead. We view this new character through Artoo's eyes as he stands, beeping off to the side. When the cloaked figure senses the droid's presence, he removes his hood and turns to face the droid (and us) with a "Hello, there!" We don't see a crazy old wizard, but a kindly, bright-eyed, elderly man with a delightfully human face. He's most reassuring to Artoo and to us—"Don't be afraid"—letting both droid and viewer know that Luke will be all right.

Luke slowly regains consciousness and finds himself staring into the face of Ben Kenobi. Luke was emotionally "struck" and knocked over by the image of the princess; now in his encounter with the primitive Sand People he has been completely knocked out and left unconscious. This will be the first of such initiatory experiences for Luke. His recovery from this particular blow begins a true awakening into himself, his past, and his future. The image of being knocked unconscious psychologically represents being hit with aspects of life that we are not ready to face but with which we must come to terms. When Ben asks Luke what brought him to the

Jundland Wastes, Luke tells him that the droid was searching for his former master and that he's "never seen such devotion in a droid before." We get another reference to a unique human quality in one of our droid heroes, and thus something very unusual going on. Devotion is a spiritual quality; we will learn that Kenobi represents the last positive connection to an old religion whose living reality is soon to be awakened in Luke.

Jung often said that when a quality falls into the unconscious because it is dismissed or rejected, it will manifest in some other way. In the first *Star Wars* trilogy, some of these "lost" human qualities become manifest in the droids. Now we have come upon a most important human figure who will challenge Luke to discover aspects of life that have not previously been available to him.

Luke tells Ben that the droid claims to belong to an Obi-Wan Kenobi. He asks Ben if he knows him, and mentions that his uncle said Obi-Wan was dead. Ben says that Obi-Wan is not dead, "at least not yet," since "he's me!" Ben informs Luke that it is a name he hasn't gone by since before Luke was born and that he doesn't ever recall owning a droid before. Thus, as Ben Kenobi awakens Luke, he himself is being awakened to a part of himself he has relegated to the past.

With hints of the return of the Sand People, they retreat to Kenobi's house, but first they find that Threepio has also had a rough time—his arm has been removed. Death and rebirth symbolism, here in the form of dismemberment, occur often and poignantly throughout the three-movie saga. The dismemberment image of "dis-arm-ament" is a frequent occurrence. In this particular instance it is an experience for Threepio similar to Luke having been knocked unconscious. He has been taken apart and will have to be put back together again. Part of the mystery of the droid characters is that they, too, "suffer," and what they go through allows the symbolic to be expressed more literally. Given their unique characterizations, emotions can be expressed in very basic, easily understandable ways.

At the home of Obi-Wan Kenobi, Luke learns more about his father and his past. The psychological implications of Luke's uncle telling him to have the droid's message for Obi-Wan Kenobi erased become clearer. We also begin to understand the implications of his aunt's statement that "Luke just isn't a farmer, he has too much of his father in him." His uncle has told Luke that his father was a navigator on a spice freighter. Now he learns that his father fought in the Clone Wars with Kenobi, was an excellent pilot (as is Luke), and was a Jedi knight.

Kenobi also gives Luke something his father wanted him to have: his father's lightsaber. His uncle had kept it from him, for fear that, like his father, Luke would follow Obi-Wan on some idealistic crusade. Obi-Wan tells him, "This is the weapon of a Jedi Knight, an elegant weapon for a more civilized time. For over a thousand generations the Jedi Knights were the guardians of peace and justice in the Old Republic. Before the dark times, before the Empire." In this scene Obi-Wan becomes the newest storyteller giving background information that exceeds the droids' knowledge and that is also very relevant to Luke personally.

This piece of history, that is both personal and galactic, moves Luke to ask how his father died. Kenobi thoughtfully tells him that a former pupil of his, Darth Vader, who turned to evil, helped the Empire hunt down and destroy the Jedi Knights. It was he who betrayed and murdered his father. "Vader," Kenobi tells Luke, "was seduced by the Dark Side of the Force."

"The Force?" Luke asks.

Ben tells him, "The Force is what gives a Jedi his power. It's an energy field created by all living things. It surrounds us, it penetrates us, it binds the galaxy together." The Force, like any symbol, can have numerous meanings. I would like to suggest here that it is a symbol for the whole of psychic energy, for what Jung called the collective unconscious, an aspect of psychic reality that all peoples share and from which religious experience, myth, symbol, and art emerge. The Force, as described in this story, expresses symbolically this layer of the human psyche in a feeling, imaginative way, offering a sense of the "other world" referred to in so many of our cosmologies and religions.

One of the impressive aspects of the symbolism of the Force is that the Jedi knight combines two archetypal figures: the knight and the priest. In the Middle Ages knights were the active fighting figures in the world, while the priests were the caretakers of souls. In the Jedi knights both roles are joined: the knights have a responsibility to the spiritual reality of the Force, and they are guardians of the people and the Republic. Lucas's notion of the Jedi knights includes both *introverted* and *extraverted* qualities. In our time a shift in the collective unconscious is challenging us to be less identified with singular roles, as humans have been in the past; the hybrid image of a Jedi carries something of this evolving psychological and spiritual complexity. A new heroic image merges Robin Hood and Friar Tuck, for example.

On a personal level for Luke, Kenobi can be seen as a representative of the Self, an embodied symbol of what Luke's personality can become, now that it has been awakened by the anima archetype and nudged into life by the droid and the message he carries. Kenobi is a man who has fulfilled his life in a way that reflects Luke's potential, which makes him an excellent carrier for a projection of the Self. At the point when Luke meets him, Obi-Wan is a man who is not overrun by the shadow figures, the Sand People, and knows how to deal with their reality. Yet he isn't about to take them as lightly as Luke had. He hasn't lost his humanity, as it seems the Sand People have, and this humanity will be a critical aspect of Luke's struggle later on. Also, Kenobi brings to Luke the personal history of his father so long withheld from him, which conveys both the unlived potential that Luke holds as well as the fear that he would suffer the same fate.

After their initial conversation Kenobi plays the message the droid carries. The princess's hologram brings a message from her father to Kenobi, who had fought with her father in the Clone Wars. She had hoped to bring Kenobi to Alderaan herself, but now that she has been captured, she asks Kenobi to deliver the droid with the secret plans for her. Kenobi ponders the message; turning to Luke, he tells him that Luke must learn the ways of the Force and come with him to Alderaan. Obi-Wan says that he is "getting too old for this sort of thing." Luke protests that he's not going anywhere because he has work to do and has gotten into enough trouble already. Kenobi suggests to Luke that this is his uncle talking—an accurate statement of an important psychological state. Luke is not developed enough to hear the voice of his "true self" and act on it, so he falls into compliance with the internalized voice of his father-figure uncle. This sequence is also accurate psychologically in that as soon as one is moved by the voice of a Self figure, typically an old voice that has blocked the connection to the true self speaks out. It usually takes an individual a long time to resolve such an internal struggle, especially when the early parental voices did not support the true self. Luke is a young man in our story, but his adventures reflect the accelerated psychological demands of our time that grip people of all ages.

The psychological situation in which his uncle's voice speaks inside of Luke repeats a pattern we saw earlier when Luke heard his aunt's voice call to him right after the image of the princess produced by Artoo disappeared. Lucas's story reflects the psychological reality that this dynamic can have both a masculine and feminine aspect to it. The forward-looking and exciting aspects of life speak, only to be followed by the old, backward-pulling *complexes.* Luke initially gives in to the voice of his uncle/father complex, rejecting the invitation to a new life direction that is actually closer to his truest nature. Luke offers to help Kenobi obtain transportation to a spaceport, but that's all. Luke is gripped by an unconscious belief that "I can't get involved" because "I have work to do," and in the wisdom of his Jedi humanity, Kenobi doesn't push the point. He's made his suggestion, lets Luke consider it, and then allows the invitation to drop. "You must do what you feel is right, of course." As we will see, this attitude of respectful allowance for individual choice contrasts starkly with the attitude of the representatives of the Empire and the dark side of the Force.

The Death Star

The scene shifts from Ben Kenobi's home to the new battle station, the Death Star, where we again meet Darth Vader, this time amongst other Imperial officers. While there are personal issues with his uncle that Luke will have to confront, we see here the bigger challenges that lie in the background. We learn more about the Force, and this dying Jedi religion. Governor Tarkin states that

Vader is the last remnant of this religion, which leads one to wonder if they realize Kenobi is still alive. As the military figures boast about their new technological power, Vader is moved to give a little demonstration of the power of the Force. If this religion is dying, the reality on which it is based is still very much alive and its power can be demonstrated. Something is present, and the audience can hear it rumble when Darth Vader uses it. In this scene we see the Force used to choke an Imperial officer, leaving him gasping for air when Vader finally stops. The frightening implications of other destructive purposes the Force might be used for are easily implied. Vader gives this little demonstration because he finds another officer's "lack of faith [in the Force] disturbing."

The dark side of politics and religion is visible in this scene with the Imperial forces. The power principle is in full display as one officer gloats that the battle station is the ultimate weapon in the universe. Tarkin announces that the Emperor has disbanded the Imperial Senate, that the last remnants of the Old Republic have been swept away, and that the regional governors will now have direct control over their territories. They will employ fear to keep the local populations in submission, fear of this new battle station. With all this gloating over technological and political power, there is also an expression of their fear of being vulnerable. This is quite interesting and important psychologically. An over-emphasis on power on any level is often a defense against disowned vulnerability, which is, whether we like it or not, an essential part of being human. Only by being vulnerable do we become capable of psychological intimacy. Only when we are vulnerable are we the most related to the deeper aspects of our psychological and spirituality realities.

This Imperial group seeks to be completely in control, to circumvent or extinguish any vulnerability. Fear of vulnerability heightens the experience of others as a threat. In response to the imagined threat, the "other" has to be eliminated rather than engaged in a more related way. Since the Imperial group believes the rebels constitute a vulnerable area for the Empire, they are eager to eliminate them—and thus, they believe, eradicate their vulnerability.[4]

Vader is criticized because his "sad devotion to that ancient religion" has not helped him to "conjure up the stolen data tapes," or given him "clairvoyance enough to find the Rebel's hidden fort." That is, his belief is rejected because it has not taken away the group's feelings of vulnerability. Their hope is to force the princess to reveal the location of the secret rebel base, but it is Vader who realizes that she would never consciously do so. This fact can be seen both as a characterization of Leia as a strong, determined, and heroic young woman and as the attitude of the deeper unconscious to a conscious attitude driven by power: it will not give up its profoundest mysteries and secrets, because, as Vader so ruthlessly demonstrated, such an attitude would not hesitate to choke off life. These men are too much in the grip of egocentric power drives to consider the mystery and vulnerability of life. The only one who has a sense of such mystery—Darth Vader—is still only interested in it for reasons of power.

At the Jawa Trawler: Point of No Return

The scene shifts back to Tatooine where Ben, Luke, and the droids have come upon slaughtered Jawas and a blasted sand trawler. Luke suspects that the Sand People did it and comments that he has never known them to hit anything so big before. Ben demonstrates that they were made to think it was the Sand People; a closer look at the formation of the tracks and the accuracy of the blaster marks indicates that it wasn't Sand People but Imperial stormtroopers.

Luke wonders why Imperial troops would want to slaughter Jawas. As he glances at the two droids the answer dawns on him, as does the fear that the troopers have traced the droids to his uncle, to whom the Jawas sold them. He rushes back home in his landspeeder as Ben shouts a warning that to do so is too dangerous. When Luke arrives home, he finds, to his horror, that the stormtroopers have indeed been there. The moisture farm has been burned and destroyed, and Luke painfully views the charred skeletal remains of his aunt and uncle. He turns his head away from the horror of what has taken place.

Luke returns to the sand trawler area where the droids and Ben are cleaning up. Ben tells Luke that there was nothing he could have done, and that if he had been there, he would have been killed, too—and the droids would now be in the hands of the Empire. In his anger and frustration Luke tells Ben that there is nothing for him on this planet now, and that he wants to go with Ben to Alderaan and learn the ways of the Force so he can become a Jedi like his father.

This is a heroic point of no return for Luke. An act of fate intervenes in his life, and the personal issues fall to the wayside—at least for a time—because a larger event has taken over: the destructive campaign of the Empire. It is into the battle against the Empire that he will now put his life energy. Only recently, while he was at Ben Kenobi's, Luke had said that he hated the Empire but that he couldn't go with Ben because he had work to do. Now that the cruel reality of the Empire has affected him in a deeply personal way, he has a new response. The impact of the larger dimensions of life often jars us into adopting new attitudes and new directions.

Had fate not intervened in the way it did, Luke might have remained paralyzed by the inner voice of his uncle. Sometimes it takes the eruption of the darker sides of life to jolt us into breaking free from the inner voices that restrain us and prevent us from becoming who we most truly are. Now something in Luke awakens in the face of this personal disaster, and he gathers himself to move forward. In Jungian language we would say that the Self has now been activated in Luke, and he has embarked on a path that is more closely aligned with his potential. Jung referred to this as the path of *individuation*, one that leads to the realization of the true *self.*

CHAPTER 3

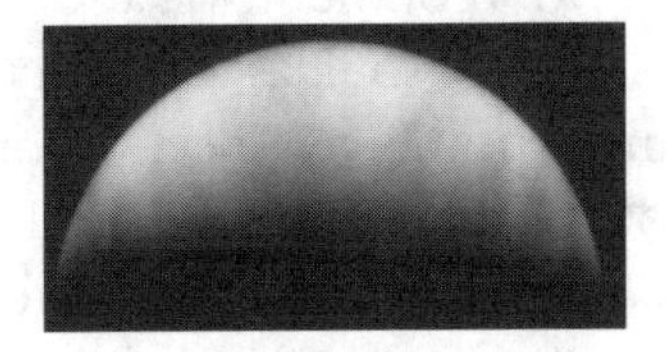

Tatooine: Mos Eisley

Before the adventure on Tatooine continues, another brief visit to the Death Star heightens the drama. Darth Vader enters the princess's prison cell with an interrogation droid in tow to attempt to extract information from her about the rebel base. The princess is in trouble. As before, we can experience this event on two levels: the literal level of the story, involving Leia the heroine, and the symbolic level of the psyche, in which the anima is imprisoned and in acute danger. At this point in the story Luke is being tested by life in a new way; inwardly this test can be seen as an interrogation of his soul. Does he have the capacity to relate to life and others with integrity, to be true to himself even when events are seemingly stacked against him? Victory that results in the loss of a man's soul is not part of the Jedi religion. Luke's ordeal on Tatooine was a test of his heart, which was awakened when he saw the image of the princess in Artoo's hologram. Having just lost his uncle and aunt, his personality is challenged much like the princess undergoing explicit interrogation.

In the next scene Ben, Luke, and the two droids stand high on a cliff overlooking Mos Eisley spaceport. Ben remarks to Luke that he will "never find a more wretched hive of scum and villainy." Psychologically, our hero—the new developing core of the personality that must make its way into the world—will now be further introduced to the world of the shadow. Confrontation with this element is another test for the soul, as the twin realities of the darker sides of life and the more primitive aspects of one's own personality shatter the illusions of youthful romanticism. In order to move forward in life with a deeper sense of purpose, these facets of our existence have to be faced. It is part of the initiation into life whereby one's ideals collide against the world *as it really is* in order for something new and creative to emerge.

Mos Eisley is a bustling desert city. George Lucas excels at creating separate worlds within the *Star Wars* universe that are hard to describe and are meant to be experienced. In the new edition of the movie Lucas expanded the Mos Eisley sequence in order to give a fuller sense of the city the characters were entering and the variety of its inhabitants. The entrance into the city now includes comic moments on the street that are particularly entertaining for children.

When Luke's landspeeder finally stops before stormtrooper guards, Obi-Wan gives a new, more subtle "demonstration" of the Force than Vader did on the Death Star. Obi-Wan is able to "suggest" to the guard questioning them that he doesn't need to see Luke's identification, that these are not the droids he's looking for, and that they can go about their business.

When the speeder stops further up the street, Luke is puzzled as to how they got past the guards. Obi-Wan remarks, "The Force has a powerful influence on the weak-minded." This sequence has important psychological implications, especially if the Force is seen in terms of the collective unconscious. In the hands of a creative personality, relationship with the collective unconscious can have a positive effect as it has through great religious figures like Moses, Christ, and Buddha. It can also have a destructive effect when a person (like Hitler, for example) connects to the darker dimensions of collective psychology and has the ability to influence people accordingly. As we will see in the next movie, it is only those who have a strong moral conscience that are not so easily influenced. Obi-Wan is able to use the Force on the masked guards who all seem the same, because people who have no individual identity are often the most susceptible to unconscious influence. They are "weak-minded" because they have no thoughts or feelings of their own. Since the unconscious is just that—unconscious and never fully knowable—everyone is subject to its influence, but some more than others. Greater awareness of this psychological reality also creates greater moral responsibility and the concomitant dangers of shirking that responsibility.

Ben takes Luke to a cantina where they are likely to meet a freighter pilot. He warns Luke that this place could be "a little rough," and Luke naively responds that he's ready for anything. Inside the cantina we encounter a wide assortment of provocative and exotic characters, the majority of which are nonhuman. A look at the imagery of medieval folklore shows that the imaginations of the artists of that era also produced an abundance of fascinating creatures (again see Figure 1). We get a touch of "racism" in this scene (a big part of any culture's shadow) when the bartender tells Luke, "We don't serve their kind here," referring to the droids.

As Ben makes contact with various characters in the cantina, Luke orders a drink and is soon harassed by two galactic desperados who "don't like him." One of these brags that he has "the death sentence on twelve systems." Ben tries to suggest to him that Luke isn't worth the trouble and offers to buy them a drink. The man becomes belligerent, pushes Luke aside, and draws a weapon. Ben quickly ignites his lightsaber in defense and literally "disarms" the man (we see a bloodied, severed arm on the floor). This is the second—and not the last—time we see this image as the story develops. Earlier in the story See Threepio lost an arm and was dismembered by the Sand People. Here, dismemberment is inflicted as an act of self-defense and in protection of another's life.

For the first time we see a lightsaber in action. It clearly cuts like a sword in an awesome way. Symbolically this would indicate that, like a sword or a knife, it has powerful discriminating aspects, which can help cut through difficult situations. In addition, it radiates light, suggesting a discrimination based on "shedding light" on a situation. It is thus closely related to the etymology of the word *phallus* meaning "shining, bright." Part of Luke's ongoing initiation will be to learn to handle this powerful, yet illuminating and mysterious, phallic weapon.

Luke is clearly not "ready for anything" as he had proclaimed outside; he requires more development before he can look after himself. It is at this moment that Ben, as he helps Luke to stand up, introduces him to Chewbacca, a tall furry creature, who is first mate on a ship that might suit them. (We later learn that Chewbacca is a Wookie. When upset, Wookies have been known to pull people's arms out of their sockets. Symbolically, Wookies represent a more direct way of "disarming" people. They don't need a weapon to do so.)

Chewbacca, who mostly growls to express himself, well exemplifies the wild man archetype. With Chewie present, a basic, instinctive dimension is added to the unfolding drama. He represents an aspect of human psychology that exists mostly on the primitive affective level and has its roots mythologically in such figures as Enkidu in the Gilgamesh Epic. The Grimm's fairy tale figure of Iron John and Jewish mysticism's Adam Kadmon are other examples of this figure's prominent place in medieval mythology (see Figures 2 and 3).[1] This archetype is still very much alive in the human imagination and finds current expression in the ongoing legends of figures such as the Sasquatch and the Abominable Snowman. If we look at Chewbacca from the standpoint of personal psychology, he represents instinctive qualities that Luke still has to come to terms with in himself.

We're soon introduced to Han Solo who is captain of the Millennium Falcon, the ship on which Chewie serves. Han represents a shadow figure for Luke, for as we soon learn, he knows how to take care of himself. Most importantly, he possesses the ship that Obi-Wan and Luke need to get to their destination. Han Solo has lived the adventurous kind of life that Luke has only dreamed about. As owner of a ship, Han is closely connected to the vehicle symbolism prominent in *Star Wars*.[2] Vehicles are also important symbols in dreams, be they planes, boats, cars, buses, bikes, spaceships, and so on. They represent a contained amount of predictable mechanical energy that enables us get around in life. This form of energy lies at the opposite end of the spectrum occupied by the instinctive energy represented by the wild man. Coming of age in our culture usually

Figure 2

The natural level of life is a critical component of our psychology. A medieval wild family. From Husband's *The Wild Man.* Drawing, Ms. francais 2374, fol.3v, cliché Bibliothèque national de France, © BnF. Reprinted with permission.

includes getting a driver's license and learning to use various forms of public transportation. It's part of modern initiation.

When Luke first sees the Millennium Falcon, he proclaims, "What a piece of junk!" Han indicates that he has made a lot of special modifications himself and that "she's got it where it counts." This is not unlike many young men who will rebuild an old "piece of junk" to their own "special modifications." Symbolically this represents someone discovering his or her own unique way of getting about in the world. There will be more vehicle symbolism to consider as we go along, particularly in *The Empire Strikes Back.*

This unlikely group of characters forms an alliance. Luke is the impatient one concerned about what this collaboration will cost them, especially since he has piloting experience of his own. Obi-Wan bargains by offering to put down less money at the start, but an amount seventy percent higher than Han has requested once they've reached their destination. Ben and Luke quietly disappear when stormtroopers come to investigate the disturbance around Obi-Wan's brief battle. Chewie leaves to prepare the ship and Han is accosted by a bounty hunter who works for Jabba the Hutt, to whom he is in debt. Here we see that when he has to, Han can take care of himself. He too is being pursued, but for very different reasons than Ben and Luke.

Another quality associated with Han Solo's character is debt. We all know about financial debt and trying to avoid it. We can also accrue a psychic debt that can even be passed on to our children. Living lopsidedly, tapping into only some forms of psychic energy while ignoring or banishing others, will usually result in life catching up with us sooner or later. Living too close to the "edge" or with the wrong company can create such a problem; drug abuse and gang memberships are examples. Solo's debt to Jabba the Hutt, who runs a smuggling operation, is a theme permeating the three movies. (In the special edition of the movie, Solo runs into Jabba at his ship. Lucas didn't create the image of Jabba until the original version of *Return of the Jedi.*)

The cantina scene, which brings together quite an assortment of characters, juxtaposes two kinds of heroic figures. First is the old, yet also futuristic, image of the knight who defends others with his

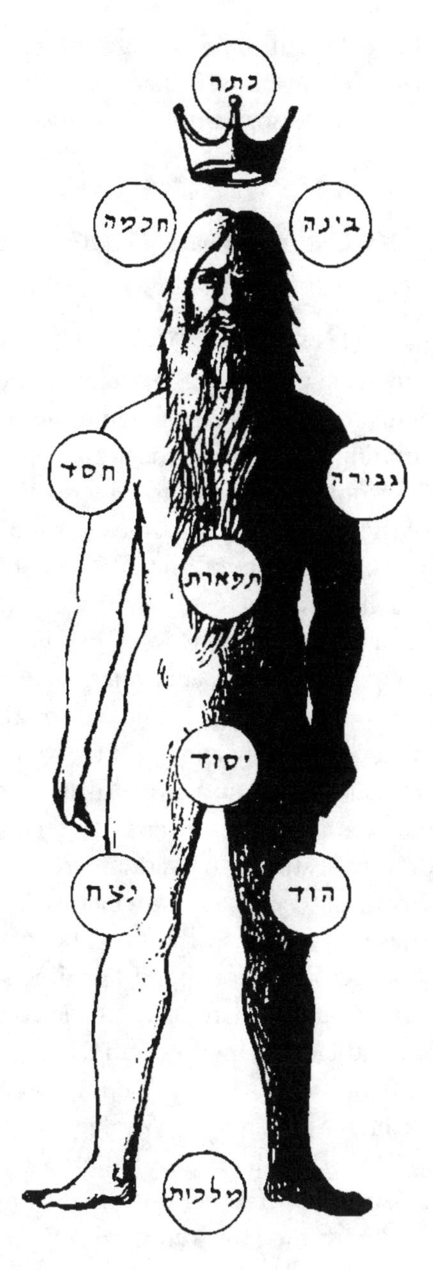

Figure 3

The archetype expresses a connection between the natural and the mystical. Adam Kadmon. From Edward Edinger's *The Mysterium Lectures*

sword. Then we have the gunslinging rogue-figure who is quick on the draw in order to defend himself. Part of Lucas's creative genius is to weave together such disparate images and make them work in a meaningful way.

On Board the *Millennium Falcon*

Imperial spies pick up the trail of Ben, Luke, and the droids, and they have to shoot their way out of Mos Eisley. Imperial ships pursue them and Han realizes that his passengers are "hotter than I thought." He begins to see them as people rather than just a source of profit. This budding sense of connection continues to grow as they escape from Tatooine and head to Alderaan.

Two aspects of the psychology of vehicle symbolism in *Star Wars* are introduced in this portion of the film. First, the vehicle has deflector shields, a limited defense mechanism, which protects it from the fire of the large Imperial cruisers. Psychologically, when we are in a vehicle mode we usually feel energized; it gives us some sense of being able to move about in the world around us in a way we can't do by using only bodily energy. If the vehicle is an enclosed vehicle that travels on the ground, we usually also feel somewhat safe and protected. We gain a false sense of security. Our modern vehicles offer comfort features that add to this sense of personal safety and security. But eventually we have to leave the vehicle world. The defenses it appears to offer can't be utilized unendingly. We can't always "deflect" life, nor spend our time solely in traveling from point to point. Sooner or later the vehicle comes to a stop and we have to get out and face the people and life-events in front of us.

The current phenomenon of "road rage" demonstrates that many people, like Han Solo, have a Wookie-like co-pilot inside of them when they drive. In the relative safety of the car primitive affects can erupt that don't emerge elsewhere. A number of people who have consulted with me have reported how shocked they have been by their own rage, which seems to appear only when they drive. This unfamiliar level of anger comes out in the relative anonymity of the car, because it is a place where it's less likely that they will be recognized, and they can't be shamed for having these feelings. Like the Wookie who will pull an opponent's arm out of its socket when he is upset, the person gripped by such rage would like to "disarm" those around him or her or eliminate them from the road altogether.

The second major element of vehicle symbolism introduced in this sequence of the film is *hyperspace*, a vehicle's ability to travel beyond the speed of light. Hyperspace is depicted in the film as entering a tunnel of space where the stars are speeding by. In this state, a vehicle seems to disappear into space and can get from one place to another without being attacked or directly pursued. This is a marvelous metaphor for using a fast-paced lifestyle as a psychological defense. Life can go so fast that there isn't time to feel or experience anything. While accelerated speed is a natural element of modern travel, we usually have to get caught up with ourselves, psychologically and physically, once we end our journey, as is implied by the term "jet lag."

The experience of hyperspace is a good example of the imaginative way Lucas has of telling a story. Our fascination with speed and space travel is stirred by this concept of going beyond the speed of light, just as breaking the sound barrier captures the imagination of both flight engineers and those who watch jet flight from a distance. The futuristic concept of hyperspace captures viewers' imaginations on various levels. Many viewers might have fantasies of space flight, while for others it serves as a symbol of the vicissitudes of modern life. By using this kind of image, Lucas can tune his story to the imaginations of a broad spectrum of people.

At Mos Eisley our heroes have linked up with other characters to form a partnership that will remain important throughout the movies. Obi-Wan has found someone to help him with the next phase of his plan to respond to the princess's call for help. Luke gives up his old landspeeder in order for them to get passage out of Tatooine, though he's not yet ready for his own vehicle. Han has found some people to help him pay off the debt that threatens his life. As separate individual characters, they, along with Chewbacca and the droids, also represent different aspects of a single male personality coming to realize its various parts, but with more significant development and adventures to come.

CHAPTER 4

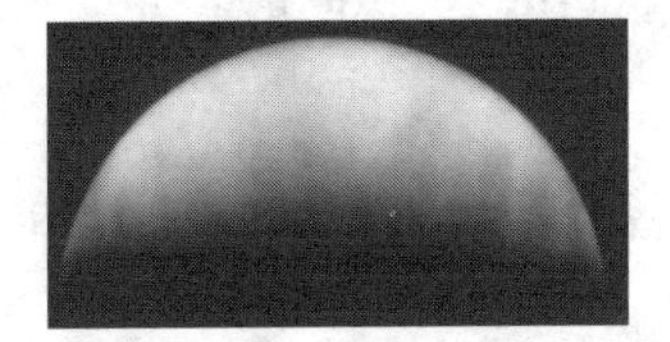

Alderaan and the Death Star

The location shifts to the Alderaan system as the Death Star arrives there. Princess Leia is brought before Governor Tarkin and does not hesitate to confront him as the one "holding Vader's leash." She "recognized his foul stench" when she was brought on board. Odor is used metaphorically throughout the movies, often in more literal contexts, as we will see. Smell functions metaphorically in everyday language too, when, for example, someone says "this stinks," or, in a more positive vein, when we say that someone "has a nose" for something.

Tarkin suggests that Leia is to blame for the choice of the location where he will test the new weapon that he has at his command. He demands that she give him a military target, the location of the rebel base, or he will test the destructive power of the new battle station on her home planet of Alderaan. Leia protests that Alderaan is peaceful and has no weapons. When faced with seemingly no choice, she tells Tarkin that the rebel base is on Dantooine. Tarkin gloats to Vader that she can be reasonable, as his alternative form of persuasion has worked, and then orders the commander to get ready to destroy Alderaan anyway.

Slowly emerging in this movie is the conflict between people who are in the grip of power and those who would live according to another principle. Psychologically we might say that Tarkin has developed powerful energy that he is itching to apply to destructive ends rather than creative or humane ones. In order to justify this kind of blatant destructiveness, a person might shift the responsibility onto someone else. In this case, Leia's sense of moral responsibility is manipulated in such a way that she is forced to make a choice that might serve the purposes of power and destruction. A subtle but important subtext of this story explores the nature of morality and conveys the message that we all must assume responsibility for the destructive aspects of ourselves and of life.

Leia is stunned by Tarkin's dismissal of any responsibility. Tarkin even chides her for being far too trusting. He claims that Dantooine is too remote for an "effective demonstration" and that he will deal with her rebel friends later. He's possessed by his power and his need to use it. He hopes to use fear to force other star systems to submit to him. Leia assures Tarkin that "the more you tighten your grip, the more star systems will slip through your fingers." This scene, like many others, may not offer the highest level of dramatic acting or writing, but it succeeds in the development of the psychological aspects of the story. The power principle, whether in the individual personality, or in the social and political sphere, would seek to control life—even destroy it if necessary—in order to achieve domination. In response to this gross distortion of the human attribute of self-expression, the soul, here represented by the young feminine figure, rebels. Life will not and cannot be controlled; it is too multifaceted and mysterious.

The Death Star fires upon the planet Alderaan and there is an enormous explosion across the screen as the planet is totally obliterated. This image of explosion has highly significant meaning psychologically—it appears frequently in dreams. On one level it reflects the situation of our own time since, with the development of nuclear weaponry, we have the capacity to destroy our own planet. As we develop the capability to generate more forms of energy—energy with more "force"—we have to be careful how we use it. It is a problem inherent in the evolution of our civilization.[1]

The issues of control and power are also personal psychological issues that greatly affect the way we relate interpersonally with other people and internally to ourselves. For example, an individual with an "explosive personality" may act out emotional energy destructively on another human being or other living creature. Other personality types may unconsciously direct negative energy in an internal way, resulting in various physical and psychological symptoms. On the other hand, such energy can be channeled creatively on both external and internal levels via healthy self-expression and mutually satisfying personal relationships. Jung liked to emphasize that psychic energy can be directed for either destructive or creative purposes and expressed through an entire spectrum of human responses from instinctual reactions to spiritual aspirations.[2] Tarkin demonstrates an extreme form of what we call "acting out behavior" that occurs when feelings are not owned, experienced and wrestled with. The tension of moral responsibility that is a natural byproduct of relational connections also does not exist. The people in the Empire don't appear to form personal relationships at all, but the main characters we come to know as part of the rebellion do, and they duly wrestle with the conflicts that come with such human connections.

The explosion of Alderaan is highly symbolic. Explosion imagery will recur in this movie and in the other movies as well. How we deal with the energy available to us, psychological and otherwise, is a critical issue of our time.[3]

The Millennium Falcon

The story shifts back to the Millennium Falcon where Obi-Wan is instructing Luke. Suddenly Obi-Wan stumbles and has to sit down. When Luke asks him if he's all right, Ben tells him, "I felt a great disturbance in the Force, as if millions of voices cried out in terror and were suddenly silenced. I feel something terrible has happened." He then suggests that Luke get back to his exercises.

This little touch of mysticism is quite important in the slowly growing sense of what it means to be a Jedi. For while this monstrous tragedy was initiated with cold ruthlessness, someone *did feel* the great pain of it. Surfacing here is the historical lesson that religion (even in the advanced form of the Jedi) has hardly been a deterrent to war and other forms of mass destruction. At certain times it has even been deeply involved, and at others it has been a passive bystander. The horrors of the Holocaust and much of the two World Wars, for example, took place in supposedly Christian societies. But except for some heroic individuals, organized religion remained silent and powerless as so many suffered. Similarly, only recently in our country's history are we beginning to come to terms with what African Americans, Native Americans, and other ethnic groups have suffered, as well as the damage done to our natural environment.[4] We are also becoming more aware of the psychological trauma suffered by many individuals who are asked to fight in wars. The negative effects of the advance of so-called scientific and technological civilization are being felt more clearly than ever before.

When Han Solo arrives on the scene to say, "Well, you can forget those Imperial slugs; I told you I'd outrun them." The audience, like Ben, knows of the great destruction that has taken place and doesn't necessarily feel safe from those "Imperial slugs." Han is disappointed there isn't more gratitude. A holographic chess game adds a little diversion here, as Artoo plays Chewbacca and we get a glimpse from Han of Chewie's emotionally explosive potential, especially his unique way of "disarming" someone. ("It's not wise to upset a Wookie. Wookies have been known to pull someone's arm out of their socket when they lose.")

The scene then shifts to Luke's exercises—his first "training" in becoming a Jedi knight. Luke is trying to use his lightsaber to deflect little bursts of laser energy fired from a small, round, flying remote. Such a sphere can be seen as a symbol of the Self. In the setting of the Death Star it is a negative manifestation, and the energy it emits is destructive and overwhelming. In the case of this little remote, the energy "stings" but is not overwhelming. Thus Luke can learn from the experience; it doesn't hit him with more than he can handle.

Ben tells Luke, "A Jedi can feel the Force flowing through him."

So Luke asks, "You mean it controls your actions?"

"Partially," Ben responds, "but it also obeys your commands." The psychology of utilizing the Force is parallel to how we connect to our psychic energy. For example, consider the two big emotions of love and hate, which both control, and are controlled by, us. When we fall in love we are totally gripped by the experience. We feel strongly moved by something beyond ourselves and invited to relate more deeply to another person. This powerful, compelling emotion partially controls what we do, but by channeling it into various behaviors related to "dating" we direct it—or in Ben's words, "it also obeys our commands." Similarly, we can feel seized by hate, as when it erupts in a family setting or in the collective forms that lead to racism and bigotry. Hatred, too, can control our actions, but if we struggle with it we can channel it, whether it be in a positive or ruinous way. Depth psychology suggests that "possession" by strong emotion may indicate conflicts within both the personal and collective levels of the psyche that need to be addressed so that they are not acted upon in destructive ways.

Next, Ben instructs Luke to "reach out with your feelings"—certainly a unique approach to training for a form of "knighthood." Soldiers are trained to be disconnected from their feelings when facing the enemy. The more feelings (other than hate) you have for someone, the less likely you are going to be able to kill them. The enemy has to be depersonalized. But on the home front such training creates a variety of problems, including the eruption of feelings in abusive ways and the incapacity to bring them to bear in intimate personal relationships. The Jedi knight is taught, in contrast, to stretch out with his feelings so as to be able to parry "stinging" attacks.

When the remote's laser stings Luke, Han Solo laughs exclaiming, "hokey religions and ancient weapons are no match for a good blaster at your side."

Luke realizes that Han is skeptical and asks, "You don't believe in the Force, do you?"

Han responds, "Kid, I've flown from one side of this galaxy to the other. I've seen a lot of strange stuff, but I've never seen anything to make me believe there's one all-powerful force controlling everything. It's all a lot of simple tricks and nonsense. There's no mystical energy field that controls my destiny." Han is the ultimate skeptic. He's very practical, which is why he's able to survive. But there is a dimension of life he remains closed to, that he can't even imagine might exist.[5] Everything has a rational explanation for him.

Rather than respond directly to Han, Obi-Wan smiles and brings a blast helmet for Luke to wear. He suggests to Luke, "Let go of your conscious self and act on instinct."

Luke complains that with the blast helmet on, he won't be able to see. Ben responds, "Your eyes can deceive you; don't trust them." Again he encourages Luke to "stretch out with [his] feelings," and as the droid fires, Luke is able to deflect each laser shot. "See, you can do it," Ben says to Luke.

Han exclaims, "I call that luck."

And Ben responds, "In my experience there is no such thing as luck."

To which Han counters, "Good against remotes, that's one thing, good against the living, that's something else." As Luke's training moment ends, we see two very contrasting views: that of the mystical wizard and that of the rogue, practical pilot. Two views will have to be reconciled in this group, whereas within the Imperial world there is only one view.

As the ship signals that they are coming upon Alderaan Luke tells Ben, "I did feel something, I could almost see the remote."

Ben responds, "That's good! You've taken your first step into a larger world." Instead of seeing things only concretely and practically, as Han does, Luke has glimpsed them through his feelings and imagination. This is similar to when we allow ourselves the inner space to experience our practical, concrete existence in more symbolic ways as well. Stretching out with our feelings poses more risks and makes us vulnerable but ultimately offers the reward of a larger, more mysterious experience of life.

Death Star Update

While our group of heroes approaches Alderaan, we are back on the Death Star. An officer reports to Tarkin that the scout ships have found the remains of a rebel base on Dantooine, which they estimate has been deserted for some time. Tarkin is upset, exclaiming, "She lied to us!" Vader tells him again that she would never consciously betray the rebellion. In his frustration Tarkin orders, "Terminate her, immediately!"

Leia isn't as trusting as Tarkin had thought. He doesn't like being fooled. The report implies that he has gained nothing and that the destruction of Alderaan was an act of horror for the sake of demonstrating power. Now he will destroy Leia as well for daring to trick him as he tried to trick her. In this totally masculine world, she was cleverer, and he can't tolerate it. With her peaceful home planet obliterated, Leia herself faces the threat of extinction. As Alderaan's sole survivor, she has unwittingly become a living symbol for all that the planet represented—for whatever time she has left to live.

The Arrival at Alderaan

When the Millennium Falcon emerges from the tunnel of hyperspace, it collides with fragments of the destroyed planet. Now the reality of the destruction that Ben glimpsed through the Force really "hits" them, and they have to come to terms with it. The anxious Luke asks, "What's going on?"

Han tells him, "Our position is correct, except . . . no Alderaan. It's been totally blown away!" Obi-Wan realizes the Empire has destroyed it. Han can't conceive how the Empire could have that much firepower.

A recurrent theme in mythology is one in which the hero, having finally arrived at his destination, doesn't find what he is searching for. In this case, it no longer even exists. Their journey now takes on far-reaching and unknowable consequences. In myth the heroic journey usually takes awhile. For example, the people of Israel get close to the Promised Land after the Exodus, but they aren't ready to make it their own and must journey through the wilderness for many more years. In Homer's *Odyssey*, Odysseus steers his ship very close to Ithaca, but then it's blown back out to sea and he must journey many more years before he actually arrives there. In the Eros and Psyche tale, Psyche at first seems to find her "dream" house, but it all comes apart; she undergoes many trials before she can have the relationship she truly desires.

On a personal psychological level this situation reflects those experiences when we get our hopes up for something, but then end up disappointed by unforeseen events. What we expected and hoped for isn't there. Or, we discover that there is much more involved in getting what we are seeking than we had previously imagined.

In the midst of the confusion on the Millennium Falcon an Imperial fighter flies past, a small, short-range fighter that could not have followed them from Tatooine. Ben wants to let it go, but Han insists on pursuing it so that its pilot cannot report their whereabouts. Han chases it towards what Luke sees as a small moon, but Ben realizes that it is a space station. Han can't believe that something that big could be a space station. When Ben urgently orders him to turn the ship around, it is already too late—they are caught in a tractor beam that is pulling them in. They have to shut down all power, because they are up against a greater power than they possess. Han protests, "They aren't going to get me without a fight." Ben points out that they can't win but that there are alternatives to fighting. As all of this ensues, Luke, who has just been taught to stretch out with his feelings, exclaims, "I have a bad feeling about this." This becomes a signature line of the main characters throughout the film. A new facet of the adventure is about to unfold.

Inside the Death Star

The Millennium Falcon is pulled into a docking bay and troops scurry to receive it. The reports to Tarkin indicate that the ship's markings match one that blasted its way out of Mos Eisley. Vader wonders if the crew is trying to return the stolen plans to the princess and remarks that she may still be of some use to them. He joins those going to meet the ship.

Once there, Vader is told that no crew was on board and that the log indicates they had jettisoned shortly after take-off. When he asks if there were any droids, he's told no; if there had been any, they must have jettisoned. Vader orders a scanning crew to be sent on board to have every inch of the ship checked. As he leaves he warily comments, "I sense something, a presence I haven't felt since . . ."

One of my personal delights in these stories is the dimension brought by "Jedi awareness." This awareness adds a hidden and mysterious element allowing for subtle but important psychological intrigue that grows in meaning through the three films (and I would expect even more so in subsequent films). In the first movie this awareness will soon lead to a duel over who is the most powerful and, more importantly, whose conscious awareness of the Force is most connected to its deepest nature.

If Vader senses Obi-Wan's presence (Ben told Luke that Vader was a former pupil of his), will the scanning crew? Will our heroes be discovered? Like them, we all need defenses from time to time, for they help preserve the most sensitive core of the personality when it is in danger. Jung developed his theory of introversion and extraversion in part by observing nature and the primary defenses of fight or flight in the animal world. As we have seen, Han Solo would rather fight, but Ben suggested an alternative approach. Using this alternative approach, they have so far succeeded in remaining hidden and escaping detection (except for the Jedi perceptions of Vader).

Luke, as the new young hero, is situated between these two approaches of very different men who have already found their places in the world. He's like most of us who have lost parts of ourselves in making early childhood adaptations and have yet to discover how to bring these parts back to life. These early adaptations help us to survive and function in the world, up to a point, but certain new experiences, most often in relationships, bring out the areas that haven't been able to develop. To allow the new growth to come forth, we must free ourselves from these outmoded adaptations that hold us back. For Luke, it is his "father complex" still holding him back, as described earlier. Fate has intervened to free him of the narrow life imposed by his uncle. Now he will have to be an active participant, fighting external, collective forces that would prevent him and the others from living life more fully.

When the initial inspection troops leave, our heroes emerge from the secret compartments that Han used for smuggling. He never thought, he tells his new companions, that he'd be using them to smuggle *himself*. Han, too, is getting initiated into a larger world than he had previously imagined. But how will they get past the tractor beam? "Leave that to me," Ben tells him.

When the scanning crew goes on board (which the viewer sees from outside the ship), we know from the sound effects that they have been jumped. Soon Han's voice calls to the two stormtrooper guards below to come up and give them a hand. Obviously they, too, are removed from the scene. Han and Luke are now in stormtrooper uniforms and helmets and they quickly gain entrance to a control room, with Han and Chewie blasting away. Luke laments that they'll alert everyone else to their presence. Han reiterates his preference for a straight fight rather than all the "sneaking around."

Through Artoo's capacity to plug into any computer system, Ben is able to get the data he needs about how to deactivate the tractor beam. (We learn Artoo has the ability to interpret the entire Imperial computer network.) Threepio helps translate what is going on. Ben realizes that he must go alone and that the others should wait there. A sense that he might not return is conveyed when he tells Luke that he can't go with him and that he (Luke) must look after the droids and see that they are safely delivered so that other star systems don't suffer the same fate as Alderaan. He tells Luke, "Your destiny lies along a different path than mine." When he departs, he utters the spiritual "signature line" of these stories, "The Force will be with you . . . always!"

As the door closes after Ben leaves, Han asks Luke, "Where did you dig up that old fossil?"

Luke responds, "Ben is a great man."

"Yeah," Han responds, "great at getting us into trouble."

"I didn't see you . . ." Luke answers, and then the beeping of Artoo interrupts them.

Each of these two different figures has a different take on the old Jedi. For Han, his involvement has gotten him into more than he bargained for. He blames the old man for this, yet, in fact, Han took the job in the first place only because of the trouble he had gotten himself into due to his problems with Jabba the Hutt. He is still Han Solo, looking after himself. Luke, in contrast, has come to idealize Ben, who has opened up his personal history and a larger world for him. His feelings for Ben constitute a form of positive identification, like those that occur in the early stages of psychotherapy or when one encounters a good teacher or mentor. The same person (therapist, teacher, mentor) will be experienced quite differently by different individuals, determined mostly by their own needs, wounds, and psychological makeup and the place they are in life when that all-important person enters it.

Now, new information is presented that means they are to do more than just wait for Ben to deactivate the tractor beam. "I've found her; she's here," Threepio excitedly proclaims.

"Who?" asks Han.

"Princess Leia."

"Princess?" questions Han, "What's going on?"

"She's the one in the message," exclaims Luke excitedly, "we have to help her! She's scheduled to be terminated."

"I'm not going anywhere," proclaims Han. "The old man told us to wait right here."

"But he didn't know she was here," counters Luke. "She'll be killed," Luke pleads.

"Better her than me," Han replies.

This is a key psychological turning point. I'm sure many "rational" viewers scoffed at the story line, sharing Han Solo's reaction to the presence of a princess. But it works, offering testament to Lucas's ability to tell stories through images that tap into the archetypal core of the human imagination. The rational mind might initially scoff, but on another level, like Luke, we are animated. Worldwide response to the death of Princess Diana in 1997 is a good example of how someone who becomes closely associated with an archetypal image can deeply move people (in her case, positively). Reports of her as a person indicate no extraordinary gifts; in fact, she had a fair share of psychological problems. But struggling with these difficulties more openly than the Royal Family of England is generally willing to do endeared Diana to countless thousands of people. Ironically, Diana was tragically killed about the same time that Nobel Peace Prize recipient Mother Teresa died. Yet Diana drew far more worldwide attention than the remarkable woman many were ready to have canonized as a saint. From a

Jungian perspective it was the fascinating power of the princess archetype that accounted for this. Lucas's creative genius for weaving such symbolic imagery into his story has enabled him to capture the imagination of more than one generation.

Hearing that the princess is in the Death Star animates and energizes Luke. He is eager to rescue her and motivated to overcome Han's resistance. In Jungian terms, showing signs of anima development and an introverted approach, he realizes how to inspire Han. "She's rich. Rich, powerful, if you were to rescue her the reward would be . . ."

"What?" the now interested Han Solo asks.

"Well, way more than you can imagine," says Luke.

"I don't know. I can imagine quite a bit," counters Han.

"You'll get it," Luke asserts.

"What's your plan?" Han asks. The two heroic figures are now working together; Luke is coming into his own—he has even gotten Han's attention.

Luke's plan is to act as if Chewie were a prisoner, putting binders on him, and in their stormtrooper garb gaining access to the detention center. The droids are to wait in the control room. Through all that follows in this sequence, there is adventure, suspense, intrigue, and a lot of Saturday matinee fun and dialogue. On the way to the detention center they start to have their doubts, naturally, expressed in bantering comments like "This is not going to work." And then, "Why didn't you say so before?" Followed by, "I did say so before."

Meanwhile, Ben is slowly making his way through the Death Star, and we can see, once again, that Vader senses his presence.

When our trio arrive at the detention center the officer in charge asks, "Where are you taking this thing?" Derogatory remarks are made about the various characters throughout the story. Han irreverently questions the character of Ben and the existence of the Force. Now the Wookie gets his. (Later on Leia will refer to him as "this big walking carpet.") The doubts of the rational mind get expressed throughout the story in this comedic tone, thereby acknowledging them and adding to the psychological integrity of the characters.

A shoot-out soon ensues and Luke races to the cell to free the princess. He stares in wonderment at Leia for a moment and she questions his stature as a stormtrooper. Luke removes the helmet and proclaims, "I'm Luke Skywalker. I'm here to rescue you."

To which Leia, responds, "You're who?" (Yet another character is regarded derogatorily.)

"I'm here with Ben Kenobi. I've got your R2 unit." These magic words propel her into action, and they dash off together.

While this story is not as rich in symbols of women's psychology as of men's, this scene does give a glimpse of *animus* development in a woman. The sudden appearance of the young Luke Skywalker is not what Leia would have expected.[6] She questions him sarcastically, "Aren't you a little short for a stormtrooper?" He's not someone she could "look up to," and falls short of what she would imagine a stormtrooper should be. Certainly this person is a far cry from General Kenobi to whom she had sent her message for help. Yet it turns out that this poor excuse for a disguised stormtrooper is connected to Kenobi and even has possession of her R2 unit. The healthy, masculine aspect of Leia's personality becomes more obvious in the subsequent movies.

"*He* Is Here"

An interlude in the prison cell rescue, away from the plight of the four characters, takes us to a conversation between Tarkin and Vader—a conversation that is central to the development of the deeper layers of the story. Vader states that "*He* is here."

To which Tarkin responds, "Obi-Wan Kenobi? What makes you think so?"

"A tremor in the Force," responds Vader. "The last time I felt it was in the presence of my former master."

"Surely he must be dead by now," Tarkin wonders.

"Don't underestimate the Force," Vader emphasizes.

To which Tarkin replies, "The Jedi are extinct. Their fire has gone out of the universe. You, my friend, are all that's left of their religion."

Then they're interrupted by the alarm signaling the emergency situation in the detention block. Tarkin realizes it concerns the princess and puts all sections on alert. Vader reiterates that Obi-Wan is here and that "the Force is with him." Tarkin clamors that he must not be allowed to escape, but Vader claims, "Escape is not his plan. I must face him *alone*."

Two very important symbolic themes are presented here that touch on the most profound psychological aspects of the story. One is the importance of the Force as a living psychic energy whose presence can be experienced. Those in contact with this reality, like Vader, can sense the presence of others, like Obi-Wan, who are connected to it as well; they can "touch" the Force. But those connected to this reality understand and utilize it in vastly different ways. We are obviously headed towards a duel between the two remaining practitioners of this "religion."

The second theme is the declaration that, but for these two Jedi, this old religion is nearly extinct, its "fire . . . has gone out." The energy (fire) for it has dissipated. The religion has failed, it seems, to connect people to the reality that it serves. New forms of energy, like those harnessed by the battle station and political wielders of power, have replaced the energy that might have gone into this religion. As Han Solo was the skeptic with Obi-Wan, so now Tarkin is the skeptic with Vader about the presence of this "mystical" energy field.

One of the key spiritual elements of the *Star Wars* myth that is relevant for our times is presented here. Currently the religious function of the psyche, which connects the soul to its archetypal layers, has slowly shifted its focus away from institutional forms of spiritual connection to those intrinsic to the individual personality.[7] The waning influence of religion (in our culture) and religious myths (in general) are signs of this momentous shift.

Jung, the son of a Swiss Reform pastor, was the first psychoanalyst to address this spiritual problem of the modern soul that has lost its fire. Even as a boy Jung felt that his father had lost faith because he no longer knew how to *experience* those ineffable qualities of transcendence that religion attempted to foster.[8] He came to realize that all myths, be they religious or otherwise, are attempts to understand the numinous experiences that occur both within and around us. Religious myths, according to Jung, must be rediscovered within the human psyche, and their psychological nature and purpose understood, their vibrancy and numinosity felt, if they are to serve their soulful function. The old images and mythological explanations must make way for the emergence of new images and the meaning they carry. Only when we have a living experience of this internal reality—what Jung called the collective unconscious, which is as "close" to us as our next dream—can we perceive its presence and its message.

In some ways traditional religion has been replaced in our age by "myths" of science and technology, which have led us to overemphasize linear thinking, technological achievement, and material gain.[9] The result is an enormous psychological imbalance that has become unsatisfying to those in tune with the deeper yearnings of the soul. Jung considered this issue to be the most pressing one now facing us.[10] Which developments in the new millennium will assist our soul-selves to connect to those deeper realities that formerly were mediated by religion? How can those of us who are no longer gripped by the old religious myths experience the mysterious archetypal roots of our psychic life and the world around us in more meaningful ways?

One important indication of the need for new myths (and a new understanding of old ones) in the modern psyche has been the reports of UFO experiences since the end of World War II. Jung interpreted this phenomenon as an expression of the need for the modern soul to find a new symbolic connection to the archetype of the Self, which had been carried in the West for the past two millennium primarily by the image of Christ, the god-man. This archetype of the Self, he proposed, was representing itself in the unconscious through new images (such as mandala-shaped UFOs).[11] The proliferation of these new images, which have appeared in many people's dreams and numerous movies, illustrates this movement in the modern psyche. The UFO phenomenon has stirred a new mythology that has gripped and fascinated many of us. It has also fostered deeper scientific yearnings to explore the near and far reaches of outer space for signs of life and other forms of intelligence in order to comprehend more deeply the mysteries of the world in which we live.

By interweaving myths of technology and religion occurring in some other galaxy, Lucas depicts a "mythic time" where there is a change in the dominant religious myth and its relationship to psychic energy. At the time of the release of the Star Wars Special Edition films, Darrin Bell, a newspaper cartoonist, captured this important aspect of the fascination with Lucas's story: the shift in the primary god-image of our world's collective unconscious. Bell's cartoon portrays an enthusiastic crowd and media types in an excited state about *Star Wars* characters (C3P0 and R2D2 are depicted). Behind the throng getting no attention is the image of the risen Christ.[12] Bell's cartoon captures the spiritual essence of our time: Fewer people are gripped by the old, pre-eminent myth (in our case, the Christian one that took hold two thousand years ago at another moment of unsettled collective psychology), and many are searching for new stories containing more meaningful truths than the old myths provided. One of the places we unconsciously look for such new images is in films.[13] Since our collective psychology responds to polarities, the question is, will we be gripped by myths that take us to the dark side of destruction or by ones that will guide us creatively into the new millenium?[14]

In Jung's psychology, as in most modern philosophies of science, it is acknowledged that we can't know things in and of themselves: we know what impacts us only indirectly—through the images that are formed either in response to our sensory perceptions or to the fantasies created in our imaginations. *Felt* encounters with the divine are mediated through the images we experience during, or subsequent to, the encounter.[15] These images give us insight into what myths we are living and which psychic realities are moving most strongly within us. The approaching battle between the two Jedi Masters will be a battle revealing which of them, both still connected to the living reality of the Force, most correctly perceives and can tap into its deepest purpose, and in what form relationship to the Force will be carried into the future.

"What An Incredible Smell You've Discovered!"

Back inside the detention area we have a new foursome, suggesting that a subtle process of transformation is taking place. While the larger issues just delineated lie in the background, there is important personal business to accomplish. The princess quickly points out the shortcomings of her rescuers. Once again, one character draws attention to the limitations of another but, in this case, her strengths complement their shortsightedness. Han and Chewie have had to join Luke in the cell corridor, and Luke discovers by comlink communication with Threepio that there is no other way out than the way they came in—a security station now filled with stormtroopers.

Leia bluntly sums up the situation. "This is some rescue. You had a way of getting in. Didn't you have any plan for getting out?"

"He's the brains, sweetheart," replies Han, reiterating that he's the man of action, not the thinker.

"Somebody has to save our skins," Leia exclaims as she blasts into an area off to the side. "Into the garbage chute, Fly Boy," she commands. Though this is not sophisticated dialogue, the conversation helps tell the story as economically and entertainingly as the images and action.

They all must descend, one by one, into the garbage chute: they literally have to dive in. Han has to prod Chewie, "Get in there, you furry oaf—I don't care what you smell." "Wonderful girl," he shouts to Luke, "Either I'm going to kill her or I'm beginning to like her." In the midst of this exhilarating adventure, he's experiencing personal feelings of like and dislike. Once in the garbage chute himself, he continues to be intensely impatient, hell-bent on action, but not very reflective. "The garbage chute was a really wonderful idea. What an incredible smell you've discovered! I had everything under control until you led us down here."

Amidst this chaotic descent and verbal bantering is important symbolism. First, up until this point, the heroes have been in a masculine mode of trying to be in control, only to land in a garbage chute. When life doesn't go as we plan or hope, we may find ourselves falling into more chaos, forced to descend further before we can get out. In mythology, while Theseus could get into the labyrinth to slay the Minotaur, it was the thread of Ariadne that enabled him to get out. In Jungian terms it is the anima function (here symbolized by Leia) within a man (in this case, Luke) that allows the man to descend into the unconscious and then helps him to get out. In Han's case anima development means being able to relate to, and work together with, other people—which he is grudgingly doing.

At this stage of the "rescue," our heroes and heroine must pass through "garbage" in order to get out. This scene makes further use of the foul odor shadow theme we've already encountered. The garbage room is quite important symbolically, for it depicts the psychological truism that if we wish to deepen our lives emotionally, sooner or later we will have to come to terms with our leftover, smelly "garbage."

The four protagonists are in a bad situation. Leia tries to put it in perspective when she exclaims, "It could be worse," but then they hear a primitive growl from the murky depths below and Han proclaims, "It's worse."

Luke wonders aloud saying, "There's something alive in here!"

"That's your imagination," Han tries to assure him.

"Something just moved past my leg," Luke exclaims. A strange creature is very much alive in the bottom of the garbage room—an uncanny eye pops out, an octopus-like tentacle appears and Luke is eventually yanked under the watery garbage. He surfaces wrapped in a giant tentacle, and they try to free him, but he is pulled under a second time. It becomes forebodingly quiet.

These are common mythological themes and also reflect the reality of internal psychological processes, in which people often feel worse before they feel better. When we are gripped by the various symptoms and problems that bring us to re-examine our lives, it means that our unconscious has become highly activated. This activation will deepen, often significantly, before we feel we are getting somewhere. Partly we are led to this deeper place, and partially it—the autonomous aspect of the psyche—pulls us in further. Luke is twice dunked, or baptized, in this primal ooze by a primordial creature. There is nothing he can do but wait it out.

On another level this scene repeats the theme enacted when the Millennium Falcon became caught in the Death Star's tractor beam. At that point we could say that a power complex generally associated with the father ensnared Luke. Now, led to a place by a feminine figure, Luke is trapped by the world of primitive instinct and primal ooze most often associated symbolically with the mother. In a sense this is the first of many experiences of rebirth for Luke, as he is eventually released from his underwater entrapment.

After this breathless interlude we hear what seems to be the sound of a large metal door opening, and Luke reappears, bewildered but unhurt. He tells the others that the creature let go of him and then disappeared. It is Leia who now says, "I've got a bad feeling about this!" Immediately the metal walls of the garbage masher start closing in on them. This double-sided threat recalls Odysseus's predicament: when his ship passes through the narrow straits of Scylla and Charybdis, it faces the dire twin possibilities of being pulled down into the whirlpool of Charybdis or being crushed on the smooth, sheer rock of Scylla.

The Droids

As the walls relentlessly press in on them, Luke suddenly remembers his comlink and tries to contact Threepio. Back in the control room we see that Threepio's comlink rests on an empty counter, as stormtroopers break into an empty room. They discover the droids in a closet and Threepio quickly diverts them. "They're madmen. They're heading for the detention area. If you hurry, you might catch them." Then he quietly grabs the comlink and tells the guard that all the excitement has overrun the circuits on his counterpart (Artoo) and he would like to take him down to maintenance.

At a corridor computer terminal Threepio asks Artoo to check if the others have been captured, frantic about where they could be. Artoo suggests he use the comlink, and Threepio, berating himself, realizes that he turned it off. But at the last moment he does connect to Luke and is able to relay instructions to Artoo to shut down all the garbage mashers on the detention level. They are able to do so just in time, although Threepio at first interprets the shouts of jubilation as those of pain and frets that he failed. Threepio certainly represents those times we succeed in an almost robotic way: despite our worries and anxieties we get through.

The foursome is able to get out of the garbage masher trouble (a symbol of a unconscious complex, in Jungian terms) because Luke succeeded at making a *connecting link*. He found a way to communicate with someone who could help him—in this case, the droids who had changed the course of his life. It had been Artoo who carried the image of the princess that had so captivated him. Here he reconnects to those elements that had opened up to him the larger dimensions of his life. The droids are symbolic parallels of the thread that leads the seeker out of the labyrinth. In other Greek myths it is a figure like Athena or Hermes who helps make this connection. In alchemical symbolism it is the spirit Mercurius. These droids have elements of all these various mythological and symbolic traditions.

Returning to the Millennium Falcon

Freed from the giant garbage compactor, Luke and Han shed their stormtrooper disguises; after their initiation in the garbage masher, they are, in some ways "returning to themselves." Now they are ready to try to get back to the ship.

The male-female bantering between Han and Leia continues. Han insists that they can get out of there if they can avoid any more "female" advice. Leia is upset with Han's blasting away at the slightest provocation and insists that he take orders from her. He makes it clear that "I take orders from just one person! Me!" (He is Han *Solo*, after all.) Leia remarks, "It's a wonder you're still alive," and makes her "walking carpet" comment about Chewie. An exasperated Han retorts, "No reward is worth this!"

As this new foursome moves towards the ship, we get glimpses of Obi-Wan at the tractor beam power controls. He is able to deactivate it and use the Force to distract the guards so that he can move along undetected. Symbolically, he has released the power of the complex that has held everyone in its grasp. They will now have a chance (if they reach their ship) to get "outside of it," which will give them a better chance to deal with it. Psychologically, this is equivalent to gaining enough objectivity about what has gripped us emotionally so that we are no longer possessed by it. Obi-Wan represents the power of consciousness, that awareness which allows us to release the powerful grasp of unconscious complexes whose hold on us keep us from our fullest potential.

Luke makes comlink contact with Threepio, who assures him that he and Artoo are all right. The foursome can see the ship from where they are, but now they must get *to* it. When they run into stormtroopers, Han chases after them (with Chewie following) and Leia remarks that he certainly has courage. Luke counters, "What good will it do him, if he gets himself killed?" For a time the two pairs of figures (Han and Chewie, Luke and Leia) become separated and will have to find a way to reunite again—a pattern that repeats the earlier scenario on Tatooine when Artoo and Threepio were separated. Luke comes a little more into his own by inventing a way to get Leia and himself over a battle station crevice, amidst all the action, in order to return to the Millennium Falcon.

The key episode of the story psychologically at this point, however, is the confrontation between Obi-Wan Kenobi and Darth Vader. Vader, sensing Obi-Wan's presence, blocks his path as he heads back to the ship. Vader stands with his lightsaber ignited, ready to engage his former mentor. It is a subtle but important factor that he has already activated his weapon. He is the aggressor and initiates the battle. This impulse will be an important part of Luke's lessons in the next two movies.

Vader is engrossed with his ability to sense Obi-Wan's presence and to engage him. "I have been waiting for you, Obi-Wan. We meet again, at last. The circle is now complete. When I left you, I was but the learner; now, I am the master."

To which Obi-Wan replies, "Only a master of evil, Darth." Then they battle. Once more dialogue inches the story along. Two views of what it means to be a Jedi master clash. One is gripped by the desire for power and dominance; the other trusts his personal integrity and a deeper knowledge of the Force.

As Vader presses the battle to a climax, he tries to play on the older man's diminishing physical strength. "Your powers are weak, old man."

To which Ben responds simply, "You can't win, Darth. If you strike me down, I shall become more powerful than you can possibly imagine."

"You should not have come back," Vader warns.

As these two figures clash—mythologically, the clash of good and evil; psychologically, the clash between a man who has developed his humanity and strengthened it by connecting to the mysterious powers of the Force, and one who has lost his humanity and become possessed by these powers—the other figures are reunited. Luke and Leia link up with Han and Chewie just outside the docking bay. The ship looks all right, if they can get to it, and the "old man" has gotten the tractor beam out of commission.

The lightsaber duel now becomes a diversion that draws the stormtroopers away from the Millennium Falcon. The two droids and four human (one a Wookie) characters see their chance and head for the ship. Luke stops abruptly when he sees Ben dueling with Vader. When Ben sees that they have all reached the ship safely, he holds his lightsaber straight up in front of him and stops fighting. As he does so, Vader strikes at him and Ben's physical body literally disappears, only clothes on the floor remain. Luke is stunned and horrified. Han has to get him to blast the door closed to cut off more troops as Vader steps around to see what has become of Obi-Wan. Leia also calls to Luke, and finally the voice of Ben speaks to him, "Run, Luke! Run!" The voice of Luke's former mentor is now a spirit guide, a living presence that talks directly to him.

This is a highly symbolic moment with important psychological implications. We observe the significance another person can play in one's life, and its most profound psychological effects. Ben, as we have seen, understood Luke's personal history and perceived his real potential more than anyone else. Luke has already learned much from Ben, and is beginning to make this instruction his own. This is born out by the fact that though Ben is physically gone, he is still able to advise Luke. Ben has helped Luke to connection to the Force, to the deeper aspects of life, and that connection remains viable despite Ben's apparent demise. In this situation his voice directs Luke to engage his "flight" instinct over his "fight" instinct, so that he and his friends can get away.

Positive role models in our outer life remain alive in our inner life to help strengthen and guide us. This is true of good parents, good teachers, good mentors, good therapists, and even good bosses. It is also an important archetypal theme on the religious level. For instance, in the Gospel of John, Christ speaks to his disciples about the necessity of his returning to the Father, so that the Father could send the Holy Spirit. This spirit would allow them to do even greater things than he has done.[16] The teacher can only do so much for the student; then it is up to the student to learn to draw directly on his or her own resources and the deeper source of wisdom that the teacher has helped him or her discover.

Before his physical death, Obi-Wan takes on the darkest figure in the Imperial command (to this point). By encountering Darth Vader directly, he is able to create a diversion whereby the others can regroup and escape their imprisonment. In psychological terms when a parent, therapist, or other important figure acts as a buffer for the darker, more troubling aspects of life, then the child or adult can use the safety of this "buffer zone" to "come together" within him or herself and feel more whole. Often these dynamics involve painful or frightening emotions that would otherwise overwhelm the child or adult. When the parent, therapist, or other figure mediates these emotions by holding, in essence, the intense psychic energy connected with them, the child or adult is able to avoid being overpowered and become more integrated once again. Here Obi-Wan, Luke's Jedi role model, engages the dark forces directly, thereby creating an opportunity for the others to reunite and escape the negative effects of the tractor beam.

Also relevant to this theme is sacrifice symbolism. Ritual sacrifice was a part of the most ancient religious customs, and reflects the earliest expression of this archetypal pattern in the human psyche. For life to be creatively sustained, sacrifices must be made. Today, for example, parents must often sacrifice personal desires and needs in order to adequately respond to their children's physical and emotional requirements. Similarly, the dominant components of an individual personality must be sacrificed at times so that other dormant or suppressed elements can come to life. Knowing the art of psychological sacrifice is extremely important to life in modern times.[17]

When the creative aspects of sacrifice are not understood, then this archetypal pattern usually turns destructive. For instance, if we aren't careful to curb our consumerism, we unwittingly sacrifice the natural environment on which we all depend. Knowing what and how to sacrifice helps keep life in balance; unawareness of this psychic principle can led to terrible destruction. When the necessity of personal psychological sacrifice isn't realized, often *people* end up sacrificed to the unconscious, hurtful actions of others. A child may become scapegoated and thus sacrificed by parents unwilling to examine their own shadow responses. The child's needs and personality are attacked or go unrecognized. Such a family system (which we now call dysfunctional) survives, but one of its members (or more) is sacrificed. Institutions, both secular and religious, sacrifice certain groups of individuals based on narrow, limiting attitudes and belief systems that deem these individuals inferior. Women and gay people, for instance, are often treated like second-class citizens in many organizations, aspects of their individuality sacrificed in order to ensure the power of those in control. Nations may attempt to sacrifice entire peoples—as the United States tried to do with Native Americans, the Turks with the Armenians, and the Nazis with the Jews and other minorities—rather than find mutual ways of understanding and coexisting.[18] In the conscious application of sacrifice to positive aims, one-sided, narrow attitudes are relinquished in order for more life-enhancing ones to emerge.

When I first saw *Star Wars: A New Hope* in 1977, both its Christian mythological parallels and its similarities to certain fantasy figures in literature struck me. I had completed C.S. Lewis's *Chronicles of Narnia* and was especially impressed by the parallels in this *Star Wars* scene with the conclusion of *The Lion, the Witch, and the Wardrobe* (a book which my nine-year-old son has been asking me to read to him). There is the sinister Vader-like figure of magical power, the White Witch, and an Obi-Wan-like character, the lion Aslan, who maintains a deep connection to life's mysteries of renewal and regeneration. Aslan offers his own life in exchange for that of a misguided boy. The vengeful witch readily accepts his proposal, believing that with Aslan out of the way she will gain complete control of Narnia. Because Aslan's sacrifice serves the deepest mysteries of life, he is completely reborn, and his renewed presence turns the tide of the great final battle. Similarly, Tolkien's *Lord of the Rings* trilogy features a wizard who, after the sacrifice of physical death, returns to the drama to help counter the dark powers.

These modern stories indicate a shift in the sacrifice motif that predates Christianity (an example is the Osiris myth in Egypt), but that has been carried primarily by Judaeo-Christian myth and ritual for the past two thousand years. The lion Aslan is the most Christ-like mythologically, since in this story it is essentially a divine figure who is being sacrificed to bring about renewal. In *Star Wars* it is a human figure who makes the sacrifice so that "divine" purposes can continue. While mythologists like Joseph Campbell can show us how ancient mythological themes still live in the modern psyche, Jung has shown how they are also *shifting*, and that it is also critical psychologically to understand such subtle changes.[19]

Lucas's imagination has grasped this collective shift in the sacrifice motif in a way that makes this theme the most important mythological one in this first movie. Because this premise of the Jedi religion was so successful in this episode, Lucas has had the opportunity to further develop the Jedi world in the other movies (and in the movies still to come). Artists often offer a first glimpse at what is happening in the collective imagination, much as our dreams offer this to us as individuals. Then, as with our dreams, we can reflect on them (or not). The re-release of Lucas's three movies in 1997, which inspired the newspaper cartoon mentioned earlier, indicates the story's power to speak to us still. The newspaper artist grasped the essence of the unconscious appeal of Lucas's story: a gradual shift in the collective imagination away from the myth of the god-man, toward stories and images that speak to human beings about the struggle to incarnate in a *human* way the powerful energies of the unconscious. The story develops this theme in the next two films.

"We're Not Out of This Yet"

Freed from the Death Star, our heroes and heroine on board the Millennium Falcon still face one more adventure in the Alderaan system. Unfortunately, the struggles of the soul—the psychological journey of development—never end, for there are always new facets. Like the people of Israel finally freed from Egypt, there is more on the journey to be encountered. This is an important transition episode representing more than merely an action scene.

A significant shift has occurred symbolically in the foursome (and two droids) that was pulled into the Death Star. While four male figures went in, now three males and a female—the rescued soul-symbol—have come out. Number symbolism is an important part of our mythological heritage. Through careful observations of his patients' dreams, Jung noted the importance of the number four or "quaternity symbolism," and attributed great significance to it as a symbol of the Self, of wholeness. Thus our four individual characters can represent aspects of a single individual personality (in this case, male), much as figures in our dreams do. The appearance of the number four implies a movement towards conscious awareness of the Self.

This shift in the make-up of the four figures is also interesting psychologically in terms of the theme of the transition in the god-image we've just discussed. Jung has written that the Western Judeo-Christian god-image is one-sidedly masculine, having eliminated the elements of the matriarchal female deities that were a part of our earliest religious heritage. The Christian deity is expressed through the symbolism of a masculine trinity, incomplete because the fourth element is missing, and also incomplete because the feminine spirit is missing.[20] Jung repeatedly noted the importance for the Western psyche of reconnecting to the feminine aspects of our inner life. He applauded the papal proclamation in 1950 of The Assumption of Mary, which celebrated the bodily assumption of Mary into heaven—a dogma long overdue, in his opinion, as it more accurately reflected the mythology of the modern soul.[21]

The quaternity of characters that escapes from the Death Star now includes a feminine figure. The old masculine wisdom has also made a sacrifice that allows for the heroic ego (Luke) to come into contact with this feminine figure (Leia) he had previously only glimpsed in the hologram. Symbolically, this male-female conjunction would imply the young man beginning to become aware of the value of the feminine aspect of his personality. This realization means both becoming aware of the reality of the unconscious (the Force) and of women as separate individual personalities (not just men's fantasies of them). Such a man is no longer identified only with heroic masculine values (as is Han Solo at this point). As Luke sadly laments Ben's fate, "I can't believe he's gone," it is Leia who is there to comfort him, listen to his *feelings*, and assure him that there wasn't anything he could have done.

Back in the cockpit Han observes that they are coming up on the Imperial sentry ships (*four* of them). He gives instructions to Chewie about the deflector shields and then calls to Luke, "Come on, buddy, we're not out of this yet," so that he can help Han with the ship's guns. They engage in an old-fashioned ship-to-ship shoot-out. Here Luke gets initiated into space battles ("They're coming in too fast!") and as he gets into it successfully ("I got him! I got him!"), Han has to temper Luke's excitement and keep him engaged in the battle. "Great, kid! Don't get cocky." Han takes on a kind of older brother mentoring role. They succeed in fighting off the sentry ships and share in the excitement of their success. "We did it! We did it!"

After this exciting victorious moment, however, the scene shifts back to the Death Star where Tarkin asks Vader if the rebel group has gotten away. When told by Vader that they've just made the jump into hyperspace, he asks if the homing beacon is secure aboard their ship. "I'm taking an awful risk, Vader. This had better work." The empire will be "tracking" them and in pursuit. Psychologically, this is quite significant, representing the fact that we may get out of the grasp of a powerful complex, but it will seek to regain its hold and can, at any opportune moment (not opportune for the conscious ego), try to regain control of us again.

Meanwhile, on the Millennium Falcon Han is gloating in his heroism. "Not a bad bit of rescuing. You know, sometimes I amaze even myself."

Leia is more sensible, clearly aware of what they are up against. "That doesn't sound too hard. They let us go. That's the only explanation for the ease of our escape." Han is flabbergasted that she would think it was easy and becomes even more so when she suggests that the Empire is *tracking* them, as if that were the primary reason for their escape.

Leia proves to be quite wise and knowledgeable about the sinister side of the political scene. In this sense she is both strong heroine and important anima figure, for the anima allows a man to experience and cope with the more complex issues of life involving both emotional conflicts and questions concerning values. Han is most clearly identified with only his heroic ego, succeeding and feeling good about himself for accomplishing the task at hand but not aware of, or even interested in, the bigger picture. He's very self-absorbed at this point.

The conversation shifts to the importance of the information in Artoo, which it turns out includes the technical readouts of the Empire's giant battle station. Leia hopes that when the data is analyzed, a weakness will be found. "It's not over yet!" she says.

"It is for me, sister!" Han emphatically replies. "Look, I ain't in this for your revolution, and I'm not in it for you, princess. I expect to be well paid. I'm in it for the money!" Han is clearly motivated by self-gratification and excitement. He is not unlike those who live for the moment, oblivious to the broader scope of either the world around them or the full reality of their own personalities.

Leia, a diplomat who knows the deeper principles underlying human behavior, responds coolly, "You needn't worry about your reward. If money is all that you love, then that's what you'll receive!" As Luke walks in she remarks to him, "Your friend is quite a mercenary. I wonder if he really cares about anything, or anybody."

To which Luke responds, "I care."

Important character differentiations are being made here. For Luke, Leia is a guide leading him to the deeper dimensions of "it's not over yet." He has a propensity to "care"—about her and about what she is fighting for—personal integrity and freedom. As we saw during their earlier trip on the Millennium Falcon, he also has the ability to "stretch out with his feelings" and touch the mysterious Force, the deeper dimension of life in the galaxy. What Luke is not good at doing, as the story continues to show is taking care of *himself*.

For Han, Leia is an irritant, challenging his lack of involvement in life. He doesn't want to develop connections to other people or to care about the quality of human existence. He lives for immediate rewards and money. He represents not only a dominant attitude of the *Star Wars* galaxy but of our own time and planet. Monetary rewards and concerns predominate; the soul is forgotten. In my own field of health care, "managed care" is a painful example. The money to be made is made by those who do *not* provide the health care services. As one colleague put it, managed care often "manages not to care." This is particularly true in the area of depth psychotherapy where the complex issues of life, like those touched on by our story, are relegated to eight sessions. The tyranny of the "Empire" can exist in any field of human endeavor.

The final dialogue in this scene involves our two male heroes. As Leia leaves, Luke joins Han in the cockpit and asks him what he thinks of her. "I'm trying not to," is Han's first response. Thinking of Leia would make him reflect on what she has said and thus reflect on himself and what he lives for. But when Luke says, "Good," he reconsiders for a moment saying, "Still, she's got a lot of spirit. I don't know—what do you think? Do you think a princess and a guy like me . . .?" "No," Luke proclaims, as Han smiles.

Leia carries the life energy in a very human and vibrant form. She has been an inspiration to Luke from the moment he first saw her image projected out by Artoo. Han testifies to her spirit, despite the challenge to his value system that she poses. But Luke's fascination gets his attention, and so Han wonders out loud a little about "a princess and a guy like me." His reflection is generic—that is, he thinks in terms of *princess*, not personally about this particular woman; but given the nature of his character, even this is a development!

There are two other subtle symbolic elements in this scene, whose relevance is brought out only after other themes emerge in the next two movies. At this point they are only hints of things to come, but they reiterate Lucas's conviction that the three movies are meant to be seen in sequence. Part of the reason for the release of the Special Edition versions was so that the movies could all be viewed in the theatre at the same time.

During the battle with the Imperial scout ships, the Millennium Falcon suffers some damage. When concern is expressed, Han responds by saying, "Don't worry, *she'll* hold together." (And then says, to himself, "Come on, baby, hold together.") Han relates to the Falcon as a feminine "other," as is common for men in naming the gender of their vehicles. In Jungian language we would say that Han's anima is projected onto his ship; an inanimate object carries the feminine. This form of anima projection is prevalent in male development, particularly in adolescence, but it must eventually shift if a man is to be able to have a meaningful relationship with an actual woman. In the subsequent movies this aspect of Han's attachment to his ship changes.

Also, during the conversation with Leia, Han refers to her as "sister." At this stage of the story it is not clear what kind of a relationship, if any, each of these two male characters will have with Leia. Ironically, in the last movie we will learn that indeed Leia is the sister of one of these men. There is some "unconscious" truth to what he calls her here, and as with some of the lines spoken on Tatooine, these statements will have greater significance later on.

CHAPTER 5

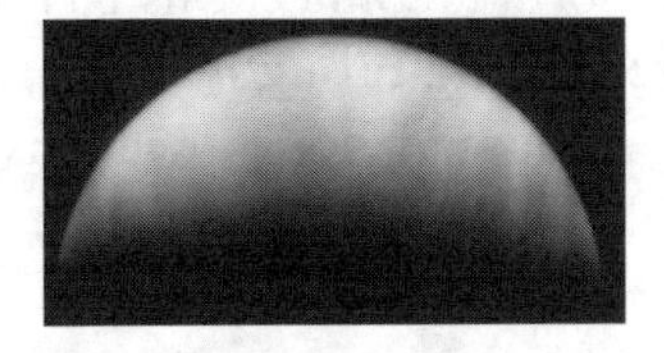

Yavin 4

The next location is a planet, Yavin, with four moons; the rebel base is located on the fourth moon. This moon location contrasts with the desert planet of Tatooine with its two suns. In symbolic terms the masculine principle at Tatooine was too strong; now the feminine principle is manifest both in the moons and the symbolism of their number, four.[1] The color of the fourth moon is blue (like earth) contrasted to the red color of the planet Yavin (which appears somewhat like Mars in our solar system). The moon is forested and full of vegetation. This symbolically connects it with Mother Nature and contrasts with the barren setting of Tatooine's deserts.

We know from the destruction of Alderaan that the Death Star can destroy an entire planet, so the Empire could easily eliminate the moon on which the rebel base is located. Psychologically, the battle represents the defense of the feminine principle from further destruction by the patriarchal cycle that has been dominating the evolution of our own civilization.[2] Symbolically then, the battle raises the question as to whether the rebels will succeed in preventing further destruction of the feminine aspects of life by the power-driven masculine principle.

Heroic figures of myth and religion usually have the support of the feminine principle in their quest or task even in patriarchal times. Odysseus was guided by Athena, Moses's birth was surrounded by many important connections to the feminine principle, and Christ was conceived and brought to life through the receptive attitude of Mary's psyche and body. Will this moon base provide enough support for the actions of the rebels . . . and their new member, Luke Skywalker?

The conclusion of this first movie plays out the drama of the battle against the new Imperial battle station. The Death Star arrives and begins orbiting the planet in preparation for targeting the moon with the rebel base. The rebels hold a briefing to plan their attack based on the information carried in Artoo. We learn that the giant battle station is heavily shielded, and that its defenses are set up against a large-scale assault. However, a small one-man fighter vehicle should be able to penetrate the outer defense, since the Empire hasn't conceived of, or prepared for, such a potential weakness. There *is* a weakness, but taking advantage of it successfully won't be easy.

Psychologically, this is a most important theme, reflecting the growing psychological, spiritual, and social perspective in Western Civilization that every individual matters.[3] Power dynamics in organizations of any kind, like the Empire in *Star Wars*, ultimately discount individuals at some level in favor of the organization. One of the important reasons that Christianity took hold when it did was the fact that unlike other "mystery" religions of that time, anyone could belong; social status didn't matter, both free men and slaves, women and children were baptized (this is not to say that there weren't serious biases within this inclusion). Much later in Christian history Martin Luther, leader of the Protestant Reformation, argued for a priesthood that was comprised of all believers, not just a selected few.

Political recognition of the value of each individual is expressed through the historical development of democracy and the right to vote. Some of the social problems within a democracy, in particular those members who are disenfranchised, are easily identified through whether or not individuals within certain groups such as women or people of color, have been deprived of the right to vote. From the point of view of depth psychology, such social problems also reveal which approaches to life are being neglected on a collective level.

The birth of depth psychotherapy at the beginning of this century is another example of this movement within the collective psyche to honor the soul of each individual human being more fully than ever before. Today through modern infant research and other psychological advances we are realizing more extensively the importance of the physical and emotional care of the tiniest infant to individual development in adulthood.

We are also more aware of the needs of many individuals to feel a connection to the spiritual or transpersonal dimensions of human existence via their own personal experience rather than via formal religious institutions. Depth psychotherapy, which accords primacy to the analytic relationship, and many other modern forums for psychological growth and development, such as recovery programs, also demonstrate how important healthy relationship with others is to our life journey's ultimate spiritual and emotional success.

The battle plan being presented to the rebel fighter pilots indicates that the "target" area is small, a thermal exhaust port only two meters wide. One pilot, Wedge Antilles, argues that such a shot is impossible for the targeting computers. Luke exclaims that it is not impossible—he used to shoot womp rats back home that weren't much bigger than two meters. We get a glimpse here that Luke has both piloting and shooting experience, and he's confident. Others, including the shrugging Han Solo, are skeptical.

Meanwhile, countdown begins on board the Death Star: Thirty minutes from now the moon hosting the rebel base will orbit clear of the planet, and the Death Star will be free to fire away. Vader proclaims that today will be a day long remembered, witnessing the end of Kenobi and soon the end of the rebellion.

In addition to the difficulty of their small target, the rebel pilots have little time and are up against great odds. In the rebel hangar bay Luke catches Han loading his ship, preparing to leave with his reward. Han reiterates that he has some debts to pay off and that it would be foolish to hang around here. He invites Luke to come with him, since he is pretty good in a fight and they could use him. Luke is upset and tells Han to look around him and see what is going on and what they are up against. They could use a good pilot, and Han is turning his back on them. Luke and Han have come to respect each other, but they are gripped by different purposes and see the situation differently. Han laments that a reward isn't any good if you aren't around to use it, and that attacking the battle station isn't his idea of courage, but more like suicide. His earlier inclination to fight rather than flee has been reversed. He chooses *flight* this time.

As they part Luke is frustrated and disappointed. "All right. Well, take care of yourself, Han. I guess that's what you're best at, isn't it?" But as Luke walks away, rather than answer defensively, Han calls, "Hey, Luke . . . may the Force be with you!" On some level Han, despite all his skepticism, is acknowledging the validity of what has gripped Luke. When Chewie growls at his decision to leave, Han retorts, "What are you looking at? I know what I'm doing!"

Luke encounters Leia as he proceeds through the hangar, and she senses that something is troubling him. When Luke laments that Han won't be joining them, Leia echoes the attitude of Obi-Wan Kenobi when Luke first turned down the old Jedi's invitation to come with him to Alderaan and learn the ways of the Force. She tells Luke that Han "has to follow his own path. No one can choose it for him." This reiterates the opposite perspective of the Empire, which discounts individual purposes, needs and desires—unless they serve the Empire's agenda. Here a leader of the rebellion expresses the same respect for each individual's freedom to make his own choices in life, as did the old wise Jedi.

In the original version Luke has lost Ben and now Han is leaving. He's alone except for Leia and the droids. In the Special Edition a scene is included in which Luke runs into Biggs, an old friend from Tatooine. Biggs is able to resolve any lingering doubts about Luke's piloting skills by recommending him highly as the best bush pilot in the outer rim. (Here it appears Lucas is tightening up his story line, just as he did earlier when Jabba the Hutt was included.) The two friends are obviously glad to be together again.

As he boards his X-wing fighter, Luke is offered a new astromech droid. However, he shows himself to be as faithful to his droid as the droid had been devoted to his "mission" when Luke first chased after him on Tatooine. The little droid and he have been through a lot together, and he will not trade him in. Here the special animated qualities of the droid are reiterated and then emphasized further when Threepio pleads with him, "Hang on tight, Artoo, you've got to come back. You wouldn't want my life to get boring, would you?" For all his earlier complaining, the human-shaped robot is emotionally attached to his little counterpart.

Finally, while still in the hangar before the fighters take off, Luke hears the voice of Ben speaking to him, "Luke, the Force will be with you." The voice of his former mentor suggests trust and faith in the deepest life principle, but it is not clear just on what such trust is to be based. This is one of many places in his journey that Luke begins to learn what it might mean that this Force will be with *him*.

As the one-man fighter spacecraft approach the Death Star, there are only fifteen minutes until the rebel base will be within its range. Wedge, a member of the "Red" squadron, which includes Luke, comments on the incredible size of the space station. As they go in, they are able to avoid the battle station's turbo lasers because their spaceships are so small. Vader orders Imperial fighters to engage them ship-to-ship. During this initial phase of the battle Luke dives and gets a "little cooked" but comes out all right. The rebels suffer their first casualty when Porkins, a member of Luke's group, goes down. These are certainly reminders of the grim reality of actual battles, but they are also a big part of the "myth" psychologically in that the hero has to continually deal with feelings of loss.

With seven minutes left Luke hears the voice of Ben again, this time saying, "Luke, *trust* your feelings." The rebel fighters, now under attack by the Imperial ones, have to help each other out. Luke is able to destroy one that is pursuing his friend Biggs who is also a member of his squadron, and then Wedge comes to Luke's rescue when an Imperial fighter that he can't shake chases after him. When Vader realizes that three rebel fighters have broken off from the main group, he takes two Imperial fighter pilots in pursuit. The three rebel fighters are a part of the Gold squadron, and the "Gold Leader" begins his attack run down the target shaft that leads to the thermal exhaust port.

With five minutes remaining in the Imperial countdown, the first rebel group zooms down the tunnel that leads to their target. The turbo lasers stop and the three rebel pilots discover the three Imperial fighters led by Vader coming in after them. Vader insists on taking them himself and all three pilots are lost. In story counterpoint an officer reports to Tarkin that an analysis of their attack indicates that there is a danger and asks if he should have Tarkin's ship standing by. "Evacuate? In our moment of triumph? I think you overestimate their chances," replies Tarkin. This man of power is convinced of victory for himself. The tension of the drama continues to build in the best *High Noon* movie tradition.

Only three minutes remain as the leader of Luke's squadron, known simply as Red Leader, takes two other fighters with him to try another run. Luke is to wait with Wedge and Biggs for his run. While his two companions are lost during his run, Red Leader, using his targeting computer, is able to get his shot off. However, it only makes impact on the surface and doesn't penetrate inside. As he instructs Luke to set up for his attack run, this pilot is also lost.

One minute is left as Luke instructs his companions to close it up and go in full throttle in hopes of keeping the Imperial fighters off their back. When asked by Biggs if he will be able to see the exhaust port at that speed, Luke responds that it will be "just like Beggar's Canyon back home." Wedge is hit and must clear out. Vader lets Wedge's ship go in order to stay in pursuit of the leader—Luke. Vader then guns down Biggs, Luke's childhood friend from Tatooine. In the midst of the intense battle Luke suffers another personal loss.

With only thirty seconds remaining, Vader is bearing down on Luke. The voice of Obi-Wan speaks again, "Use the Force, Luke. Let go, Luke." As he pursues Luke, Vader comments, "the Force is strong with this one." Ben's voice is heard again, "Luke, *trust* me." The battle fought between the two Jedi on the Death Star continues. Who has the deeper knowledge of the Force? Who knows best how to "use" it? Luke, heeding Ben's voice, turns off his targeting computer, which raises grave concerns back on the rebel base. He assures them that he is all right. But then a blast from Vader scorches his ship and Luke reports that he has lost Artoo. Except for trusting Ben's voice, he is truly all alone.

Now the Death Star has cleared the planet and Tarkin gives the order to fire when ready. A command is heard to "commence primary ignition," and Vader takes aim at Luke, exclaiming "I have you now!" A blast from somewhere else throws him off; one Imperial fighter and then another crashes. Vader exclaims, *"What?"* as his ship hurtles off into space. We then hear and see Han Solo (the gunslinger) yelling "Yahoo!" and exclaiming, "You're all clear kid. Let's blow this thing and go home!"

As we hear the command "Stand by" on the Death Star, Luke gets off his shot—a perfect hit that sails into the exhaust pipe and begins the chain reaction that explodes the Death Star (with additional special effects in the Special Edition). All the energy that had been built up and bent for destruction is now released back into the universe. "Great shot, kid. That was one in a million," exclaims Han. "Remember, the Force will be with you, always," the voice of Obi-Wan Kenobi reminds him, as Vader's ship careens off into space.

Back on the rebel base there is a lot of excitement. Leia greets Luke, and together they greet Han. Luke tells him, "I knew you'd come back—I just knew it." And Leia exclaims, "I knew there was more to you than money." In grand storytelling fashion, Lucas has created a climax that is both heart stopping and heartwarming. However more important psychologically, he has set up the next two movies by hinting at the possible progression of the themes introduced in this one.

Trusting in the Force involves not only being attuned enough to the voice of inner wisdom, but knowing when and how to trust it. It also involves the recognition that we are ultimately dependent on our fellow human beings and their ability to be transformed, changed, and redeemed. Luke succeeds not only because of his innate abilities and his encounter with this wise Jedi, but because Han Solo has a change of heart. In the end he is no longer Han *Solo*: he's a man who can respond to the needs of others whether there is a reward involved or not. In the subsequent movies we follow the ongoing development of Luke and Han as well as some other surprises. At this point the stories of transformation at the heart of *Star Wars* have only just begun.

In psychological terms this moment represents the point in a person's development when the archetype of the Self is realized in a deeper and more conscious way. We could say that the "kid," as Han calls Luke, has just touched his true personality and realized some of its potential for the first time. Han, who has "been around" for a while and knows how to take care of himself in the outer world, has opened up to a part of his personality that he has previously ignored—for whatever reasons—fear of failure or vulnerability, lack of desire, sheer ignorance of life's larger issues, and so forth.

Leia remains the princess in this movie—that is, she remains an essentially symbolic figure, an anima character, and not an individual woman. The celebration in which our heroes receive their rewards is centered on her as a symbol of the feminine principle. She presents medals to Han and Luke.[4] The setting conveys a "great hall" elegance, reinforcing the subtle subtext that each of these figures is honored with an award for selflessly serving the feminine principle—which, in turn, can help a man become more deeply connected to his true self. For Luke this means his new connection to the Force and his ability to attune to it; for Han it means working in relationship with others. The movie begins with the princess captured by the dark figure, and ends with this princess bestowing awards in a great hall on a forested moon to those men who have rescued her and served her cause.

Receiving awards can be seen as representing a stage of anima development. One still needs support and recognition in some concrete form; one is still attached to that inner child who needs to be appreciated. Fulfillment is not yet carried within as a deeper personal and spiritual satisfaction from living life well. Obi-Wan's "success" in the movie would represent that level of fulfillment. We will contrast this award level of fulfillment for Luke with a more spiritual attitude regarding transformation when we get to the end of the trilogy.

While Luke and Han received awards for their efforts, Grand Moff Tarkin and the Imperial command did not. We could say that their efforts for success literally "blew up in their faces." As it turns out, it was not other star systems that would suffer the fate of Alderaan, but the Death Star itself. As a result of one carefully placed shot, its destructive energy is turned back onto itself. Explosion symbolism occurs again, but it carries a totally different feeling response than the explosion of Alderaan.[5] Now energy that has been pent up for destructive purposes has been dispersed and released back into the galaxy.

The Death Star was built as a vehicle of power that went beyond any humane purposes. It repeats the mythological theme of the Tower of Babel story from the book of Genesis, in which the people of an early civilization built a giant structure in order to reach directly to the heavens so that they might make a name for themselves. God did not look kindly on their misguided efforts and acted to thwart them by creating all the different languages of the world, thus forcing the people to give up their project and scatter across the face of the earth.[6] The Empire had eliminated the Imperial Senate and its representatives from throughout the galaxy, attempting to establish a sole dictatorial ruler. As we will see, the rebellion represents an acceptance and appreciation of individual diversity in all its expressions.

The theme of a supposedly indestructible structure or vehicle that fails is an archetypal one. A subsequent box-office champion, *Titanic*, tells a love story with the tragic historical context of the sinking of the so-called unsinkable ship in the background.[7] A more recent real-life tragedy of this nature was the shocking explosion of the space shuttle *Challenger* shortly after blast-off. Particularly disturbing was the fact that children all across the country were attentively watching, because a teacher had been chosen as a crewmember for the first time. They—all of us—witnessed a powerful archetypal "event" involving traumatic and unexpected annihilation.

The destruction of the Death Star follows Luke's successful torpedo shot into the space station's main reactor, setting off a chain reaction culminating in its explosion. A laser blast from the Millennium Falcon frees Luke for this heroic "shot heard round the galaxy." The Millennium Falcon was the vessel that ferried into the Death Star the original quaternity of heroes, and emerged from it with a new quaternity including the rescued soul figure—a new image of wholeness, a new "god-image" in Jungian terms. (In some mythologies the falcon represents a god, for instance, Ra in Egyptian mythology and Indra in the mythology of India.) Now the Millennium Falcon carries the sole individual who began the chain reaction process of transformation required to ensure the future of a galaxy entering a new age.

Finally, two more symbols of transformation occur at the end of this movie. When Luke arrives back at the base and has greeted Leia and Han, Artoo is unloaded from his X-wing, very "cooked." Threepio frets about him, but Luke assures him that Artoo will be all right. Threepio even offers some of his own circuits, if need be, so Artoo can be repaired. He's appreciative of his counterpart in a way that is noticeably different from the beginning of the movie. We could say that he is a changed droid.

After the medals are awarded, a fully restored Artoo Detoo arrives and squeals in delight. He has made sacrifices and shown devotion, and his reward is restoration. His renewal, too, previews more profound ones that lie ahead.

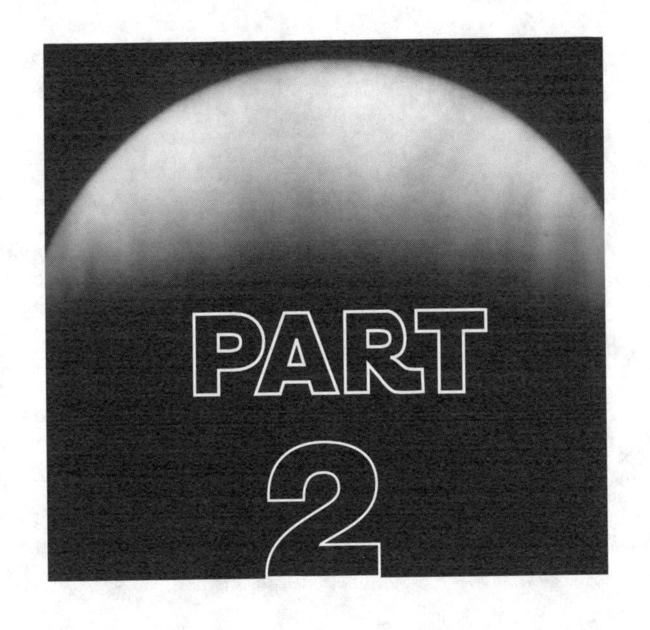

EPISODE V

THE EMPIRE STRIKES BACK

CHAPTER 6

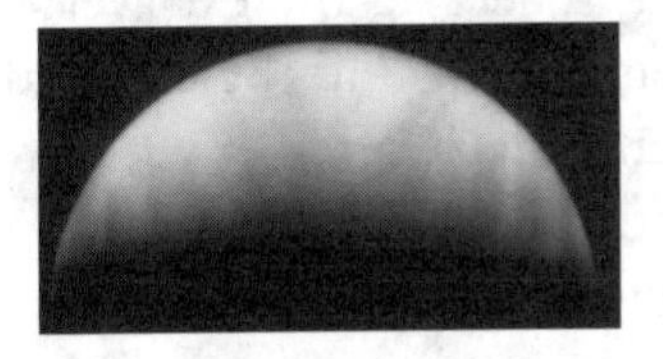

Hoth

Introduction to the Second Act

The Empire Strikes Back is an unusual sequel because it is darker than the other two movies and has no strong resolution at the end. If you've become hooked by *Star Wars,* Lucas gives you an experience that is absent from most modern religious practice. One example of a lost religious experience that comes to mind is that involving the Christian Holy Week services. Originally experienced as a whole, nowadays most people who do attend church for Easter do so only for Easter *Sunday*. Holy Thursday and especially Good Friday experiences are missing. *The Empire Strikes Back* gives us a mythological dose of the Good Friday experience. Like the *Inferno*, Book One of Dante's trilogy *The Divine Comedy,* this movie is the descent into darkness of the *Star Wars* trilogy. Such descent motifs have a long history in mythology, reflecting archetypal patterns of initiation that are still very much alive in the modern psyche.[1]

Particular pairs of opposites come more into play in this movie, especially those involving the instinctive, animal level versus the mechanical and technological level. Both have a dark side, yet both are needed for a balanced existence. The dimensions of good and evil are also more deeply drawn out in this movie.

Development takes place on two parallel levels. On one level we follow Han and Leia, reflecting the extraverted side of life: engaging in relationships and managing the ebb and flow of emotions in the midst of life's demands. The other path of development follows Luke and is more introverted, mystical, and spiritual. In this movie Luke begins the transformation from hero—a psychological mode of being that our culture and media are obsessed with—to *initiate*. The initiate learns that there is far more to life than heroic action and seeks knowledge and experience of life's deepest mysteries. Eventually these two lines of development—extraverted and introverted—must come together in any individual. This process of integration is briefly glimpsed at the end of the movie, setting the stage for the final act of the three-act drama.

The time frame for this second movie is about three years after the destruction of the Death Star. The main characters are now more familiar with each other and there has been enough time for seeds of development to sprout. Lucas opens the second part of his story using the same format that he used to begin the first part (which we discussed in Chapter 1).

A long time ago in a galaxy far,
far away. . . .

Star Wars

Episode V
THE EMPIRE STRIKES BACK

It is a dark time for the
rebellion. Although the Death
Star has been destroyed,
Imperial troops have driven the
Rebel forces from their hidden
base and pursued them across
the galaxy.

Evading the dreaded Imperial
Starfleet, a group of freedom
fighters led by Luke Skywalker
has established a new secret
base on the remote ice world
of Hoth.

The evil lord Darth Vader,
obsessed with finding young
Skywalker, has dispatched
thousands of remote probes into
the far reaches of space. . . .

The Imperial Starfleet is pursuing the Rebels and Darth Vader is obsessed with finding Luke. We begin with the motif of pursuit that also opened the first movie. Our first sighting appears in the black, star-filled sky: an Imperial Starship, from which small space pods, the remote probes, fire out into the vast void of space. We follow one as it streaks into a planet's atmosphere and then makes impact with a barren snowy terrain. Shortly afterwards a droid emerges from the point of impact, emitting beeps and signals, moving purposefully across the landscape. Along with this droid we are now on an ice planet in the Hoth system.

A camel-sized creature that is actually a tauntaun, a kind of horned snow lizard, moves across the stark terrain carrying Luke. He pulls to a stop to use his electrobinoculars to check out a meteorite that has landed (or a dreaded probe droid). He speaks to Han using his comlink, reporting that he has picked up no life readings. Han quips about the paucity of life of this "ice cube," indicates that the sensors are in place and he's returning to the base. Luke says he will see him shortly, after checking out the meteorite that has just landed.

This new location—the frozen, impenetrable ice planet—is an archetypal image of a defense system that is constructed by a person's psyche to protect itself from further attack, neglect, or other difficult emotional experiences it does not have the resources to handle. Such a psychological state often appears in dreams as a barren, frozen landscape. Dreams in which the dreamer or dream figures are numb, have been anesthetized or put to sleep—as seen in such fairy tales as Sleeping Beauty and Snow White—also reflect this kind of psychological situation. A part of the life energy of the personality is put "on hold" in order to protect it.[2]

At certain times in life, survival and self-preservation become the primary modes of existence. The darker, destructive, more sinister aspects of life seem to have the upper hand. In the story of the birth of Christ, for instance, King Herod is so intent on destroying the new "King of the Jews" that he has all newborn male babies in the realm killed when he can't find the one that the Wise Men visited.[3] Warned in a dream, Joseph is able to protect the child by taking him off to a distant land until it is safe to return. Similarly in the story of the Exodus, as Moses hears the call of God to lead the people of Israel to a more promising land in which they can most truly worship him, the current ruler, Pharaoh, becomes more angry and destructive.

Hoth is the complete opposite of Tatooine. Hoth is full of water, but it is totally frozen; Tatooine has little water and is scorching hot. Both are severely inhospitable to life. Tatooine reflects the external emotional environment that Luke was raised in: a parched and arid patriarchal wasteland. Hoth represents the internal state in Luke's unconscious, where the feminine side of his nature lies dormant—preserved but, as yet, inaccessible. Psychologically, *The Empire Strikes Back* depicts the further eruption of the old dominant complexes of the three major characters against those aspects of their personalities that have not been free to express themselves and are now fighting to be able to do so. These tyrannical complexes must be met head-on if our heroes and heroine are to survive the thawing process that must occur in order for the new life, seeded in the first movie, to blossom.

Wampa Attack

Following his conversation with Han, Luke's tauntaun becomes skittish. As Luke asks the creature if she smells something, a huge, furry snow creature strikes them down and drags away an unconscious Luke. Symbolically, a new phase of initiation from the primitive level of the psyche is erupting. Luke is totally unprepared and easily overtaken by this creature as he was by the Sand People on Tatooine. However, there are subtle but significant symbolic shifts in the story. Themes are repeated but also further amplified. In the first movie Luke rode a landspeeder, a mechanical vehicle. During his search for Artoo he encountered the Sand People, who rode Banthas—horned, elephant-sized creatures—and knocked Luke out when they jumped him. Now Luke is riding a living creature, also horned, and is knocked out by an even less human-like creature, a wild man archetypal figure, a more primitive version of Chewbacca.

We next see Han returning to the base and engaging Chewie at the Millennium Falcon. Chewie is obviously upset with the work he's left to do, but Han is able to respond to his impassioned emotional expressions—it's a world he's at home in. Luke is not at home in this world and has just been overwhelmed by it in the form of the Wampa. Chewie, working on the Millennium Falcon, combines two important elements of symbolism, animal/creature motifs and vehicle/mechanical motifs. On the Millennium Falcon these elements work well together. Han's relationship to Chewie and Chewie's mechanical abilities suggest a degree of psychic integration. We will soon see just how instinctive Han is and discover further important dimensions of vehicle symbolism in the journey of the Millennium Falcon.

Han then goes to report to General Rieekan that the sensors are in place and that there are no signs of life outside of the base. Rieekan asks if "Commander Skywalker" has reported in yet, giving us a sense of Luke's higher rank in the rebellion. When Han reports that Luke is checking out a meteorite that hit the planet nearby, Rieekan comments that, with all the meteorite activity, it will be difficult to spot approaching ships.

After his report Han tells Rieekan that he has to leave. He has a price on his head, and if he doesn't pay if off, he will be a dead man. His very life hinges on unresolved personal issues from his past. To go forward in his life Han will have to deal with his past and, in this case, the debt he owes. Serving the rebel cause, as important as it is, isn't enough for Han at this point. Rieekan understands the problem of living with a "death mark." He is also clearly aware of Han's value as a fighter and his own regret in losing him.

Leia has been eyeing Han through all of this and Han turns to her as he leaves. He's put off by her lack of feeling, and they bicker. An important theme is introduced in the dialogue, which signals the beginning development of Leia as a character (even as her "rank" is reiterated sarcastically through such lines from Solo as, "Yes, your Highnessness?"). Leia is "frozen" to her personal feelings; she can only respond to Han in terms of his abilities, which are an asset to their "cause." Leia is a woman in the grips of the animus: a fine leader, devoted to her principles, but unaware of her humanity as a person and as a woman. She's completely unaware of her personal feelings about Han, though they are clear to him. Understandably this frustrates him. Luke and Leia carry opposite poles of the emotional spectrum: Leia remains out of touch with her feelings, and Luke has just experienced his feelings erupting, symbolically speaking.

The scene shifts as the droids enter the picture with their own form of bickering and bantering. They approach Solo on behalf of the princess and the concern that Luke hasn't shown up yet. Han takes charge to determine if Luke has indeed checked in or not. When it's clear that he hasn't, Han is quick to go after him, even though the speeders aren't ready. He's told that with the temperature dropping so rapidly, his tauntaun will soon freeze. Han remains undaunted. If mechanical means aren't available, he will act in as natural a way as possible, as vulnerable as it might make him, to help his friend. (He's clearly no longer Han *Solo*.)

The Wampa Cave

We move outside the base to see Luke hanging from the ceiling in an ice cave with the primitive noises of the snow creature filling the background. Luke awakens to these disconcerting sounds and to his predicament. The Special Edition of this movie includes additional glimpses of the creature and the threat it poses. Luke is literally in danger of being eaten, of ending up like many a human before the advance of "civilization." The struggle for survival in the earliest times revolved around which creature was going to eat which creature—humans included.

Luke struggles first to free his feet, realizes he's stuck, spots his lightsaber in the snow below him, and tries to retrieve it. Recognizing that the lightsaber is out of his grasp, he turns his attention inward. By tuning in to the Force, he is slowly able to loosen the lightsaber and then finally draw it into his hand in order to cut himself free. He does so just in time, as the creature has stirred from its dinner and headed his way. Luke confronts the Wampa with his ignited lightsaber, severs its arm, and makes a frantic escape out of the cave into the frigid, windswept landscape outside. Meanwhile, Han continues his search for Luke on his tauntaun over the frozen ground, and the droids banter while Artoo scans for signs back at the base.

The wampa's lair is the first of a number of caves that we visit in this movie. Each is, on some level, a place of initiation for those who enter. Luke has been turned upside down, literally, after being knocked unconscious. To free himself he must turn within and "stretch out with his feelings," as Ben had taught him. In this way he gets the "weapon" of light—of consciousness and differentiation—that enables him to cut himself free from his dilemma, to "right himself" so to speak. Using the Force to accomplish the impossible is a delightful metaphor (repeated throughout the stories) for making a conscious, aligned connection to life amidst its vicissitudes.

During the cantina scene at Mos Eisley, ruffians had accosted Luke, and Ben had to come to his defense using a lightsaber. During the scuffle, he severed the arm of one of the assailants. Now Luke must defend himself in the same way from a primitive hostile attack. In this case he literally has to defend himself from being devoured. Symbolically, Luke struggles on the inner landscape with his primitive instincts and emotions. Being "devoured" by the creature means being overwhelmed by these instincts. Escaping from the creature's clutches means using his conscious awareness to keep them from getting a hold of him.[4] The main *Star Wars* hero and heroine, Luke and Leia, are both in a thawing process. Yet, this process holds some dangers, for as Luke "stretches out with his feelings," he is also opening himself to the powerful, raw level of primitive emotions often represented by animals and other creatures in our dreams.

This scene makes clearer the symbolism of the severed arm, which had occurred previously in *A New Hope*. Disarmed in this way, the creature is less likely to get a hold of Luke and thus devour him. It takes all the energy Luke has to accomplish this defensive maneuver. It's his first personal step in the heroic process of integrating his shadow side rather than remaining unaware of it and therefore subject to possession by it. Like the Sand People, the Wampa knocks Luke unconscious. This time, however, there is no mediator—he must face this creature himself. Afterwards, struggling to move on in the wind and snow, Luke falls and later collapses. This is all he can manage on his own at this time.

Han is still searching for Luke, and back at the base the situation becomes more dramatic when the shield doors of the base must be closed as the temperature outside continues to drop. Luke and Han must be left to fend for themselves. One recurrent theme of this movie is struggle "against all odds." Threepio informs us that Artoo figures that the odds for survival of Luke and Han are 775 to 1. Rationally it doesn't look good, and Chewie's deep wailing conveys that it doesn't feel good either. From either a *thinking* or *feeling* perspective, the situation is bleak. Leia was forced to make the reasonable decision to close the shield doors for the greater good, but her face now shows the conflict and pain of leaving these men out alone in the cold.

Luke's Vision and Rescue

Collapsed in the snow, Luke is awakened by the voice of Ben Kenobi, and when he looks up, sees him in a vision. Ben tells him, "You will go to the Dagobah system. There you will learn from Yoda, the Jedi Master who instructed me." The vision fades as Luke calls out to Ben, and then Han Solo appears on his tauntaun in its place. Han quickly comes to Luke's aid, hoping he is still alive; the tauntaun collapses from the cold as he does so. Han uses Luke's lightsaber to open up the stomach of the tauntaun and places Luke inside for warmth and protection until he can get a shelter built.

The theme of smell is repeated here, similar in meaning to its occurrence in the garbage room in *A New Hope*. Han apologizes to Luke for the smell, telling him it is necessary for his survival—it comes with the warmth. Many times in my work I've heard people say, "This stinks," when they have to work through difficult material. However, doing the difficult emotional work is necessary if one is to heal the wound—the lack of human warmth, perhaps even neglect or abuse—from earlier critical stages of development. This odor symbolism is viscerally expressed when Han exclaims after gently placing Luke inside, "Ugh, . . . I thought they smelled bad on the outside!"

In psychological terms we would say that Luke's encounter with the Wampa has opened up the unconscious, foul contents and all. He has escaped being swallowed by primitive emotions and is, in fact, receiving protective assistance from the sacrifice of instinctive life (the tauntaun) that must take place in order for the transformation that comes with conscious integration to happen. Now other layers of the psyche speak to him through the vision of his former teacher, Ben Kenobi, so that he can receive further guidance. It's not uncommon for people familiar with their dreams to discover this kind of direction from within at critical junctures in their lives. One of two things often happens when we get stuck psychologically: something emerges from within, as in a dream or inspiration, or we get help from someone outside of ourselves.

For Luke on Hoth, both of these things happen. Just as the vision fades, Han rides up. This scene is a wonderful depiction of the kind of experience Jung referred to as *synchronicity*. Vision and rescue coincide. Luke can't go on physically and must be helped. Timely assistance arrives just as the guiding vision for the future disappears. Help from Han again arrives at a critical moment, as occurred in the battle against the Death Star in the first movie. In synchronistic occurrences, inner and outer levels of experience come together in a meaningful way; archetypal phenomena manifest simultaneously on both the physical plane and the psychic one.[5] An example from my own life occurred when I dreamt that a professor friend of mine who was retired had died. The next morning his wife called from the East Coast to say he had passed away that night.

Luke is delirious from his ordeal and fragments of the vision keep misting through his mind . . . *Ben . . . Dagobah system . . . Yoda.* These elements from both his past and future are closely entwined with Luke's discovery of who he really is—his deepest and fullest self—and his connection to, and utilization of, the Force. In order for new aspects of psychic life to open up, contained—even sheltered—experiences of rebirth are necessary. On Hoth Luke is put inside the stomach of the snow lizard; back at Echo base he is placed in a bacta medical tank. Both symbolically represent being returned to the womb of intense introspection, self-knowledge, renewal, and regeneration. In the recovery room we see that the experience has left Luke with scars that will have to heal.

The bacta tank is especially interesting not only as a symbol of the womb, but also in regard to the process of psychotherapy. Psychoanalysis was discovered and developed by medical doctors, suggesting that psychic processes can be observed in an objective way—yet those doing the treatment have to be personally involved. People undergoing psychotherapy voluntarily enter a highly contained space, where they are observed as they trudge their way through the unconscious contents that have emerged, so that wounds can heal and new visions for the future can be glimpsed, grounded, and realized.

Imperial Probe Droid

Once Luke's recovery is assured, the drama shifts to the battle with the Empire upon the discovery of the Imperial probe droid. Han has been prevented from leaving because of the meteorite activity. In Luke's recovery room he kids Leia about her wanting to keep him around. She denies it, and everyone has a good laugh at his expense. Only he is aware of the hidden, underlying feelings between him and Leia

Han and Chewie go out to check on the signals they've detected. When the probe droid soon self-destructs, the rebels recognize the danger of being found by the Imperials and prepare to give up their base. They will fight, put all their energy into defending the base, only until they can (literally) take flight.

Psychologically, a frozen defense system works only if one is not discovered. But once a person is "found out," then he or she has to move on to find another defense or, as we will see later, recognize and accept the vulnerable feelings that gave rise to the defense in the first place. This often entails exploring relationship and intimacy and letting things "heat up." On Hoth Leia cannot admit to herself or others her true feelings for Han. She reflects the frozen state of the feminine principle at this point in the story, as well as this particular female character.

It is the nature of the psyche to "probe" our defenses, challenging us to live more fully by coming to terms with life as it really is. The story of the Exodus is a good example. During the drought in their homeland, the people of Israel found a safe home and refuge in Egypt. But after a while life there became oppressive and destructive, and the original reasons for being there were no longer valid. When called by God to go back to their homeland where they could live more as they were truly meant to, they came up against the resistance of Pharaoh. Egypt, the former refuge, became a place they had to escape. The more they wanted their freedom, and the more they rebelled, the more tenacious became Pharaoh's efforts to keep them there and prevent them from prospering.

The Empire represents just such an impersonal, collective form of power and control. On Vader's Star Destroyer we see this attitude clearly demonstrated. When Captain Piett reports to Admiral Ozzel that there is a lead from a probe droid on the Hoth system, Ozzel wants to dismiss it. Vader overhears them and, when he checks the monitor, he clearly realizes that the rebel base is there. Ozzel is not happy when Vader orders the Imperial fleet to precede to Hoth and gives Piett a cool look. The command ship control deck is a cold place.

Later when the fleet emerges from hyperspace too close to the Hoth system, Vader is enraged to hear that the rebels are already alerted to their presence. Considering Admiral Ozzel's actions clumsy and stupid, he activates a view screen and vents his anger, via the Force, at Ozzel—who is soon gasping for air, having failed

Vader for the last time. Unlike the Imperial officer on the Death Star that Vader had "released" from this choking, Ozzel's body slumps to the floor. In a chilling voice Vader gives his orders to the new admiral, Piett.

When Vader receives news of their arrival at the Hoth system, he is in a cold steel "meditation" chamber. The helmeted figure is further enclosed in a hard "shell." As powerful as he is, he is also very well defended. Vader's intolerance of his men's foibles reflects his intolerance of such qualities in himself. He is clearly a patriarchal tyrant who dominates through fear. Devoid of all feeling, he is the human personification of inhuman coldness.

The battle on the sixth planet of the Hoth system sets the stage for the next part of the movie. But first, will the rebels escape? The energy shield protects them from bombardment from ships in space, and an ion cannon protects ships leaving the system until they can make the jump into hyperspace. But Imperial ground troops will attack the generators that supply power to the energy shield. Can the rebels hold out long enough to safely evacuate everyone?

The battle on the planet's surface features rebel ground troops and snow speeders against giant Imperial walkers—cold hard steel against more vulnerable human fighters. The walkers' armor proves too strong for blasters, and in the battle Luke loses his gunner, Zack. Some troops and other snow speeders are also lost. Wedge and his gunner are finally able to trip up one Imperial walker by encircling its legs with a tow cable. When Luke is shot down, he's able to recover and disable a walker by throwing a grenade inside. As a pilot and warrior Luke is obviously fully recovered.

Repairs on the Millennium Falcon are shaky, and Han is concerned that Leia get out safely. When they are cut off from her transport by the aftermath of the explosion that destroys the power generators, he uses his comlink to report that he will take her out on the Falcon. They scramble to get away, with Threepio running to catch up with them, even as Imperial troops and Vader enter the remains of the rebel base. They *just* make it out. The fight to take flight has barely succeeded.

Luke watches as they take off and prepares his X-wing fighter with Artoo on board. He and Artoo leave as the remaining pilots prepare to depart for the rendezvous point. Once airborne and out into open space, Luke sets course and questions beep from Artoo. Luke informs him that they are not going to regroup with the others. Instead, they are going to the Dagobah system.

This is a critical psychological juncture. Luke is choosing his own path, different from his companions, and acting on the advice of the vision that came to him when he had collapsed after his escape from the Wampa cave. The vision called to him to explore life beyond the battle with the empire, and he will now let this vision lead him in a new direction. To trust in such an experience and follow it is a true act of faith.[6]

The Millennium Falcon, however, is still struggling to escape Imperial Star Destroyers. Finally, Han is ready to make the jump to light-speed, but nothing happens! Threepio reports that the hyperdrive motivator has been damaged. "We're in trouble!" Han exclaims. He and Chewie rush to make repairs, during which time Han tells him, "I don't know how we're going to get out of this one."

The old, reliable form of defense, speeding off into space, has failed. They have not succeeded in escaping their pursuers. This segment of the drama takes us to a new location, a new symbolic place in space.

CHAPTER 7

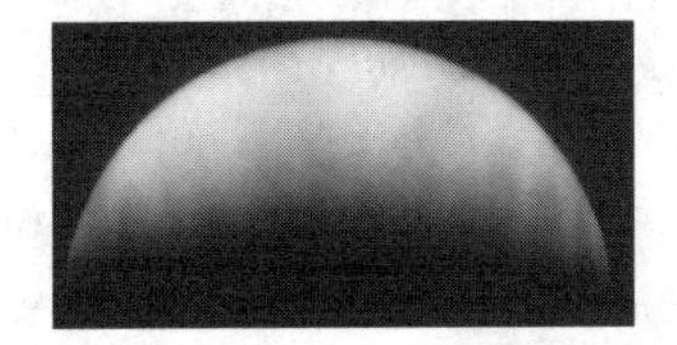

The Asteroid Field and Dagobah

"You're Not Actually Going Into An Asteroid Field?"

As Han and Chewie struggle to repair the Millennium Falcon, the ship is jolted and a toolbox falls on Han. Another blow to the ship alerts Han that it wasn't a laser blast that hit them. A call from Leia on the comlink brings Han back to the bridge. It turns out they've entered an asteroid field; *asteroids* are striking the ship. Han demonstrates his propensity for taking life on directly and sets course, to everyone else's horror, directly into the asteroids, racing past them.

"You're not actually going into an asteroid field?" questions Leia. "They'd be crazy to follow us, wouldn't they?" responds Han. "Sir," a panicked Threepio calls out, "the possibility of successfully navigating an asteroid field is approximately 3,720 to 1." "Never tell me the odds!" Han retorts. The tension of their adventure and the threat to their survival in this new location are escalating. They are all dependent on Han's courage and instincts.

In agreement with Leia, Han realizes that they can't stay out there too long. His solution, again to the dismay of the others, is to get closer to one of the big asteroids. In the process of navigating the menacing asteroid field and then the surface of the big asteroid, all the Imperial fighters chasing them ultimately crash. Han finally finds a place on the large asteroid that looks good to him, and the Millennium Falcon begins a descent into a large cave. As he goes in Leia remarks, "I hope you know what you're doing." And he responds, "Yeah, me too." He trusts his instincts for survival now, and he can't be sure where they are leading him.

The Arrival at Dagobah

As the Millennium Falcon narrowly escapes annihilation and heads into the asteroid cave where concealed threats may still await them, Luke and Artoo approach the atmosphere of the planet Dagobah. The parallel landings on unknown surfaces double the symbolic motif of descent. Descent symbolism is generally related to achieving psychological and emotional depth, entering the unconscious, and becoming more human. In Jungian terms symbols of descent in dreams often refer to becoming more grounded or down-to-earth and giving more human expression to the various archetypal energies that are becoming activated in one's life. Han and Leia represent one aspect of this process, and Luke another.

Dagobah is a fascinating location symbolically. In contrast to the asteroid field, an area of space packed with multitudinous hard fragments flinging through the void, Dagobah is a solitary, still planet, mysteriously clouded in mist. Artoo expresses hesitancy about going there, but Luke is determined to explore the realm that beckoned to him in his vision. Sensors on Luke's ship pick up no indications of cities or technology; however, there are "massive life-form readings." "There's something alive down there," Luke informs Artoo. When Artoo beeps nervously, Luke assures him, "Yes, I'm sure it's perfectly safe for droids."

Luke's attempts to land on the planet are impeded by the pervasive fog that greatly reduces his visibility. In fact, he can't see and his scopes are dead. They crash into the foliage and find themselves in the middle of a very swampy environment brimming with primitive life. It is wet and tropical, the antithesis of both Tatooine and Hoth. Symbolically it is a very feminine landscape, Most, warm, and alive.

After landing and surveying his surroundings, Luke becomes frustrated and discouraged. Despite Luke's request that he wait, Artoo emerges from his station on the X-wing, loses his balance, and falls into the water below. After a worried moment Luke relaxes as the little droid reappears with his periscope looking about. Luke points him to the shore and jumps off the ship to head there himself. A dark creature moves through the water toward Artoo, and the droid suddenly disappears again. Finally, he is jettisoned through the air onto the shoreline.

This little scene repeats the ongoing theme of the droids' escapades during their adventures with the human protagonists. When Luke and Artoo had first landed on Tatooine, Threepio had forewarned him (and us) about what would be happening to them. "We seem to be made to suffer. It's our lot in life." Artoo was hesitant about going to Dagobah—where he now has a Jonah-in-the-whale experience. He is swallowed up and eventually dumped on the shore. It might have been worse, for as Luke tells him, "You're lucky you don't taste very good."

Luke summarizes their situation and his feelings about it when he tells Artoo, "If you're saying coming here was a bad idea, I'm beginning to agree with you. Oh, Artoo, what are we doing here? It's like . . . something out of a dream, or, I don't know. Maybe I'm going crazy." Luke's vision has led him to a dreamlike place. Dagobah is to Luke what I feel the *Star Wars* trilogy is to the viewer. It is an ethereal place to be reflected on, as one would ponder a mysterious dream.

Immersed in a world so strange and new to him, Luke questions his sanity. When the unconscious is very activated, this is a natural reaction. Sanity to the modern ego is often measured by its degree of *dis*connection from the unconscious, having as little experience as possible of childhood's dreamland. Psychotherapy in general and depth psychology in particular demonstrates that the opposite is actually true. Denial and suppression of unconscious feelings and fantasies usually only causes further difficulties for people. One's first descent into the unconscious may easily evoke fears of being overwhelmed and "going crazy." There are very real dangers in approaching the unconscious, for the "dark side" of psychological experience is also very real—as this movie demonstrates—and should not be ignored. That is why a trained mediator (therapist, counselor, or spiritual director) of such experience is so important.

The Imperial Fleet Enters the Asteroid Field

Both groups of main protagonists are in unfamiliar locations at this juncture in the story. The asteroid field scene shifts to Vader's Star Destroyer, where Admiral Piett visits Vader's meditation pod. Piett catches Vader recovering his scarred head with his helmet. Because nothing is said about Vader's wound, we, like Piett, are left with our own thoughts about what this means. Vader is a man who has been seriously scarred and has known conflict. When Piett reports that the Millennium Falcon has entered an asteroid field and they can't risk entering it, Vader responds firmly that he wants no excuses; he only wants the ship. He is completely determined in his pursuit; whatever it takes is the price Vader is willing to pay.

Meanwhile, Han is preparing to fix the Falcon by shutting down all unnecessary systems, but that cannot include Threepio because Han needs him to "talk" to the Falcon to find out what's wrong with the ship's hyperdrive. The spacecraft suddenly lurches, leaving its passengers startled. Regaining their balance, Chewie and Threepio go off to begin the repairs. When the ship reels again, Leia falls into Han's arms and immediately tries to squirm out of his reach. They banter, and she hotly denies any feelings she may have simmering below the surface. Han moves on to do the repairs, leaving her in a huff. Something else is rumbling besides the reverberations of the ship.

Luke's Camp on Dagobah

For many people the process of psychological transformation unfolds in a way similar to Luke's predicament—one soon feels swamped and in a fog when one had hoped for immediate clarity. Luke establishes a power source to recharge Artoo and gloomily begins to ponder his state of affairs. With nothing else *to do,* he has to sit with himself and his own thoughts. In this isolated, mysterious, but completely natural setting, his unconscious processes begin to open up. In many ways he is like an initiate on a vision quest.

Doubts surface in Luke's mind. He is supposed to find this Yoda character, but does he even *exist*? "It's really a strange place to find a Jedi master. It gives me the creeps," he tells Artoo. "Still," he muses as he continues to examine his surroundings, "there's something familiar about this place." Being in Dagobah is much like being in the world of one's dreams. Recurring dreams or dream themes add a growing sense of familiarity to one's internal landscape. It feels strange at first, but it then becomes more familiar. Like a child's room at night, Dagobah is that kind of place—easily enlivened by the imagination.

Luke begins to experience this aspect of the planet's environment, and he tries to verbalize what he perceives to Artoo. "I feel like . . . I don't know . . ."

"Feel like what?" a strange voice asks from the tree behind him.

Quickly drawing his blaster, Luke turns towards a small, curious, robed creature and responds, "Like we're being watched!"

Both *seeing* and *being seen* are critical components of our psychological development that have personal as well as archetypal roots.[1] In *A New Hope* Luke encountered in Ben someone who saw him more fully; another human being who knew who he could become. Ben was a person Luke looked up to and admired, a man he could model himself after, despite what he had first heard about Ben from his uncle.

Now Luke is looking for an important individual he can respect, as he did Ben, to teach him. He obviously has some preconceived ideas of what this person will be like. The figure he now faces, however, is a completely unexpected sight. Covering his face a bit and turning away from the blaster pointed at him, the odd little creature tells Luke to put away his weapon, as he means him no harm. Though startled, Luke instantly realizes he isn't in any danger. Receiving such assurances—and believing them because of the genuineness of the source—is common on a religious quest. For example, in many Biblical stories when a divine figure appears, the apparition (often an angel) assures the person being greeted that he or she need not be afraid, and the person instantly recognizes the truth being conveyed.

Immediately this small creature starts up a dialogue with Luke. "I am wondering, why are you here?"

"I'm looking for someone," Luke responds. Completely without realizing it, Luke has begun the simple yet profound process of reflecting on himself and his life.

"Looking? Found someone, you have, I would say, hmmm?" The little fellow laughs, and despite himself, Luke smiles. Luke clearly, though, doesn't want to be bothered with this unusual, and even annoying, swamp dweller.

"Help you I can. Yes, hmmm," the creature continues. Luke, however, is skeptical, obviously unimpressed by him.

"I don't think so," he demurs. "I'm looking for a great warrior."

"Ah! A great warrior," the little one replies. "Wars not make one great."

Luke is quickly introduced to an idea that challenges the accepted valuation of the heroic ideal. Without his realizing it, Luke's training, and his master's evaluation of his student's capacity for this training in the deeper mysteries of life as a Jedi, have begun.

As this dialogue makes clear, Luke had expected to meet a great warrior, and this anticipation colors how he experiences the creature he encounters in the present moment. His attitude precludes experiences that could prove to be valuable. Dispelling preconceived perceptions will be a big part of Luke's training as a Jedi. For first-time viewers, this scene is also a time to examine what *we* expected as we joined Luke on his journey to Dagobah. What did we imagine this Yoda would be like when we first heard about him from Ben? Or when Luke and Artoo first arrived? What was stirred in our imaginations?

In a truly delightful, comical scene, the little cloaked creature starts rummaging around the camp, very much like a kid in the cupboards. Both Luke and Artoo are annoyed. When the creature goes after some of Luke's food, Luke becomes even more irritated, but the creature, who doesn't particularly care for the food, remains undaunted in his behavior. A very frustrated Luke says, "Listen, friend, we didn't mean to land in that puddle, and if we could get our ship out, we would, but we can't, so why don't you just . . ."

The swamp dweller plays with Luke's frustration "Aw, cannot get your ship out?" He rummages further. As the childlike figure persists in his antics, Luke tries to grab some things back. When the little fellow comes away with a small power lamp, Artoo also tries to intervene in retrieving the item. Luke's frustration builds (and sounds like many a frustrated parent), "Hey, you could have broken this. Don't do that. Oh . . . you're making a mess. Hey, give me that!"

Watching this scene with children provides the full tone of raucous amusement—as well as the profundity it contains. Viewing after viewing, children roll with laughter. For Luke, this creature is the antithesis of a great warrior; he's an annoying child who triggers Luke's impatience. Yet to a child this little creature's actions are both entertaining and heroic, and all the better since he behaves like a kid. Children readily accept the value of this magical and surprising little guy (as does the alive child in any adult).

That such child-essence is spiritually superior is expressed in many New Testament passages. In one, for example, Jesus's disciples, much like Luke seeking "a great warrior," ask him to tell them who is greatest in the Kingdom of Heaven. Bringing a child into the midst of the discussion, Jesus answers, ". . . unless you become like little children, you will never enter the Kingdom of Heaven. Whoever humbles himself like this child, he is the greatest in the Kingdom of Heaven."[2]

Psychology has discovered that traumatic aspects of childhood are closely related to many current psychological problems. Disturbances during the various stages of our early development distort our connection to life and challenge our later strivings for self-fulfillment. This childlike creature is the true link to what Luke searches for and what has been missing in his life: a mature connection to the life-force that permeates his inner world, the rich natural world in which he finds himself, and even the far reaches of the galaxy.

As Luke and Artoo try to retrieve the power lamp from the little creature, he (like a child) insists, "Mine! Or I will help you not."

Luke quickly retorts, "I don't want your help. I want my lamp back. I'll need it to get out of this slimy mud hole."

The long-eared swamp dweller takes offense. "Mud hole? Slimy? My home this is." (It bears noting that most children love to play in the mud and would heartily agree with this little creature who makes his home in this place.) As this spunky figure battles Artoo over the lamp with cries of "Mine! Mine!" Luke finally relents and tells Artoo to let him have it. His persistence has won, and he is certainly the hero of every child at this point.

This little fellow, however, is not Luke's hero. The exasperated youth tries to get him to go away—he and Artoo have work to do. "No, no, no! Stay and help you, I will." (Many children do like to stay and help, if given the chance.) "Find your friend, hmmm?"

"I'm not looking for a friend," Luke replies, "I'm looking for a Jedi master." Luke finally states why he is there.

The inquisitive creature tunes in directly, "Ooh. Jedi master. Yoda. You seek Yoda." He announces that he knows of this Jedi master and even offers to take Luke to him, but he also insists that they eat first and invites Luke to follow him. Given the opportunity to find the Jedi instructor he is looking for, Luke overrides his misgivings and agrees to go along. He tells Artoo to watch after the camp as the little animated figure waddles off into the fog, holding the light, leading the way for Luke.

Two important symbolic themes are expressed in this scene. The first is that Luke is left no choice but to follow this unknown mysterious figure who has gone off with his lamp—a strange unknown creature lights the way for him. Luke will have to learn how to expand his conscious awareness in order to know how to shed light on the dark and sinister situations he encounters. Such conscious insight is a more advanced form of illumination than that represented by the lightsaber and, as we will see in the third movie, it is ultimately more powerful and productive. Luke is challenged to follow the way of developing consciousness, of individuation, not that of the heroic warrior.[3]

The second theme is that of sharing food. The Dagobah creature, who had earlier raided Luke's cupboard and disapproved of the food he found, insists that they eat together before beginning their journey to the Jedi master. The assimilation of food, a natural bodily act that is essential for life, carries important symbolism. In the Wampa cave Luke barely escaped being devoured by the snow animal; subsequently, he had the vision of Ben instructing him to seek out Yoda. Rather than be devoured by life's primitive forces, Luke has to learn how to assimilate them in a more conscious, disciplined, and spiritual way. Eating is closely connected with the first stages of our emotional development in infancy and early childhood. For many people unresolved personal issues are partially expressed via eating disorders. Much of our early development is influenced by our relationship to food and the psychological climate surrounding feeding and mealtimes. (Luke received the frustrating news that his uncle wanted him to stay on his farm for one more season at the dinner table.) Luke's search for further training as a Jedi is to begin with such a seemingly rudimentary activity.[4]

As adults, food is one of the most common ways we forge bonds with others. Two people wanting to get to know each other will go out for lunch or dinner or meet for coffee or a drink. Food is synonymous with the relational process whereby individuals assimilate each other's viewpoints and emotions. "Breaking bread" is also an ancient form of acknowledging and cementing spiritual bonds, as seen, for example, in the Jewish Seder and the Christian Last Supper. This is how this childlike, instinctive creature suggests that they begin their journey in search of Yoda, the Jedi master—by eating together.

Inside the Asteroid Field

After delighting in the burst of childlike behavior from the swamp creature on Dagobah, we are taken back to sobering conditions on the Millennium Falcon, where another important aspect of emotional life will be expressed. The immediate concern is repair of Han Solo's spaceship; the scene revolves around vehicle symbolism, conveying the message that vehicle energy (technology) can carry us only so far in life (psychologically). Since the ship can't make the jump to light-speed, the characters on board have to stop for repairs, and Han and Leia will have to spend more time together. An added feature of their journey is traveling with the talkative, anxious, seemingly know-it-all Threepio. The annoyance that the droid creates is a comical counterpoint to the slowly emerging emotional connection between Han and Leia. Threepio is an irritating childlike presence on the Millennium Falcon, much as the Dagobah creature in Luke's camp. Grudgingly, Han has to accept the fact that Threepio can, at times, provide helpful input, as when Han quietly tells Chewie to repair the negative power coupling, as Threepio had suggested.

When Leia has trouble with some of the repairs she is doing, Han comes over to assist. She rebuffs him, and he snaps back, "Hey, Your Worship, I'm only trying to help." She asks him to stop calling her that, and he replies by saying, "Sure, Leia." Dropping our defenses for intimacy begins with dropping titles, roles, and other distancing mechanisms we typically use when we converse with others. Han would rather engage Leia as a woman than as a princess, and she is growing tired of the sarcasm to which he submits her official status.

Leia mentions that his sarcasm and general attitude makes relating difficult, which he readily admits. He is not defensive with her (he is with Threepio though, because he doesn't like being told what to do), and then he challenges her in return to acknowledge that she, too, could be a little nicer. He begins to try to thaw out the feelings between them by getting her to admit that at least *sometimes* she thinks he's all right. "Occasionally," she concurs, "maybe . . . when your aren't acting like a scoundrel." "Scoundrel? Scoundrel?" Han replies. "I like the sound of that." Han does not have an idealized view of himself and can accept that he has a shadow side to his personality.

Leia has been absently rubbing her sore hand, and Han takes it in his and gently begins to massage it as they talk. She asks him to stop, and when he asks, "Stop what?" she replies that her hands are dirty. "My hands are dirty, too," Han responds and then asks her, "What are you afraid of?" She tries to say she is not afraid, and then when he tells her she's trembling, she denies that feeling as well. As these enticing but threatening feelings emerge and are spoken about, Han and Leia slowly draw closer together. As storytelling, this love scene captures important psychological dynamics. For instance, intimacy requires being closer to our feelings and being able to admit to them. Han recognizes Leia's feelings for him and offers her an opportunity to acknowledge them as well. However, she still remains griped by the denial that had encapsulated her feelings back at Echo Base.

The interaction between Han and Leia depicts how unconscious feelings can become activated in the context of a potential love relationship. Luke's encounter with the curious figure on Dagobah evoked feelings that emerged in a different way. In both cases interactions with others compel the characters to come to terms with hidden emotions. The display of childlike antics by the tree creature evoked feelings that Luke was unaware of and uncomfortable with, otherwise he wouldn't have reacted to the impish creature the way he did. Such feelings can surface at any time but tend to be evoked most often and powerfully in intimate and other significant relationships. These feelings of discomfort are the psychological markers that signal the presence of an opportunity to come to terms with our emotions and thereby know more about ourselves.

As Yoda will do for Luke, Han begins educating Leia about herself. He tells her that she likes him *because* he's a scoundrel. "There aren't enough scoundrels in your life," he wisely tells her. He realizes that she's drawn to him because he's different, because he is able to live out some of the shadow qualities in life that she fears. Leia tells him that she likes nice men. And he responds, "I'm a nice man." She starts to tell him, "No, you're not. You're . . ." and then Han interrupts her and they kiss tenderly. The reality is that Han is a scoundrel *and* a nice man; he's a decent man who lives out some of his shadow qualities. Leia needs to realize that her "ideal" of a man is too one-dimensional and that her feelings are leading her to a more balanced experience with a man who is genuinely human and alive, not an abstraction. (We first saw this limitation in Leia when Luke arrived at her cell in *A New Hope*. He wasn't the image of rescuer she expected.)

Leia's feelings are beginning to thaw. Perhaps frozen initially in response to the objectivity and impersonality required by her role as princess, she is finally allowing her own personhood to emerge. This is an important part of anyone's development. As the feminine counterpart to Luke, Leia represents his anima development. As a female heroine, she is challenged in her own development to know her own feelings and come to terms with her animus. This doubled-sided challenge requires her (1) to realize that men are not always who she thinks they should be, and (2) to incorporate into herself those qualities that certain men (in this case, Han) represent for her. Is she aware, for example, of her own scoundrel qualities? Then as far as actual men are concerned, she has to learn to accept that a known scoundrel might also be a nice man. (Often more challenging for women is learning that a seemingly nice man, who says all the right things, is a scoundrel.)

Threepio, who has come to announce his excitement about another one of his mechanical discoveries concerning the ship, interrupts their kiss. Han is not thrilled that the moment has been spoiled; and Leia, after the intrusion, slips away, clearly in turmoil over what she is feeling.

Juxtaposing this very personal scene occurring deep within the large asteroid, we join the Imperial fleet in its search for the hidden ship. Reports are given to Vader that the Falcon is not on their scopes, and that given their damage, the ship must have been destroyed. Somehow Vader knows that they are alive and orders that the asteroid field be searched until they are found.

Admiral Piett then reports that the Emperor has commanded Vader to make contact with him. The ship is moved out of the asteroid field to assure a clear transmission. As threatening and powerful as we have seen that Vader is, it is clear that the Emperor, a cloaked, dark figure, is even more sinister. Vader kneels before the Emperor's holographic image and asks, "What is thy bidding, my master?" Both men describe having felt a great disturbance in the Force. The Emperor reports that they have a new enemy, Luke Skywalker, who, he believes, can destroy them. Vader notes that he is only a boy and that Obi-Wan can no longer help him. The Emperor asserts that he must not be allowed to become a Jedi. Vader suggests that, if he could be turned (to the dark side of the Force), Luke could be a powerful ally. The Emperor concurs that if he could be brought to their side he would be a great asset. When he asks if it can be done, Vader vows "He will join us or die, my master."

When we last saw Luke he was anything but a threat to anyone. Somehow, though, just by being on Dagobah Luke has grown strong with the Force, or at least strong enough that it can be felt by these dark Jedi figures. The conversation between Vader and the Emperor makes it clear that those trained in how to utilize the Force have the capacity to use it for perceptual purposes—in particular, to detect others who are also connected to it. (Curiously, however, they don't sense the existence of Yoda.) We also see in these powerful unearthly characters an even more intense fear of being vulnerable than shown by the Imperial officers on the Death Star in *A New Hope*. That such a threat could emanate from "just a boy" is a common mythological theme. We previously noted, for example, the Gospel story in which Herod so fears the birth of a baby that he commits mass infanticide.[5] New life poses a threat to those who are over-identified with power of any kind. This communication between the two dark figures leaves us wondering about Luke's fate. What kind of power do they possess? *Can* they get him to join them? How? Will they destroy him? Is this Yoda whom Luke seeks any match for them?

Inside the Dagobah Tree Hut

Luke's "descent" into Dagobah continues; he sits in the creature's small hut located under the large root of a giant tree. Amidst all this vegetative life, plant symbolism is ubiquitous. Besides water, the source of life, Luke is also immersed in the organic side of existence. The full realization of oneself is a process of natural growth, rooted in the depths of the psyche.

Next we see *snakes*, and Luke casually lifts one off the table in front of him. The snake represents the animating principle of psychic life, especially when it appears in conjunction with the more passive vegetative principle. Mythologically the tree and snake are linked to the Garden of Eden and thus to the origins of human consciousness. In Eden Adam and Eve eat of the tree of the knowledge of good and evil. On Dagobah Luke must begin to learn to differentiate between the dark side and the good side applications of the Force.[6]

The tree and the house of the creature it contains have maternal significance for Luke as well, as does the carefully prepared food the creature is serving. Luke, however, samples it with little real appreciation. Another sign that Luke is unaware of his surroundings and their possible significance is the casual way he handles the snake. The snake is both a fearful and numinous creature; connected to life on its most primordial level, it generates feelings of danger and awe.[7] Luke is oblivious to this.

In this richly symbolic setting Luke is increasingly impatient. It's no wonder that the robed swamp animal suggests he simply eat first. The process of learning about the Force requires being rooted in embodied existence. In order to understand the Force Luke will have to return to the basic processes of assimilation, such as eating carefully chosen, nourishing food, before he can proceed with assimilating far more complex psychological and spiritual aspects of existence.

Luke, however, is anxious to find Yoda and oblivious to all else. His education will revolve around how he relates to such impulsive feelings and emotions, teaching him how to engage and control them through conscious awareness. "Patience!" the creature suggests. "For the Jedi it is time to eat as well." Luke persists with his desires to meet the Jedi master. "How far away is Yoda? Will it take us long to get there?" The creature indicates that Yoda is not far, again exhorting patience and assuring Luke that he will be with Yoda soon.

Now the creature asks, "Why wish you become Jedi?" Luke responds, "Mostly because of my father, I guess." To Luke's surprise, the creature responds, "Ah, your father. Powerful Jedi was he, powerful Jedi." Luke is quickly upset. "Oh, come on. How could you know my father? You don't even know who I am." Now he's even more exasperated and frustrated. "Oh, I don't know what I'm doing here. We're wasting our time!"

This scene depicts the activation of a complex, an unconscious feeling-loaded issue within the personality. At the core of Luke's reaction is his father complex (also discussed in Part I). Luke realizes that his efforts to become a Jedi are somehow related to his father, but he is not sure why. Only when he met Ben did he learn that his father had been a Jedi, and furthermore, that the Jedi even *existed.* His emotions now have an infantile (unintegrated, explosive) quality to them. Emotional issues involving core life areas like this are usually touched off in interactions with others, and often by a seemingly innocuous comment or question. What adds to the situation, in Luke's case, is that this unknown little creature, whom Luke has mostly discounted, may have more intimate information about his father—and maybe even himself—than Luke has. To suddenly discover that another possesses knowledge of oneself of which one is totally unaware can feel very threatening.

Luke's outburst is related to the acute disorientation he now feels. How *does* this little creature know about his father? Could he even know about *him*? He didn't expect this! What is he doing here? In the midst of these chaotic and confusing emotions, old patterns of behavior come out. *Don't waste time!* It's his uncle's voice exhorting him again, as it did when Obi-Wan first spoke to Luke about his father and invited him to come to Alderaan.

When the old voice of his uncle/father complex is added to this turbulent mix, it changes Luke's confusion and disorientation into guilt, which is more familiar and thus easier to handle than the new feelings. Wasting time is bad—Luke can comprehend this and take appropriate action to keep busy. He also tries to deal with the frustrating feelings by unconsciously projecting them onto the creature. Psychologically, the issue isn't that the creature doesn't know who Luke is: it's that Luke doesn't know himself. He's still very unconscious and has little sense of his life's purpose and the potential for his own personal development. (He is also still very much in the dark concerning the meaning of this planet he has landed on.)

When the creature first arrives in Luke's camp, his playfulness immediately excites children who watch him. The "natural" child responds to the behavior of the creature and the symbolism of Dagobah in some instinctive way. Such a child "knows" that this is an important place. This point in the film reveals to what extent any viewer of any age might still be connected to the imaginative wisdom of childhood. This "child" knows what's coming. Anyone as surprised as Luke will be that this creature is actually the Jedi Master may be equally lost to this magical child within, as Luke is at this moment in the story.

The creature, meanwhile, has turned off to the side and speaks to someone unseen. He is clearly irritated. The emotions connected to complexes are contagious; it's hard not be affected by them when one is around them. The creature now has an emotional reaction of his own to wrestle with as a result of Luke's outburst. He laments, "I cannot teach him. The boy has no patience." Everyone realizes by now that this creature is Yoda, the Jedi Master. It is the voice of Ben Kenobi that speaks back, "He will learn patience."

Here on Dagobah, a place like "something out of a dream," the visionary world is much closer. The conversation between Ben and Yoda can be seen in many ways. One is that the unconscious issues from the previous generations are left for those surviving to deal with, but that they will be helped by the living "presence" of those who have departed. For example, certain ancient peoples believe that their ancestors are guides for healing and bring them their dreams.[8] On Hoth Ben was such a message-bearer for Luke and is now present as an "ancestor spirit" with whom Yoda consults. Jedi awareness seems to imply communication with the spiritual plane in which Ben resides.

The conversation between Ben and Yoda can also reflect a conversation within Yoda himself. Yoda clearly has concerns about this new student's potential, particularly given his tendency to be impatient. The integration of our emotions is critical to our maturation process. It is fairly common knowledge that denied or repressed feelings are bound to erupt sooner or later. The challenge for us is to bear them—that is, *not* to lose patience. Then we must understand these feelings and direct them in more differentiated ways. Yoda has become irritated with Luke's impatience. His challenge is the same as anyone working in the helping professions. Assisting others with integrating their emotions always involves the ongoing process of wrestling with one's *own*. Our deepest emotions link us to the unfathomable depths of the unconscious and the many images emanating out of it. Tolerating other's raw emotions, and our own, until creative outlets for their expression can be found, is probably the most difficult aspect of teaching, counseling, mentoring, and parenting.

The Jedi student must wrestle with his or her emotions in the process of confronting the darker and more primitive uses of the Force made possible by disowned, unconscious impulses. Yoda realizes that there is much anger in Luke, as there was in Luke's father, and he is very concerned. Ben asks, "Was I any different when you taught me?" Still Yoda fears another failure and insists that Luke is not ready. Luke bursts into the conversation having finally realized who the little creature is. He worries that the Jedi Master doesn't think he's ready and appeals to his former mentor. "Ben! I can be a Jedi. Ben, tell him I'm ready." However, as Luke tries to get up, he bumps his head on the roof of the hut. Yoda's living quarters help keep Luke in his place, preventing him from "losing his head" and getting carried away.

In order to deal with life we need energy from the psyche to find our place in the world. But if we get too filled up by it—in Jung's terms, too identified with the archetype of the Self—then we run the risk of inflation.[9] The popular term for psychiatrist, "shrink," metaphorically suggests the antidote for such hubris. Ironically, people who *don't* consult therapists and could use some "shrinking" but fear self-knowledge probably coined the term. The roof of Yoda's house serves to keep Luke "down" and thus more contained so that he doesn't get too carried away with himself.

Yoda protests Luke's eager assessment of his own readiness, refers to his *800 years* of training Jedi, and tells Luke he will keep his own counsel regarding who is to be trained. He informs Luke that a Jedi must have the deepest commitment, the most serious mind. He tells Ben that he has watched Luke for a long time. The young man has looked away towards the future all his life; he has never had his mind on where he was and what he was doing in the moment.

Yoda gives us an inner view of Luke. While he was kept busy working for his uncle, his mind was wandering off into daydreams and fantasies of the future. This is common for any child who has not been given the time or guidance to develop a genuinely introverted aspect of his or her life. Children have a natural symbolic capacity that is deeply connected to their emotions. When thwarted, it has to find outlets in some way. Luke's way was to give free reign to his imagination of future possibilities.

"Adventure. Huh! Excitement! Huh! A Jedi craves not these things. You are reckless!" Yoda tells Luke with brutal honesty. When there is no acknowledged safe place for imaginative and emotional expression, a child is more susceptible to acting-out behaviors and creating "adventures" for their own sake. Luke, it seems, developed a propensity for such behavior growing up, presumably in order to escape the barren atmosphere his uncle created at home—but, in Yoda's view, it made him reckless.

Ben counters Yoda's assessment by indicating that he, too, was reckless when he began the training. Still doubtful, Yoda expresses his misgivings in another direction: Luke is "too old. Yes, too old to begin the training." So Luke responds, "But I've learned so much." Yoda ponders it all thoughtfully. Luke is reckless, and can be naive, but he has demonstrated the ability to learn about the Force. So Yoda asks Ben (and himself), "Will he finish what he begins?" The question seems to be that if he doesn't have enough commitment: he will once again be prone to succumb to a complex that might get the better of him.

Luke responds: "I won't fail you—I'm not afraid." One of his better parts, his determination, and one of his weakest, his naiveté, both assert themselves now. Yoda's answer gravely counters Luke's denial of his fear, "Oh, you will be. You will be." Luke underestimates the depth and nature of his emotional life, especially on an archetypal level. An approach to life that invites one to "stretch out with your feelings" leaves one precariously vulnerable to eruptions of hidden emotions. Luke, according to Yoda, will experience fear he cannot even imagine. Learning about the Force has far wider ramifications than Luke is capable of envisioning . . . yet.

Before leaving this scene on Dagobah, I'd like to comment further on the rich symbolism carried in the character of Yoda. Immersed in the swamps of Dagobah and surrounded by all sorts of primordial life, Yoda is a child of nature. Mythologically, because of his close relationship to water, vegetative life, and animals, he is closely linked to the symbolism of the Great Mother the elemental, archetypal feminine principle. Yet Yoda also clearly reflects the masculine principle of spirit. In the first scene with Luke he was very childlike; now he is the old Jedi Master with the wisdom of many years. (Mythological figures are often described as having lived for hundreds of years.[10]) Yoda combines the opposite masculine archetypal energies of old wise man *(senex)* and spirited, impish child *(puer)*.[11]

Above all, however, and more symbolically "down to earth," Yoda is symbolic of *creatureliness.* Uniting masculine and feminine symbolism, he's a creature's creature. As a symbol of the Self he clearly reminds us that most important in integrating archetypal energies of all kinds is maintaining our creaturehood. When we as humans forget this aspect of our existence, we are in the most danger of becoming inflated and losing touch with our natural self and its roots in nature. In an age of burgeoning technology, whether it is on our own planet or in the *Star Wars* universe, the greatest realization of the Self comes from being the creature one is. Of all the animals in nature, the human variety has the most difficulty being itself. The realization of the Self, or individuation, ultimately means being a fully embodied human being. Yoda captures the essence of this symbolically. Individuation is not about being "great"; it's about being comfortable with one's "smallness" in the grand scheme of life and still giving full expression to the potentials within. Then the Force will be with us, as paradoxical as that feels, and as the story to unfold illustrates.

"This is No Cave!"

After this psychological drama on Dagobah, we rejoin the action in the asteroid field. Imperial ships are bombing the asteroids in their search for the Millennium Falcon. Inside the Falcon it is quiet. A creature on the cockpit window awakens Leia. Very primitive, even primeval, it has attached itself with a suction cup to the window. Startled, Leia hurries to inform Han that there's something out there. They hear banging on the hull of the ship, which ominously confirms her assessments. Han immediately announces that he's going outside the ship, despite her objections. Having just fixed the Falcon, he's not going to let anything tear it apart. Chewie and Leia follow.

They discover a strange and unexpected environment. The ground is squishy, definitely not rock, and there's a lot of moisture (much like Dagobah). Leia has a bad feeling about it. One of these creatures, like a prehistoric animal, flies by, and they shoot at it. Han identifies it as a mynock and tells Chewie to check the ship for any more of them that might be chewing on the ship's power cables.

As the ground shifts under their feet, Han becomes suspicious and fires his blaster into the ground. It rumbles again and they are all thrown off balance. Han announces that they are taking off immediately. Leia voices objections, but Han insists on action not discussion. He soon has the ship headed out of the cave. Up ahead they witness a strange sight: the cave is seemingly closing shut in front of them. They suddenly realize that they are not in a cave; what at first had seemed to be stalagmites and stalactites turn out to be *teeth*. The Millennium Falcon barely escapes the huge jaws of an enormous space slug making one last effort to devour them.

As counterpoint to the pace of Dagobah, the action of the story picks up with this narrow escape of the Millennium Falcon. Important symbolism repeats parallel motifs to those found in Luke and Artoo's adventures. First, this scene duplicates the Jonah-in-the-whale adventure that Artoo had on Dagobah. They can't stay inside this place; they must move on. Their escape also mirrors that of Luke from the Wampa, as they, too, must avoid being eaten and devoured. Han's instincts quickly recognize the dangerous situation in time to save them. This scene counterbalances the setting Luke is in. Luke discovered a challenging but nurturing, moist environment where he must remain and learn; Han, Leia, and Chewie are in a moist locale that turns out to be lethal and must make a harrowing escape in order to survive.

Symbolically the space slug is representative of any experience involving hideous fears that suddenly develop out of nowhere and threaten to consume us. One such fear, born out the context of the story, is the fear of intimacy, in particular of being overwhelmed by the feelings that are stirred in oneself, or being swallowed up by the needs and desires of the other person. As the relationship between Han and Leia heats up, Leia has shown definite discomfort and even fear of her feelings. Han displays eagerness to move on and not become pinned down. Behind the male fear of commitment often lies the fear of being trapped and engulfed by a woman—but really it's the archetypal feminine in its most elemental forms that is feared, here symbolized by the enormous slug. One keeps one's distance so as not to be consumed by the emotions involved. Both Luke and Han are engaged in activities that bring them closer to the elemental world of the Great Mother—Luke by delving into the mysteries of the Force on Dagobah, and Han by courting further intimacy with Leia.

Women fear intimacy, too, but often cover their misgivings by trying to tell a man how to be and what to do. Han is a man doing things his way, using his instincts; he can't be directed by Leia's *ideas* of what he should do—which is precisely why she is ultimately drawn to him.

As the feelings simmer between Han and Leia, the underlying fear for both of them is being swallowed up by the feelings, losing themselves in the other. The space slug represents for these characters the threat of being "devoured" by their undifferentiated, unconscious emotions. The Wampa creature represented the same fears for Luke. Han and Leia escape for now, thanks to Han's survival instincts, but once more they will have to navigate the asteroid field and continue to elude the Imperial pursuit.

The Lessons and "Cave" Initiation of a Jedi Apprentice

With Yoda riding on his back, Luke runs, climbs vines, and somersaults through the Dagobah swamps. A squawking, flying creature appears, similar to the mynocks just encountered by Han and Leia. We've left a moist but threatening environment to return to a moist and rich one, where the Jedi Master is teaching Luke about the Force and the dangers of the dark side. "A Jedi's strength flows from the Force. But beware of the dark side. Anger . . . fear . . . aggression. Easily they flow. If once you start down the dark path, forever will it dominate your destiny, consume you it will, as it did Obi-Wan's apprentice."

"Vader," Luke responds, and then asks, "Is the dark side stronger?"

To which Yoda answers, "No. Quicker, easier, more seductive."

The teachings of Yoda put in clear psychological terms the symbolism carried by the escape of the Millennium Falcon from the space slug (and the earlier Wampa scene). A Jedi's strength comes from the Force. As a metaphor for the archetypal layers of the psyche, the Force is rooted in nature and our deepest emotions. For the Jedi, primary emotions such as anger, fear, aggression, or greed, lust, and avarice can all too easily lead to sinister usage of this life energy. These menacing emotions flow easily, and because they do, they can easily consume us. One becomes devoured from within, so to speak, and once this happens, it is hard to break the emotional hold of the particular complex gripping the personality.

The wisdom of the Jedi religion has parallels in modern psychotherapy and psychoanalysis, which contend that emotional patterns established in the childhood environment affect us pervasively throughout our lives. If parents are too strongly gripped by their anger and fear, these disowned and/or out-of-control emotions will profoundly influence their children's emotional life during childhood and later as adults. Some children from these difficult environments grow into adults who act out their angry emotions on *their* children, as their parents did. Other children react in an introverted manner, paralyzed by fear, and as adults often become caught in self-destructive compulsive behaviors (such as addictions) or feel trapped in states of depression, anxiety and self-doubt. Once such emotional patterns are established they can "dominate our destiny," especially if we remain unconscious of them. We then tend to function in the world and interact with others *as if* we were still living in our troubled childhood environments.

Falling into our old patterns, our complexes—as we saw Luke do in Yoda's hut when he got frustrated—is "quicker, easier, more seductive." It takes conscious awareness to break these patterns and choose to live from more balanced emotional places within ourselves. The way these primary emotions can suddenly seize us makes them very powerful. Affects discharged without our conscious humanization of them can be extremely frightening.

Luke asks Yoda how he is to know the good side from the bad. In this swampy forest, he asks the key question of all psychological and spiritual knowledge: How do we distinguish good from evil? The more conscious self-awareness we attain, the more critical this question becomes—and the more complicated. Yoda tells Luke, "You will know. When you are calm, at peace. Passive. A Jedi uses the Force for knowledge and defense, never for attack." Yoda's advice suggests that Luke, as a man, must become more connected to the positive feminine principle, the receptive inner space wherein one can touch the wholeness of oneself not fragmented by emotional conflict. Then he will be able to "know" in the best way that he can. A "passive" yin stance balances the active, aggressive yang energies.[12]

For Yoda, who lives in the midst of the archetypal feminine world, the knowing one needs for separating the good side from the bad comes from a place of feminine wisdom. Jung suggests that the function of *feeling* is also critical in this process and that the opposite of wisdom is bitterness—a quality that certainly fits the angry Darth Vader, Obi-Wan's former apprentice. Wisdom, according to Jung, is closely connected to how we cope with life's disappointments. Earlier we saw how violently Vader dealt with being disappointed by Admiral Ozzel. Jung suggests that disappointment can generate either bitterness or "the strongest incentive to a differentiation of feeling."[13] Yoda's teaching connects Luke back to Obi-Wan's instruction on the Millennium Falcon: "Stretch out with your feelings." Without a conscious connection to our feelings, which involves careful reflection on all of our emotions, the function of feeling, which is to make value judgments, cannot operate.[14] A careful connection to feeling helps us to know the good from the bad, what harms others and what truly helps them.

When a person has lost the capacity for a humane response to situations, as Vader has, bitterness takes over, as well as anger and aggression. More often than not, these powerful emotions culminate in violence and other forms of acting-out behaviors. The opportunity for wisdom, and a more creative human solution, is lost. Yoda tells Luke that the Jedi knight seeks wisdom and knowledge but not violent action. Knowledge of the Force—of life in all its mystery including the aggressive actions that come from it—is to be used only for defense.

Luke wants to know more, "But tell me why I can't . . ."

Yoda cuts him off, "No, no, there is no *why*. Nothing more will I teach you today. Clear your mind of questions." Yoda would stop Luke from knowing only through *thinking*. The lesson concerning the knowledge of the good side from the bad has to do with feelings as well as thinking. Feeling-level discernments often take more time; they are not quick and easy because they distinguish imprecise psychological currents that swirl around us within a complex array of emotions. Relying only on thinking—and the "cleaner" either/or polarities of logical thought—can serve as a defense against feeling these conflicts within ourselves and with others that we are challenged to confront. Our culture values thinking above feeling. Many of us were raised to believe that if we know something intellectually, then we understand it. However, the larger truth is that only when we know something emotionally as well—how we are affected on a feeling level—do we really "know" it. In my psychotherapeutic work a patient—usually to relieve anxiety—will ask quickly, much like Luke on Dagobah, "Tell me what I should do." But I can't tell them anything, because what they need to know, first and foremost, can only be found inside of them. Only when *they* experience this in some way—perhaps through a feeling, an image, a dream, or a bodily sensation—can they be helped to understand and integrate what they are experiencing. Only then can they *know*.

What Luke needs most is direct psychological experience. Having ended the lesson, Yoda sits quietly, Artoo beeps, and Luke begins to settle down in a clearing. Then Luke senses a disturbance: "There is something not right here. I feel cold, death." A "chill in the air" often symbolically suggests the presence of evil of some sort. Luke feels a different kind of coldness than what he experienced on the ice planet Hoth; he feels a spiritual coldness.

Pointing to a nearby cave Yoda tells Luke, "That place . . . is strong with the dark side of the Force. A domain of evil it is. In you must go."

"What's in there?" Luke asks.

"Only what you take with you," Yoda responds. Luke warily eyes the cave entrance and starts to strap on his weapon belt. "Your weapons," Yoda tells him, "you will not need them." Luke finishes strapping them on anyway. Artoo vibrates nervously as he leaves; Yoda sighs.

Yoda, it seems, lives in a place that contains both the light and dark sides of life, of the Force. To know oneself, one must know the dark side as well as the light. Metaphorically, it is as if Luke must face his own coldness and his own mortality. As an initiate Luke is to take nothing with him; he is to experience what is within himself. When we venture into dark places, be they in the city or the wilderness, our imaginations often become very alive. Every child knows this truth all too well. It's the darker, more frightening aspects of our own psychic life that we project into the shadowy environs. It is here we must go if we are to know the depths of life more deeply. Luke must come to terms with his worst fears and the depths of his own imagination.

While just a moment earlier Luke wanted to know more from Yoda, now he ignores his instructions and takes his weapons with him anyway. He's still identified with the heroic warrior attitude. His weapons reflect another very common psychological defense in our culture: our reliance on various concrete *things* for security. Possessions, money, clothes, food, alcohol, drugs, and the whole array of consumer goods we seek to acquire are often procured for their own sake, in a compulsive way, rather than for any true practical purpose. They give us a false sense of security and protect us from the depths of our psyches and our underlying fears. In a similar way Luke takes his weapons with him.

However, what Luke will soon encounter is of a psychological nature; he won't need his weapons. But since he doesn't realize that yet, he is not ready to risk the feelings of vulnerability that would come if he were to leave his familiar means of defense behind. They make him feel more powerful, more confident. The Jedi Master does not interfere with his choice, but we wonder if Yoda isn't disappointed in this further expression of Luke's naiveté.

Luke descends into the cave and moves slowly through its primordial atmosphere. A lizard squawks as he passes by, as if announcing his presence—or maybe a warning. As Luke moves further into the darkness, a glow of light appears up ahead and then the labored, artificial breathing of Darth Vader is heard. Vader himself steps forward in front of Luke. Luke ignites his lightsaber and Vader does the same. Briefly they duel and then Luke is able to unleash a blow that decapitates the dark, helmeted figure. The helmet falls to the ground, its mask dissolves, and Luke beholds his own face inside.

The Dagobah cave is a psychological chamber of initiation. No weapons or other objects are needed; this is a state of direct inner experience only. For Luke to move forward in his training, to discern the beneficial versus harmful employment of the Force, he must know his own inclinations for evil and his own destructive impulses. We usually remain unaware of these shadow aspects of ourselves because we project them onto others. Darth Vader is clearly an evil villain, and Luke doesn't seem at all like him. In the Dagobah cave, as in a powerful dream experience, Luke is forced to see things differently, to see himself more honestly. Here is a shock: Luke has a Darth Vader side—he, too, could be lured to misuse the power of the Force.

A very subtle but important aspect of this scene is that Luke draws his weapon first. At that moment, Luke becomes like the Darth Vader on the Death Star who waited, with weapon drawn, to challenge and kill Obi-Wan Kenobi. When the worst enemy he could imagine confronted Luke, he was quickly overcome by his aggressive urge to fight and he acted impulsively, igniting his lightsaber. Thus, though it was Vader's head that rolled to the cave floor, symbolically it was Luke who "lost his head."

Decapitation is another form of the dismemberment symbolism that is prominent in the *Star Wars* films. The symbolism of beheading revolves around the psychological imperative of gaining control over destructive impulses that are acted out in the body. These can be of any sort—aggressive (as in Luke's case), sexual, addictive, and so on. Because the body and its instinctive nature is seen as the source of these impulses, removing the head from the rest of the body symbolizes the urgency of separating oneself from them. The desire and goal of such a psychological process is to understand the nature of the impulses, emotionally and imaginatively, so that they don't take us over.

Jung discusses a process of psychic integration found in alchemy called the *coniunctio* (the union of opposites) that involves this symbolism. This alchemical *coniunctio* is a three-stage process that begins with what the alchemist referred to as the *unio mentalis.*[15] According to this symbolism, before one can be at peace and at one with the world, one must first resolve the conflict between body (instinct), soul (imagination), and spirit (mind/intellect). Unconscious longings of the soul fall into the body and are lived out through instinctive impulses unless they can be understood psychologically. The union of soul and spirit, distinct from the body, symbolizes the process of separating out these longings of the soul. One of the symbols of this stage of the *coniunctio* is beheading. Spirit and soul must unite so that enacted impulses may be brought under control. According to the alchemists, soul and spirit come together in this stage—this is the first conjunction.

Psychologically, spirit (mind/intellect) helps the soul (imagination) understand what it is searching for so that it may find other ways to express its longings than through destructive instinctual enactments. Through this process the meaning of impulsive and compulsive behavior is understood and can be integrated internally instead of enacted externally. (The second conjunction involves the unification of the *unio mentalis*—soul and spirit—with the body and instinctive life. The third, called the *unus mundus,* is the unification of this second conjunction with the world.)

From the powerful symbolism of this scene, and the ending shrug from Yoda, it is clear that Luke has much more to learn.

"It's Not My Fault"

Back on the Imperial command ship Darth Vader is conversing with a motley array of men and creatures. Through Admiral Piett's comment to the Imperial crew that is present, we learn that they are bounty hunters. Vader is offering a substantial reward to the one who finds the Millennium Falcon. He wants those on board alive, but beyond that one stipulation, the bounty hunters are free to use any methods they deem necessary.

New characters with bizarre features keep popping up throughout the *Star Wars* story, thus keeping our imagination freshly engaged. Shadow symbolism suffuses this scene; we recognize bounty hunters from our westerns as mercenaries who are paid to find wanted men. These unsavory characters are very similar to those seen in the cantina where Ben and Luke discovered Chewie and Han. Vader obviously believes the bounty hunters might have more success than the highly organized and technological Imperial forces, who lack the resourcefulness that such rogue characters possess. At the moment of Vader's instructions to this new group of characters, Admiral Piett reports to him that the Imperial fleet has found the Millennium Falcon.

As they leave the asteroid field, an Imperial Star Destroyer is firing upon Han's ship. Ready to make the jump to light-speed, he pulls back on the throttle and . . . nothing happens. No light-speed. "It's not fair," Han exclaims. "It's not my fault!" They are defenseless. Once more the escape that got them away from Imperial ships near Tatooine in *A New Hope*, isn't available to them. The safety of the far reaches of space still eludes them.

When things just don't work as we would like, or we have come to expect, we often want to blame someone else. We feel that somehow someone must be held accountable; someone must "pay" for things not working out as expected. While Han doesn't blame anyone else, he doesn't want to become the brunt of such blaming by others due to the failure of the hyperdrive.[16]

Given the urgency of their situation, there isn't time to fault anyone. The Imperial ship has just knocked out their rear deflector shield; one more hit and they will be destroyed. All possibilities for defense are breaking down, but the quick-thinking Han has one more clever maneuver. Ordering Chewie to turn the ship around, Han declares he's going to put all power into the front deflector shields. Leia and Threepio are shocked at Han's decision; the Imperial officers are also quite surprised. The Star Destroyer captain orders their shields up, and they duck as the Millennium Falcon flies right past the bridge window, and . . . disappears.

While Luke is in the midst of an intensely introverted initiation, facing his own inner demons, the adventures involving Han are a test of extraverted instinct pitted against external foes. With no other choice, Han directly engages the threat that is facing them. Luke's attack of the dark figure in the cave was too impulsive, but Han's flight right into the face of the enemy is absolutely necessary at this moment.

The Millennium Falcon has seemingly completely disappeared, no longer registering on the Imperial ship's scopes. The Star Destroyer's officers cannot fathom where it could have gone, or how it could have escaped detection. Informed that Lord Vader wants an update, Captain Needa orders that his shuttle be made ready. He will assume full responsibility for losing them and apologize to Vader. His attitude is opposite to Han's, at the other end of the accountability spectrum. Han didn't want to be blamed; he didn't want to be made accountable for something beyond his control. Needa, on the other hand, takes full responsibility for losing the Millennium Falcon; he takes on *too much* responsibility. When life becomes unpredictable, there has to be a balance between what we can honestly be responsible for, and expect from others, and what we can't. Some people don't accept enough responsibility; others take on too much. Part of Luke's initiation, as outlined in the next chapter, will involve learning to evaluate just how responsible he should be for the fate of his friends.

The Recovery of the Sinking Ship

The scene now shifts back to Dagobah where Yoda is instructing Luke further about the Force. The lesson will soon revolve around the condition of Luke's spaceship, which he fears is hopelessly sunk in the swamps of Dagobah.

Once more, Luke is symbolically at a place where he has to turn his attitudes "upside down," as he was in the Wampa cave on Hoth. This time he stands on his hands with Yoda perched on his feet. Big rocks lie nearby and one of them lifts off the ground. "Use the Force. Yes," Yoda tells him. During this time Artoo is beeping nervously, as Luke's ship begins to stir in the nearby bog. "Now, the stone. Feel it." Yoda encourages. As the stone rises, Artoo becomes more frantic as the ship begins to sink further into the water. The disturbance causes Luke to lose his balance. Even as Yoda suggests that he concentrate, Luke falters; the rock, Luke, and Yoda all tumble to the ground.

Symbolically Yoda is trying to teach Luke to experience a living connection to all things, to reach for the final stage of the alchemical conjunction, which the alchemists called the *unus mundus,* a state of being one with the world.[17] If he feels the environment around him through his body and the spiritual energy that resides within him in a deeply related way, not an impulsive and reckless way, life can flow more effortlessly; life may not weigh so heavily. One strives to stay in balance, and this requires concentration.

No one stays in balance all the time. Earlier Yoda became upset with Luke's impatience when Yoda asked him about his desire to become a Jedi. He, too, had to bring himself together after becoming frustrated. The flow of life itself creates disturbances, which are particularly distressing when our complexes are aggravated in the process. Our task is to restore balance by interacting consciously with the complexes constellated by the vicissitudes of life. When Luke's ship slips further into the bog, Artoo gets increasingly worried and anxious. His reaction upsets Luke's emotional balance and distracts him, and he can no longer hold himself together and stay connected with the Force. Thus he falls into a complex. "Oh, no. We'll never get it out now." He's become disillusioned and disheartened. Unlike the resourceful Han Solo, Luke easily gets discouraged.

"So certain are you," Yoda responds. "Always with you it cannot be done. Hear you nothing that I say?" When a complex, an old emotional pattern of behavior, grips us we are often possessed by a false sense of negative certainty. We are easily defeated and frustrated. In his frustration Luke is not open to new possibility, and is dejectedly skeptical. He tells Yoda, "Moving stones around is one thing. This is totally different." Yoda insists, however, "No! No different! Only different in your mind. You must unlearn what you have learned."

Yoda's response suggests much the same awareness that depth psychology and ancient and modern religious practices discuss in their own frameworks. What we think and imagine affects how we relate to the world around us and other people and creatures in it. In Luke's mind, what he is learning can't apply to the ship, since the ship is so much bigger than the stones he is trying to move. He *believes* there is a difference, and that belief determines how he relates to the situation. What we imagine and what we can't imagine both affect how we deal with the world. Ultimately *all* systems of belief, from the religious to the scientific and technological, depend on what is imagined about the nature of life. Each accordingly facilitates or limits how we come to terms with our life experience.

Luke tells Yoda that he will "give it a try." This is too halfhearted an attitude for Yoda, who responds, "No! Try not. Do. Or do not. There is no *try*." If Luke doesn't believe that what and how he imagines things affects his reality in any way, then he limits what he can actually accomplish in life. If he doesn't *believe* he can do it, he won't be able to. Yoda's instruction urges Luke, in essence, to "unlearn" his current attitude, one that does not comprehend the relationship between his mental/imaginal life (represented by gaining knowledge of the Force), and his external, concrete life (represented by his ship). The ship, his vehicle, is also Luke's only remaining link to the rest of the galaxy and the life he has known outside of Dagobah.

Yoda's teaching, "Do. Or do not. There is no try," is easily taken out of context. Some people may interpret this particular teaching of Yoda in a way that fuels and energizes a complex, a negative life pattern, rather than as a way to help dissolve and "unlearn" it. Yoda's statement to Luke is not good advice for a workaholic, for example, a person who does too much and tries too hard all the time, an overly focused and driven person.

What Yoda suggests here applies to someone like Luke, who gets discouraged easily and can't readily conceive new life possibilities for himself. First, he must learn to imagine a potential he hasn't considered before, and second, he must find the will and desire to implement this un-imagined possibility. We've seen that this is exactly what Han Solo can do, and in an instant. Luke's lessons with Yoda here are the introverted version of what Solo is able to do in an extraverted and instinctive way.

Yoda stands wide-eyed as Luke's efforts begin to stir the ship and bring it up out of the water. Artoo is also excited. But the ship soon sinks back even deeper, and Luke quickly becomes discouraged. "I can't. It's too big," he laments.

Yoda looks down; he's dejected and disappointed, too. "Size matters not," he responds. "Judge me by my size, do you? Hm?" Luke shakes his head in recognition of the fact that he doesn't judge Yoda this way. "And well you should not," The Jedi Master continues. "For my ally is the Force. And a powerful ally it is. Life creates it, makes it grow. Its energy surrounds us and binds us. Luminous beings are we . . . [Yoda pinches Luke's upper arm] . . . not this crude matter. You must feel the Force around you. Here, between you . . . me . . . the tree . . . the rock . . . everywhere! Yes, even between this land and that ship!"

Luke has made a judgment based on a superficial observable factor that has hampered his ability to become reconnected to his ship. We might recall that when he first came to Dagobah he was looking for a "great warrior." He imagined someone larger than life, not the Jedi Master he found. While he has come to accept Yoda as the teacher he was seeking, he still is caught up in the issue of "size." (In *A New Hope* Leia had first rejected Luke as being too short when he appeared in her cell.) On one level, this is a classic male self-image issue; for many males growing up, body size and height, not to mention penis size, are viewed as defining a man's masculinity and thus his male identity. Yoda's insight applies as much to these contemporary concerns as it does on Dagobah. "Size matters not." What does matter is one's connection to life. If one is properly aligned with life, then "it" serves as a powerful ally. The creative energies and capacity for growth inherent in life are what matter most, in addition to an understanding of how life's energy is all around us.

Yoda's teaching has much in common with Jung's hypotheses about the nature of the human psyche and the various dimensions of life it touches. Though deeply rooted in nature and our bodily existence, the human psyche is not merely a by-product of the body. It is a reality in itself, much like Yoda's description of "luminous beings." For Jung modern psychological experience echoes the age-old beliefs of an immortal soul that encounters a larger spiritual and psychic dimension, the collective unconscious, within which we exist. Many people have powerful emotional experiences of transcendent dimensions of life that they cannot dismiss; however, very often such experiences are difficult to articulate. People who are connected to their dreams, for example, find that they might have more powerful emotional experiences while dreaming than in waking life. Some deeper dimension touches those who learn how to carefully cultivate a relationship to it.

Yoda's description of where the Force can be felt is one of the most succinct articulations of the fourfold symbolism of the Self that I know. These four categories are found in mythologies throughout the world (Jung outlines them in one of his later works[18]). First there is Luke as representative of anthropos or spiritual symbolism, men and women as spiritual (luminous) beings.[19] Second comes Yoda as representative of the animal or shadow level of symbolism, the importance of our existence as creatures of the natural world. Third is the tree as representative of the vegetative and plant symbolism, the organic level of life related to growth and the process of death and resurrection. Fourth is the rock as representative of mineral symbolism and the inorganic level of life, which we can mine for various uses and on which our existence is grounded. In the most recent exercise it was the rock that Yoda was teaching Luke to be connected to.

It is during his instruction about the interconnection among all forms of life that can be experienced through the Force that Yoda suggests to Luke that there is a connection between the land on which they stand and the ship. The ship is also part of inorganic symbolism, like the rock. The size is not what matters, only the aspect of life it represents. We have already discussed how animated and alive the droids are. In our contemporary world there are those who invest more emotional energy in mechanical things than in any other form of life, be it human, animal, or plant. In essence, they live primarily on the mineral level of life. Since vehicles are a relatively late addition to human civilization, the psychological task of making a spiritual relation to them is relatively new. This task seems to be the problem now challenging Luke. "You want the impossible," Luke tells Yoda, as he walks away, frustrated, to retrieve his shirt.

Meanwhile, Yoda turns towards the water, closes his eyes, and with his head bowed raises one of his arms towards the ship. Slowly and majestically the X-wing emerges from the water and floats through the air towards the land—the land and ship are truly connected. Luke carefully walks around his spaceship to examine it. "I don't . . . I don't believe it," Luke stammers. "That is why you fail," the Jedi Master enjoins. And on that breathtaking remark the scene ends.

Yoda's concluding statement punctuates the fact that it is Luke's old unconscious belief system that has failed him. He needs a new myth, a new way of understanding life if he is to move forward. Yoda's lesson reflects the essence of effective depth psychotherapy. Old unconscious myths and beliefs about life that no longer serve us in healthy ways must be recognized and given up, or they will continue to get in our way. Developing new, more expansive perspectives can connect us to the "vehicle" we need to move forward once again; a vehicle that doesn't remain immobilized and unavailable, sunk in a swampland of unconsciousness.

One More Clever Escape

Inside Vader's Star Destroyer we witness the gasping, choking demise of Captain Needa, duplicating the fate of Admiral Ozzel when the Imperial fleet arrived at Hoth. Vader accepts his apology by making him pay with his life. No forgiveness or tolerance for human limitations and failure is forthcoming. Needa's demise contrasts sharply with Yoda's response to Luke's failures, which he utilizes as opportunities for further learning and growth, not as reasons for terminating a life—even when the instructor is frustrated!

Admiral Piett reports to Vader that the Imperial fleet has scanned the area and found nothing. If the Millennium Falcon made the jump to light-speed, it would be on the other side of the galaxy by now. Vader orders that all commands be alerted to attempt to calculate their destination along their last known trajectory. When Piett assures Vader that they will find them, Vader poignantly tells Piett not to fail him again. The agent of the dark side of the Force will not tolerate feelings of disappointment; Yoda, however, will do so, as any good teacher must, in order to create more space for a student to learn.

After Piett gives the orders to deploy the fleet, the camera pans the Imperial ships and closes in on the one Needa had commanded. We see the Millennium Falcon attached to the rear of the Star Destroyer's bridge. Han has not been able to get them into hyperspace, but he's made the ship "disappear" by attaching it, undetected, to the much larger Imperial ship. Inside the Falcon, Threepio, as usual, is complaining that Solo has gone too far this time. After Chewbacca growls at him, Threepio whines that he won't shut up and continues to fret that no one listens to him. Once more he carries all the anxious, worried feelings.

Han sees that the Imperial fleet is starting to break up and tells Chewie to stand by at the manual release for the landing claw. As Chewie leaves, Threepio launches into more of his incessant chatter and concern about what Han is doing. "Surrender is a perfectly acceptable alternative," he declares. By now his blabbering is disturbing not only to Han, but to Leia, and she turns around to shut him off, for which Han is grateful.

Leia's action represents an important development in her character. Up until now she, like Threepio, has been expressing worry, concern, and disbelief regarding all of Han's actions. Now, not only has she shut off Threepio, she has also shut off this critical side of herself (her negative animus, in Jungian terms). Now she's interested in what Han has in mind for their next move. She's ready to relate to him and accept the unique way that he approaches life as being helpful to her, despite the fact that it's not an approach that would naturally occur to her. She can interact with him now as a person who has thoughts and feelings different from her own, a man who does things in a strange, compelling manner that actually intrigues her.

Han tells Leia that standard Imperial procedure before making the jump to light-speed is to dump their garbage. When they do so the Millennium Falcon will just float off with the rest of the garbage. Escape with the Imperial garbage reprises the theme of escape through the garbage chute and garbage room on the Death

Star in *A New Hope*. Symbolically, garbage represents shadow contents. What is rejected can actually bring salvation psychologically to the individual personality. In this case by hiding in the garbage—that which the Imperials reject and leave behind—no one is likely to notice the Falcon.

Now they have to find a safe port. Han establishes that they are in the Anoat system, and Leia remarks that there isn't much there. Reviewing his computer map screen, Han finds something of interest: Lando—not a system, the conversation reveals, but a man, an individual Han has known before and whom he describes to Leia as a card player, gambler, and a scoundrel. "You'd like him," he kids her. Lando is at Bespin, a Tibanna gas mining colony he won in a card game.

Han tells Leia that he and Lando "go back a long way." When she asks Han if he trusts Lando, he says, no, he doesn't; he's certain, though, that Lando has no love for the Empire. Thus they will not only "escape" through the rejected, forgotten elements of Imperial ship life, but they will seek aid from a "scoundrel," a shadow figure from Han's past.

Realizing that it's time to act, Han instructs Chewie to *detach*. Leia is grateful for his cleverness and leans over to give Han a genuine kiss on the cheek. "You do have your moments," Leia can now honestly admit. "Not many," she then hedges. "But you do have them." Leia has developed in her own way . . . she's coming around. She can more openly acknowledge her appreciation of Han, not just as a good leader for the rebel cause but as a person whose resourcefulness she can truly admire.

The Millennium Falcon floats off amidst the Imperial garbage. When the Imperial Star Fleet has made the jump into hyperspace, the Millennium Falcon ignites its engines and heads for Bespin. But then another small ship, also floating in the garbage, does the same and follows them. In the cockpit is the bounty hunter Boba Fett. This man, who also lives in the world of the galaxy shadow, knows the tricks of men like Han who have learned to hide in unexpected places. Vader knew, contrary to Piett, that the Empire did need this kind of "scum." As we heard in *A New Hope,* "It's not over yet!"

CHAPTER 8

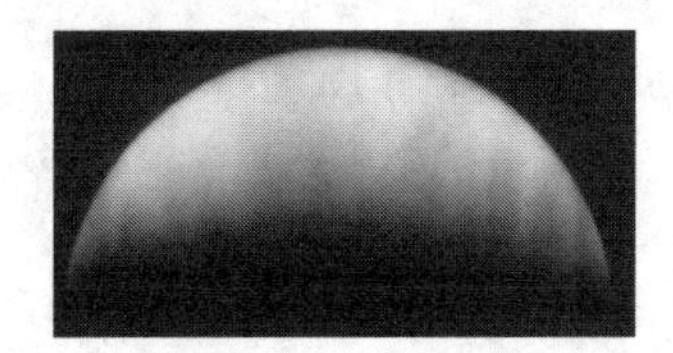

Dagobah and Bespin

New Challenges for the Jedi Apprentice

Luke is once more standing on his head in the presence of Yoda and Artoo. Equipment boxes rise off the ground, as does a beeping Artoo. "Concentrate . . . feel the Force flow. Yes. Good. Calm, yes." Yoda guides Luke through the exercise, and Luke seems more comfortable than during the previous scene. "Through the Force," Yoda tells Luke, "things you will see: Other places, the future, the past, . . .old friends long gone."

Luke suddenly becomes distressed. He calls out, "Han! Leia!" The two packing boxes and Artoo fall to the ground and Luke tumbles over.

"Control, control. You must learn control," an exasperated Yoda tells Luke.

"I saw . . . I saw a city in the clouds," Luke responds.

"Hmm. Friends you have there," Yoda tells him.

"They were in pain!" Luke exclaims.

Yoda informs him, "It is the future you see."

"Will they die?" Luke asks.

Pausing, Yoda responds, "Difficult to see. Always in motion is the future."

Luke feels his response quickly, "I've got to go to them," he exclaims.

"Decide you must," the Jedi master exhorts, "how to serve them best. If you leave now, help them you could. But you would destroy all for which they have fought and suffered." Luke's face registers the conflict he feels, as he nods sadly. Only he can decide, and the choice is most difficult. The Jedi master's assessment of the consequences seems very clear.

During the previous lesson with Yoda, Luke had become disturbed by an extraverted event: his X-wing fighter sinking deeper into the Dagobah bog. This time it is an introverted event—a vision of friends in pain—that disturbs his ability to stay focused. By losing his concentration, he loses control of his reaction and everything falls around him. Psychologically, this is equivalent to being overwhelmed by a new emotional experience, when we can't control our reactions and aren't capable of holding things together in the "old" way. Luke is being shown a broader connection to life that includes a deeper awareness of the past and future; this greater consciousness of the Force increases the psychic burden he will have to carry.

In school we are exposed to *history*, which takes us far beyond the limited parameters of our personal lives and into the varied landscapes of far-flung civilizations and cultures. We are challenged to embrace a broader understanding of life that not everyone has lived, or does live, as we do. We face similar demands psychologically whenever feelings, fantasies, or ideas previously foreign to our everyday existence emerge into awareness—either through dreams or waking state moments of insight and psychological expansion. Either way, new vistas of experience appear, awaiting integration, pushing us towards further conscious development. For instance, many people dream of symbols and cultural rituals of which they know nothing. A Christian may dream of Hebrew symbolism, or vice versa. Someone living in the United States might dream of a Native American site, like a Pueblo Kiva, and not have any conscious notion of its significance.

The deeper layers of the unconscious connect us to unknown dimensions of ourselves and to the varieties of symbolic expressions found throughout the world. Yoda teaches Luke about those mysterious layers of life that are alive in the *Star Wars* galaxy. The more deeply he experiences the Force, the more Luke sees and feels this connection to past life, future potential, and the suffering of others. (Recall how Obi-Wan felt "a great disturbance in the Force . . . as if millions of voices suddenly cried out in terror," when Alderaan was destroyed by the Death Star.) However, this deeper awareness leaves him with even more complicated life choices.

Luke is now caught between two approaches to human suffering. One approach is to accept the suffering as a part of a person's fate and seek to understand it in terms of the grand scheme of life, meanwhile continuing with one's own life course. This attitude, a more introverted one, suggests leaving others to fend for themselves and not intervening or becoming involved. The opposite attitude, a primarily extraverted one, is to intervene in human suffering whenever possible, and by so doing, "make the world a better place to live." Often it isn't clear at any given time which approach is best. However, acting too quickly to relieve suffering, especially psychological pain, often sacrifices opportunities for the soul to discover important truths about its place in the grand scheme of life and the nature of life itself.[1]

The dilemma Luke faces on Dagobah parallels the challenges of the earliest religious figures who mediated transcendent reality for others—the shamans. Usually tribal healers, shamans, are called to service by an illness of their own.[2] Shamans learn to assist others first and foremost by finding healing for themselves ("Physician, heal thyself"). Through this process and subsequent training, they learn about the transcendent reality they later act as a go-between for others for similar purposes. Luke's Wampa attack represents such a calling for him. It is in his wounded state that he has the vision that leads him to his instruction with Yoda. As Jung first realized (followed by the entire field of psychoanalysis), behind such a "calling" lies an unconscious desire and need to heal oneself. When this aspect of the call goes unrecognized, the unconscious therapist or healer can unwittingly harm those people seeking her or his help.[3]

A New Testament teaching addresses this predicament of attempting to assist others before having adequate knowledge of oneself:

> Can a blind man lead a blind man? Will they not both fall into a pit? A disciple is not above his teacher, but every one when he is fully taught will be like his teacher. Why do you see the speck that is in your brother's eye, but do not notice the log that is in your own eye? Or how can you say to your brother, "Brother, let me take out the speck that is in your eye," when you yourself do not see the log that is in your own eye? You hypocrite, first take the log out of your own eye, and then you will see clearly to take out the speck that is in your brother's eye.[4]

The approach of the Jedi masters on the "good" side is to let the apprentice make the choice about what he or she should do. Luke has shown himself to be impetuous and impatient all through his training—bringing weapons to the cave, losing his concentration when the ship sank, and now losing control when seeing the vision of his friends in pain. Is he really ready to assist others in pain, or does he need to do more work on himself? This scene on Dagobah introduces the next location, the city in the clouds. Symbolically Luke's training is still very much "up in the air." Yoda's description of the future as being "in motion" further adds to this sense of uncertainty. Both Vader and the Emperor saw Luke as powerful in their earlier visions of him. Yet here on Dagobah we have not seen much to corroborate this. Luke's best quality—his loyalty to his friends—pulls him away from the training, which Yoda believes serves a more important purpose than helping his friends.

Approaching the City in the Clouds

The arrival of the Millennium Falcon at Cloud City is fraught with apprehension. As Han declares to the spaceship pilots that intercept them that he is trying to reach Lando Calrissian, the Millennium Falcon is rattled by bursts of laser fire. "Rather touchy, aren't they?" Threepio declares. "I thought you knew this person?" Leia inquires. When Chewie growls something, Han responds, "Well, that was a long time ago. I'm sure he's forgotten about that." Once they are given permission to land, he tells the others, equally trying to assure himself, "There's nothing to worry about. We go way back, Lando and me." Because they go way back, he's hopeful, but given the nature of the former relationship, it's not clear how Lando will receive Han.

When they disembark from the ship at the landing platform, the emotional atmosphere is still very unsettled. "Oh. No one to meet us," Threepio declares. "I don't like this," says Leia. Threepio then attempts a positive view, noting that at least they were allowed to land. Again Han tells them not to worry and tries to assure them that everything will be fine. The door from the city to the landing platform opens and Lando, a splendidly cloaked black man with an assortment of supporting personnel, strides forward. To Leia and Threepio's doubts, Han enjoins, "See? My friend." But to Chewie he quietly adds, "Keep your eyes open, okay?"

Han now comes face to face with his old friend. As he approaches, Lando exclaims, "Why, you slimy, double-crossing, no-good swindler! You've got a lot of guts coming here, after what you pulled." Perplexed, pointing to himself quizzically, Han's nonverbal gestures clearly ask, "Me?" Lando approaches Han threateningly, as if he might throw a punch at him, but then suddenly Lando throws his arms around him in friendly embrace. Laughingly he asks, "How you doing, you old pirate? So good to see you!" "Well, he seems very friendly," says Threepio, as Han and Lando converse. "Yes," an unconvinced Leia warily responds, "very friendly."

It is very difficult to know where things stand with all the mixed signals in the air. Does Lando harbor anger for Han from previous encounters? Is he genuinely glad to see him? Or is it some of both, expressing the angry feelings first, and then the more positive ones? This scene captures some of the issues around male bonding, especially in adolescence and often into adulthood. Feelings of affection are feared as appearing unmanly. Angry barbs and humor are often used to convey a kind of gruff affection that simultaneously projects invulnerability. Honest, caring feelings are either flatly denied or simply well disguised. Some men, and women too, carry deep wounds from adolescent same-sex relationships when they were the brunt of others' hostility because they were too sensitive, or different in some way. Surviving often means learning how to "play the game," but there is always a price: a more authentic emotional part of one has to be put aside in order to do so.

In our culture people of color (particularly African-Americans) are especially susceptible to shadow projections from Caucasians. Dream figures portraying people of color generally represent important qualities that the dreamer has lost connection with or disowned as negative. Such qualities might be related to the expression of so-called negative emotions, to aspects of one's own personality that have been oppressed, or to other qualities that it is more comfortable to attribute to dark-skinned people than to oneself. Psychologically, Han's face-to-face encounter with Lando represents the need to become more connected to his past and his own shadow side in order to go forward in life. If a man is to develop an intimate relationship with a woman as well as cultivate a connection to his inner feminine side, honest integration of the shadow becomes essential.

Lando expresses some shadow aspects of male relationship as they interact. When Han admits that he is in need of repairs for the Millennium Falcon, Lando responds with an angry edge, "What have you done to my ship?"—as if he had some claim on it. "*Your* ship?" Han counters, "Remember, you lost her to me fair and square." First, Lando gets in a little dig as to who owns what, revealing competitive feelings over ownership of property. Then greeting Chewbacca, whom he has also known from the past, he derisively asks, "You still hanging around with this loser?"—making a jabbing comment typical of shadow snipping.

When Lando becomes aware of Leia's presence, he does a complete about-face. Aggressive bantering abruptly ceases and out pours its opposite, honey-coated flattery. "Hello! What have we here? Welcome. I'm Lando Calrissian. I'm the administrator of this facility. And who might you be?" (Notice that it is "what" not "who," a woman as object, not a person he addresses.) When Leia gives him her name, he greets her and bids her welcome. He extends his hand for hers, and then kisses it. "You old smoothie," Han responds. Han promptly takes hold of Leia's hand and steers her away from Lando, heading inside. The male shadow and anima problem are revealed succinctly in this scene. Too much latent hostility is expressed (but not owned) in the male world; and too much exaggerated charm is used to attract women, while more honest feelings remain completely hidden. Neither approach is emotionally authentic. The falsity underlying Lando's exaggerated charm is unmistakably revealed when, greeted enthusiastically by Threepio, Lando turns away, utterly disregarding him. Threepio's function is human-cyborg relations, but Lando completely dismisses this reality. He is actually more "mechanical" than the droid, and Threepio, who is understandably peeved, is actually more humanly courteous than the human.

When the conversation turns more directly to business, it becomes more genuine—as is often the case with men. When Lando learns that the problem with the Falcon is in the hyperdrive, he tells Han that he will have his people get right on it and excitedly adds to Leia, "That ship saved my life quite a few times. She's the fastest hunk of junk in the galaxy." Now, rather than play around with the feelings of envy for his friend's ship, he expresses honest appreciation for it.

Once inside the corridors of the city, Han asks Lando about his gas mine. Lando indicates that it's not paying off as well as he would like; it's a small outpost and not self-sufficient. When he mentions that he's had supply problems of every kind, not to mention labor difficulties, he draws a big grin from Han. "Listen to you," Han tells him, "you sound like a business man, a responsible leader. Who'd have thought that, huh?" Han recognizes the new person his friend has become. Lando, like Han, is not the kind of man he used to be; he's changing. Lando and Han both realize that seeing each other again "sure brings back a few things."

Psychologically, moving forward in life eventually brings up unresolved aspects of our past. Why we did what we did earlier in life to get by becomes clearer, as other parts of ourselves emerge with which we still must come to terms. Acting more responsibly in our day-to-day life eventually challenges us to become more responsible *psychologically* as human beings. Deeper, more honest relationships with others and a fuller awareness of the nature of the world in which we live become important components of such development. The reunion of old friends will soon offer both Han and Lando such challenges.

As Han, Lando, and Leia head off down the city corridor, Threepio trails along. He greets a similarly shaped droid in a friendly way but gets a rude response. Hearing the beeping of an R2 unit and determined to make a friendly contact, he goes into the room in which he hears the sound. Could it be . . .? A gruff voice suddenly questions his presence. As Threepio tries to apologize, we hear a laser blast fire and dismembered parts of the droid slide near the door. When the door closes, Chewbacca appears, having returned to look for Threepio, but seeing no signs, shrugs and follows after the others.

As the old human friends begin to reconnect, the humanoid droid is disintegrated, undergoing a more devastating dismemberment than he did in the first movie. Symbolically, Threepio represents the ability to communicate both verbally and nonverbally. When Han and Lando first meet, Lando, in particular, relates in the old, double-entendre way of their former days. This earlier style of communicating must undergo renewal and transformation on order for a more authentic one to develop. Threepio's sudden disappearance, however, also has other ominous meanings, and the fate of our main characters is still very precarious.

Departure from Dagobah

Back on Dagobah Luke is dressed in his orange flight suit and preparing his ship for departure. While he does so, Yoda sternly tells him, "Luke, you must complete the training." Luke responds, "I can't keep the vision out of my head. They're my friends. I've got to help them." But Yoda insists, "You must not go!" Tension has risen between student and teacher. The student is gripped by his vision and the emotional urge to help his friends. Does he follow his own vision? After all, the last time he did so, he found Yoda. But now the Jedi Master tells him he must complete the training first. Why? Are Luke's emotions once again disturbing his connection to the Force, like when the ship sank further into the bog, or when he lost his balance after he saw the vision of the future in which his friends were in pain? Or is this a new vision he must follow, despite the apprehensions of his mentor? Now, even on Dagobah, the situation is very uncertain.

Luke fears that Han and Leia will surely die if he doesn't go. As he expresses his distress to Yoda, the voice of Ben Kenobi suggests, "You don't know that," and a shimmering manifestation of Obi-Wan appears near Yoda. "Even Yoda cannot see their fate," Ben continues.

"But I can help them!" Luke proclaims, "I feel the Force!"

"But you cannot control it," Ben responds, "This is a dangerous time for you, when you will be tempted by the dark side of the Force."

"Yes, yes. To Obi-Wan you listen," exhorts Yoda, "The cave. Remember your failure at the cave!"

"But I've learned so much since then," counters Luke. "Master Yoda, I promise to return and finish what I've begun. You have my word."

Clearly Luke is in a vulnerable place and faced with a difficult choice. Excited by the new sense of awareness he feels inside, he deeply desires to help his friends. His Jedi instructors, however, are concerned about his vulnerability, especially evident in his characteristic impatience and his past failures. Luke does not discount his need to complete the training and pledges to honor his commitmen—and still feels compelled to do things his way. Luke's situation is common in many fields of endeavor. When we reach a certain point of learning, we feel ready for action and eager to succeed. But do we know enough?

Ben tells Luke that his friends are being made to suffer because the Emperor wants *Luke*, implying that Ben knows of the suggestion Vader made to the Emperor. This information, however, only strengthens Luke's resolve to go. He cannot tolerate the fact that others are suffering on his account. His feelings move him to have to try, to find a solution beyond all logic or even principle. Luke's earnestness is matched by Ben's concern; he doesn't want to lose Luke to the Emperor, the way he lost Vader. (The new *Star Wars* trilogy, Episodes I–III, tell the story of how this happened.) The details concerning how this loss came about are unclear at this point, but what is clear is that Ben's self-doubts and fears are influencing his judgment and the way he advises Luke. He doesn't want to fail again, so he is more directive with Luke than when they met first. This aspect of the story depicts a danger in any helping profession: the needs, fears, and goals of the person giving assistance inevitably infiltrate, to some degree, the way this help is offered. Luke assures Ben that he is different from Vader and that he won't be lost in this way.

Yoda's concern is galactic, not personal, and based on his assessment of the larger political situation. "Stopped they [Vader and the Emperor] must be. On this all depends. Only a fully trained Jedi knight with the Force as his ally will conquer Vader and his Emperor. If you end your training now, if you choose the quick and easy path, as Vader did, you will become an agent of evil."

"And sacrifice Han and Leia?" Luke asks, aghast.

"If you honor what they fight for . . . yes!" responds Yoda. Luke must choose between principle and personal friendship, between a cause of high importance and human relationships of deep feeling.

Luke's struggle is also connected to a shift in the Force in his galaxy (which will be discussed further when we get to *Return of the Jedi*), and it symbolically reflects a tremendous psychological shift occurring in the modern psyche. All the practitioners of the Force live and function in an isolated way. Ben lived alone as a hermit on Tatooine, Yoda lives without the companionship of similar sentient creatures on Dagobah. Vader serves his Emperor, acts in general disdain for his troops, and retreats to his meditation pod. Those connected to the Force are one-sidedly introverted in how they live and work. They do not function in close interpersonal relationship with anyone else.

Similarly on our planet most major religious systems, Eastern or Western, have valued the spiritual search over close personal relationships. Even those religions that offer marriage and family opportunities for religious figures, often ask that the personal parts of life be sacrificed when so demanded by the concerns of the religion. Today more and more people are discovering that delving more deeply into personal relationships can offer a path for deeper connection to psychological and spiritual depths. Lost and unrecognized spiritual gold is to be mined in the interactive fields of people in intimate partnership, and it is a different gold than that mined through the introverted methods and dutiful participation within various religious organizations. Jung recognized:

> Individuation has two principal aspects: in the first place it is an internal and subjective process of integration, and in the second it is an *equally* indispensable process of objective relationship. Neither can exist without the other, although sometimes the one and sometimes the other predominates.[5] (My italics)

Symbolically Luke's conflict entails maintaining a connection between two lines of equally indispensable psychological development. One is of an introverted, spiritual nature that establishes a connection to the archetypal layer of the psyche symbolized by the Force. The other is the interpersonal side symbolized by the relationship between Han and Leia, who also represent aspects of Luke's personal psychology, his shadow and his anima. When they departed from Hoth these two lines of development evolved separately. Now Luke is moved to try and reconnect them. In Jungian terms equal attention must be given to extraversion and introversion and to personal and archetypal aspects of the personality. We can all too easily be pulled to remain overly one-sided and out of balance. Yet ultimately we are not meant to keep these aspects of life completely separated.

It is a lonely choice for Luke, since there does not appear to be any precedent for his predicament. Ben tells Luke that, "If you choose to face Vader, you will do it alone. I cannot interfere" (as he did previously, during the battle with the Death Star and through Luke's vision at Hoth). Luke clearly understands and instructs Artoo to fire up the ship's converters. "Don't give in to hate," Ben instructs. "That leads to the dark side." Luke nods as he climbs on board the ship.

"Strong is Vader," Yoda warns, "mind what you learned. Save you it can."

"I will," Luke assures him, "and I'll return. I promise." The cockpit closes, and the two Jedi masters are left alone with their concerns for Luke.

As the ship departs, Yoda is not pleased. He repeats to Ben his sense that Luke is reckless; he assumes that matters have worsened with Luke's decision to depart. Ben surmises, "That boy is our last hope," but as they look up towards the departing ship, Yoda replies, "No. There is another." More concerns and questions are added to this point in the story, some of which won't be answered until the next film, especially who or what the "other" hope is. Luke's ship leaves the atmosphere of the planet Dagobah where, through Luke's vision, we first learned about the "city in the clouds." Through the ruminations of the Jedi who remain behind, we get a hint of what dangers await Luke and his friends on Bespin.

"Something's Wrong Here"

The first image we see as the story returns to Cloud City is a large oval building supported by a thin, scant base. Symbolically, the situation is precariously perched, at best. In Leia's guest quarters Han expresses confidence that they will soon be on their way; Leia, however, is suspicious. "Something's wrong here. No one has seen or knows anything about Threepio. He's been gone too long to have gotten lost." When Han says that he'll talk to Lando, Leia responds that she doesn't trust Lando. Neither does Han, it turns out, but he's hopeful that, since Lando is his friend, they will soon be on their way. "Then *you're* as good as gone, aren't you?" she inquires. Han's silence implies that this is probably true. While in the asteroid field, he had touched unconscious feelings in her; now she touches an unconscious place in him. Intimacy often challenges a man's undeveloped emotional side, and often leaving a relationship is deemed preferable to confronting those deeper parts of himself that are utterly foreign to him. A man, like Han, might sense the hidden feelings in a woman and even evoke them, but once he has succeeded and the relationship reaches a point where he will have to reciprocate, he abruptly leaves—and the woman feels betrayed and abandoned. Han and Leia's relationship now edges towards this painful turning point.

Meanwhile Chewie has succeeded in finding the dismembered pieces of Threepio in a junk room, just as they are to be put on a conveyer belt that leads to a melting furnace. A number of short, dwarf-like creatures (Ugnaughts) are working there and play keep-away, tossing parts back and forth, taunting an angry Chewbacca trying to collect the scattered pieces of the droid. Chewbacca returns to Leia's quarters with the recovered body parts of Threepio; Leia asks him what happened and if he can fix him. Han suggests that Lando's people can do it, to which Leia curtly responds, "No, thanks."

Lando arrives, compliments Leia on how beautiful she looks, and invites them all for "a little refreshment." Han dismisses his inquiry about concerns over the disassembled droid. As they head down the corridor outside the room, Lando narrates that they are but a small operation, are not part of the mining guild, and do not fall under the jurisdiction of the Empire. He adds, in an insinuating tone, that their customers are anxious to avoid attracting attention to themselves. When Han asks Lando if he's afraid that the Empire will find out about his little operation and shut him down, Lando responds, "That's always been a danger looming like a shadow over everything we've built here. But things have developed that will insure security. I've just made a deal that will keep the Empire out of here forever." Lando is a pragmatist and a survivor, an "everyman" trying to make a go of it in the world. Most people want to succeed and to insure security for themselves and their families; Lando's character portrays a very concrete image of a universal need.

Reaching the dining room to which their host has led them, Han, Leia and Chewbacca are shocked to discover the menacing form of Darth Vader standing at the other end of a long table. Han quickly draws his laser blaster and fires, but the gloved hand of Vader deflects the blasts, and using the Force, Vader draws Han's weapon into his own hand. Boba Fett, the bounty hunter, steps forward from the background, and Vader calmly remarks, "We would be honored if you would join us." When Han looks Lando squarely in the eye, his friend responds, "I had no choice. They arrived right before you did. I'm sorry." "I'm sorry, too," replies Han.

Most of us have probably been in Lando's situation, knowingly or unknowingly betraying someone, and justifying the betrayal—or denying it as a betrayal—on the grounds of just trying to survive and get through life. We don't believe we have a choice. We have to do the best we can, but it may not be satisfactory for those with whom we are involved; they are betrayed and given over to the darker forces of life. Such betrayals may involve individuals or entire groups of people.

Vader proves to be a cunning and powerful adversary; his use of the bounty hunters has paid off and he quickly disarms Han Solo. He is a man who gets what he wants, and remains impervious to the ramifications of his actions, which brutally disrupt the lives of those he encounters and forces them into difficult—even life-and-death—choices.

The next image to appear is that of Luke's ship making its entry into Bespin's City in the Clouds—we view the same precarious structure in the air seen earlier. Now as Luke arrives at the planet, we see what Luke "envisioned" while on Dagobah: the way his friends are made to suffer. Chewie is tortured by loud screeching sounds that fill his cell. Finally, they subside and, following Leia's earlier request, he begins to reassemble Threepio by first fitting the head back on the torso. As Threepio's voice function returns, we hear what happened to him: He stumbled upon stormtroopers and tried to warn the others, but was shot.

Meanwhile, Vader is devoting himself to a hi-tech torture of Han by which the unwilling hero is zapped by various electrical charges. Outside of the room Lando hears his screams and becomes visibly upset. When Vader emerges from the cell, Lando tries to address him. Vader, all business, speaks directly to the bounty hunter, Boba Fett, telling him that he can have Solo to take to Jabba the Hutt after the arrival of Skywalker. Fett laments that Solo is no good to him dead; Vader replies that he will not be permanently damaged.

Han Solo's past has caught up to him. Psychologically the timing is significant: as the opportunity for intimacy increases with Leia, so too do the consequences of the unresolved issues from his past. Whenever we become involved in personal relationships, painful, often long-buried feelings are likely to surface, and we have to come to terms with them—often an emotionally torturous process. Han's deepening relationships, first with Luke and now with Leia, coincide with his past, symbolically speaking, catching up with him. Except for the brief sonic assault on Chewie, it is Han who is enduring the pain of Vader's plan to lure Luke.

A concerned Lando requests an update from Vader on Leia and Chewbacca. Vader snaps out a terse, "They must never again leave this city."

An angry Lando retorts "That was never a condition of our agreement, nor was giving Han to this bounty hunter!"

Vader responds, "Perhaps you think you're being treated unfairly."

"No," an obviously frustrated Lando answers.

"Good," Vader declares, "it would be unfortunate if I had to leave a garrison here."

As he moves down the corridor away from Vader and Boba Fett, an irritated Lando exclaims, "This deal's getting worse all the time."

The Lando character is now becoming the moral compass of the story. He's made an agreement to insure the security of his business, but because of it people are being hurt and conditions of the original agreement are being violated. The price Lando is paying rises steadily, ominously. The deal is becoming more and more corrupt, and to Lando's credit he is clearly unhappy about it.

The scene shifts back to the cell where Chewie is proceeding with the repair of Threepio, whose impatience and verbal chatter leave Chewie wondering why he is bothering to reactivate the annoying droid. Imperial troops deliver an exhausted, bedraggled Han Solo to the room, and Chewie gently places him on a platform to rest. Leia is then shoved into the room, and walking on her own power, moves towards Han to tend to him. "*Why* are they doing this?" she wonders. "They never even asked me any questions," Han replies weakly.

The cell door opens once more and Lando and two guards enter. "Get out of here, Lando!" Han barks. "Shut up and listen," Lando replies, proceeding to update them on Vader's plans to turn Leia and Chewie over to him and Han over to the bounty hunter. Leia doesn't buy it, protesting, "Vader wants us all dead."

"He doesn't want you at all," Lando informs her. "He's after somebody called Skywalker. Lord Vader has set a trap for him."

"And we're the bait," Leia responds.

"Well, he's on his way," Lando confirms.

Han's Wookie-like anger erupts, "You fixed us all pretty good, didn't you? My friend!" He then hauls off and punches Lando. The guards strike Han in return, and he slumps to the floor. "Stop!" Lando orders, wanting to put an end to it, "I've done all I can. I'm sorry I couldn't do better, but I have my own problems." "Yeah," Han answers, "you're a real hero." Lando and his men depart.

The drama on Bespin lays forth the details of the troubles Luke and his Jedi masters could only glimpse on Dagobah. It is Luke who Vader and the Emperor want, and the others were made to suffer only to get him to come. Vader is playing on Luke's compassion and concern for others, his desire to help and preserve all life forms. Part of the immorality of those driven by power is using the humanity of others only for personal gain. Thus Vader seeks to use Luke, just as he has used Lando.

Lando, who has proven a disappointment to Han, represents to the cocky pilot the necessity of coming to terms with his own shadow qualities and his humanity. Han came to Lando in need of help but uncertain as to whether he could trust him. Yet he is indignant that Lando let the Empire move in—as if, as Lando told him earlier, he really had another choice. Lando has become more than an every man; he has done all that he can to help and would have liked to do more, but like all of us, he has his own problems, and there are limits to what he can do. The everyday demands of life limit what we can do for others, even when we care to do more. The painful reality of life sets in for Han. Like many people who begin giving more to others, he unconsciously hopes for help himself—and when it is not forthcoming, he explodes. Han has spent so much of his life *on the go,* running to and from things. Now life is catching up to him, so to speak, and bringing him more down-to-earth. The heroic mode does not eliminate life's darker complexities. Han can run longer.

Inside the Carbon-Freezing Chamber

The drama shifts to a dark carbon-freezing chamber where Vader, meeting with Lando Calrissian in his capacity as the city administrator, makes plans to freeze Luke in preparation for the trip to the Emperor. Lando tells Vader that the carbon-freezing equipment might kill him. Vader, not wanting to risk harming Skywalker unnecessarily, announces that they will test the equipment on Captain Solo. Meanwhile we glimpse Luke's ship approaching the precariously perched building that looms amidst the clouds in the city's atmosphere.

Guards bring in Han, Leia, and Chewie—who carries the pieces of a partially assembled but fully communicative Threepio on his back. Lando informs Han that he's being put into carbon freeze, and the bounty hunter complains to Vader that Solo is not worth anything to him dead. Vader assures him that the Empire will compensate him if Solo dies. The procedure in this dark chamber is risky and poses a threat to the lives of both Han and Luke. When they begin moving Han into position, Chewie erupts and begins tossing stormtroopers aside in his fury. Han is eventually able to calm Chewie, urging him to save his strength, and suggesting to him that there will be another time to fight. Han tells Chewie that he (Chewie) has to take care of the princess. He expresses concern for Leia, but phrases it only in terms of her important role. His personal feelings are still somewhat frozen, yet to be fully thawed. This man of action, however, does bend over to kiss Leia and she passionately reciprocates. But when they are pulled apart and Han is placed on the carbon-freeze platform, he can only reply to her declaration, "I love you," by saying, "I know." Their facial expressions say far more.

Han is lowered down into the carbon-freezing chamber—an intense moment with looks of grave concern on all present. The atmosphere lightens only a bit when Threepio is finally able to get a glimpse of the proceedings and announces that Han "should be quite well-protected—if he survives the freezing process." Up until this point the symbolism in *The Empire Strikes Back* has carried the theme of thawing; once again, it now turns cold and dark. The slab of frozen carbonite is raised and eventually dropped by the

Ugnaught workers with a booming thud on the chamber floor. As Lando checks the controls on the side, Vader asks the question that is in everyone's mind. "Well, Calrissian, did he survive?" "Yes," Lando reports, greatly relieved, "he's alive. And in perfect hibernation."

Vader immediately resumes Imperial business. "He's all yours, bounty hunter. Reset the chamber for Skywalker." An Imperial officer reports to Vader that Skywalker has just landed, and Vader orders that they be sure to see that he finds his way into the carbon-freezing chamber. As Lando begins to lead Leia and Chewie out of the room, Vader orders him to take them to his ship. A shocked Lando replies, "You said they'd be left in the city under my supervision." "I am altering the deal," Vader boldly announces, "Pray I don't alter it any further." Lando is dismayed and, as if knowing how Vader acts on his displeasure with people, instinctively covers his throat with his hand.

The Action in the City Corridors

Having landed his ship, Luke moves inside the city with Artoo and watches a group of guards and the bounty hunter marching down a corridor escorting the floating slab in which Han Solo lies frozen. In the past Luke has gotten help from both Ben and Han. Ben has told him that he can't help him this time, and Han is clearly out of commission. Is Luke psychologically ready to take care of himself *and* help his friends? As Luke tries to follow this party, he is greeted by a laser blast from Boba Fett as the small company disappears behind automatic doors.

Meanwhile, using his wrist communicator, Lando inconspicuously signals a message received by his assistant, Lobot, who wears a pair of headphones. Luke then comes across the Imperial squad guarding Leia and Chewie and accompanied by Lando. They, too, quickly disappear, but not before Leia turns to shout a warning to Luke that it's a trap as she's pulled through a closing blast door. Luke then passes through another doorway that shuts quickly behind him before Artoo can follow him through. Once again, he is separated from everyone and on his own.

Other doors mysteriously open and close, and Luke eventually finds himself on a hydraulic lift that stops to deliver him to the floor housing the carbon-freeze chamber. Feeling his way into the room, he holsters his blaster and turns to discover the figure of Darth Vader on the platform above him. Vader ignominiously declares, "The Force is with you, young Skywalker. But you are not a Jedi yet." Luke ascends and confidently stands to face the dark figure; he then ignites his lightsaber. Vader follows suit, and after a moment's pause Luke begins the duel and Vader counters his first blow.

An important concern hangs in the air at the carbon-freezing chamber as the scene shifts back to Leia, Lando, and Chewie: before Luke departed from Dagobah, Yoda had reminded him about his failure in the cave. Luke had unnecessarily taken his weapons with him and initiated a battle with the Vader-like figure he encountered there. He has now done the same thing on Bespin with the actual personage. Is Luke making a mistake? Has he already forgotten what he has learned? Has he gotten too engrossed with defeating Vader and forgotten why he is there?

As the Imperial troops escort Leia and Chewie to Vader's ship, Lando's men suddenly appear with blasters drawn to surprise and disarm the guards without having to fire a shot. Lando orders that the stormtroopers be held in the security tower and that his men keep it quiet. He begins to undo the binders that had been placed on Chewie to restrain him. When Leia asks him what he thinks he's doing, he informs her, "we're getting out of here." Threepio is delighted and claims to have known it all along. Finally, there is a rescuer! However, the now unshackled Chewie is furious and begins to choke Lando, as Leia asks, "Do you think that after what you did to Han, we're going to trust you?" As Lando tries to free himself from the Wookie's grasp, he attempts to reiterate to her what he had earlier told Han: "I had no choice." Threepio pleads with Chewie to "trust him, trust him," but Leia is not so sympathetic. She is also furious, especially given the fact that she is now fully awakened to her feelings for Han. When Lando pleads that he was only trying to help, she tells him that they don't need any of his help. Her attitude has an angry "solo" quality expressing characteristics of both Han and Chewie in her usual sharp-tongued way.

Lando tries hard to speak through the Wookie's choking grasp, and Threepio realizes he's trying to say something about Han. Finally, Lando is able to gasp that there's still a chance to save Han at the East Platform. Only then do Leia and Chewie let go of their outrage at Lando and head off in the direction of the landing platform that holds the bounty hunter's ship. As he's carried off on the Wookie's back, Threepio tries to apologize to Lando, remarking, "I'm terribly sorry about all this. After all, he's only a Wookie."

Lando now assumes the burden of a crucial role similar to the one Han Solo took on in the first movie. In order for Leia and Chewie to succeed, they will have to gain assistance from someone. In *Star Wars: A New Hope* Han Solo returned at a critical moment to help Luke—an act that required a complete "change of heart," for in doing so, Han was no longer the smuggler who looked out only for himself. Now in *The Empire Strikes Back* Lando undergoes a similar dramatic transformation when he rejects the business arrangement that has been imposed on him, recognizing the treachery behind it. At last Lando "comes to himself" in order to "do the right thing" and assist those who are being wronged.

Without strong moral responses to destructive behaviors, the underlying malevolence is perpetuated. Lando's desire to save Han eventually dissipates Chewie's and Leia's distrust of his motives. Ultimately to move forward in life, we all have to be able to trust others. Knowing who to trust can involve a difficult and complex process of discernment. Lando steps forward to try to save Han, offering hope that they all might escape from the clutches of Darth Vader—and Leia and Chewie, forced to make a life-altering decision in a split second, give assent.

The trio of characters heads for the landing platform; Artoo joins them and Threepio gives him an update from his perch aboard Chewbacca. Unfortunately, they arrive just as Boba Fett's ship is departing and their laser blasts prove unable to stop it. As they retreat back into the city, they are fired on by stormtroopers. As had happened so often to Luke in *A New Hope,* they are now running for their own escape and survival amid deadly foes and acute feelings of loss.

The Duel in the Carbon-Freezing Chamber

Luke is pressing for the advantage in his duel with Vader. The dark Jedi seems impressed and remarks, "You have learned much, young one." The interior psychology of characters in the story is often revealed in the dialogue of the Jedi, not from subtleties of acting. The insight of the Jedi represents the function of *intuition*—the ability to know things that cannot be known on conscious, sensate levels. Having sized up this "young one," Vader now takes the initiative. Luke's lightsaber is twisted out of his grasp; another move from the dark figure drives him further backwards and he tumbles down to the platform above the carbon-freezing equipment. Sprawled on the floor, Luke quickly rolls to the side to avoid being crushed by the leaping figure of Vader. "Your destiny lies with me, Skywalker," Vader tells him, "Obi-Wan knew this to be true."

"No!" Luke firmly tells him.

Vader continues his attack and, in attempting to retreat, Luke falls into the open carbon-freezing shaft. Using the Force, Vader activates a switch off to the side to initiate the carbon-freezing process. "All too easy," he says to himself, "Perhaps you are not as strong as the Emperor thought." Behind him, though, a blurred figure rises out of the carbon-freezing cylinder and lodges in the hoses and other apparatus that hang above it. Luke has summoned the Force on his own behalf, and when Vader realizes what he's done, he murmurs, "Impressive . . . most impressive."

Luke uses the steam from a nearby hose to distract Vader, then swings down to the platform and uses the Force to retrieve his lightsaber in time to parry the next blow coming from Vader's weapon. "Obi-Wan has taught you well," Vader tells him. "You have controlled your fear . . . now release your anger."

Luke escaped the carbon-freeze cylinder trap because he did not become paralyzed by fear. Symbolically speaking, the "Han Solo within" has come alive; now he can access the Force as he has been taught to do by Ben and Yoda.

The dark Jedi now goads Luke into an impossible double bind when he hisses, "Only your hatred can destroy me." But Luke has been taught that to give into his anger is to risk becoming that which he hates, as the lesson in the cave pointed out. Now Vader tells him that this is the *only* way to destroy him. Either way, Luke loses—or so Vader makes it appear. How should he deal with the dark figure before him? Vader destroyed whoever failed or disappointed him during his pursuit of Luke and his friends. What will Luke do with his angry feelings? No longer afraid, Luke is able to parry Vader's lightsaber and knock him off the platform. Seeing or hearing no sign of him, he deactivates his own sword, hooks it on his belt, and goes in search of his formidable adversary.

The Confrontation in the Corridor

A metal tunnel opens before Luke and illuminates his way to the next phase of his confrontation with Vader. Traversing a corridor that passes by a large, circular window, Luke is alerted to the presence of Vader and imminent attack by the sound of heavy breathing. The assault takes on a new form as Vader nods his head and points his weapon, indicating he's using the Force in a new way. Various objects detach from walls and fly at Luke. At first, he's able to dodge and deflect them, but he is soon overwhelmed. The large window is shattered and the resulting vacuum sucks Luke out the opening as the wind roars all around. Vader grabs equipment attached to the corridor wall to hang on to so that he is able to stay put. Luke ends up suspended on a walkway that hangs over an enormous abyss. He hooks his lightsaber on his belt and begins to pull himself up onto this catwalk.

It is obviously a turbulent time for Luke as a clearer sense of the power he's confronting becomes evident to him. Symbolically the scene depicts the feeling that "the whole world is against me." One participant in a lecture after the release of the *Star Wars* Special Edition perceived this scene as indicating that Luke was bringing the assault of the objects on himself; Luke caused everything to come at him. This man's reaction underscores the importance of each of us experiencing the story in our own way. It's like the cave on Dagobah: We find only what we bring in. While I interpret this scene differently, this man's experience conveys an equally valid and important psychological insight. When life seems overwhelming, many people blame themselves and believe that they are causing their own misfortune. Such debilitating complexes make difficult situations even worse. These complexes usually stem from attempts during early childhood to cope with unmanageable and disturbing experiences. Failure to do so generates self-recriminating explanations when the child eventually acquires the cognitive ability to formulate reasons. In later life these recriminations typically remain internalized, so that the person repeatedly blames him or herself for each and every misfortune.

On another level this scene depicts Luke coming to terms with his own naiveté. The realization that some people have the capacity to behave in powerfully destructive ways can feel overwhelming and utterly disillusioning. Vader is no longer toying with this "young one"; he is avidly demonstrating his power so as to leave no doubt as to who is the stronger of the two.

Meanwhile Leia, Chewie, and Lando are seeking to make their escape with the two droids. Pursued by stormtroopers, Lando is dismayed to find that the security code on a door panel has been changed. Threepio suggests that Artoo can tell the computer to override the security system. When Artoo tries to engage the computer terminal, however, he gets zapped by electricity—apparently, he has inadvertently engaged a power socket. Threepio protests that he didn't know better because he's only an interpreter. Meanwhile, before the party moves on, Lando announces over the public intercom that the Empire has taken over the city and he advises everyone to leave.

Amidst all the turmoil of mass exit our trio-cum-droids arrive at another gate and Artoo plugs into another terminal. When he beeps about the hyperdrive on the Millennium Falcon, Threepio dismisses such talk; understanding the hyperdrive to be fixed, he anxiously tells Artoo to concentrate on opening the door to the landing platform where the ship is docked. When Artoo succeeds, they manage to hold off the Imperial stormtroopers, board the ship, and make their escape. Luke remains behind all alone.

The Battle Over the Great Abyss

Luke succeeds in climbing back onto the catwalk and returns to the adjoining control room. Immediately he hears Vader's labored breathing and the hiss of the dark Jedi's lightsaber. As Vader presses the attack, Luke activates his own weapon and tries to defend himself. Vader battles more aggressively this time and Luke, driven back out onto the narrow walkway, is knocked flat on his back. "You are beaten," Vader tells him, "It is useless to resist. Don't let yourself be destroyed, as Obi-Wan did."

Vader fights in order to demonstrate his power, and he relishes his capacity to vanquish an opponent. Clearly he has no sense of the carefully chosen sacrifice Obi-Wan made at the end of their battle on the Death Star. He is also offended by anyone who attempts to differ from him or stand up to him. Luke is still determined; perhaps, because he knows Obi-Wan has not been defeated, he still has hope. He rolls to the side, gets back on his feet, and continues the duel. In the process of defying Vader's assessment of his certain defeat, he nicks Vader on the shoulder with his lightsaber. Angered, Vader slashes violently, driving Luke back near the end of the catwalk, and with cruel vengeance severs Luke's right hand, the hand that holds his lightsaber. Cradling his dismembered forearm Luke collapses on the platform. To get as far from Vader as possible, he inches out to the extreme end of the walkway where he holds himself in place with his remaining good hand, hanging precariously over the great abyss with no place to go.

Once more dismemberment occurs in the story, this time symbolically depicting Luke's current predicament. (The theme of hand loss and dismemberment is found in fairy tales and other stories.[6]) Luke has been clearly overwhelmed and unable to fully "grasp" the situation in which he has found himself. Vader is right—he's *not* a Jedi yet; he can't handle himself fully. Because he cannot, he is *disarmed*, literally unable to hold onto the weapon that could assist him the most. Luke is alone and frightened, menaced by the powerful figure before him.

Now, having seemingly attained complete control of the situation, Vader gloats over his victory, intoning, "There is no escape."

Then he puts the responsibility for his possible destructive actions onto Luke, warning him, "Don't make me destroy you," as if Luke were forcing him into the actions he has taken—and might still take. Like Tarkin destroying Alderaan, Vader does not accept moral accountability for his destructive acts, even when someone like Captain Needa is willing to accept responsibility for a situation beyond his control.

An interesting shift in the dialogue begins to occur when Vader tells Luke, "You do not yet realize your importance. You have only begun to discover your power. Join me and I will complete your training. With our combined strength, we can end this destructive conflict and bring order to the galaxy."

"I'll never join you!" Luke quickly retorts.

Symbolically, we begin to see the "shadow side" of the dark power-driven figure. Isolated from his own humanity and that of others, he does not wish to remain alone; he desires, even *needs*, someone to "join" with him. The offering of knowledge along with power is part of the seduction; fulfill your unknown potential, end all destructive conflict, and bring order everywhere. However, Vader is interested in Luke's potential only to the extent that it can be used towards Vader's own ends—the classic position of the consummate tyrant. People who feel isolated and alienated are often lured into cults or gangs in this same way. By joining, they believe they no longer have to feel so alone and vulnerable; they now "belong" and are given secret knowledge and a sense of power that, they are told, will serve some greater purpose. In exchange for this "boon," members give up all personal freedom and become bound together by the destructive illusion that all others who are not a part of their group pose a threat.

Since the time of the Roman Empire, Western civilization has been pulled, mythologically speaking, by two polarities of the *anthropos* myth. Caesar, the man of power, ruled as a god, not as a man; as such, he attempted to bring his view of order to the known world. Such an attitude, however, left the general populace open to a compensatory myth—that of the god-man (eventually Christ won out over other such figures of that time), who was both divine and human. The god-man myth represents the process of *human* transformation through *divine* means and, according to Jung, *divine* transformation through the ongoing psychological process of conscious human integration of the archetypal level of the unconscious. Throughout the history of the Common Era the power myth of a man identified with god-likeness has battled, as it were, the myth of the god-man, one centered on the mysteries of transformation. In the Christ myth (and others) the god-man is tempted by the power myth but successfully resists its lure of dominion. Recall the story of Satan offering Christ sovereignty to rule the world if he would forego his life's mission of teaching and healing.[7] In this myth Christ refused Satan's temptations. Many people throughout history, however, have misinterpreted the divine spark that is a part of each person's humanity and become gripped by the seductive power myth. Hitler is one contemporary example of the horror that can result from succumbing to this ultimate temptation of the misuse of power.

Luke is now tempted in a similar way. "If you only knew the power of the dark side," Vader offers, "Obi-Wan never told you what happened to your father." Now the subject is getting personal.

"He told me enough," Luke insists, "He told me you killed him."

"No," retorts Vader, "*I* am your father."

Luke is absolutely stunned, "No! No! That's not true! That's impossible!"

"Search your feelings," Vader suggests, "you know it to be true." He continues to entice the horrified, and dumbfounded youth. "Luke. You can destroy the Emperor. He has foreseen this. It is your destiny. Join me, and together we can rule the galaxy as father and son. Come with me. It is the only way." Vader seeks this alliance with Luke only because of Luke's potential to use the Force in destructive ways, as Vader does.

We recall how exposed and upset Luke became when he realized that the strange Dagobah creature knew about him and his father. Now the most feared figure he can imagine claims an even more intimate relationship with Luke; he claims he *is* his father. In the Dagobah cave Luke encountered the cloaked Vader figure, only to find his own face in the helmet of the severed head. Now this experience takes on further meaning: Luke not only faces the archetypal challenge of not succumbing to the dark side of the Force, but he faces the more personal one of not ending up like his own father.

Psychologically, this is a universal theme. Who doesn't dread "turning out" just like one or both parents? Many children imagine themselves to be everything that the "bad" parent isn't, and later, painfully discover that qualities they disliked in that parent reside in them and have to be wrestled with in order to be integrated in a new and different way.

Cartoonist Mike Peters cleverly captured this aspect of parent-child psychology in a cartoon drawn shortly after the release of the Special Edition movies (see Figure 4.) The Bible expresses this theme in its injunction that the sins of the parents are visited on the children for three and four generations.[8] Psychologically this implies that it takes a number of generations to rectify the loss of connection to the Self that is passed on from parent to child. Jung was the first psychoanalyst to recognize that children carry the burden of their parents' unconscious and unlived potentials.[9] Luke is thus suddenly presented with the shocking reality that he is intimately related to a man who is his worse enemy and who, by implication, has passed onto Luke the same destructive life patterns that now threaten the freedom of the galaxy. Luke's only alternative: somehow breaking a tragic family precedent and reconnecting, unequivocally, to the full reach of the Force and thus establishing an authentic relationship to the Self.

This scene in which Vader "invites" Luke to join him also captures the dark side of mentoring, spiritual direction, and psychotherapy. No one really knows what life has in store for another person, but it is easy to think we do. Taken to the extreme, the student becomes the pawn of the *mentor's* aspirations. Vader, who has been totally loyal to the Emperor, now considers a close partnership with the son he never knew, in order to defeat the Emperor—but nevertheless perpetuate a rule through fear, intimidation, and power. As the Empire fears the rebels, the Emperor fears the new Jedi. Aware of the Emperor's fear, Vader is tempted to form an alliance whereby he would become the central figure of power. However, he doesn't teach Luke, as Yoda did. Vader claims to know

Figure 4

A modern artist amplifies the psychology of a modern myth. "Dork Vader" Cartoon by Mike Peters, *Mother Goose and Grimm* (*Los Angeles Times*, 31 March 1997).

Luke's destiny; he leaves no room for discovery of who Luke really is as a person.

Terribly shaken, Luke ponders this invitation as Vader extends his hand to him. Slowly he draws away to the edge of the platform, looks out into the abyss, and lets go. Like Obi-Wan fighting Vader on the Death Star, he trusts in a greater mystery. Letting go and falling into an abyss is highly symbolic. Dreams involving the themes of *letting go* and *falling* depict the need to let go of the old ways of doing things in order for more creative and *grounded* ways of being to emerge.

In *A New Hope* fate broke the hold of Luke's father complex, forcing him to leave the life created for him by his uncle, and move on. By choosing now to reject the offer of his power-driven father rather than join him, *he* alone acts to break the hold of the old dominant complex. He can now take this greatest risk because of his experiences with Ben and Yoda, whose very way of living has given Luke a far more expanded view of reality.

To where does Luke drop? Soon after his loud "primal scream," he ends up sliding through a large metal chute at the bottom of the abyss. When he comes to a stop, the hatch below him suddenly opens; he drops through it and finds himself hanging precariously on the cross-pole of a weather vane. For the fourth time since he hung in the Wampa cave on Hoth, he is upside down! Symbolically, he descends to the ground of his own being. Throughout this descent, we encounter rebirth imagery: a passage down a "birth canal," dropped out into the air through an opening in the tunnel, and left hanging precariously in the sky. He's as vulnerable and alone as a newborn infant. He tries to climb back inside, but the hatch closes and his way back is blocked. He cries out for Ben, but there is only silence. Ben had told him he couldn't help him if he chose to try and save his friends. Then another name comes across his lips, "Leia. Hear me, Leia."

Leia, meanwhile, is piloting the Millennium Falcon; she sits in Han's old seat. Through the Force she hears Luke's call and realizes they have to go back. "I know where Luke is," she tells the others. Overcoming the objections of first Chewie and then Lando, she orders Chewie to turn the ship around. Luke's rescue, symbolically, comes through his turning his attention to the feminine principle. Staying connected to the feminine allows a man to chose alternatives to the grip of a power principle that serves itself but not life's fullest potential.

While Vader is boarding his shuttle to leave the city and return to his command ship, the Millennium Falcon arrives to pick up Luke. Lando opens the top hatch and receives Luke into the ship; he's wrapped in a blanket and Leia briefly tends to him. As the ship departs, Imperial fighters give chase and Vader arrives back aboard his Star Destroyer. Luke's difficult rebirth is completed, the feminine principle has heard his cry and responded, and a vessel that can carry him away from his precarious predicament and, hopefully, out into a renewed—and yet unknown—life has received him.

Tractor Beam or Hyperspace?

During *A New Hope* the Millennium Falcon served as a vessel of both transformation and rescue. A new foursome emerged from the Death Star on it, and the "new" Han Solo later used the Falcon to act on behalf of another, not just for himself. The Millennium Falcon helped save Leia from the Death Star and Luke from Imperial fighters. In *The Empire Strikes* the Millennium Falcon has also been a vessel of transformation: in it Leia has awakened to her feelings for Han. Now, once more, it is a vehicle of rescue: Luke is saved.

Ironically the would-be-rescuer, Luke, once more has to be helped by others. This stage of his initiation parallels that of many people who enter the helping professions ostensibly to assist and work with others. As they do so, they discover that it is they who need help and guidance (though, unfortunately, many do not wake up to this fact). Jung was the first psychoanalyst to recognize this dynamic and to suggest that every analyst must first work on him or herself. Desires to assist others are usually indicative of more than altruism; often there is a need for further self-recognition. As one sets off to aid others, as Luke did, one discovers that there is much more about oneself and about life that has to be learned. One discovers unknown vulnerable aspects of one's own personality. In order to touch these places of vulnerability, old defenses have to be dropped—as we saw with Leia and Han. However, there still may be times when we need these defenses; such is the case with those on-board the Millennium Falcon now. They must rely on the ship's hyperdrive—its ability to avoid direct pursuit—to complete their escape from the Imperial fleet.

However, when they try to use the hyperdrive it doesn't work. Lando is upset; his people had told him they had fixed it. Like Han earlier, he is defensive, saying, "I trusted them. It's not my fault." Naturally he wants his new traveling companions to have faith in him. Meanwhile, on Vader's command ship, Admiral Piett is preparing to activate a tractor beam that would capture the Millennium Falcon. Assured that the admiral's men have deactivated the hyperdrive on the Falcon, Vader orders that a boarding party be prepared with weapons set for stun.

Chewie rushes around inside the ship, trying to fix the hyperdrive. Artoo, busily finishing the reassembly of Threepio, indicates as they converse (as usual we hear Threepio's translation and commentary) that the hyperdrive has been deactivated—information he acquired from the city's central computer. Threepio snaps at Artoo, telling him he should know not to listen to strange computers but to pay attention to fixing *him*.

Through the Force, Vader and Luke, father and son, now communicate. Vader calls to Luke, and Luke responds, "Father." He experiences his deeply buried longing for a father, accepting on some level, that what Vader told him is true. Vader clearly wants his son to come with him, but not necessarily for familial reasons. Luke struggles with the fact that Ben never told him what had really happened to his father. As the Falcon tries to gain time, Luke joins the others in the cockpit to inform them that it is Vader who is pursuing them. Through the Force, Vader again tells Luke that it is his destiny to join him. Luke is filled with confusion that Ben hadn't told him the truth about this father. Part of Luke's inner turmoil comes from feeling disillusionment concerning his first mentor, someone he trusted, and the natural attraction to his own father, who in every other way he despises. Will the negative father complex (so vividly symbolized by the tractor beam), once again, pull him in, or will he be able to escape and claim his full identity and autonomy?

Admiral Piett and his crew are now ready to activate the tractor beam. On board the Falcon, Artoo darts away from Threepio, who criticizes him for not finishing with his reassembly and tells him that he can't fix the hyperdrive. According to Threepio, Artoo should let Chewbacca fix it; this is no time for "delusions of grandeur." But Artoo pulls down the right switch, and they successfully make the jump to light-speed. The mercurial droid succeeds at just the right moment—a most timely impulse for life emerges from the mineral level of existence to keep them moving forward.

On the Star Destroyer Vader stares out the view-port into empty space. Slowly he walks back past Piett and the bridge crew. Oddly, unexpectedly, there is no retribution for their failure. Are the Dark Jedi's thoughts with his son? As Vader walks off with his musings, we are left with our own.

Preparations for a New Rendezvous

In the final scene the Millennium Falcon is docked at a Rebel Star Cruiser. Chewie and Lando are in the cockpit of Han's ship, talking by comlink to Luke, who is having his hand attended to by a medical droid. Chewie and Lando are heading to find Jabba the Hutt and the bounty hunter; they will contact Luke to set up a rendezvous back on Tatooine. The first order of business remains the rescue of Han, and Lando assures the princess that they will find him.

The medical droid is in the final stages of giving Luke a bionic hand, checking to see if feeling is restored to the end of his fingers. When finished, he closes the lid to the mechanism in the wrist: Luke has a new hand. The futuristic setting of his story allows Lucas to continue to weave dismemberment symbolism into the drama. Thus we witness the regeneration of Luke's ability to grasp and get a hold of things.

As the Falcon prepares to leave, Luke joins Leia at the large window of the medical center which looks out into the bright, wide spiral of a luminous galaxy. The two droids stand together next to them forming a second pair. Quaternity symbolism once more appears, this time with two pairs of opposites: young man and young woman; tall, golden, humanoid droid and short, silver cylindrical one. The spiral in the background is a form of mandala which, juxtaposed with the quaternity, creates a symbol of the Self.[10] Such symbolism represents the psyche's way of bringing order and balance out of chaos and life's inequities.

The Millennium Falcon heads off into the great spiral and the camera pans away from our figures in the window as we watch the Rebel Cruiser dart off into hyperspace. The adventure will continue, but only after a three-year wait for those who first saw the original film in the theater. Various questions remain to be answered; for some, like my *Star Wars* fan brother, there is the intriguing question about the "other" hope that Yoda mentioned to Ben when Luke left Dagobah. Just what and whom will we encounter as this mysterious saga continues?

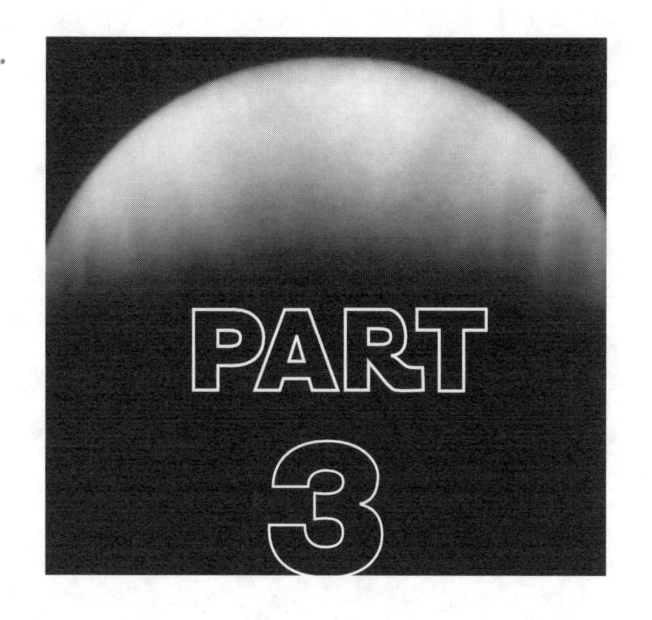

EPISODE VI

RETURN OF THE JEDI

CHAPTER 9

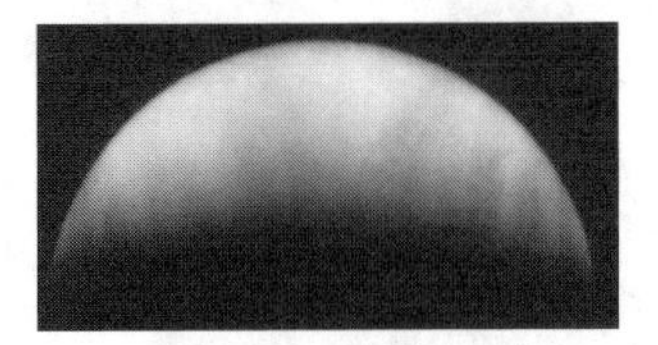

Return to Tatooine

Introduction to the Third Act

Initially this third installment of the first *Star Wars* trilogy was entitled *Revenge of the Jedi;* T-shirts were even printed with that title prior to the movie's completion. Screenwriter and former movie critic Jay Cocks reports that Lucas changed the movie title, because "revenge" is not a Jedi concept.[1] Our human view of life is typically limited, our sense of balance—of righting any wrong—is generally skewed by our own needs and desires. The Jedi knight, however, has hopefully learned to see beyond the narrow confines of a subjective human perspective to a larger source of wisdom, trusting the Force to bring life into balance, not his own will.

The time frame for the break in the story line between *A New Hope* and *The Empire Strikes Back* encompasses three years; that between *The Empire Strikes Back* and *Return of the Jedi* is one year. As we will soon see, Luke has made progress as a Jedi apprentice since we last saw him barely escaping the clutches of Darth Vader along with his companions and the droids. A question throughout the third movie is whether Luke is a Jedi knight yet, and if not, whether he will succeed in becoming one. Lucas uses his customary opening format to catch us up on the story.

A long time ago in a galaxy far,
far away. . . .

Star Wars

Episode VI
RETURN OF THE JEDI

Luke Skywalker has returned to
his home planet of Tatooine in
an attempt to rescue his
friend Han Solo from the
clutches of the vile gangster
Jabba the Hutt.

Little does Luke know that the
Galactic Empire has secretly
begun construction on a new
armored space station even
more powerful than the first
dreaded Death Star.

When completed, this ultimate
weapon will spell certain doom
for the small band of rebels
struggling to restore freedom
to the galaxy . . .

The declaration that Luke is returning to Tatooine brings up an immediate irony: when Luke sold his landspeeder in Mos Eisley so that he and Ben could make the trip to Alderaan, Luke vowed that he would never come back. Obviously, like most of us, he has unfinished psychological business back in the place of his childhood. Given all his struggles in Bespin, will he be able to help a friend? Admirably, Luke hopes to help the person who consistently has gone out of his way to help him when he most needed it. Han Solo's unfinished business has caught up to him before he could take care of it himself and now, for the first time in the story, he needs help.

The story update also brings the larger galactic struggles into focus. The Empire persists in building destructive weaponry and the rebels are in mortal danger. But before we find out how Luke will fare, we find ourselves looking over the rim of a large blue planet where we see a partially assembled battle station, in the Death Star mode, looming over the horizon. A large Star Destroyer passes overhead and a shuttle emerges from its underside, its wings unfolding as it heads to the new armored space station.

The story introduces an Imperial procedure that will have dramatic significance later in the film. The shuttle pilot requests deactivation of the energy shield protecting the space station. The Death Star controller requires clearance of a code transmission before the shield can be deactivated. When the code clears they are given permission to land, and an officer orders that the commander be informed that Lord Vader's shuttle has arrived.

The tense expression on the face of the young commander and the elaborate staging of Vader's arrival mark this event as an ominous occasion. Vader is there to put them "back on schedule." The commander contends that his men are working as fast as possible; Vader retorts, "Perhaps I can find new ways to motivate them." The commander insists that the station will be operational as planned, but Vader informs him that the Emperor does not share his optimistic appraisal of the situation. When the young officer protests that the Emperor asks the impossible and that he needs more men, Vader suggests that he tell the Emperor directly when he arrives. The commander is dumbfounded. After confirming with Vader that he has heard correctly about the Emperor's imminent arrival and displeasure with their progress, he pledges that they will redouble their efforts. Vader indicates that he hopes they do, since "the Emperor is not as forgiving" as he is.

Previously we have experienced the Emperor only through one holographic communication. At that time the ruthless Vader was most deferential to his superior. Only later, when Vader proposed to Luke that they join forces as father and son, destroy the Emperor and rule the galaxy together, did we see any sign of disloyalty.

Obviously no signs of such second thoughts are evident here. This scene leads us to anticipate a figure more powerful, unscrupulous, and inhuman than is Vader or any other Imperial figure we have yet to encounter. Left to ponder the meaning of the Emperor's arrival, we now make the return visit to Tatooine heralded in the opening story line.

Old Symbolism for a New Age

Before doing so, however, I would like to take a moment to explore Luke's newest challenges in order to understand further what it means in psychological terms to be a Jedi knight. To complete his initiate's journey, Luke will have to grapple with embodiments of the deepest, most unconscious shadow elements of the primordial psyche to which all humans may be made vulnerable. Such manifestations may occur in the most personal arenas of life, such as family relationships, and lead to various forms of traumatic abuse, or in larger cultural or sub-cultural arenas whenever a major shift takes place in the predominant ethos of a group, society, or civilization. With such a shift, the morals, values, and social and religious practices that had contained these most primitive impulses are no longer sufficient, and many individuals find themselves directly confronting these overwhelming aspects of human existence.

In his first major work illuminating the crucial psychological relevance of mythology in understanding the human psyche, Jung wrote:

> At a time when a large part of mankind is beginning to discard Christianity, it may be worth our while to try to understand why it was accepted in the first place. It was accepted as a means of escape from the brutality and unconsciousness of the ancient world. As soon as we discard it, the old brutality returns in force, as has been made overwhelmingly clear by contemporary events. [Jung is referring to events in the first half of our century.] This is not a step forwards, but a long step backwards into the past.[2]

Jung indicates that, in addition to offering us a means of connecting to a transcendent reality, religion also offers the illusion of refuge from brutality. While historically religion has *not* been able to provide an "escape from the brutality and unconsciousness," it nevertheless represents a critical *attempt* to do so. Abandoning such religious practices without replacing them with suitable alternatives produces a vacuum quickly filled by self-destructive forces. World events subsequent to these words of Jung testify to their validity: All continents with significant human populations suffer from outbreaks of large-scale brutality. Jung summarizes this point in blunt terms:

> Anyone who throws Christianity overboard and with it the whole basis of morality, is bound to be entangled with the age-old problem of brutality . . . The beast breaks lose, and a frenzy of demoralization sweeps over the civilized world.[3]

Jung's descriptions of this collective psychological problem are vividly captured by the nineteenth-century artist William Blake in his paintings of images from the Book of Job (see Figure 5.)[4] Blake depicts the father-god in the heavens showing the human Job the dilemma of earthly beastliness, the shadow side of his creation. Jung interprets the Christian myth as an unconscious attempt to resolve this very problem in those societies that adopted it. The myth of god-becoming-man offers people the hope of transcending the beastliness of their lives. The myth's appeal still reaches across nationalities and offers meaning to people from a variety of cultural backgrounds. But this myth, according to Jung, as alive as it still is in many parts of the world, no longer speaks psychologically to many modern souls in the condition in which they find themselves. Jung suggests, however, that we should not simply abandon Christianity (or any religious system) before its purpose is *consciously understood*. Once consciousness is brought into the picture, the psychological and existential aspects carried by the myth can be assimilated and integrated by individuals—which, in turn, opens the psyche to generate a new mythology that more richly expresses both this assimilation and what is "up next" for human consciousness. The newspaper cartoon discussed in Chapter 4 captures the fact that the *Star Wars* story speaks to the modern soul's search for new, more relevant mythology that reflects the psychological problems we encounter in our time. Jung reminds us, "We like to imagine that our primitive traits have long since disappeared without a trace. In this case we are cruelly disappointed, for never before has our civilization been so swamped with evil."[5]

On Tatooine Luke will soon encounter two very primitive and powerful beastly figures, much like those in Blake's painting. Later he will have to come face to face with the Emperor, a personification of an evil more sinister than any that has yet appeared. To face these various powerful figures and come to terms with them is necessary to restore human freedom and dignity—a dignity afforded, in the *Star Wars* Universe, to a great variety of other creatures as well.

Entering Jabba's Palace

The two droids, Threepio and Artoo, travel the brown, dusty road on Tatooine that leads to Jabba's isolated palace-fortress. As usual, Threepio is worried and supports his concerns with the news that Lando and Chewie never returned from this place, and he's heard some awful things about this Jabba. Artoo, as always, is determined and presses forward.

At the huge metal gate Threepio knocks quite tentatively; he quickly comments that no one seems to be there and recommends that they leave. However, a long, thin mechanical arm soon appears out of a small hatch with an electronic eyeball on the end. This mechanism inspects the two droids and questions them. Threepio explains that they are there with a message for Jabba the Hutt. When the eye abruptly disappears, Threepio concludes that they aren't going to be granted admittance and again urges that they leave. Suddenly, there is a loud clamor and the huge metal gate rises, revealing a wide, dark interior. The adventurous Artoo immediately starts moving in. Rather than be left alone, the anxious Threepio hastens to follow. Various creatures lurk in the shadows and, soon after they have entered, the massive door shuts behind them with a loud slamming screech.

Though we are entering a strange, unknown, and intimidating place, we are also in familiar territory. We first journeyed to

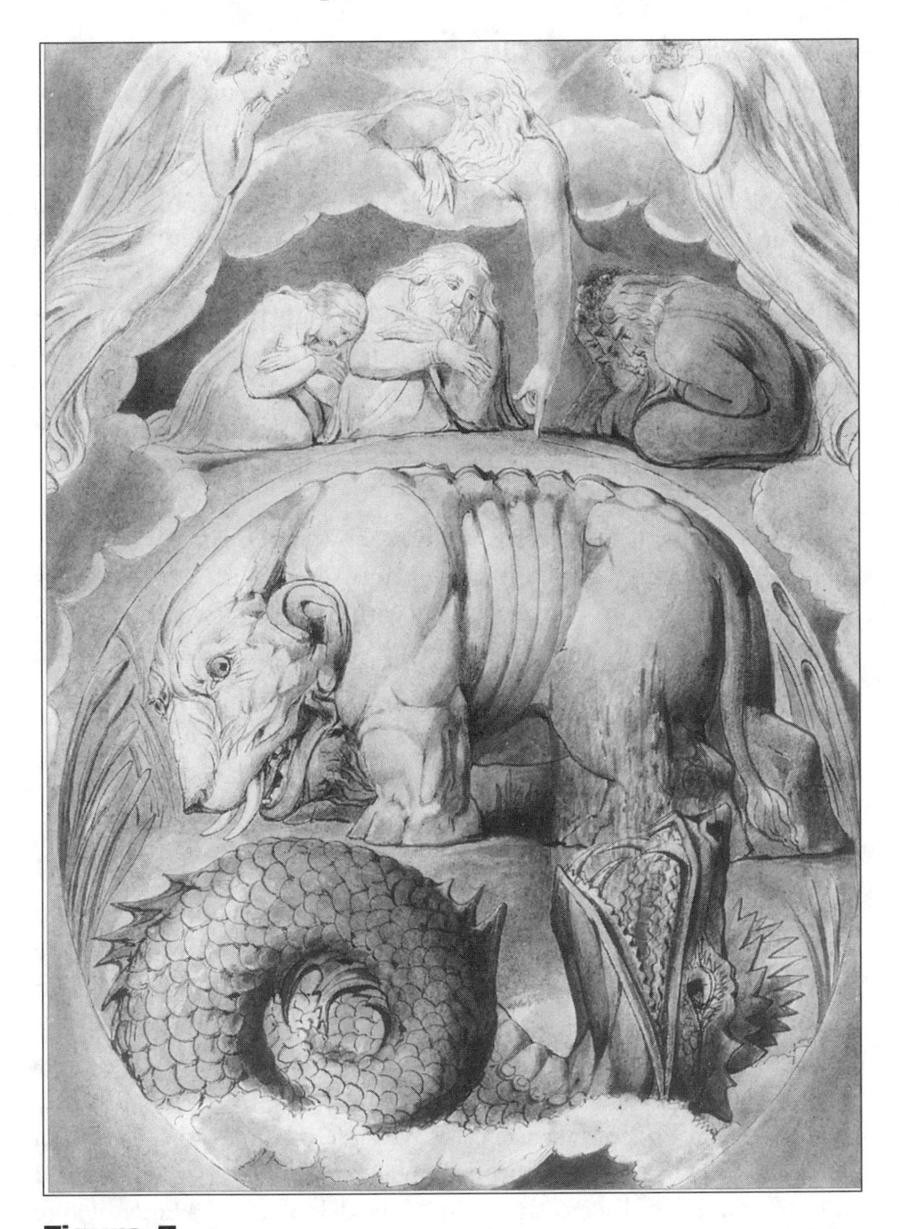

Figure 5

Yahweh reveals to Job his monstrous aspects.
Behemoth and Leviathan depicted by William Blake.

Tatooine with the two droids; now, through them, we discover the foreboding world of Jabba the Hutt. Artoo and Threepio are soon stopped by two large Gamorrean guards, a rather hideous-looking pair of brutes. Walking towards them is Bib Fortuna, a human-like alien with two tentacles that protrude from the back of his head and wrap around his neck. Threepio translates for Artoo that they bring a message for the alien's master, Jabba the Hutt, and, to Threepio's sudden surprise, a gift. When the alien demands that the message be given to him, Artoo protests, much to Threepio's unease, that his instructions are to deliver the message only to Jabba himself. Their angered greeter motions for them to follow, and Threepio utters the emotional signature line of the story, "I have a bad feeling about this."

Symbolically, it is even clearer now how much the droids carry the childlike feeling quality of these adventures. With Artoo, we are excited and eager for the challenge; with Threepio, we are anxious and nervous and worried about what will happen. As a pair they bring together both sets of feelings that usually emerge when we face new challenges in life. Threepio makes it acceptable—even endearing—to feel nervous, scared, and worried.

Jabba's Throne Room

The figure on the throne-podium overlooking the audience room is a giant slug with a tremendous face, huge eyes, and a large wide mouth. He is disgusting and despicable, as are many of the great variety of characters that surround him. While some are human, the majority are aliens and a few are of a human-alien mix. In the original movie versions he first appears in this scene of the final movie. In the Special Edition version of *A New Hope* Han Solo speaks with Jabba outside the Millennium Falcon as he waits for Ben, Luke, and the droids. They discuss the money owed Jabba and Han's pledge to pay. When Jabba agrees to give him more time, Solo remarks, "Jabba, you're a real human being." The vulgar-looking slug, having proven to be reasonable, receives an ironic compliment that contrasts the qualities connoted by his appearance with those demonstrated via his behavior.

Fortuna, Jabba's alien lieutenant, quietly announces the droid's arrival, and a nervous Threepio urges Artoo to quickly produce the message. A hologram of Luke in Jedi garb appears greeting Jabba and announcing himself as a Jedi Knight and friend of Captain Solo. First he acknowledges Jabba's powerful position, as well as his anger at Solo, and then he requests an audience with "Your Greatness" to bargain for Solo's life. Luke hopes they can work out a mutually beneficial arrangement and avoid any unpleasant confrontation. As a token of his goodwill, he offers the two droids as a gift! This comes as a complete shock to the incredulous Threepio, who bangs his hand on the top of Artoo, sure that his counterpart must be playing the wrong message.

Luke is not as naive as he was in the Mos Eisley cantina. He tries to engage Jabba's grandiosity and self-absorption and does not underestimate the power of this bizarre and strange character. His proposal sounds reasonable as he speaks, but the laughs from those present during the playing of the message hint that Jabba will scoff at Luke's offer. When the hologram disappears, Jabba laughs and immediately declares that there will be no bargain, as he likes his favorite decoration right where it is. The camera pans to the wall of an adjacent alcove where the figure of Han Solo hangs upright, still frozen in carbonite, as laughter from the crowd echoes in the background.

Those who are unconsciously ruled by the inner beast scoff at attempts for human connection and relationship. They insist on devouring life on their own terms, which generally means disregarding the reality and desires of others. The figure that most poignantly expresses this dynamic is that of the female dancer, half human and half alien, chained to Jabba's throne. The feminine principle is not allowed to live freely; it is enslaved to the lusts of others and treated with disrespect. Men gripped by this beastliness—the Behemoth and Leviathan figures Blake recreated (Figure 5)—have a general disregard for others, but especially for women, and an overall irreverence toward all life forms.

One figure close to Jabba is a little, noisy bug-like creature who seems to get the most pleasure out of others misfortune. Salacious Crumb's obnoxious, screeching laugh often permeates the proceedings in the throne room, carrying the sense of sadistic pleasure gained here at the expense of those less fortunate.

Visit to the Dungeon Machine Room

Gamorrean guards take Artoo and Threepio through a dungeon corridor where various creatures are being held; a menacing tentacle darts out and briefly encircles Threepio's neck. The protocol droid is utterly distraught at the turn of events—surely he has done something to displease his master and warrant his shameful treatment, though he can't imagine what that might be.

They are led into a room with a variety of droids—where some are even being tortured—and are brought before a humanoid droid who asks if Threepio is a protocol droid. When this fact is confirmed, he quickly assigns him to Jabba, who has recently become displeased with his interpreter and is having him destroyed. A worried Threepio is fitted with a restraining bolt and ordered back to service in the throne room. The feisty Artoo, warned that he will soon learn some respect, is assigned to Jabba's sail barge. Their plight is reminiscent of their first visit to Tatooine when the Jawas captured them. Becoming separated once more becomes an issue too; as a panicked Threepio is led off, he cries out, "Artoo, don't leave me!"

As symbols of childlike qualities, Artoo and Threepio's current plight represents the challenge to children and the child in each adult of surviving the brutal aspects of life. Family violence, abuse, and neglect are registered in the psyche in both personal and archetypal ways. Children, depending on their natural dispositions, will try to cope through a variety of means. In the broadest categories: Some become numb and frozen by fear and shame. Others may erupt, unable to contain the overwhelming pressure of their instincts and emotions. As young adults, the "frozen" ones will have to let in warmth to thaw out their emotions and make connection to others possible; "volcanic" personalities will need to seek ways of containing their raw emotions, whereby these powerful feelings can be integrated into the conscious personality. Most of us, at times, have to deal with a little of each of these struggles.

New Visitors to the Throne Room

Jabba's audience room, like the Mos Eisley cantina, features a band. Rather than an ensemble of similar alien musicians, this one is a motley assortment of different creatures. Jabba's throne room is one setting in *Return of the Jedi* to which Lucas added more colorful touches in the Special Edition. As the music blares and the camera scans the various characters and creatures in the room (including glimpses of Boba Fett, the bounty hunter who brought Han to Jabba), the dancer chained to Jabba's throne tries to thwart Jabba's desires. Angered by her opposition, Jabba pounds a nearby button; the floor opens beneath the distraught young dancer and she falls into a cavernous room. The growls of some hideous creature are heard, and those present, especially Jabba and Salacious Crumb, take vicarious, sadistic pleasure in the young woman's certain demise. As if in celebration Jabba reaches for a large bug in a nearby bowl and chomps down in disgusting fashion on this distasteful (to us!) morsel.

A laser blast interrupts the event, and a guard at the entryway to the throne room is shoved aside. A very short, helmeted bounty hunter appears with a shackled Chewbacca in tow, demanding the reward for his capture. Jabba offers twenty-five thousand (no specific galactic currency is mentioned); the bounty hunter, however, insists on fifty. An outraged Jabba inadvertently knocks Threepio, who is translating for him, off the dais in his fury. When Threepio regains his position, Jabba asks the bounty hunter why he should meet his demands. Chewbacca's captor pulls out a thermal detonator, which, if activated, would destroy everyone in the room. Jabba's big laugh soon permeates the silence, and he remarks that this bounty hunter is "my kind of scum. Fearless and inventive." Jabba offers him a reward of thirty-five thousand. Threepio finishes his translation by suggesting to the bounty hunter that he take Jabba's offer. After a moment of consideration the bounty hunter puts away the thermal detonator and accepts the offer.

The lively sounds of music and conversation continue as Chewbacca is led away by the guards. After he passes into the dungeon corridor we gain a glimpse of a masked figure lowering his face guard to get a better look—it is the face of Lando Calrissian. The despair of Chewie's capture is offset by the hope that maybe something is up and Luke and his friends have a plan. A growling Chewbacca is led to the dark, dingy hallway and placed in one of the cells.

Return from Hibernation

Later, once the raucous proceedings have subsided, a quiet, dark atmosphere descends on the audience chamber. A figure moves stealthily through the shadows; it's Boushh, the new fearless bounty hunter. Slowly he makes his way to the alcove where the frozen Han Solo hangs in carbonite. He pushes a button and the heavy casing, released from its mooring, drops to the floor with a thud. More maneuvering of the control panel buttons and dials begins the thawing process of Captain Solo. Circulation in his face and hands is restored and, eventually, his whole body slumps forward on the floor, shaking from the cold. The bounty hunter rolls Han towards himself, tries to get him to relax, and lets him know what has happened in a strange, electronically processed voice: "You're free of the carbonite. You have hibernation sickness." When Han complains that he can't see, the bounty hunter reassures him that his eyesight will return in time.

"Where am I?" Han wants to know. Told he's in Jabba's palace, Han realizes the figure speaking to him is wearing a helmet that filters his voice. "Who are *you?*" he asks. The bounty hunter, sensing the emotional distance the helmet creates, slowly removes it over his head. We see a beautiful woman's face and hear her say, "Someone who loves you." Han utters the name of the person we see, "Leia!"

This scene continues the thawing process that began in *The Empire Strikes Back.* Han rescued Luke from death by freezing, and Leia's feelings for Han thawed and became fully evident when he was put into the carbonite. Now her love is once more openly expressed as the frozen aspects of him are released. As with Luke in the previous movie, Han experiences a symbolic rebirth and will eventually see everything in this new and different light. He will also be free of the hold that elements from his past have had on him.

Personal expressions of love from a woman who has come to rescue him literally also rescues him from the binds of his former life that have kept parts of him immobilized.[6] But he must still get free from those agents of life that have "left him cold."

As they are reunited, Leia tells him she has to get him out of there. Their reunion is short-lived, for they soon hear the distinctive deep laugh of Jabba. A curtain is pulled away, revealing the giant slug in the company of various other aliens who join boisterously in his laughter. Recognizing Jabba's big belly-laugh, Solo quickly turns to face in his direction and tells him that he was on his way to pay Jabba back when he got sidetracked, unconvincingly concluding "It's not my fault." (This echoes the "signature line" protest of misfortune in *The Empire Strikes Back.*) Delighting in Solo's plight, Jabba ignores all pleas to bargain or receive higher payment. All attempts to relate are swiftly cut off, reminiscent of Jabba's offhanded dismissal of the dancer for annoying him. Disdain for the feminine (or yin) aspect of life is reflected in relationships with men who don't value working out solutions that are amicable to all parties. Instead, the other person is but fodder for such a man and not allowed any inherent value as a person in his own right.

Jabba orders that Han be led away but that Leia be brought to him. His desire symbolically represents another shadow aspect of relationships between men. If one man has a healthy connection to a woman, especially one who genuinely loves him, another man might easily envy the situation and try to destroy his imagined rival and possess the woman for himself. This is an old theme in the drama of human existence still very much alive today; it is often at the root of jealous quarrels that lead to various forms of domestic violence.[7] Brought close to Jabba, Leia expresses her disgust, as does Threepio, about his behavior and very presence. Once more the symbolic mood of evoking an emotional reaction is used along with dramatic acting.

Reunion in the Dungeon Cell

Han is led to a dungeon cell and stumbles in; a monstrous growl is heard. "Chewie? Chewie, is that you?" Han asks. There's an enthusiastic Wookie reception, which Han tries to tone down while letting Chewie know that he can't see. He asks Chewie, "What's going on?" He's flabbergasted by the Wookie's response. "*Luke*? Luke's crazy," he tells Chewie, "He can't even take care of himself, much less rescue anybody." We recall how much help Luke has needed in his previous adventures, especially from Han, and what happened on Bespin when he attempted to rescue his friends.

When Chewie gives Han more information about what's going on, he is even more incredulous. "A—a Jedi Knight? I—I'm out of it for a little while and everybody gets delusions of grandeur." In symbolic terms Han's statement summarizes his role as a key personal shadow component of Luke's personality. Han has demonstrated the capacity to take care of himself; this is, as Luke told him in *A New Hope,* what he's good at. He has also shown himself subsequently to be good at looking after others, especially Luke and Leia. He knows how to help others because he knows how to look after himself. Since Luke seemingly hasn't learned the first basic life skill—personal survival—how can he now try to help others? Han's character represents the biggest counterpoint to Luke's plan and reminds us of Luke's previous limitations. We also recall what Darth Vader told Luke on Bespin, "The Force is with you, young Skywalker. But you are not a Jedi yet."

All the principal protagonists are reunited in this beastly place, awaiting the arrival of Luke. The primitivity is visually underscored by the scene outside the fortress where a giant, brutish frog reaches out with its tongue to retrieve its prey. The circumstance parallels that in the Death Star in which the characters were reunited after the rescue of the princess, but required the help of a Jedi, Obi-Wan Kenobi, to get them out. Is a Jedi coming for them now? Or is Luke, once again, in over his head?

Luke Skywalker, Jedi Knight?!

Back inside the dark entrance to Jabba's palace, we watch the giant gate rattle open as the cloaked figure of what appears to be a young Jedi enters, backlit by the bright daylight outside. When confronted by the two boar-faced Gamorrean guards, we recognize Luke as he confidently uses the Force to push their weapons aside and drive them back. When Luke reaches the entrance to the audience room where the others all sleep, Bib Fortuna approaches to intercept him. Luke uses the Force to counter the orders Jabba gave the alien, insisting, "I must speak with Jabba." And after a pause, "You will take me to Jabba now." When Fortuna verbally reiterates these suggestions, Luke assures him that "You serve your master well. And you will be rewarded."

So far Luke acts very much like the Jedi we've seen, demonstrating the ability to use the Force as both Ben and Vader did in the earlier movies. Luke uses the Force to counter the intent of the "weak-minded" Bib Fortuna, just as Obi Wan used it on stormtroopers in *A New Hope*. A vital connection to the Force, the living source of all creative mental activity, is far stronger than weak mental abilities—in this case, relying on instructions received from someone else. The Gamorrean guards, like stormtroopers, are only doing their duty; Bib Fortuna is following specific orders given to him. They live and act in accordance with the directions they receive from somebody else; it isn't their own thoughts and instincts that they follow. This level of thinking is easily overridden by higher mental activity that has deeper psychological roots. In the case of Bib Fortuna, he is left to believe that following Luke's suggestion is serving his master well and will earn him a reward. Luke demonstrates a clever influence that taps into Fortuna's primary psychological incentive: serving another person and receiving a reward for subservience. (Recall that in *A New Hope* the primary motivation for Han Solo's initial involvement was the reward he would receive if he helped the rebels.)

When Luke arrives in the audience room, he encounters a scene that vividly symbolizes this part of his challenge. Leia, dressed only in a very skimpy outfit, is now chained to Jabba's throne. The dilemma facing Luke is to rescue not only Han Solo but also Leia, the story's feminine figure. This time, though, she is not an unknown princess trapped in political and social struggles, but a woman he knows personally whom he now finds imprisoned in the world of masculine power dominated by primitive instinct. It is the positive anima in a man that keeps him from being overwhelmed by his primal instinctuality, the inner beast, and maintains a connection to his humanity—if the man succeeds in holding an honest, respectful attitude to this inner dimension. Now Threepio expresses the hope of the moment, "At last! Master Luke has come to rescue me!" (He is very self-centered in his wish, given that Leia, Han, and Chewie have it worse.)

As Bib Fortuna awakens Jabba and tries to introduce "Luke Skywalker, Jedi Knight," Jabba becomes furious, especially when he sees that Bib has succumbed to "an old Jedi mind trick." He rebukes his assistant as a "weak-minded fool." When Luke tries the same Jedi technique on Jabba, insisting that he bring Captain Solo and the Wookie to him, Jabba informs Luke that the mind trick won't work on him. We could assume that this is because Jabba is more strong-minded than the others, and this certainly is one interpretation of this encounter, as Jabba does his own thinking. But symbolically, Jabba represents the leviathan level of body and psyche that is not affected by mental processes and can't be "tricked" away. For example, when we have to urinate, we might postpone the necessity of relieving ourselves, but eventually we have to give expression to this basic instinct. The same is true with our hunger and thirst and other bodily functions governed by the autonomic nervous system. We have to satisfy these needs; our mental processes can't eliminate them, though they can help us find creative and enjoyable ways to meet them. However, this aspect of our physical life can take over aspects of our emotional and spiritual life. For instance, in food disorders and other addictions, various substances are consumed as if they were essential for a person's survival. Yet their consumption is physically and psychologically destructive. Primitive instinct has taken over the capacity to satisfy emotional needs through other avenues, and this satisfaction is narrowed down to a very constricted means of gratification.

Similarly, as with basic physical needs, certain essential emotional desires cannot be overridden by the rational mind. When we fall in love, we can't make those feelings go away. Or when we become angry, we have to recognize the emotion and find ways to express it. The rational mind can help us do this, but it can't really "trick" us out of it. Symbolically, Jabba the Hutt represents those primitive instincts and emotions that we can't "play mind games with" and that we have to integrate into our personal lives and humanize. Otherwise they threaten to possess us and even devour us. Luke once again, but now on a deeper level, faces the aspects of instinctuality that he faced on Hoth when he was attacked by the Wampa. Now, though, it is not his life that is at stake, but the lives of his closest friends.

The Confrontation with the Rancor

Luke insists nevertheless that he is taking Captain Solo and his friends with him, and that Jabba can either profit by this, or be destroyed. Jabba believes that he alone will dictate how his life proceeds and that he does not need to bargain; he tells Luke that he will enjoy watching him die. As we've already seen with the young dancer who refused him, he gets sadistic pleasure out of the suffering of others.

When Luke attempts to use the Force to draw the blaster off one of the guards, Jabba punches the button to the trap door in the floor and Luke, together with a Gamorrean guard wrestling for the weapon, falls through it. Inside the cavernous dungeon room into which they descend we hear the deep growls of the creature that is kept there. A huge gate opens and the hideous, giant beast emerges. He goes for the Gamorrean guard first and quickly devours him. Then he goes for Luke. Unlike in the carbon-freeze chamber, when Luke could use the Force to ascend out of harm's way, he has no such escape available to him now. Relying solely on his wits, he grabs a large bone and holds it courageously as the gruesome beast lifts him toward its huge mouth. Once in position the resourceful Luke wedges the bone inside the creature's jaws so that it can't close them. The frustrated beast drops Luke and tries to free itself of the bone wedged firmly inside its mouth.

Luke then attempts to hide under a crevice at the bottom of the pit. When the creature finally breaks the bone that is wedging its jaws open, it tries to grab Luke with its claws. Spying a door on the other side of the cave, Luke uses a rock to smash one of its finger-like claws. As the beast writhes in pain for a moment, Luke dashes across the enclosure. Though he succeeds in lifting the door panel, a barred gate remains which he cannot budge. Luke turns to watch the ravenous monster approach, then notices a huge metal gate poised above it and a control button on a nearby wall. Reaching for a nearby stone, he hurls it at the panel holding the button and the huge gate crashes down on the giant beast, crushing and killing it. The raucous laughter from Jabba and his guests ends, and only Leia's face beams with delight.

As slug-like Jabba represents the serpentine leviathan, the devouring monster represents the archetypal, beast-like figure of behemoth. Like the knights of medieval times who had to slay the dragon, Luke Skywalker, Jedi knight, has slain a great beast and lives to try to free his friend and his young woman companion. When Luke fell into the pit, Threepio, in his fear for Luke, told us the creature's name. "Oh, no! The rancor!" he fretted. The word *rancor* means "deep-seated ill will," and "bitter long-lasting resentment." Its roots are also connected to the Latin word *rancere*, which means to stink; thus we have our word *rancid*. Jabba's palace and the rancor pit repeat the theme of foulness experienced in the Death Star garbage chute and Luke's refuge in the belly of the slain tauntaun on Hoth.

The rancor, as Jabba's pet, represents Jabba's disowned resentment, embitterment, and overall emotional monstrosity. Jabba's approach to life is the opposite of Yoda's perspective that pain and suffering can lead to wisdom when they are transmuted by human feeling—something that does not exist in Jabba. For Luke to confront such raw emotions inside himself during his isolated retreat on Dagobah was one thing; to have to face such primitivity as it is lived out by a gangster such as Jabba represents a whole new challenge.

Symbolically, Luke twice used a rock to help him in his battle with the rancor. On Dagobah Yoda taught Luke to feel the connection to all forms of life, even the rock. A rock served Luke well in both thwarting the rancor's attempt to grab him under the crevice, and to finally send the pit's huge gate crashing down on the monster. In the rock Luke found something "solid" he could depend on.

Of course, Jabba is outraged at what has transpired, as are the rancor's keepers, one of whom weeps at his death. Jabba is more closely linked to the rancor symbolically than to any other figure in his entourage. He orders that Solo and the Wookie be brought from their dungeon cell and decrees that they, along with Luke, are to be terminated. Jabba deals with emotional pain—in this case the loss of his rancor—in true sadistic fashion: He makes others suffer. As Han and Luke are brought together, a verbal bantering between them begins that continues through the final resolution of the situation on Tatooine. As they are reunited, Leia is still chained to Jabba, unable to take action against the terror she feels for them.

This scene also reflects a psychological problem that occurs in relationships between men, especially when those emotions represented by the Jabba character are present. The feminine soul-side of the other man is repudiated, his sensitivity, his vulnerability, and any genuine connection he might feel to a woman or other person disparaged. Sadistic pleasure is obtained at the expense of these qualities in another man. Thus, as when Luke discovered the princess's presence on the Death Star, his task, once again, is to free the feminine figure that represents not only his own soul but the helpful and supportive connection that has grown between him and Han.[8]

Jabba orders that they be "taken to the Dune Sea and cast into the Pit of Carkoon, the nesting place of the all-powerful Sarlacc." In the Sarlacc's belly they "will find a new definition of pain and suffering," as they "are slowly digested over a thousand years." Once more the image of being devoured is presented, this time in a much broader context. The awful sadism of gaining pleasure at others' pain is further amplified in the image of the "all-powerful Sarlacc." In mythological terms this creature represents the Great Mother in her most negative and devouring manifestation.[9] In the darker times of life on earth, whenever mankind had to endure war, disease, famine, and numerous natural catastrophes, the primordial aspects of life seem to prey on human existence, sometimes for extended periods. Now Luke will face this final image of the dark feminine in his attempt to free his friends.

The scene at Jabba's palace seems to imply a gangster cult that is heavily male-dominated. However, the images of Jabba, the rancor, and now the Sarlacc suggest that it is really a primitive society in service of the dark feminine. Confusion as to which archetypal power one is dealing with usually makes its manifestation that much more destructive. Conversely, consciousness of what archetypal elements are present can help one hold on to one's humanity and find a way to mediate them creatively rather than succumbing to their devouring power. For example, the experience of separation is a critical emotional component of our early relationship with our mothers and thus provides our earliest experiences of the mother archetype. If early separation experiences are not handled in an understanding and related way, then the anxieties of separation may become mixed with the terrors of feared abandonment. Later experiences in adulthood around separation may become overloaded with panic and dread that do not seem to "fit" the situation. Such experiences are the product of a negative archetypal constellation of the feminine principle.

Luke succinctly reminds Jabba of a way out of their dilemma. "You should have bargained, Jabba. That's the last mistake you'll ever make." Bargaining means relating, conversing, and finding a solution equitable for all parties. It reflects the positive feminine values, which Jabba keeps in chains.

The scene shifts to the dry sands of Tatooine—so completely devoid of feminine moisture. Over this parched landscape move Jabba's sail barge, a large anti-gravity ship, and two accompanying skiffs. On one skiff Luke, Han, and Chewie are handcuffed and Lando rides in disguise as a guard. Luke tries to assure Han that he's taken care of everything; Han, however, is very dubious.

On the sail barge Jabba yanks back on the chain around Leia's neck when she tries to see her friends on the skiff. "Soon you will learn to appreciate me," he claims in overstated grandiosity, as if he could somehow dictate how another person might feel about him. Elsewhere on the ship, Threepio accidentally knocks over a tray of drinks that Artoo is carrying. As they interact, he is his usual worried self and expresses envy of Artoo's confidence.

The Pit of Carkoon is a huge gaping hole in the sand. In the middle is a creature that looks like an open and alive digestive tract. The Special Edition adds a more active creature that emerges to devour anything that falls into the pit. Over this the skiff holding the prisoners stops; a plank is extended off one side. Guards release Luke's binders and shove him out onto the plank.

Jabba offers to listen to any pleas for mercy, but Han is quick to respond (hoping Chewie agrees) that he'll get no such pleasure from them, reiterating the depiction of Jabba as a creature who gains pleasure from others' pain. Luke calmly reverses the situation and tells Jabba, "This is your last chance. Free us or die." He nods slightly to Lando, and after a moment of mystery hangs in the air, he salutes Artoo, who opens a flap on his domed top. When the order is given to push Luke into the pit, the guard pokes at him with his spear. Luke jumps off the end of the plank, spins, and using his hands to grab the end of the board, springs in a somersault back into the center of the ship. He lands just in time to receive the lightsaber that Artoo has sent arching towards him. The battle for their freedom is on!

With great skill and occasional good fortune, Luke carries the battle, first on the prisoner skiff, then fighting those on the other skiff, and finally by assaulting the sail barge directly. While wrestling for the weapon of the guard next to him, Lando ends up falling off the skiff near the side of the pit. Han and Chewie spend the duration of the battle trying to rescue him. With inadvertent assistance from Han, Luke is able to thwart the attempt of Boba Fett to intervene; an accidental blow from the spear Han holds to the back of Fett's rocket pack sends the bounty hunter bouncing off the sail barge and into the belly of the Sarlacc. For all intent and purposes, Luke wins this battle single-handedly. The kid who couldn't "even take care of himself, much less rescue anybody," succeeds at both.

There is one very significant exception. On the sail barge, it is Leia who shuts down Jabba's command room and turns the tables on him by choking him to death with the chain that had shackled her. Symbolically, this is a vital image, as it is the positive anima in a man that allows him to cut off the hold that his primitivity might have on him. If a man can connect to his own human feelings and make a genuine, emotional connection to others, then he is well on his way to transforming the beastly instincts that Jabba represents. Usually psychological integration of instinctuality happens over a period of many years and begins with a healthy mother-child relationship. The less personal experience one has over time with an attentive and loving mother (as we will see later is the case with

Luke), the harder this battle with primitive instinctuality becomes in adult life. The connection Luke has made to Han and Leia as loving and related companions, and they to him, allows Luke to succeed in this challenging psychological task.

Luke's attack on the main barge allows Han and Chewie to complete the rescue of Lando at the skiff. Artoo frees Leia from her chains and rescues Threepio from the annoying Salacious Crumb who has removed one of Threepio's eyes (his third dismemberment). When Leia joins Luke on the main deck, he has her aim a large barge cannon toward the ship's deck. At this moment one of the guards gets a shot off that hits Luke on his bionic hand, revealing some of the underlying mechanisms. Despite the pain, he is able to parry the last threats and join Leia at the gun. Artoo pushes Threepio off the barge, and Luke fires the cannon into the deck of the ship, triggering an explosion. Luke swings with Leia—reminiscent of their swing over the chasm on the Death Star—onto the skiff now piloted by Lando. Once more, energy that had been gathered for destructive, self-serving, sadistic purposes—as was the case with the first Death Star—is released. Meanwhile, as he lands on the skiff with Leia, Luke reminds Lando to pick up the droids (which they do, using two large electromagnets) and they are soon on their way, as Jabba's barge continues to disintegrate behind them.

The final scene of this sequence on Tatooine shows Luke's X-wing and the Millennium Falcon leaving the planet's atmosphere. Luke tells the others over his comlink that he will meet them back at the fleet. Leia asks him to hurry, as the Alliance should be assembled by now; Luke assures her that he will. Han expresses his gratitude for Luke's rescue. "Now I owe you one," he tells Luke. The roles have been reversed, and now each man has come to the aid of the other during the course of their relationship. Luke can "solo" if he has to, and Han, like all of us, can get into the kind of trouble where he requires the help of others to resolve it.

As Luke pulls a glove over his wounded mechanical hand, he responds to an inquiry from Artoo. "We're going to the Dagobah system. I have a promise to keep . . . to an old friend."

CHAPTER 10

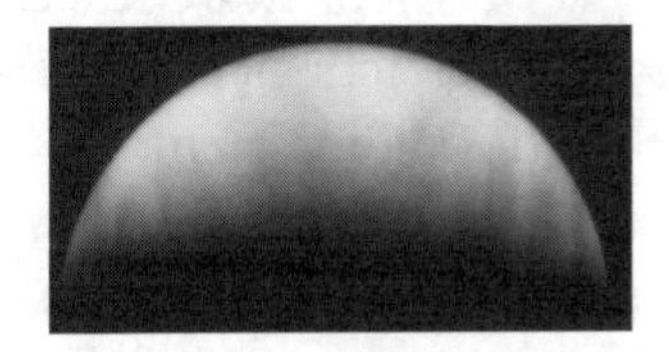

Dagobah/Rebel Fleet

New Arrival on the Death Star

A large Imperial contingent awaits the Emperor as he follows red-robed royal guards off his shuttle. Vader and the battle station commander kneel on the walkway awaiting his descent from the spacecraft. The Emperor is a black-robed, elderly man with shriveled facial skin. The somber, eerie music in the background adds evil solemnity to the occasion.

The Emperor instructs Vader to rise, and they walk together down the passageway between the gathered troops. Vader reports, "The Death Star will be completed on schedule."

The Emperor commends him on his work and then voices his intuitive perception that Vader wishes to continue his search for "young Skywalker." "Yes, my master," Vader responds.

The Emperor counsels patience and tells Vader that, in time, Luke will seek him out, and when he does, Vader is to bring him to the Emperor. "He has grown strong," the Emperor asserts. "Only together can we turn him to the dark side of the Force."

"As you wish," Vader answers.

"Everything is proceeding as I have foreseen," the eerie figure proclaims.

The Emperor both demonstrates and proclaims intuitive prescience. We see that those with Jedi awareness can perceive the inner thoughts and feelings of other Jedi. We catch a glimpse of Vader's inner life for the first time through the Emperor's Jedi awareness; we acquire an inkling of the man behind the mask. The Emperor declares that the son he seeks will search for him; he is quite confident in his knowledge, believing that events will unfold as he sees them doing. He laughs hauntingly at the thought of it. He is a sinister, inflated man, but at the same time mesmerizing and convincing.

The threat that Luke faces shifts from that of death at the hands of Jabba, to being turned to the dark side and becoming an agent of destructive energy. As we will see, such a fate is spiritually and psychologically worse than death.

Return to Dagobah

The reality of mortality is immediately brought home as Yoda and Luke talk within Yoda's little house. Yoda reads the look on Luke's face in reaction to how old Yoda now appears to him. Luke tries to deny it, but Yoda affirms, "I do, yes, I do! Sick have I become. Old and weak. When nine hundred years old you reach, look as good you will not. Hmm?" As he hobbles towards his bed, he continues, "Soon will I rest. Yes, forever sleep. Earned it, I have."

Luke is obviously disconcerted at suffering yet another loss. "Master Yoda, you can't die," he tries to tell his mentor.

"Strong am I with the Force," Yoda replies, "but not that strong! Twilight is upon me and soon night must fall. That is the way of things . . . the way of the Force."

Even the deepest connection to life and its transcendent realities does not eliminate the inevitability of physical death; the eternal lives through the physical, especially its cycles of death and rebirth. We have already seen how Obi-Wan's death helped sustain life in a creative way. Then, Luke faced loss of a Jedi mentor through a consciously chosen sacrificial death; now he faces such loss from natural causes. The elderly Yoda peacefully facing the end of his life contrasts with the elderly, feebly embodied, but power-driven Emperor we have just met.

Luke expresses his desire for Yoda's help to complete the training. Somewhat surprisingly Yoda tells him that he does not require further training. "Already know you that which you need."

"Then I am a Jedi?" Luke asks.

But Luke is a little too carried away. "Not yet," Yoda informs him, "One thing remains: Vader. You must confront Vader. Then, only then, a Jedi will you be. And confront him you will." In this statement Yoda shares some of the perception of the Emperor: Luke and Vader will face each other again. So far there have been two confrontations between Luke and Vader, and Luke has failed both times: first, in the cave when he encountered the image of Vader that lives inside himself, and later when he dueled with Vader on Bespin.

The subject of Vader having been broached, Luke asks Yoda the pressing personal question raised so dramatically in the previous movie, "Is Darth Vader my father?" Yoda, who usually addresses issues directly, rolls over on his side turning away from Luke, insisting that he needs rest. Luke persists, "Yoda, I must know."

"Your father he is," Yoda confirms to a disheartened Luke. "Told you, did he?" Yoda inquires. When Luke confirms this, Yoda declares, "Unexpected this is, and unfortunate."

"Unfortunate that I know the truth?" Luke breaks in."

A more animated Yoda replies, "No. Unfortunate that you rushed to face him . . . that incomplete was your training. Not ready for the burden were you."

"I'm sorry," Luke replies.

The story theme at this point reflects the critical psychological reality of the intersection of the personal and archetypal elements of the psyche. Every man and woman must face the archetypal problem of engaging and integrating the dark masculine energies of the unconscious, and avoiding being possessed by them. Spiritual disciplines of all kinds have been developed over the ages to aid in this process by gaining an understanding of the nature of these energies and learning how to thwart the darker ones and channel the positive. In modern times with the advent of depth psychology the profound link between our struggles with such energies and our personal histories has been elucidated far more than it has ever been before. While hints of this connection are found in myth and story from long ago, the personal side has only recently been explored in detail.

For instance, Freud found the Oedipal myth very relevant to his own psychology, so much so that he tried to universalize it. However, there are many other father-son-mother paradigms in myth. Even within Greek mythology other versions, like that of Odysseus and his son Telemachus, exist. The mythological theme of the death of the son at the hands of the father is included in the Christian myth, and earlier roots of this myth are evident in the Hebrew Bible story of Abraham and his son Isaac. The mythology reflects the problem of competition between the two and the possible resolutions: coexistence versus the killing of either father or son by the other to ensure the existence of only one. The Abraham story appears to be the earliest that works through a solution whereby neither father nor son has to be literally sacrificed for both to be fulfilled.[1] Psychologically, this problem is still very much alive in many families, as was discussed earlier, when an individual personality, in this case father or son, is sacrificed.

Luke's personal struggles and the preservation of the Jedi religion can't be separated, but their interface makes the emotional burden and the psychological task greater than if only one or the other was being engaged. Jungian psychology introduces to the general field of psychoanalysis and psychotherapy the awareness that both levels of the psyche are always present and that neglecting one to the detriment of the other can be dangerous. Knowing which archetypes are activated or what piece of personal history is involved is never enough by itself; it is in the area of our complexes, where personal experience and archetypal energy are mixed, that transformation usually occurs and the soul is redeemed (as we will soon see).

One important irony in Luke's situation is that the figure who has seemed the most impersonal throughout this story, at least until the Emperor arrived, is Darth Vader. Yet it was he who unexpectedly brought in this personal equation. Luke is no longer dealing with a masked "enemy"; he's dealing with an unknown father, whom he believed was dead. Lucas's story, I believe, subtly catches this shift in our age from dealing with life solely through large-scale belief systems and ways of looking at the world, to doing so more directly through our personal relationships and significant interactions with others. This is where the most profound transformations take place.

In *The Empire Strikes Back* Luke responded to the visions he had of his friends' suffering by interrupting his Jedi training to see if he could be of assistance to them. In doing so he discovered important personal information of which he was still unconscious: the horrible reality of what his father had become. Previously, in all religious systems, this information would have been seen as irrelevant. Today such information, when we are ready for the burden of it, is critical for psychological and spiritual transformation of the individual personality.

Yoda now reiterates to Luke key points of his training. "Remember, a Jedi's strength flows from the Force. But beware: anger, fear, aggression. The dark side are they. Once you start down the dark path, forever will it dominate your destiny." In psychological terms Yoda is reminding Luke to rely on all of life's energies, not just that which can easily possess him or paralyze him. "Giving into them," as Obi-Wan called it, leads to the dark side and loss of some humanity. Once we've done so, it is easier to give in again. Probably the clearest example is the case of addictions. Once a person is hooked on some substance in order to unconsciously deal with difficult feelings and emotions, the more these unconscious emotions and the behaviors they elicit control the person and take over his or her life.

As Yoda's energy continues to fail, he quietly warns Luke, "Do not underestimate the powers of the Emperor, or suffer your father's fate, you will." His warning reminds Luke that he faces a very powerful foe—and the danger is not death but possession by the darker, more destructive emotions that can be evoked in all of us.

As his energy wanes further, Yoda passes on to Luke one last bit of instruction and mysterious information. "When gone am I, the last of the Jedi will you be. Luke, the Force runs strong in your family. Pass on what you have learned. Luke . . . There is . . . another .

. . Sky . . . Sky . . . walker." Then Yoda dies, much as Obi-Wan did; his physical being disappears and only his clothes, which collapse on the little bed, remain.

Most startling of his last words is that there is "another Skywalker." We heard Yoda tell Ben that there was another hope when Luke left Dagobah to try to help his friends. More specifically, we now learn there is *another Skywalker;* that is, there is yet another member of Luke's family besides the father he has only recently learned is still alive. Yoda indicates that the Force, being strong in his family, would be present with this other Skywalker and Luke should pass on what he has learned. Yoda is passing his mantle as teacher on to Luke.

Yoda's death visually conveys his passing into the Force, becoming a "luminous being" in that "energy field," as we have seen with Ben. Because, like Ben, his physical body disappears at death, we might surmise that his life has been lived well while he was embodied in a way that now allows his luminosity, his soul quality, to make a transition to some other form of reality, like many of the world's religious beliefs suggest that see death as the last physical journey of the soul.

Conversation with a Former Mentor

Back at his ship Luke is forlorn and dejected. "I can't do it, Artoo," he tells his faithful droid, "I can't go on alone." Luke expresses the angst of a person who has opened up to the vibrant tutelage of others—teachers who have helped enliven his life immensely—and now faces the despair of life without them. His journey to keep a promise to "an old friend" has unfortunately left him feeling more alone than ever.

"Yoda will always be with you," the voice of Ben offers. Luke looks up to see the shimmering form of his first Jedi instructor.

Luke gets right to the point of expressing his biggest concern, "Obi-Wan! Why didn't you tell me? You told me Vader betrayed and murdered my father."

Obi-Wan responds, "Your father was seduced by the dark side of the Force. He ceased to be Anakin Skywalker and became Darth

Vader. When that happened, the good man who was your father was destroyed. So what I told you was true . . . from a certain point of view."

"A certain point of view!" an upset Luke retorts.

"Luke," Ben responds, "You're going to find that many of the truths we cling to depend greatly on our own point of view. Anakin was a good friend. When I first knew him, your father was already a great pilot. But I was amazed how strongly the Force was with him. I took it upon myself to train him as a Jedi. I thought that I could instruct him just as well as Yoda. I was wrong."

The sudden appearance of Ben's luminous image recalls Yoda's earlier teaching that through the Force, among the things he would see would be friends long gone. As we discussed earlier, the theme of the connection to past figures in one's life comes into play here. Ben gives Luke a lesson in subjectivity, the reality that we see the world through our own point of view, and this subjectivity, by its very nature, limits us. After his break with Freud, Jung was able to recognize the subjectivity of each psychology, including his own, as being limited to the personality of the theorist. He refers to an inner figure, Philemon, who helped him realize the limits our subjectivity poses to each of us.[2] Recipients of any psychology or form of personal teaching eventually have to find their own connection to reality through their own sense of self and move beyond what they received from a teacher. Ben recounts his own failing due to overconfidence—in his case, believing that he could instruct a Jedi as well as Yoda. He is now willing and able to admit his shortcomings and accept responsibility for them. His sense of failure, though, also informs the subjectivity through which he perceives Vader, which is different from Luke's perception. But which is closer to the inner reality of the former Anakin Skywalker?

Having encountered Vader directly, Luke now has his own view. "There is still good in him. I've felt it."

Ben replies with great sadness, "He's more machine now than man. Twisted and evil." Earlier Ben introduced a new concept of "death" to Luke, a view that outlines the current threat Luke must face. How does he confront the dark figures and not lose his own humanity—suffer the loss of his soul by becoming an agent of evil himself—and die inside. Luke and Ben differ on how "lost" Vader has become as a person, how dead he really is. For the second time in this third film we get a glimpse of Vader's inner life from the perceptions of a person, this time Luke, who can see behind the mask—an insight we can neither confirm nor refute.

A conflicted Luke tells Ben, "I can't do it."

Ben, however, like Yoda, affirms, "You cannot escape your destiny. You must face Darth Vader again."

"I can't kill my own father," Luke protests.

"Then," Ben responds after thoughtful pause, "the Emperor has already won. You were our only hope." A very subtle subtext exists in this dialogue. Ben, like Yoda, tells Luke that he must "face" Vader, but Luke is still stuck in the assumption that had gripped him in the Dagobah cave: that to "face" or "confront" someone means to attack and kill. In order to sort out his feelings, he will once again have to face the figure directly, since in his own mind he continues to imagine only one scenario: killing his opponent. Psychologically, Luke now wrestles with the primitive masculine dilemma of "kill or be killed" when confronting a powerful adversary, as if no other solution exists. The father-son implications of this conflict further complicate the dilemma Luke faces.

The "answer" emerges in the next twist of the conversation. Luke asks Ben about the other of whom Yoda spoke. "The other he spoke of," Ben replies, "is your twin sister."

"But I have no sister," Luke responds.

"Hmm," Ben begins, "To protect you both from the Emperor, you were hidden from your father when you were born. The Emperor knew, as I did, that if Anakin were to have any offspring, they would be a threat to him. That is the reason why your sister remains safely anonymous."

After a quick moment of thought, Luke exclaims, "Leia! Leia's my sister."

"Your insight serves you well," Ben tells him, "Bury your feelings deep down, Luke. They do you credit. But they could be made to serve the Emperor." At this point the scene on Dagobah ends.

The symbolic living "other" in a man is the anima, which he comes to know through his emotional life and the images related to her. In the complex process of forming an ego-identity, certain aspects of the personality are inevitably left undeveloped or unacknowledged and only emerge later in life. Plato suggested that we are all androgynous at birth; then we are cut in two and spend the rest of our life looking for our other half. Thus psychologically, a boy is separated at birth from the anima, his inner sister, so that his masculine identity can be formed. His relationship with his parents (and others) colors the unconscious development of this aspect of him, but it essentially remains "anonymous" and unknown unless it is discovered later, if at all. Usually its discovery is mediated by the process of psychological projection—which Lucas captures visually in the scene where Luke "discovered" Leia in projected holographic form when he inadvertently came across the message in Artoo.

Part of the challenge of growing up for a boy raised in a patriarchal society is learning to express his anima aspects—his feelings, his vulnerability, his own unique humanness. He learns to hide them fairly early in life, so that others can't use this side of himself against him. Yet to succeed in the most difficult tasks of life, especially in one's later years, this is the side that a man needs most; even then, it leaves him vulnerable, and others still might use this vulnerability against him. As we discussed earlier, people who thrive on exercising power—be they parents like Vader or societal figures like the Emperor, are threatened by others who have the same or greater abilities. In this scene with Ben, Luke symbolically deepens the connection he made to Leia when he hung onto the weather vane on Bespin. He now acknowledges her as a counterpart, a woman to whom he's directly related, and an equal.

Luke's vulnerability has a paradoxical twist to it. When he first taught Luke, Ben suggested that he "stretch out with his feelings." Now he warns Luke that though these feelings do him credit, he should bury them "deep down," or else they could be made to serve the Emperor. Burying feelings is the old way of masculine development in the world. But will it serve Luke now? What are the dangers that his feelings pose? When does it help to be vulnerable? These issues surface during the final confrontation between father and son.

One further note on the story's development is worth mentioning at this point. When our tale began, a dark-cloaked warlord chased and captured a young princess. A young man was unwittingly brought into the adventure and he succeeded, along with his new companions, to rescue her and thwart her enemies. Now we discover that these very impersonal, archetypal figures are related as father and son, brother and sister. The myth is also a family affair. Subtly Lucas has brought archetypal symbolism closer to bear on the drama of some of our most important personal relationships as well.

The Gathering of the Rebel Fleet

We rejoin the other main protagonists as the rebels meet to discuss their strategy against the Emperor and the new Death Star. We get caught up on the proceedings through the bantering of Han and Lando, as Han discovers that Lando is now a general and involved in leading the fighter attack. When Lando remarks that he's surprised they didn't ask Han, Han responds, "Well, who says they didn't. But I ain't crazy. You're the respectable one, remember?"

The buzz in the room subsides as a regal, soft-spoken woman, Mon Mothma, steps forward to speak. She is clearly the leader of the rebel group, and her presence and name (Mon Moth[er]ma) symbolically reflect the connection to the feminine principle that permeated the rebel cause during the battle against the original Death Star. The diversity of humans and aliens present at this gathering symbolizes the life principle, in all of its variety, which is struggling against the power-driven, tyrannical Emperor.

Mon Mothma announces that the Emperor has made a critical error and the time for their attack has come. The information they have received, shown through a holographic image, reveals the location of the Emperor's new battle station now in the process of being constructed. The rebel leader reports that the weapons systems of this station are not yet operational, and that because the Imperial Fleet is spread throughout the galaxy in their efforts to engage them, the Death Star is relatively unprotected. But most important, she reports, the Emperor himself is personally overseeing the final stages of construction. She gravely notes that many Bothans died to bring them this information, and defers to Admiral Ackbar for the next phase of their presentation.

Ackbar, a salmon-colored, amphibian-like alien, points to the Death Star in the holograph as it orbits the nearby forest moon of Endor. He demonstrates that while its weapon systems are not operational, the Death Star has a strong defense mechanism in the form of an energy shield generated from the nearby moon. The shield must be deactivated before the attack can commence. Once the shield is down, the cruisers will create a perimeter around the battle station while the fighters fly into its superstructure and attempt to knock out the main reactor. Ackbar announces that General Calrissian has volunteered to lead the fighter attack. Han, his bantering buddy, tells him, "Good luck. You're going to need it," as Ackbar asks for General Madine to come forward.

Madine announces that they have stolen a small Imperial shuttle, which, disguised as a cargo ship and using a secret Imperial code, will carry a strike team to the moon and deactivate the shield generator.

"Sounds dangerous," Threepio proclaims.

"I wonder who they found to pull that off," Leia ponders aloud.

"General Solo," Madine asks, "is your strike team assembled?"

"Uh, my team's ready," Han replies, "I don't have a command crew for the shuttle." One by one, Chewie, Leia, and a newly arriving Luke agree without hesitation to join him. The foursome that escaped the original Death Star together is reunited for a new mission. They will be joined, of course, by the two droids, whose contrasting attitudes are summed up by Threepio's sarcastic translation of Artoo's beeps, "'Exciting' is hardly the word I would use."

Luke arrives at the last moment, to the others' delight, and Leia greets him warmly with a hug. Sensing something different in him, she asks, "What is it?"

"Ask me again sometime," he replies. Fuller development of the meaning of Leia being his sister will have to wait until later, and a more private moment.

As Han and the others board the shuttle, Han pauses to talk to Lando and offer him the Millennium Falcon. "Look," he tells his friend, "I want you to take her. I mean it. Take her. You need all the help you can get. She's the fastest ship in the fleet."

"All right, old buddy," Lando replies, "You know, I know what she means to you. I'll take good care of her. She—she won't get a scratch. All right?" An obviously vulnerable Han Solo responds, "Right. I got your promise now. Not a scratch." They each say their final goodbyes and wish each other luck.

As Luke is moving toward a deeper personal relationship to Leia on one level, Han's character is developing also. Having come to value his relationships with his rebel friends, he can let go of the "anima" attachment to his ship we discussed earlier. He can share "her," offering "her" assistance to a friend and trusting that his friend values "her" importance to him. The scene also symbolically depicts psychological development in the relationship between two men: in this case, one recognizing a way to help another with the vessel that is so important to him, and the other fully appreciative of the emotional attachment involved in the gesture. They are working together and not competing.

Once on-board the shuttle, Han gets another glimpse of the Falcon and pauses quietly. Leia picks up on his state of mind and asks, "Hey, are you awake?"

"Yeah," he tells her, as he peers out at the Falcon, "I just got a funny feeling. Like I'm not gonna see her again."

She understandingly puts her hand on his shoulder and suggests softly, "Come on, General, let's move." This modest scene adds drama to the later battle when the Millennium Falcon first flies against Imperial fighters and then penetrates the Death Star superstructure. We wonder if the ship will make it. But this moment also reflects Han's psychological development, as he is gripped by an unconscious fantasy of not seeing the ship that has served as a "container" for his feminine attributes. We usually take such fears literally when they arise, but often they signal deeper psychological (nonliteral) change. In Han's case he is further letting go of his old life, from which he has just been rescued—Leia was the one who released him from his carbonite prison—and moving closer to acknowledging feelings of vulnerability that he has avoided previously. In this way he will be "losing" his older, primary attachments in order to discover more intimate ones. By offering to lend Lando his customized ship, his personal development moves to a deeper emotional level.

Threepio utters an introduction to the final adventure, "Here we go again," as Han moves the ship out of the docking bay, telling everyone to "hang on." They make the jump to hyperspace and head to the forest moon of Endor.

CHAPTER 11

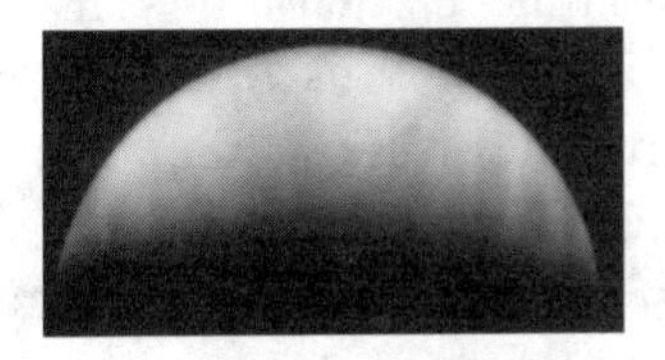

Endor

The Emperor's Throne Room

The drama around the planet Endor begins with a brief meeting between Vader and the Emperor on the Death Star. The Emperor has now assumed complete control of the Death Star's construction. He orders the Imperial fleet moved to the far side of Endor, where it is to stay until he calls for it. He dismisses Vader's reports of a rebel fleet building near Sullust; they do not concern him. The hideous figure assures Vader that "soon the rebellion will be crushed and young Skywalker will be one of us!" He informs Vader that his work on the Death Star is finished and orders him to wait on the command ship for further orders. Vader dutifully bows and departs.

The Arrival of the Stolen Imperial Shuttle

Meanwhile, Han, Chewie, Luke, Leia, and the droids enter the Endor system inside the shuttle carrying the rebel strike team. Amidst all the Imperial traffic, they are rightly nervous about their situation as they prepare to test the code that has been stolen along with the spaceship. This point in the drama is heightened as Luke, through the Force, senses Vader's presence on the Imperial command ship. He knows full well that if he can sense Vader's presence, Vader will also be aware of *his.* Luke expresses concern to his friends that he's endangering the mission; the always practical Han Solo claims it's just his imagination.

On the bridge of the Imperial ship Luke's fears are confirmed, however, as Vader suddenly becomes interested in the proceedings at the controller's station. He walks towards it and demands to know where the shuttle is going. Admiral Piett inquires over the comlink system as to the ship's cargo and destination. Han responds that they carry parts and technical crew for the forest moon. Vader demands to know if they have a code clearance; Piett tells him that the ship's code, though an older one, does checks out and he is about to clear their passage. In the pause that follows, Vader clearly detects Luke's presence. When Piett asks if he should hold them, Vader responds, "No. Leave them to me. I will deal with them myself." Piett gives the order for the controller to proceed and clearance is given to the stolen shuttle. While most are relieved—Han says, "I told you it was gonna work"—the look on Luke's face shows he's puzzled and concerned.

The Speeder Bike Chase

Once on the forested moon, our heroes and heroine move over the terrain along with the rebel squad they lead. They come upon two Imperial scouts at work and decide that it would take too long to go around them, yet they can't risk detection. Han tells Luke and Leia that he and Chewie will take care of the two troopers. Despite a warning by Luke to keep it quiet, Han accidentally steps on a twig as he sneaks up on his Imperial target. The alerted soldier is able to turn and knock Han back against a tree, setting off Han's drawn blaster. The sound alerts the Imperial scout's partner to the danger, and he takes off on his speeder bike. Chewie is able to get off a blaster shot that sends the trooper and the bike crashing.

As Luke and Leia rush up to help, they discover two more Imperial scouts racing off into the forest on their anti-gravity vehicles. Leia quickly hops on the remaining bike, and calling after her,

Luke quickly jumps on behind. An exciting chase ensues, and the tense action brings Luke and Leia together as equals working side-by-side to defeat their common enemy. As they pull up next to one Imperial biker, Luke is able to dislodge the driver and take possession of the vehicle. As he and Leia pursue the remaining biker, two more scouts keeping sentry on bikes parked in the forest take off after them. Luke tells Leia to keep on tailing the biker in front of them; he drops back behind everyone to take on their new pursuers. Using the laser blaster on his bike, Luke is able to knock out one of the two troopers he is following. Now he and Leia each have one more of these Imperials left to defeat.

Leia attempts different maneuvers to overtake the trooper she's pursuing, but has little success. When she tries pulling off to the side, he draws a blaster and hits the engine section of her bike, causing Leia to lose control of it and plummet to the forest floor. As the scout turns around to see what is happening to her, he inadvertently crashes into a tree. Leia watches his demise, sprawled on the ground on her stomach, with head raised; then her head drops as she slips into unconsciousness.

Luke pulls up next to the scout he is pursuing, and as they try to knock each other off their vehicles, the bikes become entangled. In order to avoid crashing into an approaching tree, Luke dives to the ground, abandoning his bike. The trooper, able to stay aboard his bike, circles back and charges Luke while firing the bike's blaster at him. Using his lightsaber to deflect each blast, Luke severs the rudder system of the bike when it speeds past; both bike and rider crash. As he takes a deep breath Luke deactivates his lightsaber and prepares to head back to meet the others.

When Luke catches up with Han, Chewie, and the squad they lead, it becomes clear that Leia has not returned. "I thought she was with you," says Han.

"We got separated," Luke responds. They quickly decide to go look for her and make arrangements to meet the rest of the rebel unit at the shield generators at a specified time. Han, Luke, Chewie, and the two droids head off into the forest in search of Leia.

Symbolically, this search is important on two levels. First, it recreates the sibling situation Obi-Wan has recently informed Luke about. Just as he and his sister were separated at birth, they have become separated again. Psychologically, it is critical that Luke search for her, not only because she is the sister he never had, but for what she represents as his own feminine counterpart. The symbolic foursome that has also been broken up represents a second motif of reunion: the one consisting of Han, Chewie, Luke, and Leia (accompanied by the droid pair). The search for Leia repeats the theme of the rescue of the feminine figure, the missing fourth (in the symbolism of a male personality), in the first movie. An important shift in this search, though, is that these men now seek Leia as a *person* and not as a princess, as they did in *A New Hope*.

Leia and the Ewok

Next we rejoin Leia, who is still lying unconscious on the forest floor. A short, chubby, furry creature wearing a leather head and shoulder garment prods her tentatively on the back with a primitive spear—a pointed stone tied to the end of a long stick. (He's about three feet tall and the stick maybe four feet long.) As she begins to stir, he continues to poke in a very annoying manner. "Cut it out!" she exclaims as she realizes what is going on. But seeing that this creature spooks quickly, Leia becomes reassuring, "I'm not going to hurt you." As she takes stock of her predicament, she talks openly about it. "Well, looks like I'm stuck here. Trouble is, I don't know where here is." Working some of the stiffness out from her body, she settles on top of a large fallen log and invites him to join her. "Maybe you can help me," Leia says. "Come on, sit down."

The creature (already known to people familiar with this film as Wicket, an Ewok), still very wary, circles his spear in front of him and even growls a bit as he continues to shuffle about beside the log. Leia again assures him that she won't hurt him and invites him to come over and sit down. "All right," she wonders, "You want something to eat?" She reaches for a scrap of food from her rations, and the Ewok, though still hesitant, shows interest. Sniffing the food curiously, he slowly approaches and eventually sits beside her on the log, nibbling a little of the food.

As they sit Leia removes her field helmet, an action that spooks the Ewok once more and sends him running about, chattering and pointing his spear at her again. Leia assures him that "it's a hat. It's not going to hurt you," and offers him a clear look at it while remarking how jittery he is. Wicket rejoins her on the log but soon goes on the alert again, quickly standing on the fallen tree and sniffing the air. He continues to sniff and chatter in an alarmed way. As Leia asks him, "What is it?" a laser blast slashes through the forest, hitting the log on which they sit. They both roll off behind the far side of the log, and peer back over it to scan the forest for the source of the blasting. Leia stays acutely alert with her blaster. Another blast strikes the log, and this time the frightened Ewok dives into a hollow underneath it.

As Leia once more peers over the log to survey the forest, a voice behind her suddenly barks, "Freeze." A stormtrooper reaches out for her weapon and instructs his partner to get his bike and take her back to base. As the second trooper moves away, an infuriated Wicket strikes the leg of the remaining trooper with his spear. As the startled man bends to check out this unexpected interference, Leia grabs a loose branch, knocks him out, and quickly grabs his blaster to shoot the speeder bike now carrying the second trooper. Bike and rider explode in a crash in the woods. As Wicket chatters through the action, Leia takes his hand and sets off in one direction, declaring that they have to get out of there. Wicket, who concurs with the gist of her plan but not her direction, pulls on her hand to lead her another way. She quickly follows.

The arrival of the first Ewok into this film's story introduces a wealth of new symbolism. Like Yoda in the previous movie, Wicket is a childlike character to whom children readily relate; his emotional world is very resonant with theirs. As in many previous scenes, symbolism that has occurred earlier is reintroduced with important new twists. For instance, in the previous two movies Luke was knocked unconscious and awakened to the presence of a helpful figure: On Tatooine it was Ben, and on Hoth, the vision of Ben coupled with the arrival of Han Solo. Here on Endor Leia is knocked unconscious and is awakened by an unknown—but benign—figure.

Leia's introduction to Wicket is also similar to Luke's encounter with Yoda, but with important differences. Both Luke and Leia meet a small and essentially harmless creature; Luke did not believe that the creature he encountered could help him in any way, whereas Leia surmises that this unknown creature might be able to help her and immediately seeks to establish a relationship with him. In Luke and Leia we see archetypal masculine and feminine attitudes symbolically juxtaposed. Luke, like many men who become lost while driving a car, doesn't want help and won't consider asking for assistance. In addition, Luke evidences a type of masculine psychological rigidity when he dismisses Yoda as a source of aid because Yoda doesn't match his expectations. Leia, in contrast, quickly recognizes she's lost and in trouble, does not discount help on any level (even from a creature like Wicket, who is initially very annoying, as was Yoda), and interjects a relational quality.

Another theme repeated here is that of establishing a bond through the sharing of food. On Dagobah Yoda insisted that he and Luke eat first and *then* find the Jedi Master. Leia instinctively offers Wicket food in order to gain his confidence and overcome his fear of her. As we discussed in the Dagobah section, the assimilation of food has many symbolic meanings. Here we see it as a means of creating a basic connection between two creatures.

The bond Leia forms with Wicket soon proves very helpful to her. While he may be jittery, he has heightened instincts that can alert her to the danger in the woods. He can sniff things out in an uncanny way, and she is not hesitant to follow him when he offers a way out. In contrast, Luke was very reluctant to follow Yoda to his home. Throughout the new adventures of the central female character in this movie, we are offered a depiction of the development of the feminine principle in the human psyche. Since Leia has now been identified as Luke's sister, symbolically we are seeing further indications of anima development in Luke as we watch Leia's personality unfold. Qualities missing in the earlier movies, especially during Luke's arrival on Dagobah, now appear embodied by Leia on Endor.

When Luke attunes to the Force, he taps into a source of unique spiritual and mental abilities. We saw in Jabba's palace, however, that there are certain instinctive levels that even this kind of ability doesn't touch. Now we discover a creature with heightened natural instincts that the human character who meets him, Leia, doesn't possess. However, rather than being used destructively as they are by Jabba, these instinctive capacities are channeled in a helpful manner. The introduction of Wicket's highly differentiated sense of smell is a striking counterpoint to the scenes in the previous movies involving grossly overwhelming odors, especially in the garbage room on the original Death Star. Anyone could smell how bad that was. On Endor only Wicket can smell the trouble brewing in the woods.

The Emperor's Throne Room

Darth Vader returns to the dark, foreboding throne room and waits for the Emperor's attention. Slowly swiveling around in his revolving chair, disengaging his view out into space, the Emperor snaps icily, "I told you to wait on the command ship."

Vader gets right to the point. "A small rebel force has penetrated the shield and landed on Endor."

"Yes, I know," the Emperor curtly replies.

"My *son* is with them," Vader continues.

The Emperor questions Vader's perception, "Are you sure?"

"I have *felt* him, my Master," Vader assures him.

"Strange that I have not," the Emperor ponders, "I wonder if your feelings on this matter are clear, Lord Vader."

"They are clear, my Master," Vader asserts. Without pausing to reflect on his own lack of perception, the Emperor quickly orders Vader to go to the Sanctuary Moon and wait for Luke. "He will come to me?" Vader wonders.

"I have foreseen it," the Emperor quickly pronounces. "His compassion for you will be his undoing. He will come to you and then you will bring him before me."

Vader bows, answers "As you wish," and departs.

We get two noteworthy glimpses into the workings of the Emperor and Vader in this scene. The first is that Vader *felt* Luke's presence, and that he refers to Luke as his son in the company of the

Emperor. The Emperor, who obviously prides himself on his heightened perception, has not felt Luke's presence. Second, while the Emperor briefly acknowledges that this is strange, he proceeds to operate as if his perceptions were infallible, an assumption that Vader also accepts. Their dialogue suggests that there is a connection between Luke and Vader, father and son, to which the Emperor is not privy. He dismisses this connection only as a weakness of Luke's that can be manipulated for his own purposes, and nothing more. The Emperor believes that Luke's feelings for his father make him vulnerable, and that such emotional openness will allow the Emperor to defeat him.

The Search for Leia

In the meantime, back on Endor, Han, Luke, Chewie, and the droids are at the site of Leia's mishap. They have found the helmet she removed while with Wicket and the wrecked bikes. Artoo's sensors pick up nothing and everyone is perplexed and worried about where she is. Suddenly Chewie gets wind of something, not unlike Wicket earlier, and they all take off after him as he charges through the forest. They arrive at a place where a dead animal hangs above the ground. "Hey, I don't get it," Han exclaims. But Chewie can't resist, and he grabs for the animal before Luke has called out his warning for Chewie to wait. Suddenly the whole group finds itself hanging in a net high above the ground. Han sums up their situation through the movie's tongue-in-cheek dialogue, "Nice work. Great, Chewie! Great! Always thinking with your stomach." As they try to figure a way out—Luke asks Han if he can reach his lightsaber—Artoo soon frees them using an extended cutting saw. As quickly as Chewie had acted to get them caught in the net, Artoo has them all falling down to the ground before Threepio can even finish voicing his concerns about the length of the drop.

Unceremoniously returned to earth, they recover from their fall to face the reality of being surrounded by a tribe of creatures like the one Leia had met earlier. Han, like Leia before him, is irritated by one Ewok poking annoyingly at him with his spear. Luke perceives that it would be wise not to resist. "It'll be all right," he says and urges his companions to give up their weapons. This is a subtle but important shift for Luke, who previously ignored Yoda's suggestion to forego his weapons when entering the Dagobah cave.

At this point Threepio—still trying to recover from their fall—sits up. When the Ewoks see him, they let out a collective gasp and begin chattering among themselves in an excited manner. Soon they are all on their knees bowing down to him and joined in a rhythmic chant. Perplexed at what is happening, Luke asks Threepio if he understands anything they are saying.

"Oh, yes, Master Luke! Remember that I am fluent in over six million forms of communication." (Threepio always seems to have to remind someone of this.)

"What are you telling them?" asks Han.

"Hello, I think," responds Threepio, "I could be mistaken. They're using a very primitive dialect. But I do believe they think I am some sort of god." This pronouncement is totally amusing to all of Threepio's companions. Once more, as happened especially in *A New Hope*, Lucas introduces important symbolism—but in such a childlike way that we can laugh along with the other characters. This attitude in the storytelling reflects the early impish behavior of Yoda as well.

Han, ever the practical one, suggests to Threepio, "Well, why don't you use your divine influence and get us out of this?

"I beg your pardon, General Solo," replies Threepio, "but that just wouldn't be proper."

"Proper?!" wonders Han.

"It's against my programming to impersonate a deity," an indignant Threepio responds.

As Han moves towards Threepio menacingly, the Ewoks intervene by encircling Han with raised spears. Han quickly backs off, "My mistake. He's an old friend of mine." The Ewoks obviously take the connection to their new god-figure very seriously.

Symbolically the story now presents a tribe in the midst of a new religious experience. A new deity has literally dropped into their midst and gripped their imaginations. The introduction of human characteristics to religious imagination is actually relatively late historically. Animals were the primary creatures of the myths and legends of earliest people. For example, Native American mythology shows a great abundance of animal heroes—coyote and raven, for instance. In the rich mythology of the Bushmen of South Africa, Mantis is the most important divine figure.[1] In the *Star Wars* story the Ewoks are introduced to a human-divine form in a highly transcendent manner: he suddenly appears in their midst, he's pure gold, and he can communicate directly with them!

Mythologically speaking, the Ewoks are at an early stage of religious development: the human form as reflective of the divine is just beginning to enter their mythology. An important example of this kind of symbolic evolution is the vision of Ezekiel found in the Hebrew Bible. The transcendent figure in the prophet's vision has four heads with four faces; only one face of each of these four-faced heads is human. Images of the divine at that time were just beginning to manifest in human form. By the time of Christ, the human-formed god-figure in the West was believed to be manifest not only in a divine abode, but also living on earth as well. Yet animal symbolism is still important in the modern psyche. One place it continues in our culture is in sports, where most school and professional teams use animal names and logos to represent their athletic identity. Such symbolism demonstrates the continual psychological need (discussed earlier) to humanize the instinctive energies in the psyche by finding socially acceptable outlets for them.

Fortunately Threepio, the new Ewok divinity, has been programmed to know his limits, even if practical demands dictate acting otherwise. His attitude contrasts sharply with that of the Emperor who thinks and acts as if he were an omnipotent deity. Threepio, pure gold in human form, has no "delusions of grandeur" as he feared Artoo might have at the end of *The Empire Strikes Back*. It's the Emperor who has delusions of grandeur—who is, in fact, possessed by the power principle—which has left his physical humanity in a state of deterioration.

A procession now weaves its way through the forest to the Ewok village set high up in the trees. Threepio is carried on a litter, while the others are carried underneath poles to which they have been lashed (except for Artoo who is tied to a primitive dolly). Once inside the village the shaman or medicine man seems to be directing things. Han mutters that he has a "really bad feeling about this." As wood is piled underneath those hanging from the poles, Threepio finally understands what is going on. "I'm rather embarrassed," he tells his companions, "but it appears you are to be the main course at a banquet in my honor." As the drums start beating, Leia emerges—much to their shocked relief—from one of the huts wearing an animal skin dress, her long hair hanging beautifully down her back. She tries to tell the Ewoks "these are my friends" and urges Threepio to tell the Ewoks that they must be set free. Threepio does not succeed in convincing the leaders, and the banquet proceedings continue; the roasting fires are being lit.

Bound to his pole, Luke suggests that Threepio try a different approach. "Tell them if they don't do as you wish, you'll become angry and use your magic."

"But, Master Luke," Threepio protests, "what magic? I couldn't possibly . . ."

"Just tell them," Luke insists.

Threepio tries, but his words seem to have no effect. Luke, however, makes sure there is magic to be seen. Turning within himself, he tunes into the Force and lifts the litter or throne holding Threepio, suspending it above the startled and frightened Ewoks. Even though Threepio panics too, the impressed tribal leaders order their prisoners to be released, and Luke sets the forest throne back down. After some brief electronic venting by Artoo, there is a reuniting of Leia with her friends and a general exchange of "no hard feelings" with the Ewoks.

The numinous experience of discovering a new "god" has stirred the ancient ceremonial customs of the Ewoks. Animal mythology was a profound part of hunting cultures, and the animals hunted and eaten were considered to be the divinity. The legacy of such early religious practice is found, for example, in the Christian Eucharist, where the body and blood of Christ are symbolically consumed in the form of the bread and wine. (In Roman Catholic doctrine the bread and wine are believed to *be* the body and blood of Christ through the "transubstantiation" rite performed by the priest during the Mass.) Using the Force—finding a way to link his imagination with the Ewoks' in a manifestable way—enables Luke to facilitate the further development of the tribe's religious instincts (begun with the "revelation" of Threepio to them) in new, dramatic ways. The next scene shows what such a "new way" of assimilating a spiritual "revelation" might be.

That evening finds our rebel protagonists sitting together with the Ewoks for a tribal gathering. The group is gathered around Threepio who is excitedly telling the story of his friends' adventures, including sound effects! The Ewoks are captivated and, after he's finished, animated conversation ignites the members of the tribe. The chief calls for everyone's attention, the drums beat, and anticipation fills the air. Threepio then informs his perplexed companions that the chief has announced "we are now a part of the tribe." The new "god" has brought to this tribal culture a living myth, a story to be added to their tribal lore.

Having learned to appreciate the wisdom of my children's imaginations, I asked my older son (when he was about eight years old) how he would describe the Ewoks. Without a pause he said, "they're animal Indians." I have yet to hear a better symbolic summary of these characters! They are close to nature and they have customs that reflect the communal practices of earliest humanity. Symbolically, the Ewoks have offered "sanctuary" to our protagonists. The Emperor had referred to this forest moon as the sanctuary moon when he sent Vader to it. It is the spiritual wonder and sense of community that is still alive in the Ewoks that is missing in the attitude of the Empire. But it's in just such a place that the human soul can find refuge. This tribal-communal setting, amidst the verdant feminine symbolism of forest and moon, augments the introverted feminine setting of Dagobah where Yoda lives. Luke has begun the process of bringing what he has learned from Yoda back to the galaxy community.

As this ceremony is taking place, Luke steps outside and away from the others. Leia, sensing something might be troubling him, follows. Meanwhile Han tends to their immediate business, bantering impatiently with Threepio to get fresh supplies and retrieve their weapons. He tells Chewie that "short help is better than no help," as Threepio informs him that the Ewok scouts will show them the quickest way to the power generator.

Luke and Leia

Leia discovers Luke alone on the walkway, high among the trees in the midst of the Ewok village. She asks him what is wrong. Remaining quiet and reflective at first, he asks her if she has any memories of her mother, her "real mother."

"Just a little bit," Leia answers, "she died when I was very young."

"What do you remember?" Luke inquires.

"Just . . . images, really. Feelings," recounts Leia.

"Tell me," Luke encourages.

Leia soulfully reminisces, "She was very beautiful, kind, but . . . sad. "Why are you asking me this," she curiously queries.

"I have no memory of my mother," Luke laments, "I never knew her."

This is a very significant moment in the story. Leia's presence as "sister" and, more importantly as a feminine figure, evokes Luke's earliest loss: he recalls no experience of his mother. For a brief, soul-searching moment he reflects on his personal origins and the void he suffered there. Loss of bonding between mother and child, especially when it occurs early in development, has profound effects on the development of a sense of self, a capacity to relate to others, and a connection to the archetypal dimension of life. Such a primal loss usually makes life that much more challenging. This scene suggests that Luke had to encounter the raw, primitive realities of Jabba and the rancor—beasts reflecting the dark feminine principle we discussed in Chapter 9—in part, as a result of the loss of the maternal function of mediating the deeper layers of the psyche that these creatures symbolize. Without close maternal contact the nascent personality is directly exposed to archetypal realities and may easily be overwhelmed by them.

Though briefly, Luke is now turning toward a consideration of his personal history and very early maternal loss. This is a vital part of anima development for a man and it usually takes a long period of reflection and emotional processing to work through the issues that lie buried there.[2] Because the task of establishing a place in the world usually comes first, the urge to explore and deepen this side of the personality comes later in a man's life. If Luke's story were to continue beyond this movie, a fuller realization of the anima would be a crucial component of his continuing psychological development.

Leia calls Luke back to the situation at hand. "What's troubling you?" she asks.

"Vader is here," Luke informs her, "now, on this moon. I felt his presence. He's come for me. He can feel when I'm near. That's why I have to go. As long as I stay, I'm endangering the group and our mission here. I have to face him."

"Why?" a distraught and perplexed Leia responds.

"He's my father," Luke replies.

Leia is, of course, aghast at such astonishing news. Luke quickly adds that there is more she needs to hear that won't be easy. "If I don't come back," he says, "you're the only hope for the Alliance."

A dismayed Leia tells him, "Luke, don't talk that way. You have a power I . . . I don't understand and could never have."

"You're wrong, Leia," Luke insists, "you have that power, too. In time you'll learn to use it, as I have. The Force is strong in my family. My father has it . . . I have it . . . and . . . my sister has it." As he looks into her perplexed faced, Luke persists, "Yes. It's you, Leia."

Slowly acknowledging some perception deep within herself Leia replies, "I know. Somehow . . . I've always known."

The issue of Luke's loss of his mother must lie in the background for now, because he must still confront his father. Not to do so would endanger his friends and their mission. Psychologically, he must further engage the complex that continues to disrupt his life and impede its fulfillment, and to do that he must come face to face with the man from whom he most inherited it. As he comes closer to making contact with the feminine element in his life, represented by Leia who offers a connection to his personal mother, he also zeroes in on the reality that his female counterpart, his "sister," has the same potential for fulfillment in life as he does.

This scene symbolically expresses another critical part of a man's relationship to the feminine side of life. He must recognize the possibilities of fulfillment for a woman as a *person* and not just as a carrier of his corporeal fantasies. If the story were to continue, it would need to focus on the psychological process whereby the "sister" half of this brother-sister pair realized the equality of their shared potential; mythologically, it would bring us to the edge of an age that would witness a more complete shift away from patriarchal culture and its hero myths and toward a more balanced world wherein the female has equality with the male and the feminine self is as fully realized and developed as the masculine.[3]

While Leia understands that she and Luke are indeed brother and sister, she does not comprehend why he has to face their father. In simple terms and with quiet certainty Luke explains that Vader isn't *all* bad. "There is good in him," Luke tells her, "I've *felt* it. He won't turn me over to the Emperor," Luke states, "I can save him. I can turn him back to the good side. *I have to try.*" The two embrace, slowly let go of each other, and Luke heads off to meet their father.

I'd like to suggest that Luke is introducing a new myth to the Jedi religion (and to our own age)—the myth of transformation.[4] He is trusting his own instincts above everything he's been told. He does so even though previously such action almost cost his friends everything they were striving to accomplish. When he spoke with Ben on Dagobah, Luke revealed what he felt in his father. Ben was unconvinced; he too had once felt as Luke did. In this attempt, in contrast with his feeble effort to raise his ship on Dagobah, Luke is more determined, though certainly not completely confident. He is not taking action in response to what anyone told him, but out of his own creative inspiration to attempt to change a difficult situation. Psychologically, we might say that Luke is investigating to what extent a person can be "saved"—recover their lost humanity—when gripped by a power complex. Most importantly Luke has shown that, not only does he have greater abilities—as demonstrated on Tatooine when he defeated Jabba—to use the Force, but he has changed inwardly as well. His goal is no longer to battle and defeat Vader; it is to invite him to return to himself and be transformed in the process.

Leia and Han

As Luke leaves and Leia is by herself with her own thoughts and feelings, Han appears and asks her what is going on. Still trying to absorb everything, she says simply, "Nothing," and that she just wants to be alone for a little while. Understandably she has a lot of emotions to sort out; for many people it is necessary to be alone first, before they can begin to share with someone else what they are experiencing. It is obvious to Han, however, that *something* is going on, and he invites her to tell him. But Leia, still too upset, responds, "I . . . I can't tell you."

Feeling rebuked, Han gets angry, and pointing to where Luke has departed asks, "Did you tell Luke? Is that who you could tell?" Leia is still too overcome by her feelings to reply, and Han becomes frustrated by the apparent rejection and begins to leave. However, he catches himself, turns, and walks back towards her. "I'm sorry," he says.

Leia pulls herself away from the rail of the walkway and goes towards him. "Hold me," she asks. Solo obliges, though he is obviously a little new to this kind of intimacy.

Though but a brief moment, it reveals an important psychological component of the story. For here we see Han's development as a counterpart to Luke's. We see an example of anima development in a relational context, as Han becomes more vulnerable in his feelings for Leia. When he extends himself, he feels jilted by perceived rejection. For a moment a jealousy complex takes over, but he catches himself and offers his heartfelt availability to the woman he is growing closer to emotionally. By doing so she can now find a way to avail herself of his presence. She can't find the words to express herself, but he can help her hold these feelings until she has been able to understand and assimilate them more. Through Han we see extraverted elements of anima development that balance the more introverted ones happening within Luke.

Luke and Vader, Son and Father

Vader's shuttle arrives on the landing platform of the heavily guarded Imperial base. Inside, as Vader enters the facility, he is met by an Imperial detachment with Luke in binders in the forefront. While Luke gazes inside the "mask" of his father, the commander reports his findings to Vader. This rebel surrendered to them, and though he denies it, the commander believes there are more rebels present. He requests permission to conduct a further search of the area. He hands Vader Luke's lightsaber, the only weapon found in his possession. Vader commends the commander on his work, asks that he and Luke be left alone, and orders the commander to conduct his search and bring Luke's companions directly to him.

"The Emperor has been expecting you," Vader tells Luke.

"I know, Father," Luke calmly replies.

"So," Vader exclaims, "you've accepted the truth."

"I've accepted the truth," Luke specifies, "that you were once Anakin Skywalker, my father."

An irritated Vader proclaims, "That name no longer has any meaning for me."

"It is the name of your true self," Luke protests, "You've only forgotten. I know there is good in you. The Emperor hasn't driven it from you fully. That is why you couldn't destroy me. That's why you won't bring me to your Emperor now."

As Luke speaks, his back is to his father. Vader fingers the lightsaber he has been handed, and suddenly ignites it. After a pause, Vader speaks, "I see you have constructed a new lightsaber. Your skills are complete. Indeed, you are powerful, as the Emperor has foreseen."

The lightsaber Luke now carries is his own and of his own making. Previously he had used his father's lightsaber, given to him by Obi-Wan on Tatooine. When Vader severed Luke's hand on the platform at Bespin, he also severed the only connection that Luke had to the father Ben had told him about. Now Luke is trying to make a connection to the living father that he can feel hidden within the masked figure he confronts. He has accepted the truth that his human father resides in there somewhere, and it is only through Luke's perception that we glimpse this possibility. We can't see for ourselves what Luke sees. Vader has discarded his former identity and become captivated by the powers of the Emperor. As Vader extinguishes the lightsaber, Luke invites him to come with him. He offers the opposite invitation that Vader had extended near the end of their duel on Bespin: a relationship foregoing the desire for power. "Obi-Wan once thought as you do," Vader explains, "You don't know the power of the Dark Side. I must obey my master."

"I will not turn," Luke asserts, "and you'll be forced to kill me."

Vader remains unmoved. "If that is your destiny," he replies. A fatalistic response is given, even in the face of moral choice. "It was meant to be," becomes an excuse for destruction, to avoid any examination of personal responsibility.

Luke tries to reach through the power that grips his father. "Search your feelings, Father. You can't do this. I feel the conflict within you. Let go of your hate." The son once more attempts to turn the tables on his father. On Bespin, Vader knew that if Luke searched his feelings, he would know the truth concerning their relationship. Now Luke presses Vader to search his own feelings for the truth about himself and his inner conflicts.

Unfortunately, much as Jabba remained possessed by bitterness and sadistic pleasure, Vader seems unable to release the dark, powerful emotions that bind him, and which in turn keep him bound to the will and purpose of the Emperor. Vader is an extraordinarily powerful and capable man, but still a puppet of another and thus an unrealized human being in his own right. "It is too late for me, son," Vader replies. "The Emperor will show you the true nature of the Force. *He* is your master now."

As Vader signals to stormtroopers to take Luke, their conversation ends with Luke remarking, "Then my father is truly dead." Ben's "point of view," which had been so upsetting to Luke on Dagobah, is now painfully clear. Yes, his father is dead, lost in denial of personal conflicts, filled with anger and hate, and possessed by his own and another's quest for power and domination.

Rebels on the Move

As the shuttle carrying Luke and Vader to the Death Star lifts off from the landing platform, Chewie, Han, and Leia are surveying the Imperial facility with their Ewok scouts. Leia remarks on how heavily guarded the base is, but Han assures her that he and Chewie have gotten through more difficult defenses before. Then Threepio conveys information from the Ewoks indicating that there is a secret entrance on the other side of a nearby ridge.

Meanwhile the rebel fleet has gathered and prepares to head for Endor. Lando assures Admiral Ackbar that all the fighters are accounted for; Ackbar then gives the order to begin the countdown and for all groups to assume the attack coordinates. Lando responds to the anxious concerns of his new alien co-pilot by assuring him that his friends are on the Endor moon and will have the shield down in time ("or," to himself, "this'll be the shortest offensive of all time"). Lando carries one important psychological theme throughout the battle: the belief and trust in friendship as a foundation for handling the vicissitudes of life. Soon Ackbar gives the final order for the fleet's jump to hyperspace, and a multitude of ships of all sizes and shapes heads to Endor.

Back on the forest moon Han, Chewie, Leia, and the squad they lead survey the lightly guarded Imperial bunker to which the Ewok scouts have taken them. As they prepare a strategy to quietly "handle" the few posted guards so as not to sound any alarm, Threepio conveys the disconcerting news that one of the Ewoks has gone off to try something on his own. As they watch the impetuous Ewok scurry on top of one of the parked speeder bikes, they despair at having lost any element of surprise. But somehow the Ewok gets the bike going and speeds off into the forest. All but one of the Imperial scouts pursue him on their bikes, and an entertaining chase ensues. "Not bad for a little fur ball," Han remarks, impressed with the Ewok's ingenuity. Meanwhile, the Ewok finally swings to safety on a forest vine as Han and the squad easily divert the remaining guard. The rebel group gains access to the bunker door controls and stands poised and ready to enter the Imperial facility and fulfill their mission.

Luke Meets the Emperor

Luke and Vader, father and son, arrive at the Emperor's audience chambers and ascend the stairs toward the Emperor. The dark, cloaked figure swivels around in his throne chair and greets Luke. "Welcome, young Skywalker. I have been expecting you." The two stare at each other for a moment and the Emperor, remarking that Luke will no longer need his binders, uses the Force to remove them. Clearly he, too, knows how to manipulate this energy field for his own purposes. He orders his guards to leave the three of them, and the red-cloaked figures silently comply with his command.

"I'm looking forward to completing your training," he tells Luke. "In time you will call *me* Master."

"You're gravely mistaken," Luke calmly responds, "You won't convert me, as you did my father."

The Emperor slowly leaves his seat and walks towards Luke; his evil, cloaked visage glowers into Luke's face. "Oh, no, my young Jedi," he menacingly asserts, "You will find that it is you who are mistaken . . . about . . . a great . . . many . . . things."

Their encounter is more than a battle of wits; it is a struggle over the range of human consciousness. In reality *all* human awareness is limited, even "enlightened" consciousness, and it is important that these limits be recognized and accepted. In truth no one knows fully, as Ben and Yoda asserted on Dagobah, how life will unfold. The struggle between these two major players on the galaxy stage not only revolves around the range of consciousness, but also the very basis for such consciousness. On what aspect of life do they ground their awareness, and from whence do they receive their answers? Is it simply themselves, or something beyond each of them?

In his reply Luke indicates that he will not be "converted," as his father was. At issue here is the nature of the human personality: Can external forces alter the personality, or do such changes have to be generated from within the individual? We have just witnessed a spontaneous "conversion" experience for the Ewoks, a transformation that arose naturally from within them, and through which they discovered a new "god-image" and a new myth. For the Ewoks the catalyst for their conversion was the sudden appearance of Threepio. What made the response to this catalyst so powerful was the *living internal symbolic resonance* that followed. Luke, through his experiences with Ben and Yoda, knows that true conversion must happen spontaneously in such a way; it cannot be imposed on someone. Indoctrination and intimidation do not lead to true transformation.

Vader now hands the Emperor Luke's lightsaber. "A Jedi's weapon," the Emperor notes, "much like your father's. By now," he ominously asserts, "you must know your father can never be turned from the dark side. So will it be with you."

"You're wrong," Luke confidently counters, "Soon I'll be dead . . . and you with me." Obviously, Luke expects to sacrifice himself to enable his friends to complete their mission. Anticipating their success, he believes he will be destroyed along with the Death Star. (Recall that Luke watched Ben make a similar sacrifice on the first Death Star.)

The Emperor laughs at his prediction. "Perhaps you refer to the imminent attack of your rebel fleet. Yes . . . I assure you, we are quite safe from your friends here."

Luke is a little startled but not flustered, "Your overconfidence is your weakness," he succinctly observes.

"Your faith in your friends is yours," the Emperor quickly retorts.

A hitherto quiet Vader adds, "It is pointless to resist, my son."

Vader has given up, as he had indicated to Luke earlier; he is now a subdued bystander. The Jedi awareness in Luke and the Emperor search for each other's weakness and accurately identify where each is vulnerable. An angry, assertive Emperor states, "*Everything* that has transpired has done so according to *my* design. Your friends up there on the Sanctuary Moon"—Luke is a bit startled that the Emperor knows about the squad on the forest moon—"are walking into a trap. As is your fleet! It was I who allowed the Alliance to know the location of the shield generator. It is quite safe from your pitiful little band. An entire legion of my best troops awaits them. Oh . . . I'm afraid the deflector shield will be quite operational when your friends arrive."

We leave Luke with a worried look on his face and our own ponderings as to whether Luke might be right that this evil Emperor's overconfidence is also his weakness.

The Battle for Endor Begins

Han, Leia, Chewie, and the rebel strike team have entered the main control room of the Imperial bunker and gained the upper hand over the personnel. Han urges them to move quickly and Leia too underscores the urgency of their actions by reminding Han that the fleet will be arriving at any minute.

Outside, we watch in dismay with Threepio and Artoo as additional Imperial personnel rush into the bunker. "Oh, my! They'll be captured," Threepio declares. Wicket meanwhile chatters away in his Ewok tongue and then rushes off into the forest. An anxious Threepio, feeling abandoned, whimpers for Artoo to stay with him.

Back inside the bunker dozens of Imperial troops and their officers surround the rebel squad and capture them. There is nothing Han, Leia, and Chewie can do.

Meanwhile the rebel fleet has come out of hyperspace into the Endor system. Lando converses with his copilot, the alien Nien Nunb, about getting a reading on the Death Star's defensive shield. Nunb complains that they can't get a reading on the shield because the Imperials are jamming them. "How could they be jamming us if they don't know if . . . we're coming?" Lando catches what he is saying in mid-sentence and quickly orders that the attack be broken off, announcing that the shield is still up. They all veer off from the course at the Death Star and come face to face with the waiting Imperial fleet, whose fighters immediately begin swarming in. "It's a trap!" Ackbar declares. The Emperor's prediction to Luke is proving to be all too true.

Lando leads his fighters against the attacking Imperial ships to draw their fire away from the rebel cruisers. The battle is off to a terrible start for the rebels.

The View from the Emperor's Throne Room

The Emperor is gloating. "Come, boy," he goads Luke, "see for yourself." Luke moves closer to the throne chair on which the Emperor sits and looks out the large round window situated behind the throne. "From here," the Emperor continues," you will witness the final destruction of the Alliance and the end of your insignificant rebellion."

Luke is now obviously upset and in turmoil. Having no other way to turn, he glances at his lightsaber lying on the armrest of the throne. Displaying his evil grin and touching the lightsaber, the Emperor sadistically delights in Luke's conflict. "You want this, don't you?" he says, "The hate is swelling in you now. Take your Jedi weapon. Use it. I am unarmed. Strike me down with it. Give in to your anger. With each passing moment, you make yourself more my servant."

Luke is desperate. The only thing he has to reach for is his weapon, but as he painfully learned in the Dagobah cave, this is not the solution. The Emperor, with a more subtle and vengeful sadism than Jabba, gloats over Luke's agony. The only feelings Luke can summon now would lead him to act out of the dark side—yet he has no other place to channel them. As he watches everything he believes in face possible annihilation—a destruction that would leave him all alone—he cries out in anguish.

"No!"

"It is unavoidable," the Emperor smugly declares. "It is your destiny. You, like your father, are now mine!"

In psychological terms the Emperor has manipulated Luke to the point where he loses hold of his conscious resolve and falls into a complex filled with anger and hate. Once overwhelmed by these powerful, destructive parts of his emotional life, there won't be any way out. For if he becomes gripped by these emotions, he will simultaneously come under the control of the same man who now commands the services of his father.

The Ewoks Enter the Battle

Back on the forest moon Imperial troops lead Han, Leia, Chewie, and the members of their strike team to the front of the bunker. The area is now surrounded by hundreds of Imperial troops and numerous small-scale Imperial walkers—more agile than they faced on Hoth (two-legged rather than four and only about two stories tall). Their situation looks bleak.

On a forest hill above the clearing in front of the bunker, Threepio, with Artoo at his side, waves to those in the clearing and cheerily calls out, "Hello! I say, over there! Were you looking for me?" The commander orders that the droids be brought down, and a number of stormtroopers climb up the hill to get them. "Well, they're on their way," Threepio confides to his counterpart. "Artoo, are you sure this was a good idea?"

When the troopers arrive Threepio gladly announces their surrender but at the same moment the stormtroopers are jumped by a band of Ewoks and summarily defeated. Clearly the entire Ewok tribe is involved, and the air is soon filled with the sound of Ewok horns calling these devoted creatures to battle. The Imperials are now surrounded by hundreds of Ewoks who attack with their primitive weapons—spears, arrows, slings, ropes, rocks, and catapults. The Imperial troops scatter into the forest on foot, using speeder bikes, and with Imperial walkers. The battle for Endor is on!

Psychologically and symbolically, this is an important development. Because the figure who represents a new sense of divinity to them is threatened, the Ewoks are fighting for their souls, just as Luke, threatened by the Emperor's desire to control him, struggles inside the Death Star to preserve his. The developments on Endor are clearly something the Emperor did not foresee. The positive instinctive element of life (here represented by the Ewoks) fights for freedom and self-expression against the negative inflated and power-driven side.

In the forest the Ewoks meet with some success but also with much frustration, as their attempts to halt Imperial walkers too often prove fruitless. As during the end of *Star Wars: A New Hope*, here the extended battle on Endor and in outer space to conclude *Return of the Jedi* creates an *emotional* experience that helps viewers participate more on the symbolic than the rational level. Any rational prediction that the Ewoks couldn't possibly defeat their Imperial foes misses the symbolic and mythological intent of the battle and the entire story.

As the Ewoks battle Imperials in the forest, Han and Leia are trapped at the entrance to the bunker and struggling to get back inside. They discover that the door's security code has been changed and call, via comlink, for Artoo, who is still on top of the hill with Threepio. The golden droid is not eager to go or have Artoo leave him and pleads to his companion, "Oh, this is no time for heroics. Come *back*!" Once more, the irrepressible Artoo is off to see what he can do to help save the day.

The Battle in Space

The rebel fleet, meanwhile, awaiting the destruction of the Death Star deflector shield, engages Imperial fighters in intense combat. As the battle rages, Lando wonders why only fighters are attacking and what the Imperial Star Destroyers might be waiting for.

On the bridge of the largest Star Destroyer a commander reports to Admiral Piett that they are in attack position. "Hold here," Piett orders. When questioned about why they aren't going to attack, Piett explains that he has direct orders from the Emperor himself. They only need to keep the rebel ships from escaping; the Emperor has something special planned for them.

The answer to what this something "special" might be comes from the Emperor himself as he continues to delight in watching the progress of the battle out in space through the throne room window, with Vader and a horrified Luke also looking on. "As you can see, my young apprentice," the Emperor gloats, "your friends have failed. Now witness the firepower of this fully armed and operational battle station." Once more it is clear that the Emperor has succeeded in misleading the Alliance. Now he orders the Death Star commander to "fire at will." Imperial firing procedures commence, and eventually a giant laser blast from the Death Star completely destroys one of the large rebel cruisers.

"That blast came from the Death Star!" exclaims Lando from his pilot seat on the Millennium Falcon. "That thing's operational!"

This reality is painfully clear to Admiral Ackbar as well, and he gives the order for all craft to prepare to retreat.

"You won't get another chance at this, Admiral," Lando protests.

"We have no choice, General Calrissian," Ackbar replies. "Our cruisers can't repel firepower of that magnitude."

"Han will have that shield down," Lando urges. "We've got to give him more time."

Three important psychological themes are reflected in the fleet's dilemma. One is the fight-or-flight issue that has appeared in earlier parts of the story. What's the best course of action here? Which should they choose? Lando would stay and fight, whereas Ackbar believes that flight is more prudent—given what they have just witnessed.

The second important psychological theme is that of "faith" in one's friends. To what extent can we depend on other people to come through so that joint success can be achieved? On the Death Star the Emperor perceived such faith as Luke's weakness: by attempting to destroy Luke's friends he hopes to exploit this faith to his advantage. Lando, who was the moral compass that turned the direction of the adventures on Bespin, is now the character carrying the banner for such faith. He suggests that in this particular circumstance, belief that Han will come through should supersede the inclination to flee that Ackbar would choose in the face of a fully operational Death Star.

The third psychological element of importance is the theme of *more time*. On Dagobah Yoda taught Luke that the dark side was "quicker, easier, more seductive." Working together with others often requires a patience that allows a given situation time to unfold and develop. Trusting in the more vital aspects of life, as symbolized by the terrain on both Dagobah and Endor, takes time and patience, a "wait and see" attitude. That is what Lando lobbies for now: that they wait and see.

Meanwhile, back at the Imperial bunker on Endor, Artoo arrives with Threepio reluctantly in tow and plugs himself into the door's computer terminal. As he does so an Imperial stormtrooper hits him with a laser blast that sends him reeling and completely short-circuits him. Threepio laments, "Artoo, why did you have to be so brave?" and a dismayed Han Solo prepares to try and hotwire the door's electronic panels as Leia offers to cover for him. The little droid hero from the Bespin escape won't carry the day this time, and Han will definitely need more time if he is to succeed.

Elsewhere on Endor the Ewoks battle courageously and with some success, but their efforts prove largely ineffective against the Imperial walkers. A blast in the woods sends two Ewoks to the ground. One gets up and tries to awaken the other. Sadly realizing that his companion is dead, he slumps in mourning.

The battle in space is also looking desperate for the rebels as a second blast from the Death Star destroys another one of their large ships. Lando urges them to move in closer to the Star Destroyers to engage them at point-blank range and avoid the Death Star's devastating weapon. When Ackbar objects that they won't last long against the Star Destroyers at such close range, Lando responds that they'll last longer than going up against the Death Star—and maybe take a few of the enemy ships with them. The fight for life hangs precariously close to being a dance to the death as more rebel fighters are lost in the battle.

Pushed to the Breaking Point by the Evil Emperor

Luke peers out in disbelief at the battle scene. The Emperor articulates his dismal view of the proceedings. "Your fleet has lost. And your friends on the Endor moon will not survive. There is no escape, my young apprentice. The Alliance will die . . . as will your friends." The Emperor boasts over the battle scene and his belief that he has accomplished total demoralization of Luke. As things look now, Luke will be all alone and the friends he has relied on since his journey began will no longer be available.

Luke's face is flushed with rage as Vader stands and watches. Luke obviously detests with all his being this evil Emperor and what he is doing. He would like nothing better than to strike him down right then and there, to destroy him as he has destroyed so many others. Yet this is just what the hideous Emperor wants him to do! "Good," he exults, "I can feel your anger. I am defenseless. Take your weapon! Strike me down with all your hatred, and your journey toward the dark side will be complete." As he becomes increasingly enraged, Luke is taunted to become more like the Emperor and Vader—to be possessed by these powerful dark impulses and thus lost to his own humanity.

It works. Luke can resist no longer. His aggressive feelings take hold and, using the Force, he snatches his lightsaber up into his hand, ignites it, and lashes down at the Emperor seated in front of him. Vader's lightsaber immediately appears to block Luke's blow and defend his master. The Emperor laughs in glee at what has transpired, relishing all the more his success at manipulating Luke. Once again, Luke has "lost his head" and fallen into the grip of a powerful complex—but worse, he may have lost himself this time. And, as we have seen, the battle situations on Endor and in surrounding space also look very bleak. Has the Emperor won? Can *anything* turn things around? This is the most dismal moment of the entire story.

Surprising Developments on the Endor Moon

Back on Endor, Chewbacca and two Ewoks make their way through the forest and come up behind one of the Imperial walkers. Using a vine to swing across the terrain, they manage to land on top of the Imperial armored vehicle. One of the Ewoks draws the attention of the driver through the front window, and the driver immediately sends his partner up to get the little creature off the roof. The Imperial soldier is no match for Chewbacca, however, and soon Chewie and the Ewoks have gained control of the vehicle. This is both the dramatic and symbolic turning point in the story.

Despite the enthusiastic efforts of the Ewoks, they were no match for the technology turned against them, especially these large mechanical vehicles—which, just like playground bullies, can "walk all over them." Now these two species (Wookie and Ewok), representing nature and instinct, are *inside* this cold steel walker and can use it for *their* own purposes. Chewbacca, a mechanic and pilot, represents a balance between instinct, the wild man, and technology. He now brings this balance to his Ewok friends in a way in which they can use it against their enemies. Their captured Imperial vehicle soon destroys a walker manned by the Empire, the other Ewoks are quickly re-energized, and the battle on Endor begins to turn.

Originally, George Lucas envisioned the final battle as involving Wookies, then later "cut them in half" to create Ewoks.[5] (A seminar participant in one of my lectures noted that the word *E-wok* reverses the syllables for the word *Wook-ie.*)[6] These additional creatures add to the symbolic texture of the films—they convey a family and societal element to the wild man symbolism (see Figure 2)—and bring a more spontaneous, childlike feeling to the drama on Endor. Thus Chewbacca brings something to them, and they to him.

Spurred by the success of Chewbacca and their two fellow Ewoks, the Ewoks on the ground become much more ingenious and determined in their efforts. A playful cleverness is expressed more fully in a community that is fighting hard together. For instance, by rolling a stack of large logs down a hill onto a passing Imperial walker, they force the walker to lose balance, stumble, and fall. It is a comedic moment that evokes delight. The Ewoks are finding their own ways to defeat the technological Imperial menace. When we left Luke, he was in the grip of his own anger in the contaminated atmosphere of the Emperor's throne room. Positive emotions can also be contagious, as is demonstrated on Endor through the increased enthusiasm the Ewoks bring to the battle.

Meanwhile, Han finally believes he has finished his hot-wiring job but then discovers that he has mistakenly rigged the controls to close a second door, not open the one that blocks their way! As he resumes work, a stormtrooper's laser blast wounds Leia on the shoulder. Han rushes to tend to her and she assures him that it's not serious. Suddenly, a stormtrooper shouts: "Freeze!" With his back to the two stormtroopers who have arrived on the scene, Han smiles as he eyes the blaster Leia holds in front of her. "I love you," he declares as they look into each other's eyes for a moment. "I know," she replies with a sly grin, echoing their exchange when Han was about to be put in carbonite on Bespin. For the first time Han openly admits his feelings for Leia, and she reciprocates using his tongue-in-cheek style. Then she quickly dispenses with the two stormtroopers, taking the necessary action to ward off the threat of their enemy. (Recall that Leia also initiated their escape through the garbage chute on the first Death Star.)

As the Ewoks in the forest become more resourceful, Han and Leia find further mutuality in their relationship. There is no time to relish either, though, for just as Han gets up, an Imperial walker approaches. Han urges Leia to stay back in a safe corner. When the hatch of the walker pops open, all are surprised—and relieved—to see that it is Chewie who is inside. Pausing for a moment to ponder how to best utilize Chewie's arrival, Han exclaims, "I've got an idea!" Inspiration is catching. First Chewie, then the Ewoks, and now Han—everyone is getting more energized.

The Father and Son Duel

Luke battles Vader aggressively and with more confidence than he did on Bespin. He sends Vader somersaulting down the stairs that lead up to the throne room. The Emperor is obviously delighted to see father and son engaged in mortal combat. "Good," he declares, "use your aggressive feelings, boy! Let the hate flow through you." Now that he has succeeded in stirring up these dark responses, he adds further "fuel" to Luke's "fire."

Luke, however, regains control of his rageful and vengeful reactions. He catches his breath and turns off his lightsaber. "Obi-Wan has taught you well," Vader asserts (oblivious, it seems, to Yoda's role).

"I will not fight you, Father," Luke replies.

Vader ascends the stairs. "You are unwise to lower your defenses," he warns as he launches another attack.

Luke quickly parries the blow, proving himself quite able to stand up to Vader's assaults. Suddenly Luke does a reverse somersault up onto a catwalk and addresses Vader, still standing below. "Your thoughts betray you, Father," he says with a glimmer of hope in his eye. "I feel the good in you . . . the conflict."

"There is no conflict," Vader quickly asserts.

Luke, with simple yet unyielding clarity, tells Vader that he can sense the tension of ambivalence within the dark Jedi who was once his father: the pull inside him to do good, and not evil. If Vader could consciously acknowledge the reality of this inner battle, he would be able to make a choice for himself. Without conscious awareness of this internal disharmony, however, he remains possessed by the greed to "have it all."

This is an important psychological insight that Luke introduces to Vader and to all of us. If we can consciously own our warring emotions and admit how they pull us in different directions, we can make choices that do not cause harm to others. If we ignore or deny these internal conflicts and the painful feelings that are involved, as Vader does, then we are more likely to fall sway to the destructive ones.

Once more, as he did at the Imperial base on Endor, Luke takes a chance with his father. "You couldn't bring yourself to kill me before," he says, "and I don't believe you'll destroy me now."

"You underestimate the power of the dark side," Vader insists. "If you will not fight, then you will meet your destiny." He hurls his ignited lightsaber at the catwalk on which Luke stands, severing some of the supports holding up the structure. Off to the side Luke slides down to the ground and disappears out of sight amidst many flying sparks. Vader searches for Luke.

"Good, good," the Emperor declares through his sadistic laugh. Obviously he cares only for the battle and the hatred that he can provoke. It is of no concern to him whether father or son wins. He simply wants to control the survivor as the one with the greater power. If one does not serve the Emperor's desires, "destiny" is equated solely with death—not with one's innate purpose in life. Vader demonstrates how possession by the dark side moves one to act destructively even towards his own son, his own "flesh and blood."

The Outside Battle for Endor

While Luke struggles to stay aligned with the integrity of his own soul and to bring his father back to the good side, the spaceship battle around Endor rages on. For the time being, the rebel forces are holding their own. Lando expresses the hope they are clinging to while fighting when he says, "Come on, Han, old buddy. Don't let me down." However, it's clear that they cannot continue fighting under these circumstances forever.

Meanwhile, Han has instigated a clever ruse. Using the radio on the Imperial walker that Chewie and the Ewoks captured, he tells the Imperial commander inside the bunker that the rebels have been routed and are fleeing into the woods, and he requests more reinforcements to continue the pursuit. A delighted Imperial officer orders three squads to be sent out the back door to help.

As the Imperial troops rush out the bunker door, they find themselves surrounded by rebel troops and Ewoks and have no choice but to surrender. Han and Chewie rush inside with the rebel squad and are soon setting up the charges that will blow up the energy shield.

Luke and Vader: Their Last Battle

With ignited lightsaber in hand Vader continues searching for Luke, who remains hidden in the area below the Emperor's throne. "You cannot hide forever, Luke," he taunts.

"I will not fight you," Luke insists.

"Give yourself to the Dark Side," Vader persists. "It is the only way you can save your friends." First, the Emperor preyed on Luke's personal vulnerability of losing his friends. Now Vader toys with Luke's concern over the well-being of those he cares most deeply about, suggesting that turning to the dark side is the only way he can save them. (Recall that Tarkin tried a similar ploy with Leia to get the information he wanted in *A New Hope*.)

The Jedi awareness that Luke used to try to get his father to look more honestly at himself is now used against him, as Vader turns his Force-enhanced focus to Luke. Vader's unvoiced thoughts betrayed the literal and symbolic mask he wears; he's actually a human being with human conflicts—though he completely denies any ambivalence. Luke's unspoken thoughts reveal his core feelings, not only making him more vulnerable but also exposing those he cares for most deeply to perilous danger.

Vader mocks Luke, "Yes, your thoughts betray you. Your feelings for them [his friends] are strong. Especially for . . ." Vader senses he is on to something, an even more sensitive area of Luke's feelings. Luke tries to shut his mind and heart tight to the probing of Vader's Jedi awareness. But it's no use. "Sister!" Vader proclaims, "So . . . you have a twin sister. Your feelings have now betrayed her, too. Obi-Wan was wise to hide her from me. Now his failure is complete. If you will not turn to the dark side, then perhaps *she will.*"

This sinister threat to his sister combined with Vader's disparagement of his first mentor is too much for Luke to bear. "Noooo!" he shouts as he springs forth in a fury, pressing the attack with his ignited lightsaber. The most vulnerable spot in Luke's soul has been touched and he charges forward with a ferocity that we have not seen in him before. Relentlessly he drives Vader back as the sparks fly from their battling lightsabers. Vader stumbles on a walkway and falls against the railing; Luke presses his advantage, flailing away with his own weapon. In his frenzy he severs the hand of his adversary, revealing a bionic stump. He has dismembered his father as his father had done to him in their battle on the catwalk on Bespin.

The Emperor is sadistically delighted with the proceedings. "Good!" he says as he comes down from the throne area to the battle scene. "Your hate has made your powerful," he smugly tells Luke. "Now, fulfill your destiny and take your father's place at my side!" The Emperor's only interest is in his own greedy glee at controlling the life of the more powerful of the two Jedi. It means nothing to him if father destroys son or son destroys father.

Luke stands still, in a moment of shock, slowly realizing how much he has become filled with rage. He glances at his own gloved bionic hand, and then at the stump that remains of his father's. Clearly giving in to his rage is making him more like the man who was lost to him as a father so long ago. Pulling himself together, he switches off his lightsaber and stands to face the Emperor. "Never!" Luke proclaims, throwing the lightsaber handle off to the side. "I'll never turn to the Dark Side," he declares still catching his breath. "You've failed, Your Highness. I am a Jedi, like my father before me."

Luke has succeeded in holding on to his humanity despite the threat posed to his sister and to his own soul; he will serve the Force and not be taken over by yearnings for an easy and alluring path toward power, dominion, and destruction. The delight the Emperor showed at Luke's hateful eruption leaves his face, replaced by angry disappointment. "So be it . . . Jedi," he replies in scathing denigration, adding a bitter "Amen" to Luke's courageous decision, acknowledging the fact that Luke has truly become a Jedi and will remain one.

Completion of the Endor Mission

Just at the moment Luke makes the bold decision that aligns all of himself with the Force, staying centered in a larger wholeness in which he is connected to all life forms, as Yoda had instructed, Han comes rushing out of the Imperial bunker on the Endor moon, urging his companions to stand clear. As he does so, an explosion erupts inside, followed by the total destruction of the huge shield-generator dish that had provided the defense for the Death Star. Precisely when Luke successfully renounces the Emperor's efforts to turn him to the dark side, the external defenses that the Emperor had thought impregnable are destroyed. This is a highly synchronistic event similar to the timely arrival of Han Solo on Hoth, just as Luke's vision of Ben faded and he collapsed in the snow. An inner event—Luke preserving his personal integrity—corresponds in time to an outer triumph.

Noting quickly that the energy shield is down, Admiral Ackbar orders the attack on the Death Star's main reactor, which is its main source of power. The rebels can now attempt to complete their original battle plan. Lando rallies the fighters for the attack and leads the way, delighting that his faith in his friend has panned out. "Told you they'd do it," he exclaims.

The Emperor's Final Retaliation

Though the Emperor has accepted the fact that Luke will remain a Jedi, he is not done with him. No one else can have the last word with someone so gripped by power and control. "If you will not be turned," the Emperor declares, slowing raising his arms towards Luke, "you will be destroyed!" Electric bolts of energy flash from the Emperor's hands and quickly encircle Luke, catapulting him to the floor writhing in pain. Slowly the wounded Vader rises to stand beside his evil master.

"Young fool," the Emperor waxes on, "only now, at the end, do you understand." More discharges of electric energy—released with increasing sadistic pleasure—course through Luke's body, leaving him in unbearable pain. "Your feeble skills are no match for the power of the dark side," the Emperor pontificates. "You have paid the price for your lack of vision." More painful energy jolts sear through Luke as if the Emperor were trying to brand his vision into Luke's very cells.

Luke's lack of vision is, of course, due to the fact that he does not share the Emperor's outlook on life. For such a despot there can be no other viewpoints. As upset as Yoda had been that Luke had followed through with his desire to help his friends, Yoda did not discount or discredit Luke's need to follow his own inner counsel. It was a noble effort, as it turned out, that enabled Luke to complete most of the remaining work involved in becoming a Jedi. Ultimately each person must find his or her own destiny by responding to the vision that comes from within, not that which someone else imposes. The Emperor is so enraged by Luke's choice that he has become intent on destroying Luke, oblivious to the fact that his own so-called vision—his arrogant certainty of victory on Endor—has begun to crumble all around him.

The fact that the Emperor discharges all his rage and anger through electrifying bolts of energy symbolizes his loss of his own humanity and his total identification with the dark side of the archetypal masculine energy seen in such mythological figures as Zeus, Yahweh, and Odin. People who have suffered physical abuse will sometimes dream of being attacked by such bolts of electrical energy, as if the perpetrator were simply discharging energy at the victim's expense rather than finding outlets for it that did not harm others.

In his pain Luke seems hopelessly lost. "Father, please," he cries out, "help me." Vader stands motionless; the helmeted-visage turns to look at his son writhing in agony on the floor and then toward the sadistic, vengeful Emperor discharging the intense energy bolts into Luke. Subsequently Vader turns back to look at his son squirming in horrifying spasms that may bring him close to death. Having become a Jedi, will Luke now die as one?

The Emperor, as much as he seems to have enjoyed making Luke suffer, now grows tired of this horrific game. "Now, young Skywalker," he announces to Luke, "you will die." He resumes his deadly attack with even greater ferocity, and Luke groans in agony. Again Vader watches helplessly, glancing first at Luke, then at his master, and then his son once more. How can he just stand there? Is he truly merely his master's servant? Electric charges of energy fly out of the Emperor's hands, searing the helpless Luke who writhes even more wildly in agony and pain . . . and still Vader watches. Suddenly, as if a light had been switched on inside him, Vader turns towards the raging Emperor, grabs a hold of him, lifts him over his head, and throws him down the deep abyss at the central core of the throne room. A screaming Emperor, with energy bolts still firing out all around him, tumults to the bottom, whereupon there is a violent explosion. At the top of the deep tunnel, where the explosion's effects shake the very walls, Vader hangs by the rail gasping for air, wheezing heavily. As he grabbed and then hurled the Emperor, energy bolts encompassed him. He took on all the power that was being directed at Luke until he had mustered the strength to eradicate the enraged Emperor once and for all. Luke slowly recovers from his ordeal, relieved of the violent assaults of energy by his father's intervention, and slowly moves towards the dark-cloaked, helmeted figure struggling now to breathe. Luke holds his father in his arms.

Literally and symbolically Darth Vader has now become Luke's personal father. He has mediated powerful psychic energy that threatened to overwhelm his son so that his son could survive and come back to himself. In doing so Vader has broken the hold of the evil, power-mad Emperor. Only Luke believed that the Emperor had not succeeded in banishing all traces of humanity from his father. Just as Han Solo has justified Lando's faith in him, Darth Vader has gone through an even more dramatic transformation that now legitimizes Luke's feelings that the good in his father was still reachable. Anakin Skywalker, father of Luke Skywalker, made himself into a living lightsaber to come to his son's defense. Now his son embraces him in his pain.

Transformation Through Fire

The demise of the Emperor is one of a number of images of *calcinatio*, the alchemical process of transformation through fire, which occurs at the end of this film.[7] The Emperor is so completely identified with the pulse of the power principle that the energy he represents must be returned to the source from whence it came. In Tolkien's fantasy trilogy *The Lord of the Rings* the ring of power must be similarly disposed off—returned to the fires that forged it. By throwing the Emperor into the power core of the Death Star, Vader succeeds in freeing Luke from destructive attack and himself from unconscious identification with the dark side of himself.

The Emperor must undergo the process of *calcinatio* because he cannot comprehend any reason to change himself in any way. He is completely content to be identified with the power motive and the blatant, arbitrary use of authority. This theme also occurs in Lucas's first Indiana Jones adventure film *Raiders of the Lost Ark,* when the malevolent archaeologist and the Nazis act on their power motives and open the ark; they are swiftly overwhelmed and destroyed by the energies that *they* have released and sought to possess.

Luke also has endured a *calcinatio* experience while being helplessly seared by the Emperor's electric discharges. By standing up to the Emperor, he became the recipient of all the Emperor's primitive rage (fire). But because Luke confronted the Emperor while maintaining proper attitude toward the Force to which he was attuned, something changes at the last minute (in this case, in Vader) and Luke is rescued from what would have been certain death.[8] A similar theme is found in the Hebrew Bible when the Babylonian King Nebuchadnezzar decrees that everyone must worship a giant gold statue he has erected. Anyone who refuses will be thrown into a furnace of blazing fire. When three Hebrew officials refuse, the furious Nebuchadnezzar orders the furnace heated even hotter and the three men thrown in. The heat of the furnace was so intense it destroyed those who threw the Hebrews into it. A fourth figure appeared in the furnace and they were not harmed in any way. They were able to walk out freely and the king himself paid homage to their divine protector.[9]

Another *calcinatio* experience, as we shall see, will involve Lando and the Millennium Falcon. Once the Imperial energy shield protecting the Death Star is destroyed, Lando leads the rebel fighters in an attack on the Death Star. Their target is the power generator, the largest power source running the giant space station. In their first penetration into the battle station's superstructure, a few Imperial and rebel fighters are incinerated in the pursuit. Frustrated by this initial attempt, Lando and Wedge, who is flying nearby in his X-wing, split off from the others and try again. The Millennium Falcon, which Han had been so concerned about before they left for Endor, has a close call as its roof bangs up against the space station's superstructure.

Meanwhile Ackbar, wanting to give the fighters attacking the Death Star more time, orders the rebel fleet to concentrate its fire on the largest Imperial Star Destroyer—the ship commanded by Piett that Vader used. They succeed in knocking out the ship's bridge deflector shield and before the Imperial crew can make necessary adjustments, a damaged rebel fighter, flying completely out of control, crashes through the bridge. The giant battleship also loses control and crashes into the Death Star, igniting an enormous explosion. The Super Star Destroyer and its crew suffer the same *calcinatio* experience as the Emperor.

During this time, as personnel now scurry in all directions on the Death Star, Luke drags the heavy and weakened body of his father towards the ramp of an Imperial shuttle. He pauses to rest from his efforts at the foot of the ramp and gently lays his father down. Vader slowly raises his head. "Luke," he rasps, "help me take my mask off."

"But you'll die," a concerned Luke replies.

"Nothing can stop that now," Vader confides. "Just for once . . . let me look on you with *my own* eyes." Hesitantly, Luke carefully removes the helmet cover and the facemask that have shrouded his father. A very scarred yet extraordinarily human face graciously smiles back at Luke. Then, as if that was all he needed, he orders, "Now . . . go, my son. Leave me."

The unmasking of Darth Vader is a very powerful symbolic moment. We all wear "masks" out in the world—we cannot reveal everything about ourselves to everyone. Jung called this aspect of the personality the *persona*. The persona can be authentically connected to who we are, or, at the other extreme, it can be completely disassociated from one's true personality. Darth Vader epitomizes the latter; now, having saved his son from a terrible death, he longs to see his son, not as the Emperor saw Luke—as a pawn in his quest for power—or through the mask that had come to signify his own seduction to the Dark Side, but through his human eyes.

To allow oneself to be truly "seen" makes one more vulnerable, for it is not possible to always hide behind a mask of any kind. To those who are completely identified with a false self presented by a psychological mask, losing it feels like death. Vader now faces his own death, his own mortality. He realizes that living inside such a mask has left him cut off from genuine contact with others. This is something he will not let himself miss now—but, like many people who open themselves up to a new level of intimacy, the first glimmer of it is all they believe they deserve or feel they can tolerate. Vader, having abandoned his son for so long, now requests that his son leave him.

Luke, however, won't hear of it. "No," he replies. "You're coming with me. I can't leave you here. I've got to *save* you."

In a surprising and profound response, Luke's father, Anakin Skywalker, assures him "You already have, Luke. You were right. You were right about me. Tell your sister . . . you were right." Luke's belief, which was part perception and part hope—that there was still good in Darth Vader and that he could thus be turned to the Good Side, back to his true human self—eventually led to the transformation of evil energies. It was not Luke's ability with his lightsaber that saved the day but his trust in human transformation and his perceptive use of the Force.

Acknowledging the truth of Luke's insight and its transformative effect, Anakin Skywalker dies in Luke's arms even as Luke tries to assure his father, "I won't leave you." Luke bows his head in grief over the body of his now deceased father. During the course of his journey, which began when he discovered the remains of his uncle and aunt back on their Tatooine moisture farm, Luke has also lost Ben, Yoda, and now his father. Symbolically he has become the healing agent of a split spiritual legacy—one split between good and evil and thus one fighting itself.

True to his promise not to leave his father, Luke begins to carry Vader/Anakin's body up the shuttle ramp. Suddenly, chaos is all around him as explosions rock the docking bay.

Meanwhile Lando and Wedge have found the main reactor within the core of the Death Star and, still pursued by Imperial fighters, initiate their attack. Lando instructs Wedge to target a power regulator as he guns for the main reactor. Both score direct hits and then proceed to race out of the space station, trying to stay ahead of the explosion raging behind them. Out in space Ackbar orders the fleet to move away from the exploding Death Star; in the docking bay, Luke pilots the Imperial shuttle free just as the structure collapses behind him. Wedge, who flies ahead of the Millennium Falcon, escapes from the Death Star inferno, but the Imperial fighter directly behind the Millennium Falcon becomes consumed in flames.

Will the Falcon—the ship Han feared he would never see again—make it? As the fireball reaches the edge of the battle station, the Millennium Falcon is jettisoned into the void of space outside, and Lando gives a jubilant cry of relief. The energy released from the exploding Death Star expands in a great circle through space, and the hate that had gone into creating it now turns into the joy and jubilation of the successful rebels. Lando's cry announces a new birth by fire, both for himself and the ship he pilots, further symbolism for a new age we first discussed in reflections on *A New Hope.*

Final Resolutions on Endor

After Luke and Lando's successful escape from the Death Star explosion, the final scene shifts to the forest moon of Endor. "They did it," Threepio exults in the company of Han, Leia, Chewie, other rebels, and the Ewoks. The heroic group watches the explosion high in space above them.

Han's face expresses sudden concern as Leia continues to glance into space but with her attention clearly turned inward. "I'm sure Luke wasn't on that thing when it blew," he tries to assure her—and himself.

"He wasn't," she calmly announces, "I can feel it." (She has now linked her perception into the unseen reaches of the Force.)

"You love him," a suddenly concerned Solo inquires, "don't you?"

A bit puzzled, Leia smiles. "Yes," she clearly acknowledges.

"All right. I understand. Fine," a disappointed Han replies. "When he comes back, I won't get in the way."

"Oh. No, it's not like that at all," a gently amused Leia responds as she realizes Han's misperception. "He's my brother," she reassures him.

Han is at first stunned, then delighted. He understands some of the mystery of the previous night when Leia had been unable to communicate, but most importantly his declaration of selflessness in the context of his relationship with Leia is rewarded.

Solo has taken a significant step by revealing his vulnerable feelings to Leia, and when he fears that they might not be reciprocated, he does not resort to angry outbursts or negative responses of any kind—as often happens in such circumstances. If she feels differently than he, he will accept that she has feelings for someone else, as painful as it is—clearly indicating that it is Leia for whom he truly cares. He will not try to interfere if the feelings are not mutual.

Leia's clarification to Han that Luke is her brother and not a personal love interest, as Han fears he is, helps the story delineate two important aspects of a man's anima development. The first aspect is represented by Han's newly attained ability to share intimate love with a woman in an open way that is reciprocated. Neither is coerced into the relationship or driven by a complex to become so involved. In fact, both Han and Leia each had to face and overcome complexes that precluded deep involvement, as we saw throughout the movies.

The second aspect of anima development is contained in Luke's discovery that Leia is not only his sister but also his equal in every way, including spiritually. When a man reaches a certain stage of emotional development, he can experience women as equals on all levels, no longer devaluing them as sexual objects (as was symbolized by Jabba the Hutt), or as pawns to be dominated (as symbolized by the Emperor). Han and Luke represent two parallel modes in which a man can relate to a woman in a healthy way—modes that move far beyond our patriarchal "legacy."

With matters cleared up for Han as to how Leia is related to Luke, he kisses her and they hold each other, only to be interrupted in their intimate moment by a jubilant Wicket. Even as they celebrate their personal relationship, a larger celebration is in the making.

With twilight approaching we find Luke standing solemnly by the funeral pyre of his father, where he ignites a blaze with the torch he holds. Flames consume the body, dressed in the helmet and clothes of Darth Vader, as fireworks burst in the sky above and small spaceships speed overhead. The funeral pyre of Darth Vader/Anakin Skywalker is another important *calcinatio* image.

Ben and Yoda passed easily into the Force when they died, but it seems that because Anakin Skywalker assumed an identity that was so far from who he truly was, the trappings associated with his one-sided, archetypal identification must be purged. Here the *calcinatio* process offers a purification and restoration, as Anakin Skywalker is cleansed of the trappings of ruthlessness and power with which he had become so identified. Such a psychological process allows the individual to experience more vividly his or her own true state.[10] As we glimpse Luke's final act on behalf of his father, the jubilant celebration on Endor commences.

Revelations of Joy

The liberation of the energy that had been harnessed for destructive purposes now brings forth an outburst of joy and jubilation. Begun with Ewok drumming, the festivities on Endor center on the celebration of those who have worked together in death-defying defense of their galaxy. Fireworks in the sky and fires in the Ewok village celebrate what they have accomplished on a deeper level: using life's vital energies constructively and in conjunction with other animate elements of the universe.

In the Special Edition Lucas extends the celebration on the Endor moon to sites throughout the galaxy. For me, this is the most important psychological dimension added to the original movies. Joy and religious ecstasy expressed on a natural level, a joy that must be shared with others to be most deeply felt (as symbolized by the Ewoks), is the counterpart to the drive to power.[11] The sadistic pleasures of Jabba and the Emperor, who experienced joy only through the suffering of others, are the dark backdrop for this exuberant finale of love and fellowship.

In the Special Edition it is clear that the celebration on Endor is felt far and wide: on Bespin, where the Empire had tried to trap Luke and where Lando joined the rebel cause; on Tatooine, where Luke's journey began and where he rescued Han from Jabba; and on the galaxy's capital planet of Coruscant (not actually mentioned in the films, but sure to be seen in the prequels), where a giant statue of the Emperor is toppled. The festivities at each of these sites are reminiscent of our New Year's Eve rites.

On Endor there are many touching reunions as those who fought in space join those who fought on the Endor moon. Lando hugs Han and Chewie, Luke and Leia embrace, Luke and Han, Luke and Wedge, and Han and Leia. The droids are also active in the great celebration, as are the effervescent Ewoks, who quintessentially convey the exuberance of the galactic triumph. The music added to this ending sequence also enhances the feeling quality of the finale by combining the grandeur of symphonic themes with the playful antics of instruments that evoke Ewok sensibility. The utter release of feeling that comes through good will and freedom from destructive power is conveyed more fully in the ineffable rhythms of the music.

Amidst the final celebration, Luke steps off to the side where he has a vision. His father Anakin Skywalker, Yoda, and Obi-Wan are all luminous beings who convey genuine pride in what Luke has accomplished. Most importantly Anakin Skywalker, much like Ben

Kenobi, appears in the garb of a Jedi knight; there is no sign of his Darth Vader identity.

In the first film Darth Vader appeared as an evil villain, juxtaposed against the feisty, but cornered, princess dressed all in white. He seemed the personification of evil. Later on Bespin, to the shock of Luke and everyone, he reveals that he is Luke's father. How could such a dark figure be the human father to anyone? Finally, at the end it is revealed that he is truly a human being, one who had become lost in a powerful and destructive archetypal identification. Through the efforts of his son he is "saved" from this identification.

Lucas has indicated that his movie trilogy is really about the *redemption* of Anakin Skywalker.[12] Psychologically, I would suggest that the story is about redemption from identification with archetypal energies, especially destructive ones, which can cause the loss of our humanity. These archetypal energies are expressed in our myths, both old and new. To fail to recognize them for what they are and to identify with them is to lose one's soul. When this happens, as this story demonstrates, we need the help of others—as well as a conscious understanding of the nature of the transformation of archetypal energy—so that lost aspects of the human personality can be restored.

Luke's final vision suggests that he has succeeded in healing wounds that have been carried forward from the past, in particular Ben and Yoda's loss of Anakin Skywalker to the dark practitioners of the Force. This task of redemption is completed. Significantly it is Leia, the central feminine figure, who comes to pull Luke back to the celebration and to the whole group—a group symbolically representative of one complete personality; a group connected to a galaxy of which Luke is still very much a part, and which now must look forward to the future.

Luke's vision contains a masculine trinity, symbolism we discussed in Chapter 4. In our age this symbolism reflects an old dominant religious image that is now shifting. Leia's original rescue from the Death Star by Luke, Han, and Chewie created a new feminine fourth. Now Leia steps forward to invite Luke back to the celebration and to what may lie ahead for all of them. The film ends with the theme that initially awakened the young hero: a beckoning of the feminine principle to enter a new age—an invitation to go forward in life in conjunction with the transformation of problems held over from the past. This brother-sister pair and their companions become new symbols for the future.

CHAPTER 12

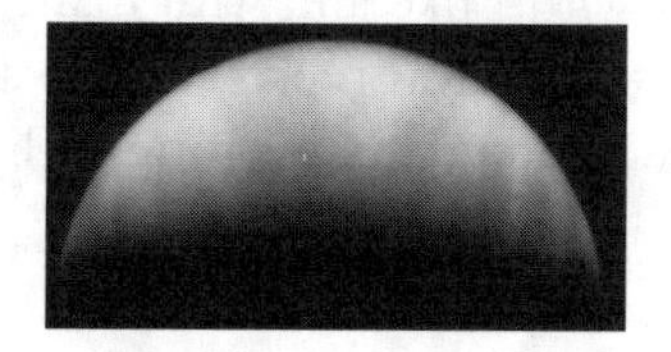

Final Thoughts: Why the Force Is Still with Us

Jung provides an incisive summary of what has been called "the religious function of the psyche":

> The religious myth is one of man's greatest and most significant achievements, giving him the security and inner strength not to be crushed by the monstrousness of the universe. Considered from the standpoint of realism, the symbol is not of course an external truth, but it is psychologically true, for it was and is the bridge to all that is best in humanity.[1]

Jung's statement suggests an answer to the question posed by the journalist quoted in the Introduction to this commentary on the first *Star Wars* trilogy: "Why is the Force still with us?" For one thing, the Force is still with us because we still need religious myths and stories, especially those of us who no longer find satisfactory meaning in the old stories and hunger for something more. Another reason that the Force is still with us is that the world in which Lucas sets his story offers a "realism" more advanced than our own, since it encompasses a technology far more evolved than ours. People can receive these movies' religious myth—that of the Jedi—because they believe it as a "technological myth."

It also my experience that many people today, both men and women, identify with Luke and with many of the other characters, either in a direct way or as representing various parts of themselves. Consider these comments by Jung in light of Luke's entire journey:

> . . . we are still swamped [compare Dagobah] with projected illusions. If you imagine someone who is brave enough to withdraw all these projections [Luke's challenge in the cave], then you get an individual who is conscious of a pretty thick shadow. Such a person is saddled with new problems and conflicts [Luke's journey became even more challenging] . . . Such a man knows that whatever is wrong in the world is in himself, and if he only learns to deal with his own shadow he has done something real for the world. He has succeeded in shouldering at least an infinitesimal part of the gigantic, unresolved social problems of our day.[2]

Luke's redemption of Anakin Skywalker, the father from whom he had become totally disconnected, can be seen in this light. In psychological terms to be a Jedi means to guard against being possessed by power, greed, lust, and other primal impulses and to work for individual human transformation, not just in society, but within one's personal life as well. Men (Luke) and women (Leia) have the same ability to work towards this noble goal.

What started out as purely a mythological adventure—a princess, an evil villain, a young innocent hero—evolved into a family affair. Archetypal dramas are lived out not just in history or myths; they are enacted in the psychology of individual personalities and family units. Jung noted:

> The collective unconscious—so far as we can say anything about it at all—appears to consist of mythological motifs or primordial images, for which reason the myths of all nations are its real exponents . . . We can therefore study the collective unconscious in two ways, either in mythology or in the analysis of the individual.[3]

Lucas's story uniquely blends these two elements, though, obviously, it is more heavily weighted on the mythological side. Yet it offers enough individual psychology so that many viewers experience aspects of themselves through this drama.

It is important to note the limits of any single approach, including a Jungian approach, and to do this I would once more quote Jung:

> The psyche, as a reflection of the world and man, is a thing of such infinite complexity that it can be observed and studied from a great many sides. It faces us with the same problem that the world does: because a systematic study of the world is beyond our powers, we have to content ourselves with mere rules of thumb and with aspects that particularly interest us. Everyone makes for himself his own segment of world and constructs his own private system, often with air-tight compartments, so that after a time it seems to him that he has grasped the meaning and structure of the whole. But the finite will never be able to grasp the infinite.[4]

Thus a Jungian approach to this story of Luke Skywalker's journey is but one approach and my own suggestions of its meaning are but the eyes of only one Jungian; others might see it differently.[5] Ultimately the film is what we each subjectively experience and take away with us, just as is the case with any other imaginative work.

The approach I've taken cannot possibly cover all the psychological or artistic nuances. For instance, in film criticism the role of the director as primary "auteur" is generally a given. But in this trilogy Lucas brought his unique creativity in the capacity of director only in the first film. Others, Irvin Kerschner in *The Empire Strikes Back* and Richard Marquand in *Return of the Jedi,* painted for us the story Lucas wanted to tell.[6] My amplification of the drama has had to stay within the context of the three films as a whole, telling one story, and thus from the perspective of viewing George Lucas in his various roles as the primary artist.

Whichever way one might understand these films, I hope that the efforts I have made offer a psychological panorama as to why the story, with its rich, if at times simplistic, mythological underpinnings, has had such an enduring effect on so many people now spanning more than one generation.

To conclude my commentary I would like to pass on one more story! It comes to us from adventurer and author Laurens van der Post, who first heard it from his African nurse who was half Bushman and half Hottentot:

> Once in the days of the early race, there was a man who captured a superb herd of cattle, all stippled in black and white. He loved them very much. Every day he took them out to graze, and brought them home in the evenings, put them in his thorn shelter, and milked them in the morning. One morning, he found that they had already been milked; their udders which had been sleek the night before were wrinkled and dry. He thought, "Well, this is very extraordinary. I couldn't have looked after them very well yesterday," and he took them to better grazing. But again the next morning he found that they had been milked. That night, bringing them back after a good feed, he sat up to watch. About midnight, he saw a cord come down from the stars, and down this cord, hand over hand, came young women of the people of the stars. He saw them with calabashes and baskets, whispering among themselves, creep into the shelter and start to milk his cattle. He took up his stick and he ran for them. Immediately they scattered and running for the cord they went up as fast as they could.
>
> He managed to catch one of them by the leg and pull her back. She was the loveliest of them all and he married her. Their life would have been happy but for one thing. She had with her, when he caught her, a tightly woven basket with a lid fitted tightly into its neck. She said to him, "There is only one thing I ask of you and that is, that you will never look into this basket without my permission." He promised. Every day she went out to cultivate the fields and he went to look after the cattle and to hunt. This went on for some months, but gradually the sight of this basket in the corner began to annoy him. One day, coming back for a drink of water in the middle of the day, when his wife was away in the fields, he saw the basket standing there and he said, "Well, really, this is too much. I'm going to have a look into it." He pulled up the lid of the basket, looked inside, and began to laugh. In the evening his wife came back and after one look at him she knew what had happened. She said, "You've looked in the basket." He said, "Yes, I have," and then added, "You silly, silly woman. The

> basket is empty." She said, "You saw nothing in the basket?" "No, nothing." Thereupon looking very sad, she turned her back on him and vanished into the sunset.
>
> My old nurse said to me, "You know, it didn't matter so much his breaking his promise not to look in the basket. What was so awful was that looking in the basket he saw nothing in it. That he couldn't see all the wonderful things that she had brought from the stars for them both."[7]

Van der Post suggests that this story depicts the situation of the modern soul: " . . . we lift the lid of our own particular basket and look inside and see nothing in it." According to him our narrow rational awareness has cut us off from the value of the imaginative aspects of the psyche that create our dreams. It's through the images and symbols generated there that we derive meaning in life, a meaning that is far greater than any intellectual concept to which we might try to reduce such rich imagery. These images are the source of an enormous spiritual and psychic energy, if we learn to access them creatively. When we are cut off from them, we lose connection to their transforming energies, and our souls feel empty.

Within the journey of Luke Skywalker the exuberant Ewoks depict this aspect of the soul, its yearning for stories that engage the more mysterious aspects of existence. This has always been the power behind our myths.

Many people have opened the *Star Wars* basket, a story set in the stars, and have been stirred and enlivened. The enthusiastic reaction of two generations of viewers suggests that George Lucas has succeeded in replenishing the basket of our mythological heritage, enriching the imaginations of so many people in a uniquely creative way. The journey of Luke Skywalker, and the prequels which are now being added to the saga, offer an exciting, well-told story, but more than this, a deeply meaningful myth for our time.

EPILOGUE

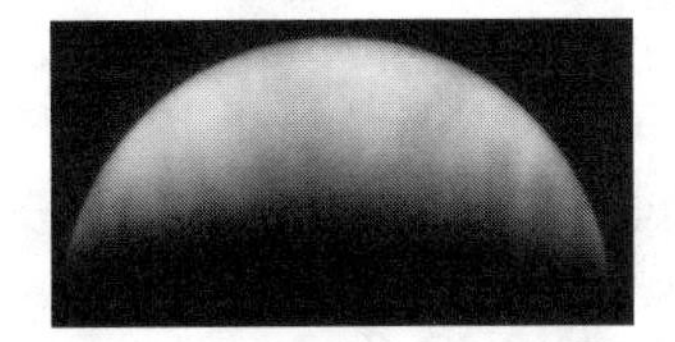

The Phantom Menace

As the music fanfare announces the start of Lucas's newest *Star Wars* feature[1] and we read once again, "Long ago, in a galaxy far, far way . . . " the excitement of the audience for more of this saga is palpable. We re-enter this unique story time and place—a galactic "dreamland." The opening script sets the stage for us. A greedy Trade Federation has set up a blockade over the peaceful planet of Naboo. With the Republic Congress caught in endless debate on this and related matters, the Supreme Chancellor sends two Jedi knights, the guardians of peace and justice in the galaxy, to try to settle the dispute. We join Jedi Qui-Gon Jinn and his apprentice Obi-Wan Kenobi aboard their starship as they approach the Trade Federation blockade.

We quickly learn that there is much more involved here than a trade dispute. The trade federation leaders are taking orders from Darth Sidious, a black-cloaked figure who first appears in holographic communications, who has ominous political designs on taking control of the planet. When Darth Sidious learns that the ambassadors sent by the Supreme Chancellor are Jedi, he orders the Trade Federation viceroy to have them destroyed and the invasion of the planet to commence immediately. However, the Jedi prove elusive and resourceful. Their ship destroyed, they find a way down to the planet, quickly secure the help of the Gungan—sentient creatures who live beneath the water—and make an underwater journey to the palace where the queen is imprisoned and being coerced to sign a treaty unfavorable to her people. The clever Jedi are able to rescue the queen and help her escape. They successfully clear the Trade Federation blockade with the aid of an unusually resourceful astromech droid called R2D2. However, their hyperdrive is damaged and they must land at the remote planet of Tatooine in order to repair the ship.

New characters and locales are introduced and woven together with ones familiar from the earlier films. For example, as in the other films there are three primary locations: Naboo, a planet filled with vegetation including both forested swamps and rolling grass hills, plus a regal, Mediterranean-style city; Tatooine, where the initial *Star Wars* movie *(A New Hope)* began, and to which Luke came back in *Return of the Jedi;* and Coruscant, the capital of the Republic, a planet that is one entire city. (This planet is briefly glimpsed at the end of the Special Edition of the original trilogy.)

On Tatooine Qui-Gon Jinn discovers a young nine-year-old slave boy, Anakin Skywalker, whom he senses is strongly empowered with the Force, the mystical energy field with which the Jedi are deeply connected. Qui-Gon wonders if this young boy might be the answer to a Jedi prophecy of one who will bring balance to the Force.

Anakin offers Qui-Gon's little group shelter from a sand storm in the small home he shares with his mother. Here it is determined that the only way to raise the necessary money for the replacement parts they need is through the local propensity for gambling which centers around dangerous, high-speed pod racing—at which young Anakin excels.

With the aid of his innate Jedi reflexes and mechanical abilities, young Anakin succeeds in winning a pod race against an assortment of alien pilots who are more at home at such intense high speeds than most humans. His victory wins the parts needed to fix his new friends' spaceship, and due to a clever bet by Qui-Gon, young Anakin's freedom as well.

Once the ship is repaired, they travel to Coruscant to plead the case of the Naboo people—but encounter only failure and the ineffectiveness of the government. The courageous young queen returns to Naboo with the two Jedi to see if she can resolve the situation herself. She proves to be quite clever, ingenious, and determined—another mysterious representative of the feminine symbolism that, as we have seen, permeates all the *Star Wars* movies.

After forming an alliance with the Gungan, the queen hatches a plan that creates a diversion allowing her to develop a three-pronged attack. Meanwhile the two Jedi become engaged in an intense duel with Darth Maul, the intimidating apprentice of Darth Sidious sent to thwart their efforts, and young Anakin is inadvertently swept into the battle in space where he proves more lucky than skilled.

Archetypal Evolution

The basic storyline contains ample action and intrigue for all ages, but as with *Star Wars Episodes IV–VI,* archetypal themes are also introduced that make the movie intriguing psychologically. For example, while on Tatooine, we learn that Anakin Skywalker has no father. His mother tells Qui-Gon Jinn, when he asks about the boy's father, "I carried him, I gave birth . . . I can't explain what happened." Later we learn that Anakin's blood contains an unusually high midi-chlorian count, and that midi-chlorians are "a microscopic life form that resides within all living ceils and communicates with the Force. . . . Without the midi-chlorians, life could not exist, and we would have no knowledge of the Force."

Lucas has boldly introduced a slightly altered version of the myth of the virgin birth and also an image of a living organism that is the seat of consciousness and links organic life with psychic life. Such images are associated mythologically with the mystery of incarnation and psychologically with the ongoing integration of archetypal energies through their engagement by human consciousness—themes of great importance to Jung. In Greek myth, for example, many new gods and heroes were of half-divine and half-human conception. For instance, Asklepios, the god of healing, was the son of a mortal woman, Coronis, and the god Apollo. Such unions, while often creating difficulties (especially for the humans involved), generally led to situations in which humans could become more beneficially related to the gods—that is, to the archetypal levels of the psyche.

Jung saw the Judeo-Christian myth as reflective of the ongoing evolution of the divine/human drama: As more of the archetypal levels of the psyche are increasingly integrated and humanized, the psyche is also likely to erupt in more primitive ways that create an ongoing shadow problem. For Jung, the end of the last millennium and the beginning of our new one signify the dawning recognition that along with the development of the "good" side of humans is the dark side that also has to be integrated. In Luke 10:18 Christ remarks, "I saw Satan fall like lightning from heaven." Even as Christ walks the earth as the embodiment of God's newest incarnation, he describes this other divine descent into human existence. (We might recall that near the end of *Return of the Jedi,* an enraged Emperor assaults Luke Skywalker with lightning bolts when he refuses to be turned to the Dark Side.)

Noting that events in the Book of Revelation belong to the end of the Christian aeon (which is now upon us), Edinger points out: "It is interesting that the image of the fall of Satan from heaven should come up in the same scriptures that announce the incarnation of God in Christ."[2] Edinger suggests that our time is an apocalyptic one. My sense is that Lucas, as an artist, draws upon these apocalyptic energies in creating his story.

In *The Phantom Menace,* just when the Jedi Qui-Gon Jinn becomes aware of the possibility that this young boy—with a midichlorian count higher than any of the Jedi—might be the answer to a prophecy of one who will bring balance to the Force, dark figures are already mobilizing for other purposes. The Jedi first learn of one of them, the dark apprentice Darth Maul, after he "descends" to Tatooine and challenges Qui-Gon Jinn, just at the moment that Qui-Gon is bringing the boy to their ship.

The Jedi Council on Coruscant, though recognizing that the Force is strong within this boy, remains very dubious about his training to be a Jedi. They sense much danger in him as well.

The theme of ambivalence concerning the "special one," young Anakin Skywalker, will obviously be central to *Star Wars* Episodes II and III, which are scheduled for release in 2002 and 2005—in the opening decade of our new millennium. This theme mirrors both the messianic myths and the psychic turmoil that were afoot in Western civilization two thousand years ago—and which, according to Edinger, are upon us now.

While such symbolism has rich mythological undertones, it can also prove problematic to modern viewers who have lost a natural appreciation for the symbolic language of the soul, the language of dreams and myth. I encountered this problem in a young man in his twenties who had befriended my older son for a number of years in their mutual quest for *Star Wars* figures from the original trilogy. At an early age this young man had become captivated by the story. However, after seeing *The Phantom Menace* he expressed disappointment in Lucas's story, in particular because he had difficulty with the theme of the virgin birth. To his way of thinking, now as a young adult, Lucas was just artificially intruding religion into his story, and this felt like a "cop-out" to him. In his mind the archetypal image had become equated with dogmatic religious beliefs that his rational mind had long ago dismissed as meaningless. But to the younger psyche—one still at home in the archetypal world—such an image "works" naturally, it simply *belongs*, it doesn't have to be dismissed.

Jar Jar Binks and the Gungans

Another rich area of symbolism in this film—the amphibious Gungan people and the digitally created character Jar Jar Binks—generated collective controversy. I have to admit that it took me a second viewing to be able to fully appreciate all the digitally created efforts of Lucas and Lucasfilm (my wife and two sons, however, had no such difficulty). While rationally I could appreciate that new technology made it more feasible to create products of the author's creative imagination on film, it nevertheless took a little getting use to. Yet I realized that the compelling symbolic qualities of the story still remained.

Once more it is important to remember that Lucas's menagerie of exotic characters has a direct appeal to children's imaginations, much as animals often do. The controversial Jar Jar Binks, the outcast Gungan the Jedi first meet when they land on the planet Naboo, is an excellent example. Most young people readily identify with such a character; my two sons immediately fell into their own version of Jar Jar's "Gungan speak" at the dinner table after they had seen the movie. Emotional qualities can be expressed in this highly idiosyncratic method of characterization that are hard to express in other ways.

Jar Jar Binks is a highly ambivalent character, which is precisely the point. After all, his own people don't like him, and, at first, neither do the Jedi. Thus it is not surprising that many viewers didn't like Jar Jar either, and it is he that received the most derision from critics, including an accusation of racism by at least one journalist. As Jar Jar is ostracized by the Gungans (and the Gungans, in turn, by the Naboo), the character becomes a "hook" for people's projections of their own unconscious racial stereotypes. Such attitudes are not only offensive to the meaning of the character's part in the story but also to the African-American actor who was given much latitude in voicing and creating the character. This form of criticism misses the symbolic point of the character even as it inadvertently offers an unconscious recognition of the psychological source of racism: the projection of such unconscious aspects of the human personality onto certain individuals or entire groups of people, thereby denying those unwanted aspects in ourselves. Fortunately, in *The Phantom Menace*, a wise Jedi, a young boy, and a valiant young queen demonstrate other approaches to relating to such an "ungainly" creature.

Jar Jar Binks captures the vulnerability, awkwardness, and naiveté that children and adolescents feel and try to hide for fear of being shamed, ridiculed, and ostracized. He is member of a tall, frog-like amphibious society, one that feels condescended to by the seemingly more civilized Naboo. Jar Jar and the Gungan, a "people" living in an underwater city, serve as a symbolic connection to those who live more closely to the unconscious in unassuming ways. Yet even amongst his own kind, the Gungan, Jar Jar is an outcast banished to the surface world. His crime? He's clumsy.

Jar Jar thus carries numerous significant psychological characteristics best appreciated by children. Curiously Jung remarked that the frog is animal symbolism for the child.[3] Children are not yet equipped with the tools to free themselves from an identification with their psychological "clumsiness," which, like Jar Jar, can get them in trouble with their own families and amongst their peers because they are still raw, unformed and not "cool." The ridiculed aspect of the personality can't help being any other way, especially at early stages of its formation and growth.[4]

Jar Jar carries the same qualities as the dumbling or stumblebum figure found in our fairy tale lore who becomes either the true hero or possesses qualities that must be included together with the hero. Because he is clumsy, Jar Jar needs the hero's help—first that of Qui-Gon Jinn on Naboo and later that of young Anakin on Tatooine. Jar Jar and the Gungan represent those aspects of the psyche that are still in the process of development and which are crucial for individuation. When Queen Amidala realizes the importance of establishing an alliance with the Gungan, assuring them that the Naboo do not look down on them, a significant psychological bond is realized.

In the adult personality a figure like Jar Jar represents material that has fallen into the general realm of the shadow—and, I believe, more specifically into the realm of the inferior function.[5] This aspect of the personality must be brought within the ego's conscious awareness, though it is not seen as heroic in relation to the ego's current standards. Those components of the personality represented by characters like the Gungan embody our chthonic roots, creatures "of the depths of the earth, . . . always a bit comical or grotesque—in vivid contrast to the world of light."[6] When we face these roots, we acknowledge important components of ourselves. When we deny our own chthonic components, we usually project them onto others in a negative way; these "others" become carriers of our shadow qualities on both a personal and collective level. Jar Jar, whose dumbling qualities drew ridicule from members of his society, evoked similar responses from members of ours as well. This is exactly what we fear will happen when we expose this side of ourselves (or an artist exposes this side of his creative vision).

Returning to the Force

One other image deserves our attention from this movie, for it demonstrates how the story stirs people's imagination. A young woman who saw *The Phantom Menace* and knew I had been writing on the symbolism of the films asked me the meaning of the funeral pyre for Qui-Gon Jinn. She recalled that when Obi-Wan Kenobi and Yoda died in the original trilogy, their bodies disappeared, suggesting the peaceful passing of their spirits into the Force. But when Darth Vader/Anakin Skywalker died, a funeral pyre was built in which he would be fully transformed into his original identity.

What does it mean, she wondered, that a funeral fire was also lit for Qui-Gon Jinn? His passing was more similar to Darth Vader's than to Obi-Wan's and Yoda's. Honestly, I said, I don't really know. That is part of the mystery of this unfolding saga. As Lucas tells more of the story, there is more to ponder. The coming films will almost certainly offer some further differentiation of this symbolism he is using. This scene got her thinking; it stirred her imagination. That's what, at its best, a good story will do, much as our dreams offer, if we take the time to ponder them.

From what the story gives us to this point, I would guess that this symbolism is related to the archetypal theme of dual incarnation that I spoke of earlier. As wise and skilled as he was, Qui-Gon, like all of us, had more he could learn—about himself and about the life force. He was too certain of the fate of the boy he discovered. As Yoda reminds us, "difficult to see the dark side is."

Notes

Preface

1. My thanks to Shana Crystie of San Francisco for her letter in response to my 1997 lecture tape on *Star Wars: A New Hope.*

Introduction: "Why Is the Force Still with Us?"

1. C.G. Jung, *Psychology and Alchemy. Collected Works,* Vol. 12, par. 74. References to volumes in Jung's *Collected Works* (hereafter CW) are indicated by paragraph numbers and not page numbers.

Jungian terms are listed in the glossary and are italicized in the text when they appear for the first time. While many terms coined by Jung, such as "shadow" and "collective unconscious," have entered common usage, some may not be familiar to the reader and can be quickly found in the back of the book.

Most of Jung's writings were directed to those involved in medical psychotherapy and the then-new field of psychoanalysis. After his interests turned toward the importance of mythology and he formulated his concept of a collective unconscious (in addition to the personal unconscious postulated by Freud), he was rejected by mainstream psychoanalysis. Jung's initial writings linking mythology and psychology can be found in *Symbols of Transformation* (CW, Vol. 5).

In later years Jung's interests expanded to include the symbolism of ancient and medieval alchemical literature. The general assumption today is that alchemical concepts have no relevance to the modern mind. As the forerunner of modern chemistry, alchemy is dismissed as obsolete. Jung was able to discern that this was a big mistake from a psychological perspective. By comparing dream symbolism to alchemical symbolism, Jung demonstrated that although alchemical texts do not make sense *chemically*, they can be seen as making much sense *symbolically.* He realized that alchemy reflects an important mythological tradition that has become lost to modern times. An excellent and more recent summary of Jung's approach to alchemy is Edward Edinger's *Anatomy of the Psyche: Alchemical Symbolism in Psychotherapy.*

Because many of his colleagues and most of the academic world had great difficulties with aspects of his thinking, Jung believed that the general public would reject his work as well. Thus, despite the fact that many people from diverse fields were drawn to his work, he did not attempt to make his writing more accessible. A dream late in his life led him to reconsider his attitude about speaking to a wider audience. He then conceived and edited the book *Man and His Symbols*, which is a wonderful starting point for a newcomer to Jungian psychology.

Murray Stein's *Jung's Map of the Soul* is an excellent new introduction to Jung's work. *The Cambridge Companion to Jung*, edited by Polly Young-Eisendrath and Terence Dawson, offers a variety of examples of current Jungian thought and includes an article, "Freud, Jung and Psychoanalysis," that discusses past psychoanalytic and academic rejection of Jung.

2. John Seabrook, "Why Is the Force Still with Us?" *New Yorker*, Vol. LXXII, No. 41 (6 January 1997), p. 48.

3. Ibid, p. 50.

4. Ibid, p. 45.

5. Ibid, p. 50.

6. For examples, see Ann Belford Ulanov's book *The Functioning Transcendent: A Study in Analytical Psychology*.

7. Jungians have a long tradition of amplifying fairy tales, myths, and other creative products of the imagination. Jung's close collaborator, Marie-Louise von Franz, a prolific author herself, wrote many books on fairy tales in which she elaborated on the central psychological themes explored by Jung (see "References and Further Resources" below). Probably the best-known Jungian commentaries on fairy tales, legends, and myths can be found in Clarissa Pinkola Estes's *Women Who Run With the Wolves* and Robert Johnson's *He* (based on the legend of Parsifal and his search for the Holy Grail) and *She* (based on the myth of Eros and Psyche).

8. *Return of the Jedi: Official Collectors' Edition*. Lucasfilm, Ltd. Newton, CT: Paradise Press, 1983.

9. William Hall, "A Draught of Guinness at the Connaught." *Los Angeles Times* (20 March 1983).

10. 1995 interview with Leonard Maltin, Part I. The original *Star Wars* trilogy was last released on video on digitally mastered versions in 1995. Each of the three films begins with part of the interview Maltin did with George Lucas about the trilogy. The Special Edition videos include interviews with Lucas and numerous other people concerning the making of the 1997 Special Edition versions of the films.

11. See note 2. Of the numerous articles I came across at the time of the release of the three *Star Wars* Special Edition movies, this one was the most comprehensive and interesting. There were a great many others, including a *Time* cover story on 10 February 1997.

12. Charles Champlin's *George Lucas: The Creative Impulse* (revised and updated edition) covers the Lucas and Lucasfilm creative corpus of the first twenty-five years, including the *Star Wars* Special Edition movies. Dale Pollock wrote a biography of Lucas called *Skywalking* in 1983; an updated version was published in 1999.

13. Seabrook, p. 40.
14. Seabrook, p. 48.
15. Joseph Campbell's *Hero with a Thousand Faces* is an excellent starting point to explore his work, as is *The Power of Myth* by Campbell and Bill Moyers (based on the PBS television interviews Moyers did with Campbell at Skywalker Ranch). *Star Wars: The Magic of Myth,* the companion volume to the year-long exhibition on *Star Wars* at the National Air and Space Museum of the Smithsonian Institution, which opened 31 October 1997, nicely blends an illustrative text with wonderful images from the three movies and from various myths to elucidate the mythological aspects of *Star Wars.*

1 Setting the Stage: The Story Unfolds

1. My commentary is based of the content of the three films. I assume that you have seen the films and I summarize the story to refresh your memory. If you have not seen them, the summary provides the gist of the story, which I hope will entice you to view the films in their entirety so as to fully appreciate their symbolic value first hand.
2. From his study of dreams, alchemy, and other symbolism Jung perceived the interplay of psychic opposites—light and dark, good and evil, masculine and feminine—to be critical to our psychic life. Many Jungians consider *Mysterium Coniunctionis* (CW, Vol. 14), subtitled *An Inquiry into the Separation and Synthesis of Psychic Opposites in Alchemy* to be Jung's most comprehensive work. See Edinger's *The Mystery of the Coniunctio* and *The Mysterium Lectures* for an introduction to this very rich and complicated book.

2 Tatooine: A Desolate Place

1. John Sanford's *The Invisible Partners* is a good introduction to the anima (and, to a lesser extent, its counterpart in a woman, the animus). Claire Douglas's *The Woman in the Mirror* is a thorough review of all Jungian work on the subject of the feminine principle (through 1990) in general, with excellent material on the anima and animus. Polly Young-Eisendrath's *Gender and Desire* is a more recent study by a Jungian analyst examining how the unconscious fantasies projected onto women in our culture negatively affect women and male-female relationships.
2. There's also a dark side to the anima experience. For example, Homer's *Odyssey* contains a great variety of anima figures, whom the hero, Odysseus, must come to terms with in order to return home and reestablish his relationship to his wife. The Sirens lure men to their death, Circe turns men into beasts, and Calypso attempts to possess Odysseus for herself. The goddess Athena is the guide that allows him to eventually complete his journey.

3. Two recent books on the shadow are worth the reader's attention: *Your Shadow* by Robin Robertson and *Romancing the Shadow* by Connie Zweig and Steve Wolf.

4. The experience of vulnerability as intrinsic to life in general is often expressed via science fiction. Two of the most successful films in the past few years—*Independence Day* and *Men in Black*—depicted the threat of aliens from outer space and the heroes' special efforts to deal with them. We project onto "aliens" in such stories the fears that reside in our own unconscious.

3 Tatooine: Mos Eisley

1. Timothy Husband's *The Wild Man* offers an excellent overview of this figure, complete with pictures from an exhibit at the Metropolitan Museum of Art. Robert Bly popularized the wild man in his book *Iron John*. As Figure 2 shows, there are also wild *women*. This archetype is explored thoroughly in Estes's *Women Who Run With the Wolves*.

2. Jung writes, "The type of vehicle in a dream illustrates the kind of movement or the manner in which the dreamer moves forward in time—in other words, how he lives his psychic life, whether individually or collectively, whether on his own or on borrowed means, whether spontaneously or mechanically" (CW, Vol. 14, par 153).

4 Alderaan and the Death Star

1. Michael Ortiz Hill's *Dreaming the End of the World* weaves the author's stories related to the making of the atom bomb with modern apocalyptic dreams. The horrors and fears generated by the first use of "the bomb" still reside deeply in the human psyche.

2. See Jung's article "On Psychic Energy" in *The Structure and Dynamics of the Psyche,* CW Vol. 8, for a first-hand approach to this concept and Chapter 3 of Murray Stein's *Jung's Map of the Soul* for an excellent summary.

3. See Redfearn's *The Exploding Self* for further amplification of this image. Many of the symbols and images from these movies appear in this insightful book about the nature of psychic energy in the individual personality and across human history.

4. Roots, the television special mini-series based on the book by Alex Haley, brought the issues around Black American History to the small screen many years ago. The Los Angeles riots following the first Rodney King verdict revealed just how much explosive racial tension still exists in this country. Films such as *Dances With Wolves, Schindler's List,* and *Amistad* have helped bring the history of various racial issues more viscerally to modern awareness.

5. Many films do a wonderful job of keeping the imaginative element alive for us. Classics like *The Wizard of Oz* and Disney's *Peter Pan* feature a journey to another colorful, adventuresome world, followed by a return to our world's reality. More recently, movies such as *The Indian in the Cupboard* and *A Fairytale: A True Story* have continued this tradition of keeping the imaginative world closely linked to our daily life experience.

Even the sports figure (Michael Jordan) movie *Space Jam* succeeds using this motif. A disturbance in the imaginative world of the cartoon figures eventually affects the performance of five professional basketball players. Michael Jordan must play with familiar cartoon characters against those who have stolen the "essence" of his professional colleagues in order to restore the balance of the cartoon world and the lost energy of the professional players.

6. Young-Eisendrath's book *You're Not What I Expected* explores couple relationships in depth through this theme of the unconscious expectations placed on the opposite sex.

7. See Lionel Corbett's *The Religious Function of the Psyche* for an excellent exposition of this aspect of human psychology brought to light by Jung.

8. See Jung's autobiography, *Memories, Dreams, Reflections,* Chapters 1 and 2, "First Years" and "School Years."

9. David Noble in *The Religion of Technology* shows that the myth of technology is linked to ancient and medieval theological ideas rooted in desires for religious fulfillment. Rampant technology, however, is a signal that we, as it wielders, have lost contact with the deeper purposes it was originally intended to serve.

10. One of the earliest anthologies of Jung's writing was called *Modern Man in Search of a Soul.* Thomas Moore's bestseller *The Care of the Soul* explores the hunger of the modern soul that is easily neglected by the technological demands of contemporary life.

11. See Jung's "Flying Saucers: A Modern Myth" in *Civilization in Transition,* CW Vol. 10.

12. *Los Angeles Times* (8 February 1997).

13. John Beebe is a Jungian analyst who has explored the psychology of film for many years. He is a former editor of *The San Francisco Jung Institute Library Journal,* which often features reviews of films from a Jungian perspective.

14. The books by Michael Ortiz Hill and Joseph Redfearn reflect the fact that we are in an age of apocalyptic myths. Some of our recent social tragedies, like the death of the Branch Davidians in Waco, Texas (which, in turn, influenced the Oklahoma City bomber) and the Heaven's Gate suicides, involved groups in the grip of apocalyptic mythology. In the latter case the group was caught between two myths, a version of the old Christian myth and a UFO myth. Unconscious confusion concerning the myths that enthrall us can lead to destructive behavior on a large scale.

15. Jung outlined two primary forms of perception, *sensation* and *intuition*, by which we take in information from the world around us and

through which we process our subjective experience. He was also deeply influenced by theologian Rudolph Otto's concept of the *numinosum*, which is a directly felt experience of the divine (see Lionel Corbett's book). Myths help us articulate what we have experienced on this level.

16. John 16:17

17. Redfearn devotes a chapter to the theme of sacrifice in *The Explosive Self.* Jung discusses sacrifice symbolism in his article "Transformation Symbolism in the Mass" (in CW Vol. 11).

18. Redfearn discusses "History Seen Partly as Concretized Mythology" in a chapter of his book.

19. These themes are found in Jung's most complex works, such as *Aion: Researches into the Phenomenology of the Self* (CW Vol. 9ii) and "Answer to Job" (CW Vol. 11). Fortunately, Edinger's work helps make these aspects of Jung's thinking more accessible in such books as *The Aion Lectures, Transformation of the God Image,* and *The New God Image.* Jung's article "Flying Saucers: A Modern Myth" is probably the best place to start.

20. Jung discusses this theme in his article "A Psychological Approach to the Trinity" (CW Vol. 11).

21. See the conclusion of Jung's "Answer to Job" for his discussion of this aspect of the evolution of the Western god image. Raphael Patai's book *The Hebrew Goddess* is a comprehensive study of the neglected feminine component in the Hebrew tradition.

5 Yavin 4

1. Jung offers an in-depth discussion of the symbolism of Sol and Luna in *Mysterium Coniunctionis.* Edinger's discussion of this symbolism in *The Mysterium Lectures* provides helpful elucidation.

2. See Erich Neumann's *The Origins and History of Consciousness* for a discussion of the mythological and psychological evolution from matriarchal to patriarchal forms of social structures. Neumann's work is an excellent place to explore Jungian psychology as it relates to mythology and the works of others in this area, like Joseph Campbell.

3. See my book *Transforming Body and Soul: Therapeutic Wisdom in the Gospel Healing Stories* for an examination of the dynamics that occur when a more developed level of consciousness enters a religious or social context: *individual* spiritual and physical health benefits.

4. Unfortunately, an oversight of this award ceremony was that no medal was presented to Chewbacca. This omission was corrected at an MTV Award ceremony in 1997 when Princess Leia (Carrie Fisher) showed up to give Chewbacca his justly earned medal. After all, one of the functions of Chewbacca is to help keep Han emotionally honest.

5. See Redfearn's *The Exploding Self* for further discussion of both the positive and negative sides of explosion symbolism.

6. Genesis 11:1–9.

7. See Francis Lu's review article "At the Movies: *Titanic*" (in *The San Francisco Jung Institute Library Journal*) for an examination of the love story in this film and its psychological meaning.

6 Hoth

1. Sylvia Brinton Perera's book *Descent to the Goddess,* based on the Sumerian myth of the descent of the goddess Inanna to the underworld, offers an excellent example of the link between ancient myth and modern psychological patterns of initiation.

2. *The Inner World of Trauma: Archetypal Defenses of the Personal Spirit* by Donald Kalsched offers an excellent overview of this psychological dynamic, which he deftly exemplifies with a number of fairy tales and myths.

3. Matthew 2:1–21.

4. I am especially grateful for Edinger's elaboration of this psychological theme involving the more complicated areas of symbolism in Jung's work. Edinger's *The Aion Lectures* introduces this aspect of our psychology on pages 40–41, where he explores the ego's assimilation of unconscious contents versus *being devoured* by them. This theme recurs in *Return of the Jedi,* where the story offers further amplification of these dynamics.

5. For further background reading, see Jung's articles "Synchronicity: An Acausal Connecting Principle" and "On the Nature of the Psyche" in *The Structure and Dynamics of the Psyche,* CW Vol. 8.

6. See Corbett's book, Chapter 2 on "Personal Spirituality Based on Contact with the Numinosum," for further discussion of trusting and understanding this kind of experience. Also see Chapter 8 ("Healing and Faith") of my book *Transforming Body and Soul: Therapeutic Wisdom in the Gospel Healing Stories.*

7 The Asteroid Field and Dagobah

1. These two levels of *seeing* and *being seen* are profoundly intertwined in the development of a sense of self. Mario Jacoby explores both levels in his book *Individuation and Narcissism.* The personal level is examined on pages 62–69, where the need for "mirroring" is discussed. Examples of an archetypal experience of this nature can be found in Corbett's *Religious Function of the Psyche* (pp. 6–8) and in Edinger's *The Living Psyche* (pp. 21–22).

2. Matthew 18:3–4

3. See Edinger's *Creation of Consciousness* for a discussion of the importance of consciousness in human psychology.

4. See "The Primal Relationship," the first chapter of Erich Neumann's *The Child,* for an excellent overview of the importance of the early psyche-soma relationship. Marion Woodman's *The Owl Was a Baker's Daughter*

discusses modern eating disorders as signs of psychic imbalance in both individuals and the culture.

5. Matthew 2:1–21. *Willow*, another mythological film produced by Lucas, also includes this motif: the fear of the special predestined child.

6. See Jung's article "The Philosophical Tree" in *Alchemical Studies* (CW Vol. 13), an in-depth study of tree symbolism that includes examples of patient's drawings of trees and Jung's comments on their symbolism.

7. Edinger's *Aion Lectures,* pages 142–44, summarizes snake symbolism as found in Jung's work.

8. As an example, see M. Vera Buhrmann's *Living in Two Worlds* for a discussion of this form of cosmology in the Xhosa people of South Africa and a description of the work of their healers.

9. The psychology of the inflated ego is described in detail in Chapter 1 of Edinger's *Ego and Archetype.*

10. Merlin is one well-known example from mythology; the Bible describes Noah, who lived to be 950 years old, as being 600 years old when he built the ark.

11. See James Hillman's "Senex and Puer" in *Puer Papers* by Hillman et al.

12. Eastern influences are apparent in Lucas's work. Jung also developed an interest in Eastern spirituality. For example, see his "Commentary on 'The Secret of the Golden Flower'," in *Alchemical Studies* (CW Vol. 13).

13. *Mysterium Coniunctionis* (CW Vol. 14), par. 330.

14. See William Willeford's article, "Towards a Dynamic Concept of Feeling," and later articles by Willeford in the same journal.

15. Extensive discussion of the *unio mentalis* is found in Jung's *Mysterium Coniunctionis.* Edinger's *The Mysterium Lectures* provides an excellent commentary on this alchemical image.

16. The psychology of blame is related to the archetypal dynamic of scapegoating. Perera's *The Scapegoat Complex* provides an excellent examination of the broader cultural and archetypal dimensions of blaming and scapegoating.

17. The *unus mundus* is the third of three conjunctions that constitute the coniunctio process discussed earlier: (1) the unio mentalis (the union of soul and spirit); (2) the union of the unio mentalis with the body; and (3) the union of this second conjunction with the world to form the unus mundus. See the Jung and Edinger references in note 15 for further background.

18. See Jung's *Aion* (CW, 9ii), Chapter XIV, "The Structure and Dynamics of the Self," and Edinger's exposition of this chapter in T*he Aion Lectures.*

19. Anthropos symbolism refers to the use of human form to represent some aspect of divine reality; Adam, Christ, and Buddha are examples. See the Jung references in notes 15 and 18 for further discussion of this symbolism.

8 Dagobah and Bespin

1. See Young-Eisendrath's book *The Gifts of Suffering* for a religious (Buddhist) and psychological discussion of this theme, and also Corbett's *The Religious Function of the Psyche.*

2. See Neihardt's *Black Elk Speaks* for a Native American example of the call to become a healer; and Buhrmann's *Living in Two Worlds* for a general discussion of this cultural aspect of the Xhosa healers of South Africa.

3. See Adolph Guggenbuhl-Craig's *Power in the Helping Professions* for a general discussion of this problem; and Peter Rutter's *Sex in the Forbidden Zone* for a discussion of the problem of sexual acting out in relationships of trust, a particularly prevalent and destructive form of this kind of abuse.

4. Luke 6:39–42. See "The Call to Healing" in Chapter 12 of my book *Transforming Body and Soul* for further elaboration of this passage.

5. C.G. Jung, *The Practice of Psychotherapy,* CW Vol. 16, par. 448.

6. For example, see the fairy tale "The Handless Maiden" (first discussed in the Jungian literature by von Franz) and the Gospel story of the "Man with a Withered Hand" (Mark 3:1–6; discussed in Chapter 5 "Healing and Religion" of my book on the Gospel healing stories).

7. Matthew 4:1–11.

8. For example, see Exodus 20:5 and Deuteronomy 5:9.

9. See Wickes's *Inner World of Childhood,* the first major work by an analyst inspired by Jung; see especially Jung's Introduction and Chapter 2, "Influence of Parental Difficulties Upon the Unconscious of the Child."

10. See Jung's article "Concerning Mandala Symbolism" in CW Vol. 9i, in which he discusses numerous paintings depicting this form of symbolism. Also, Redfearn discusses the role of the mandala in tempering overwhelming experience in his book.

9 Return to Tatooine

1. Reported in an interview excerpt of Cocks shown on the 1997 Fox television special *Star Wars: The Magic and the Mystery.* This production offered an excellent overview of the impact of the original *Star Wars* trilogy on a great variety of people.

2. *Symbols of Transformation,* CW Vol. 5, par. 341.

3. Ibid. Jung refers to Christianity because that was the religious myth and god-image with which he was raised. The same would apply to those raised in other religious traditions that no longer offered meaning to them.

4. Picture 15 of Blake's *Illustrations of the Book of Job.* See Edinger's *Encounter with the Self* for a commentary on the complete series of illustrations by Blake, and *The Aion Lectures,* pp. 95–98, for further elaboration of this particular image.

5. Jung, par. 342.

6. The 1998 movie *Good Will Hunting* depicts this dynamic on a dramatic personal level rather than a symbolic one. By struggling to accept a woman's genuine love for him, and his therapist's honest connection to his suffering, a young man breaks out of the past adaptation he's made, which, if he clung to it, would keep him from living more fully.

7. An ancient example is found in the Hebrew Bible where King David desires Bathsheba, the wife of one of his generals, for himself. He sends her husband to the front line of battle so that he will be killed and David can have her for his wife. *The Golden Ass of Apuleius* is a first-century adventure story in which a young man must journey through the primitivity of the ancient world in order to find spiritual fulfillment. It, too, contains a story of the murder of a husband by a jealous suitor so as to claim the other man's wife as his own, as well as other tales of infidelity and betrayal.

8. In *Gender and Desire* Polly Young-Eisendrath explores the meaning of the myth of Pandora as underlying modern sexual issues such as gender bias towards women and competition between men.

9. See Erich Neumann's *The Great Mother* for an extensive examination of the multiple aspects of this archetype.

10 Dagobah/Rebel Fleet

1. See *Abraham* by Gustav Dreifuss and Judith Riemer for an exploration of the meaning of this story and its relationship to modern struggles with the archetype of sacrifice.

2. See *Memories, Dreams, Reflections,* pp. 182–85.

11 Endor

1. See Laurens Van der Post's *The Heart of the Hunter* for an excellent overview of the mythology of these desert people of South Africa.

2. Jung refers to such retrospective psychological work as a "remembering that is also a re-experiencing." He notes that when such issues emerge a great deal of psychological work is necessary to become free of the effects of one's childhood. (*Psychology and Alchemy,* CW Vol. 12, par 81)

3. One place such development of the feminine principle can be observed is in film. For examples see Beebe's article "The Anima in Film" and reviews of film from a Jungian perspective in *The San Francisco Jung Institute Library Journal.* Particularly noteworthy in this context are Jane Alexander Stewart's "The Feminine Hero of *The Silence of the Lambs*" (Issue 55) and Francis Lu's "At the Movies: *Titanic*" (Issue 64).

4. See Stein's *Transformation* for an insightful exposition of this theme.

5. Interview with Leonard Maltin, Part III.

6. My thanks to Arthur Taussig for this insight.

7. See Chapter 2, "Calcinatio," of Edinger's *Anatomy of the Psyche* for

an excellent summary of the symbolism of this alchemical procedure.

8. Ibid., p. 24.

9. Daniel 3:1–30.

10. Edinger, p. 44.

11. See Kast's *Joy, Inspiration, and Hope* for an insightful overview of this emotion that is often overlooked by psychological writers.

12. Interview with Leonard Maltin, Part III.

12 Final Thoughts: Why the Force Is Still with Us

1. *Symbols of Transformation,* CW Vol. 5, par. 343.

2. *Psychology and Religion,* CW Vol. 11, par. 140.

3. *The Structure and Dynamics of the Psyche,* CW Vol. 8, par. 325. My thanks to my colleague Barbara Stephens for calling my attention to this passage. In his book *Jung on Mythology* Robert A. Segal has collected all of Jung's writings on this topic and included those of a number of prominent Jungians.

4. Ibid., par. 283.

5. For instance see Beebe's comments on the garbage room scene in *A New Hope* in *The Wisdom of the Dream* edited by Stephen Segaller and Merril Beyer (pp. 167–68). I'd also like to acknowledge the approaches of Shana Christie, Jon Snodgrass, and Mary Trouba who shared papers they wrote on *Star Wars* themes with me.

6. My thanks to John Beebe for his discussions with me clarifying this distinction in the art of filmmaking.

7. While the most complete version of this story is found in *The Heart of the Hunter,* this version follows closely that found in the booklet by van der Post entitled *Patterns of Renewal.*

Epilogue: The Phantom Menace

1. Some of the comments in this Epilogue are extracted from "The Return of a Millennium Space Saga," a film review by me of *The Phantom Menace* found on the Jung, Analytical Psychology, and Culture Website at www.cgjung.com/films/phantom.html.

2. Edinger, *The Aion Lectures,* p. 115.

3. Jung, *Visions: Notes of the Seminar Given in 1930–1934,* p. 543.

4. The movie *The Sixth Sense* displays a powerful aspect of this dimension of ridicule. A young boy is branded as a *freak* by his peers for his peculiar personality; it turns out that he is tormented by a unique gift he does not know how to use.

5. The inferior function is the least developed of the four functions in the personality (thinking, feeling, sensation, and intuition) and always lags

behind the others in its development. It is always opposite to the superior function and the superior attitude of the personality (extraversion or introversion). For example, if one is primarily an extraverted thinking type, then one's inferior function will be introverted feeling. Because it is "inferior" in oneself, this aspect is likely to be ridiculed and rejected by the person when it is encountered in others, and blatantly denied as an attribute of oneself. See Marie Louise von Franz's "The Inferior Function" in *Jung's Typology.*

6. Jung, ibid, p. 533.

Glossary

anima "Soul" in Latin. Feminine images in a man's dreams or fantasies representing the unconscious contrasexual side of the male psyche. Described by Jung as "the archetype of life" and "the archetype of all divine mothers (at least in the masculine psyche)." A key part of a man's development is learning to distinguish anima projections from what actually takes place in relational exchanges with a woman.

animus "Spirit" in Latin. Masculine images in a woman's dreams or fantasies representing the unconscious contrasexual side of the female psyche. Described by Jung as "the archetype of meaning," it reflects the nature of a woman's connection to ideas and spirit. A key part of a woman's development is learning to distinguish animus projections from what actually takes place in relational exchanges with a man.

archetype/archetypal The concept of the archetype is a hypothetical one posited by Jung to explain the universal motifs of psychological experience found in religions, myth, legends, fairy tales, art, as well as in our dreams and fantasies. Basic archetypes delineated by Jung include the ego, persona, shadow, hero, Great Mother, Wise Old Man, child, anima, animus, and Self.

collective unconscious The sum of all levels of archetypal processes that is shared by all human cultures and reflects a reality that appears to transcend the parameters of space and time.

complex An autonomous content of the personal unconscious that interferes with the conscious functioning of the personality. At the core of a complex is an emotionally charged archetype. Integration of our various complexes into conscious awareness is an important aspect of individuation.

ego The center of waking consciousness that gives a person a sense of "I" and that contains the self-reflective capacities that mediate the integration of unconscious complexes.

extraversion A basic attitude toward life characterized by investment of interest and energy in areas external to the individual (other people, the environment, material objects, and so forth).

feeling One of the four functions of consciousness delineated by Jung and one of the two rational functions. The feeling function (not to be confused with feelings or emotions) makes judgments about what is perceived based on personal values and preferences.

individuation The process of psychological development that leads to the conscious awareness of one's own unique personality, including its strengths and inherent human limitations. Individuation emerges out of an ongoing dialogue of the ego with the Self and other archetypal aspects of the unconscious.

introversion A basic attitude toward life characterized by an orientation focused on one's subjective experience as mediated via thoughts, feelings, sensations, and images.

intuition One of the four functions of consciousness in Jungian psychology and one of the two perceptive (non-rational) functions. Intuition perceives possibilities and potentials without specific reference to facts and details.

persona "Actor's mask" in Latin. A person's social identity derived from the expectations of society and one's upbringing. Too much identification with one's persona inhibits psychological development.

psyche An all-embracing term used in Jungian psychology to describe the totality of psychic processes, both conscious and unconscious.

shadow The unconscious personal and collective/archetypal parts of the psyche that appear in dreams as dark or negative figures of the same sex as the dreamer.

Self Jung's word for the archetype of individual "wholeness" experienced as a transpersonal power that serves as both the center and the totality of the personality and which underlies the process of individuation.

self The authentic human personality created through conscious relationship to the Self and the ongoing process of individuation.

sensation One of the four functions of consciousness and one of the two perceptive (non-rational) functions. Using sensation, we take in information about reality through the senses.

soul Jung noted that the earliest meanings of the word indicate that soul is a "moving force, that is, life-force." Soul is the life-giving energy that enlivens all aspects of reality and links a person to all life, psychic and otherwise.

synchronicity A term used by Jung to designate the meaningful intersection of psychic and physical states or events which have no causal relationship to one another, but seem to be connected primarily by activated unconscious archetypal processes.

thinking One of the four functions of consciousness and one of the two rational functions. The thinking function makes judgments about what is perceived on the basis of logical analysis and objective data.

References and Further Resources

Beebe, John. The Anima in Film. In *Gender and Soul in Psychotherapy.* Wilmette, IL: Chiron, 1992.

Bly, Robert. *Iron John: A Book About Men.* Reading, MA: Addison-Wesley, 1990.

Burhmann, M. Vera. *Living in Two Worlds.* Wilmette, IL: Chiron, 1986.

Campbell, Joseph. *The Hero with a Thousand Faces.* 2nd edition. Princeton: Princeton University Press, 1973.

Campbell, Joseph, and Bill Moyers. *The Power of Myth.* New York: Doubleday, 1988.

Champlin, Charles. *George Lucas: The Creative Impulse.* Revised and Updated Version. New York: Harry N. Abrams, 1997.

Collins, Alfred. At the Movies: *The Star Wars* Trilogy. *The San Francisco Jung Institute Library Journal,* Vol. 4, No. 3, 1983.

Corbett, Lionel. *The Religious Function of the Psyche.* London: Routledge, 1996.

Douglas, Claire. *The Woman in the Mirror: Analytical Psychology and the Feminine.* Boston: Sigo Press, 1990.

Dreifuss, Gustav, and Judith Riemer. *Abraham: The Man and the Symbol.* Wilmette, IL: Chiron, 1995.

Edinger, Edward. *The Aion Lectures: Exploring the Self in C.G. Jung's* Aion. Toronto: Inner City Books, 1996.

———. *Anatomy of the Psyche: Alchemical Symbolism in Psychotherapy.* La Salle, IL: Open Court, 1985.

———. *Archetype of the Apocalypse: A Jungian Study of the Book of Revelation.* Chicago: Open Court, 1999.

———. *The Creation of Consciousness.* Toronto: Inner City Books, 1984.

———. *Ego and Archetype.* New York: Putnam's, 1972.

———. *Encounter with the Self.* Toronto: Inner City Books, 1986.

———. *The Living Psyche.* Wilmette, IL: Chiron, 1990.

———. *The Mysterium Lectures: A Journey Through C.G. Jung's Mysterium Coniunctionis.* Toronto: Inner City Books, 1995.

———. *The Mystery of the Coniunctio: Alchemical Image of Individuation.* Toronto: Inner City Books, 1994.

———. *The New God Image: A Study of Jung's Key Letters concerning the Evolution of the Western God-Image.* Wilmette, IL: Chiron, 1996.

———. *Transformation of the God Image: An Elucidation of Jung's Answer to Job.* Toronto: Inner City Books, 1992.

Estes, Clarissa Pinkola. *Women Who Run with the Wolves: Myths and Stories of the Wild Woman Archetype.* New York: Ballantine, 1992.

Galipeau, Steven A. *Transforming Body and Soul: Therapeutic Wisdom in the Gospel Healing Stories.* Mahwah, NJ: Paulist Press, 1990.

———. Jungian *Star Wars:* Human Tale of Psychic Wholeness. *UFO Magazine,* Vol. 3, No. 1, March–April 1988.

Guggenbuhl-Craig, Adolph. *Power in the Helping Professions.* New York: Spring Publications, 1971.

Henderson, Mary. *Star Wars: The Magic of Myth.* New York: Bantam, 1997.

Hill, Michael Ortiz. *Dreaming the End of the World: Apocalypse as a Rite of Passage.* Dallas, TX: Spring Publications, 1994.

Hillman, James. Senex and Puer. In Hillman et al., *Puer Papers.* Irving, TX: Spring Publications, 1979.

Husband, Timothy. *The Wild Man: Medieval Myth and Symbolism.* New York: Metropolitan Museum of Art, 1980.

Jacoby, Mario. *Individuation and Narcissism: The Psychology of the Self in Jung and Kohut.* London: Routledge, 1990.

Johnson, Margaret. African Dreamers and Healers. *Psychological Perspectives,* Issue 36, Winter, 1997.

Johnson, Robert. *He: Understanding Masculine Psychology.* Revised edition. New York: Harper and Row, 1989.

———. *She: Understanding Feminine Psychology.* Revised edition. New York: Harper and Row, 1989.

Jung, C.G. *The Collected Works of C.G. Jung.* Translated by R.F.C. Hull. Bollingen Series XX. Princeton: Princeton University Press.
Vol. 5. *Symbols of Transformation,* 1970.
Vol. 6. *Psychological Types,* 1971.
Vol. 8. *The Structure and Dynamics of the Psyche,* 1969.
Vol. 9i. *The Archetypes and the Collective Unconscious,* 1969.
Vol. 9ii. *Aion: Researches into the Phenomenology of the Self,* 1968.
Vol. 10. *Civilization and Transition,* 1970.
Vol. 11. *Psychology and Religion: West and East,* 1969.

Vol. 12. *Psychology and Alchemy,* 1968.

Vol. 13. *Alchemical Studies,* 1967.

Vol. 14. *Mysterium Coniunctionis,* 1963.

Vol. 16. *The Practice of Psychotherapy,* 1966.

———. *Man and His Symbols.* Garden City, NY: Doubleday, 1964.

———. *Memories, Dreams, Reflections.* New York: Pantheon, 1973.

———. *Modern Man in Search of a Soul.* New York: Harvest, 1933.

———. *Visions: Notes of the Seminar Given in 1930–1934.* Edited by Claire Douglas. Princeton: Princeton University Press, 1997.

Kalsched, Donald. *The Inner World of Trauma: Archetypal Defenses of the Personal Spirit.* New York: Routledge, 1996.

Kast, Verena. *Joy, Inspiration, and Hope.* New York: Fromm International, 1994.

Lu, Frances G. At the Movies: T*itanic. San Francisco Jung Institute Library Journal* (Issue 64), Vol. 16, No. 4, 1998.

Moore, Thomas. *The Care of the Soul.* New York: HarperCollins, 1992.

Neihardt, John G. *Black Elk Speaks.* Lincoln, Nebraska: University of Nebraska Press, 1961.

Neumann, Erich. *The Child.* London: Maresfield Library, 1973.

———. *The Great Mother.* Princeton: Princeton University Press, 1963.

———. *The Origins and History of Consciousness.* Princeton: Princeton University Press, 1973.

Noble, David F. *The Religion of Technology: The Divinity of Man and the Spirit of Invention.* New York: Knopf, 1997.

Perera, Silvia Brinton. *Descent to the Goddess: A Way of Initiation for Women.* Toronto: Inner City Books, 1981.

———. *The Scapegoat Complex: Toward a Mythology of Shadow and Guilt.* Toronto: Inner City Books, 1986.

Patai, Raphael. *The Hebrew Goddess.* Detroit: Wayne State University Press, 1990.

Pollock, Dale. *Skywalking: The Life and Films of George Lucas.* Updated edition. New York: Da Capo, 1999.

Redfearn, Joseph. *The Exploding Self: The Creative and Destructive Nucleus of the Personality.* Wilmette, IL: Chiron, 1992.

Robertson, Robin. *Your Shadow.* Virginia Beach, VA: A.R.E. Press, 1997.

Rutter, Peter. *Sex in the Forbidden Zone: When Men in Power—Therapists, Doctors, Clergy, Teachers, and Others—Betray Women's Trust.* Los Angeles: Tarcher, 1989.

Ryback, David. Movie Commentary *(Return of the Jedi)*: Jedi and Jungian Forces. *Psychological Perspectives,* Vol. 14, No. 2, 1983.

Sanford, John A. *The Invisible Partners: How the Male and Female in Each of Us Affects Our Relationships.* New York: Paulist Press, 1980.

Seabrook, John. Why Is the Force Still with Us? *The New Yorker,* Vol. LXXII, No. 41, January 6, 1997.

Segaller, Stephen, and Merrill Berger. *The Wisdom of the Dream: The World of C.G. Jung.* Boston: Shambhala, 1990.

Stein, Murray. *Jung's Map of the Soul: An Introduction.* Chicago: Open Court, 1998.

———. *Transformation: Emergence of the Self.* College Station, TX: Texas A&M University Press, 1998.

Stewart, Jane Alexander. The Feminine Hero of *The Silence of the Lambs. San Francisco Jung Institute Library Journal* (Issue 55) Vol. 14, No. 3, 1995.

Ulanov, Ann Belford. *The Functioning Transcendent: A Study in Analytical Psychology.* Wilmette, IL: Chiron, 1996.

Van der Post, Laurens. *The Heart of the Hunter.* New York: Harvest/HBJ Books, 1961.

———. *Patterns of Renewal.* Wallingford, PA: Pendle Hill Publications, 1962.

von Franz, Marie-Louise. *The Interpretation of Fairytales* Revised edition. Boston: Shambhala, 1996.

———. *Shadow and Evil in Fairytales.* Revised edition. Boston: Shambhala, 1995.

———. T*he Psychological Meaning of Redemption Motifs in Fairytales.* Toronto: Inner City Books, 1980.

———. *Archetypal Patterns in Fairytales.* Toronto: Inner City Books, 1997.

von Franz, Marie-Louise, and James Hillman. *Jung's Typology.* Woodstock, CT: Spring Publications, 1998.

Wickes, Frances G. *The Inner World of Childhood.* New York: Signet, 1968.

Willeford, William. Towards a Dynamic Concept of Feeling. *Journal of Analytical Psychology,* Vol.20, No. 1, 1975.

Woodman, Marion. *The Owl Was a Baker's Daughter: Obesity, Anorexia Nervosa, and the Repressed Feminine.* Toronto: Inner City Books, 1980.

Young-Eisendrath, Polly. *Gender and Desire: Uncursing Pandora.* College Station, TX: Texas A&M University Press, 1997.

———. *The Gifts of Suffering: A Guide to Resilience and Renewal.* Menlo Park, CA: Addison-Wesley, 1996.

———. *You're Not What I Expected: Love After the Romance Has Ended.* New York: Morrow, 1993.

Young-Eisendrath, Polly, and Terence Dawson, Eds. *The Cambridge Companion to Jung.* Cambridge: Cambridge University Press, 1997.

Zweig, Connie, and Steve Wolf. *Romancing the Shadow: Illuminating the Dark Side of the Soul.* New York: Ballantine, 1997

Index